I0788462

OPERATION BAKA

Also by Richard Joyce, featuring Johnny Vince

Operation Last Assault
Operation Blue Halo
Operation Poppy Pride
Operation Edge

OPERATION
BAKA

Richard Joyce

OLIVER & LEWIS

ACKNOWLEDGEMENTS

Although there are references made to true military operations and people in this book, none of those in this story happened. Nor do any of the characters exist. However, I have tried to make the book as factually accurate as possible.

If I haven't mentioned you on this page, please accept my apologies, and at the same time, my sincere thanks.

Firstly, I would like to thank those who have continued supporting by purchasing my Johnny Vince novels; without whom I would not be able to continue to write and raise funds for military charities.

A huge 'cheers' for your Triumph motorbike detail, Martyn Griffiths.

And finally, but not the least, a mention for the amazing Jane Tatam at Amolibros.

*I dedicate this book to my dad who loved my writing.
Rest in peace.*

ABOUT THE AUTHOR

Inspired in 2013 by his favourite author, Damien Lewis, Richard Joyce began to write his first of the Johnny Vince series. Right from the first book, *Operation Blue Halo*, he continues to finely blend historical facts and events, combined with raw emotion, suspense, and unexpected twists.

When not writing, researching, and editing in his 'man shed', Richard enjoys time with his wife and dog on beach walks; oh, and a sneaky beer. As well as raising funds for charitable affairs that are connected to his writing, he is now busy typing away for a new book, away from the Johnny Vince series.

PROLOGUE

Those horrid conditions and gory scenes that I had been a small part of had not left my thoughts on that awful trip back to Britain. It had been obvious that every man on that cattle boat was reliving their Somme ordeal. Some were in shell-shock distress. However, many did not even make the journey home and a burial at sea had been ordered.

When passing huge ships full of soldiers going to battle, pride, guilt, and loss consumed me. Also was the fear of German U-boats. I kept telling myself I was only here to get back to Afghanistan 2013.

Back on home soil, we were segregated like cattle in order of who was injured the worst. I, Georges, Jason, and Mark had managed to stay together; although, it had become a little heated with the orderlies when they tried to split us up. Again, Sergeant Rowe had used his hard-bastard personality for them to agree. Georges' imposture rank had also helped. I wondered how long those two could keep up the pretence.

The train to Birmingham was packed. A group of people lined the station, waving, cheering, and offering food and beer. The Salvation Army mingled through the carriages, but no one was up for talking. It wasn't long before I fell asleep.

The five of us ended up at Hollymoor Hospital where we had removed our fake bandages. Symptoms there ranged from delousing, dehydration, malnutrition, minor injuries, and trench foot. One main problem was who we were, but Sergeant Rowe used the paperwork that requested him, and now unofficially us, for the Egypt mission. Obviously, Mark and Jason were genuine soldiers of this era.

Before we had docked, we had told Rowe that Georges Demblon wasn't a Field Marshal. Instead, Georges had come back in time, like me. Strangely, Rowe had not questioned it. Had he let the black dogs in? However, at the hospital, Rowe barked his orders for Georges to remove all his insignia. Georges would now be known as Private William

Hewitt from the South African Heavy Artillery: a young man missing in action at the Somme. Rowe came up with the nickname 'Scrappy' due to Hewitt always getting into fights. Georges got wound-up about his new nickname, so we shortened it to 'Scrap'. Georges hated that as well. 'Scrap' it was. The biggest piss-take was when Jason had his beard shaved off, the look he had managed to keep during his time at the Somme. The hilarity soon stopped as we were all shaved from head to toe.

With Rowe back on the pedestal, he was enjoying us mere grunts beneath him. Rowe gave me the pseudo rank and name of another MIA soldier from the frontline: Corporal Jim Hurst from 14th Brigade, Devonshire Regiment. Rowe knew that it would be impossible for me to stomach this, being from Cornwall. My pleas only drew a sinister smile from him. Bastard. There was to be no using the nickname 'Sikes' for Rowe. We still called him that. Well, behind his back.

As soon as Sikes' wounds were treated and the lice infestation sorted, he was granted leave. His R&R was not down to him flirting with the nurses and Matron. Sikes was as harsh to them as he was to us. Blister also turned a blind-eye to the beautiful staff, thinking of his wife. Titan missed every opportunity because all he spoke about was what the frontline had been like. Not me though, it took my mind off all the gruesome hospital sights that provoked my recent memories. Sleep was not an option for most unless you had been sedated. Many would yell at night or quietly sob.

In front of the lads, I quizzed Sikes on his PTSD and his ordeal of being thrown in prison to face the firing squad after killing Second Lieutenant Bridge and smashing up Lieutenant Taylor. 'This fuckery stops now,' he said, 'or it will be you four facing the firing squad for shooting dead Private Adrian L'Estrange.'

I couldn't tell him or the others that I hadn't really killed L'Estrange.

A few days later, Sikes came thundering in with a new officer. Sikes growled his orders for us to get into our presented new kit. This new officer turned out to be Sikes' uncle, General Rowe, the "high ranking darling" Sikes had mentioned on the return trip.

We were given new orders in the way of a letter to meet up at General Rowe's London headquarters. In the meantime, we had been given three weeks R&R. Blister and Titan were delighted as they had family. Me and Scrap, or should I say Corporal Jim Hurst and Private William Hewitt, did not have any family to go to. Apparently, we were orphans. I am sure Sikes was getting a kick of our new identities.

Titan invited us back to his family's home: a mansion in Nottingham. Blister went home to his wife and dog in Devon. All of us were given pay and an extra bonus to live well. Ruining this for me was over-hearing Sikes and his uncle having a conversation about us not returning from this dangerous Egypt mission. I didn't tell the others.

CHAPTER ONE

March 24th, 1917. I was relaxing on my own away from the normal Saturday night mess party in the camouflaged marquee. I didn't feel like partying as a strange and unnerved presence had come over me. I could not explain it. Instead, I observed the beautiful sunset over the Sinai Desert camp here in Ismailia. I took another sip of my third 'blood and iron' cocktail. Yet, I never really liked the mixture of a shot of whisky, twice the amount of gin, two sloshes of Angostura bitter, three spoons of sugar, and topped up with Umbra mineral. The sugar and water spoiled it. Ice was a luxury for the RFC officers, as was the Champagne. However, this drink would suffice. It took the edge off the ten-degree chill, and it washed down the amazing food prepared by the Sudanese chefs.

Leaving for the laborious ten-day journey to Egypt at the beginning of August had given me and the lads time to study further German and Arabic. When I was alone, the trip had encouraged me to reflect on L'Estrange, his nickname 'Bruce'. Has Bruce still got his quirky but endearing personality? I do miss him. It's a shame it ended how it had, but at least he was free. I still had to endure the lie that I had killed him and his boyfriend.

I am still annoyed why I ended up at the miserable Somme, nearly losing my life. However, I had to remain positively focused on why I am in the Sinai Desert: find the link to whatever it is that was to get me back to Afghanistan 2013. Although I desperately wanted to see my family, Ella, and the SBS squad again, I still had to put every skill I had into completing this mission. No matter how ominous the challenge seemed, I had to keep myself and my new squad alive. I also couldn't let any new black dogs even get a sniff of me.

The trip to Canada and the death of Ant, Monkfish, and Roy seemed ages ago. Or was it just overshadowed by the Somme? I suppose a small positive mercy was my suffering of being an alcoholic and tramp was now suppressed. From time to time, I still wondered what were my family's thoughts of the letters I had left before disappearing?

The sea voyage had also given me time to think about the mission ahead. Purposely, I had not decided on a mission name as I wanted the timing right, like previously on other missions. Many names had been put forward by the lads. Interestingly, Blister had come up with Operation Desert Storm straight after a horrendous sandstorm. I told him it had been used before by the Yanks. However, the official name, Operation Exploit, had been chosen by General Rowe.

Tonight, Titan, Blister, and Scrap were enjoying themselves in the marquee along with some of the new squad handpicked for this mission. These fresh seven recruits were from different working backgrounds, religions, and countries. They all knew Sikes, but not all would say the connection. They had only been out here a month.

Although I was trying to chill out, one of these new soldiers could be heard partying hard: Lance Corporal Andrew 'Scouse' Price, Kings Liverpool Regiment. He had a thick Liverpudlian accent. Scouse was laddish and up for a laugh. He spoke fast, especially when he regularly became feisty. If anything had gone missing, it was normally found under his bunk. Scouse had been injured at Thiepval Ridge, losing part of his hand, and injuring his left side. Still, though, he had continued to attack and destroy a German trench gunnery position. He had saved his troop who had been pinned down for three days without rations and low ammo. Scouse had been due a medal, but stupidly, he was caught stealing silverware from the barracks. Because of his previous courageous feat, Scouse was given pity. However, the only options were to join the Egypt mission, or leave the army for prison. I'm pleased that he was in Sikes' squad, not mine.

The mission was a right old mish-mash of squads, like a loosely organised PMC mission from Will. One thing our squad had over them was our intense training to date. Pulling up the blanket made of mongoose, I closed my eyes, thinking back…

★

The first few days at Titan's mansion was just one big piss-up. It also made the sleep at night bearable as the bed was too clean and comfortable. The main diet was of hearty foods with lashings of lard and dripping in every conceivable type of dish known. It was difficult to stomach at first. With home-made puddings with masses of thick custard, I am sure I doubled in size after the first week.

Me and Scrap had tried to flirt with the maids. We left alone the big old cook; she had a face like a punched lasagne. I had a little crush on a stunning maid, Tina Dobson. She always would blush when around me. The butler, Henry Wynne, saw this and gave Maid Dobson the kitchen and washroom duties. We were forbidden to go in there.

Titan's mum listened to his stories of the frontline, albeit a watered-down version. In the smoking room, Titan's dad, Brian, was told how his hunting gun had killed many Germans. Albeit, a slightly exaggerated version. Even though there was much celebrating, we had to become highly trained for what lay ahead. We needed the whole squad back together. Titan had the luxury of horses and carriages. Whereas, Blister did not. Brian sent Henry to fetch Blister. I gave the orders for no more drinking, much to the disbelief of Scrap and Titan, resulting in a near mutiny.

Six days passed. Eventually, Blister turned up in a fine horse-drawn carriage. Of course, me and Scrap took the piss that he had become Queen Elizabeth. Titan and Blister didn't get it.

We began to resemble convicts where our hair was starting to grow back. Blister had been given an ultimatum by his wife: he was not to leave for this mission but to stay at home. If not, his wife and dog would not be there when Blister returned. Blister chose the army, promising he would return and that she would be all right. Some things never change.

That afternoon, there was an intense argument as the three hit the cellar again, against what I had ordered. The excuse was the homecoming of Blister. Rather than demand respect from them, I walked away and sat in the library with the smell of leather-bound books and burning logs. Mrs Bentley came in with a glass of Champagne. I refused. Instead, I asked for milk and some fresh fruit. She did not disappoint; furthermore, bringing me a selection of meats and bread.

Half a minute after she had left, Brian entered with Henry. Both were smoking cigars, and both were pissed. They gave a look of confusion to the food and drinks on the table. Was it because I was eating on Brian's desk? Perhaps Mrs Bentley was not allowed in here. Maybe it was because I was not celebrating with them all.

I politely declined a cigar and wafted the smoke. I asked Brian for any books on Egypt, Arabic, religions, and maps. It changed the disgruntled look on his face. Brian proudly went through the wall-to-wall stacked bookcase. Along with the cigar ash, he placed the pile in front of me at this huge, mahogany table. The last items on my list were: a pen, highlighters, pencil, scale ruler, and notepad. Brian frowned inquisitively. Henry opened a bureau and then came over with some thick writing paper, envelopes, and a pen and ink pot. By their pitiful look, I guessed they thought I wanted to write home. I sighed.

Daring to push my luck and perhaps outstay my welcome, I asked if they had anything modern. Brian whispered for Henry to retrieve something from the study. Trying to keep his composure for being worse for wear, Henry left. A large crash echoed down the main hall. Fits of laughter came from the lads. Brian said they needed to let off steam. It was like a eureka moment for him, and he slapped his thigh and went over to a mahogany double-doored unit. He pulled out two pheasant-guns and shouted for Henry, the cigar falling from Brian's mouth.

Henry came in holding some sort of weird contraption. Brian held out his weapons. Henry strode over to me with his arms out holding the object, nearly slipping over on the cigar on the wooden floorboards. The antiquated typewriter was placed in front of me. I spotted the brand 'Oliver'. I looked up with despair, and Henry proudly smiled. Brian coughed, and it dawned on Henry that his master was still standing there with his arms out. Brian then loaded Henry up with satchels of cartridges. Brian said he was taking the lads out on a shooting expedition. I said it was too quick, and could ignite their bad memories of the frontline. Also, someone could be seriously injured or die with all of them being drunk. Apparently, my arguments were "preposterous". Again, my pleas were ignored, and I was told to leave first thing in the morning.

Alone with the cigar odour, I started reading the books. I tried to get used to making notes with the ink pen and pot as the typewriter looked too confusing. Concentrating on studying wasn't easy with the sounds of shotguns being fired off somewhere in the vast acres. It also brought back visions I didn't want.

Someone disturbed me by gently patting my head. I opened my drained eyes. Beyond the candle on the desk, a long nightgown disappeared through the oak door. I stretched away the awkward position I had been slumped in. Mrs Bentley had placed a glass of milk and a hot bowl of porridge. I moved closer to the newly laid logs on the fire. The large grandfather clock chimed, taking my stare off the low sun coming through the single-paned windows. Time check: 06:00 hours.

Whilst I scoffed my porridge and jam, I thought it was time for an

SAS selection process. Although, a very weakened and cut version of the normal six months. Plus, the lads would pass anyway. I wryly smiled.

Straight after breakfast, I went down to the pantry to find Henry. To Henry's horror, I had caught him having sex with maid Dobson up against the large oak table. Maid Dobson was as blushed as the salmon she had been preparing. I made a quip about the pheasant getting plucked, adding further awkwardness to the situation.

Maid Dobson pulled down her outfit. I waited for Henry to pull up his trousers and then handed him a list of items I urgently wanted. After he read it, he nodded gentlemanly-like and hurried out. Maid Dobson looked at me flirtatiously and teased the string to her blouse.

Selection, day one: I dragged Titan, Blister, and Georges out for a brisk jog. Albeit, in shirts, trousers, and shoes. Within less than a mile, they were sick from their night's indulgence. It didn't matter how much they objected and threatened me, I ignored them. I then made them do squats, press-ups, and the like. They were pitiful.

That night, being cast out, I sat studying in the library. Unbelievably, the three of them were in the main lounge getting rowdy and drunk. I reckoned Mrs Bentley had put Brian in the doghouse, literally, as I had watched him walk out the back door with a blanket and pillow. Not surprisingly, Henry had got everything on my list. He said he would cover the cost. I wonder why.

Day two: again, I hauled them out of their hungover pits. A slight shock to them was that I was in a white running vest, shorts, and black plimsolls. They then took the piss.

On the run, they could not keep up. I enjoyed the routine of them being sick and moaning. I cut them a deal: if they followed me for another six miles, they would then get a reward. I showed them the inside of my haversack that was laden with pies and six bottles of Evans Stout—it had worked.

After about ten miles or so, they were all spent. Knowing their main drive was the beer, I said they had to answer one question between them to earn it. It got their attention. I asked them what was the first town that the main railway ran from Port Said. Whilst they had a conflab, not having a fucking clue, I found a tree about ten metres away and started to do some pull-ups on a branch.

After a few good reps, I returned. All of them were laid with their hands behind their heads, dressed like three muddy and sweaty Gypsies after hare coursing. They had the pleasure of telling me they did not know the answer. And, furthermore, didn't give a flying fuck. I snatched up the haversack and moodily started to jog back. I mentally smiled at their harsh banter that followed.

Laid out on the croquet lawn were heavy items that Henry had asked their blacksmith to set up whilst we were gone. The look on the merry men's faces as they returned was priceless. I knew they would steal the drink when I was doing pull-ups. Objections were futile as Henry and Dobson said there would be no dinner served unless my physical workout was completed.

For stealing the beer, for not knowing the answer to my simple question, and for drinking again last night, I put the squad through a cruel workout. Yet, nothing I didn't do myself.

Day three: Being allowed back in my bedroom, and in the squad, I was disturbed early in my bed. All three of them were enthusiastic, sober, and in their running gear. Scrap had got my quip about *Chariots of Fire* cast. I sat up and laughed at Titan in his white shorts and T-shirt that were about three sizes too small. His new beer pot-belly made it look worse. Swinging my legs over, an empty bottle of champagne fell off the bed. I acted all embarrassed. Once the air of murmured disbelief calmed, I reminded them it was Sunday and that the Lord said no training on the day of rest. They were furious, but why tell them I hadn't really had any alcohol.

Day four: Having heard them up the previous night till the early hours of this morning getting pissed, I had to drag them out of bed. Standing shambolic in line outside, I began with a good warm up. Surprisingly, they kept up.

Halfway through the fast-paced run in the woods, the squad kept on my heels. Titan said he knew a more challenging route. I had to turn back to follow them. Just as I jogged level with a stand of trees, Titan's huge hands came around and grabbed me. I was bundled to the floor and a haversack placed over my head. Against my struggling, I was thrown into chilly water. Stagnant fumes rose. Objects hit me hard in the body and face. Ripping the sack off my head, I was waist height in a muddy pond. A beer bottle landed in front, splashing the shit over my face. They then threw the weights and a book at me.

'We've all done our studying last night,' Titan said.

'This squad had even laid off the alcohol,' Scrap said. 'Looks like someone was tricked into thinking we were partying.'

The three of them walked away.

Over the remaining couple of weeks, we had studied, trained hard with hand-to-hand combat, and experimented with weapons drills. We even did a little escape and evade. I had tried to subject them to similar experiences to my SAS selection, although much of it was theory. The only part we did not get to try was the RTI training, but they had listened to the briefing.

We were all dreading meeting Sikes and his uncle in London, but at the same time we were excited to learn our mission objectives. We decided to have one more night on the lash. Brian and Henry were allowed to join us. Mrs Bentley kept the tone respectful, until she took Brian away to bed.

At the end of the evening, I took a stroll with the lovely maid Dobson. If by chance, the sky was a pure star-lit night. Even though I had remembered her early flirting, I kept it on a friend's basis. I was hoping I would return to Ella.

My spring in the step mood was dampened the next day as we had the meeting with Sikes. He did not hold back with his harsh tone and insults. His hair and large sideburns had grown back quicker than ours, looking more malicious than ever. We were still dressed in smart civies that Henry had to source, unlike Sikes' pristine military uniform. As he showed us to his uncle's office, he pulled back my arm and shut the door on the others. Thankfully, he didn't have his club to hand.

'Johnny, I want to thank you for getting me back,' he said.

Fuck me, he had called me by my real name and praised me. 'No worries. I just hope the black dogs don't return.'

I held my hand out, but he slapped my hand away, snarling,

'This fuckery stops now. Get in there, Corporal Jim Hurst.'

Opening the door, I wondered if he had meant "I want to thank you for getting me back", as in back from France, and not his mind. Bollocks. However, I will take that short-lived "thank you". And, so much for being Corporal Johnny Vince.

With large-scale maps, we were given the details of the mission: twelve men had to destroy an aeroplane hangar and blow-up a railway station to stop the advancing German and Ottoman Empire. The Royal Flying Corps had been surveying and bombing as much as possible, but they had encountered a heavy loss of pilots. Because of the gentlemanly way both German and British pilots respected each other, any prisoners on both sides had been returned.

Sikes had been tasked for a ground offensive away from the other advancing multinational cavalry and troops. In short: The Ottoman Empire was gaining more ground. It was rumoured they had been building secret weapons and using the rail network to move supplies. We were set to arrive on February 20th next year. However, I had different plans: I wanted our squad to acclimatise. Not just the climate, but to learn the ways of the locals; hopefully, with some hearts and minds. It was paramount to learn the lie of the land, weapons, vehicles, horses, and camels. We also had to accustom ourselves with the established base.

Once the briefing details were finishing, Sikes' uncle entered. We were sharply ordered to leave. Being last out, I shut the door on the lads and turned around. The two officers were shocked.

'What the dickens do you want, Hurst?' Sikes said.

I looked at the uncle and said, 'As you know, your nephew is one hell of a man. Fighting many battles…'

'Get out…'

'Let the man finish, Sean,' General Rowe interrupted.

'Thank you, sir,' I said. 'I've never met such a courageous but caring for his men person. It was an honour to save Sergeant Rowe from the firing squad.'

'Go on, corporal,' the general said.

'Obviously, our squad has to keep our gobs shut about all that nasty stuff with Bridges and Taylor.'

Sikes looked fit to burst.

'And I am sure you will prevail,' General Rowe said. 'Perhaps in the way of a medal or extra pay. Or both.'

'No, sir, that would be uncouth and immoral,' I said, remembering Mrs Bentley saying it.

General Rowe took off his cap and placed it on the table. He took two steps closer to me. I remembered the trick Sikes had done before headbutting me.

'And what would it take to dismiss that business from your mind?' Rowe asked.

'Our squad would like to leave for Egypt this week,' I said.

'Oh. Is that all, Jim?' he said.

'No, Albert,' I casually replied, as we were now on a first name basis.

Sikes took a sharp intake of breath. Albert stared hard into my eyes. I retrieved a list from my pocket and handed it at arm's length to Albert.

'I would like everything on that list, Albert,' I demanded. 'I'm sure that would erase our memories of Bridge and Taylor.'

Albert stopped his nephew coming any closer. 'I will have it ordered and with you on the next available armoured frigate.'

I shook his hand, keeping well back. He squeezed hard, furiously glowering.

'Never address me like that again,' he said.

Leaving the barracks, I rubbed the side of my head. I lied to Scrap that I had bumped into something; it had been worth the pain.

BOOOM!

I came to on my back. The frenetic noise came to a crescendo of further explosions, screams, and wild horses. Looking back from the stars, I frantically shoved off the blanket that was on fire. The smell was pungent. Scrambling off my chair, I stood up, pushing my tumbler into the sand. Small objects burned all around me and far beyond. Between the main flames, silhouettes were running, shouting, and screaming. Fuck, my mates.

CHAPTER TWO

Heart pounding and fingers working at my boot laces at treble-speed, I then sprinted towards the carnage and dodged the petrified chefs running in all sorts of directions.

BOOOM!

The shock wave flattened me on my back, again. Screams and yelling became muffled. Weird shapes streaked across, momentarily blacking out the stars. That had been the first bombing raid at night. Half-sitting and dazed, the intense smoke and raging fire engulfed a truck. My shins became heavy and hot.

'Fuck,' I said.

Having seen the smouldering torso, I frantically kicked it off. Scuttling backwards, I burnt my hand on a twisted piece of metal. I continued to work out who it was, then I recognised the burnt red hair and mashed face of Scouse. I looked down at the gore on my trousers. I spat out the 'blood and iron' cocktail that had come into my mouth—not the best name to have given it.

My arm was yanked up. Standing and slightly dizzy, I came face to face with Sikes.

'This fuckery stops now,' he yelled.

The ringing in my ears had muffled it. After Rowe looked at Scouse, he stood between me and the corpse. Picking up my rifle, he slammed it into my chest.

The 12-pounder AA-gun thumped into action. The vibrations came through the compact ground. Looking back at the stars, black objects whizzed by like fleeting bats. Another explosion ripped further to the west towards the main hangar. Fuck. That was where I had our transport and extra kit stored. Machine guns strafed the area from planes buzzing in. The search-lights from the far-back hangars waved, catching ghostly objects in a split-second. The 13-pounder started hammering the sky, not that they could fix a target. It encapsulated the cacophony of panic. Sikes strode off, still yelling.

Jumping the littered bodies and dodging the medics in service, I ran to what was left of the burning wreckage. Sand had been kicked over some of the smouldering bodies. Who and why had someone driven a truck in? Sikes was barking at those wasting precious water on the already burnt-out lorry. But instead, to go and save the injured or capture the frightened horses. Some of the soldiers took a few steps back and looked east into the black sky: a drone reverberated from beyond the abyss.

'What's that?' Trish asked.

'Sounds like a…shit,' I said, interrupted by a sting to my arm.

Trish held up a small bit of bone and said, 'I hope this is not yours.'

'Go see to the others, Patrizia.'

'Back to my real name, hey. Try not to bleed to death.'

'Oh my Lord,' an RFC officer said, 'that must be the German Gotha bomber.'

'And more than one by the sounds of it,' I added.

The officer ran over to another burning wreckage. 'Put the fires out,' he yelled. 'Put the ruddy fires out.'

Many started to whack the flames and throw water. A new rumble came from behind. From the shadows a combination of neighs and snorting echoed. Screams followed. Just as the officer's oppo shouted to man the rest of the anti-aircraft guns, he stopped. He froze to the spot to watch the haras plaguing through like locusts. He was mowed down. I grabbed Trish and pulled her back over the sandbags that surrounded a water pump. Those who did not react were trampled.

Someone from the far side started shooting. Others joined in, probably thinking it was an Ottoman ground raid. One soldier went to help another screaming after he had been crushed. That soldier spun around clutching his throat, blood spurting between his fingers as he hit the floor. Holding Trish back as she instinctively went to help, Sikes began screaming orders to cease firing. Strolling into view in the middle of the bloodshed, Sikes yelled for stretcher-bearers. Suddenly he stopped. A loan camel thundered by, just missing him. How the fuck does he get away with it?

With the last of the stampede gone, the dust started to settle. Trish tightly held my shirt.

'Have you ever made love to an Italian?' she asked.

'No, especially if you're from the Palermo region. I've heard about Salvatore Inzerillo.'

She frowned. 'But I am from the Spiga family.'

'Can you ride a motorbike?'

'I can ride anything, you know that.'

'Now's not the time for your laddish banter. Get back to the hospital and tell everyone to turn out the lights.'

'Hospital?' Trish said.

'You know what I mean,' I retorted. 'The advanced dressing station.'

'Can you please abbreviate it to ADS,' she said, impersonating me.

I laughed inside, having said this to her before.

Trish got up and jumped the sandbags. Soon after, a motorbike started and then it headed west.

I sprinted over to Sikes who was checking the bodies littered around. He stood up and wiped the blood onto his shorts.

'Nothing you can do for this lad,' he said.

I looked away from the lad's smashed-in face.

'Grab your weapons and take arms against those incoming…'

'No, Sarge,' I interrupted—Sikes was raging. 'Small arms fire will alert the bombers to our muzzle flashes. Why don't you order the Lewis gunners to take that far right ridge over there, and one of the Pierce-Arrow lorries as far east as possible. To draw the enemy away.'

Sikes' eyes narrowed towards the oncoming hum, and then he nodded at me. Jesus, another recognition. I could not wait to tell the lads. Oh shit, did they get out of the marquee in time? Whilst Sikes arranged for the defence, I quickly left.

Small planes still zipped about unleashing their hail of lead, but at least they had stopped throwing bombs over the side. All that was left of the mess party was a smouldering mass of tarpaulin. Parts that had not caught fire lay in strange heaps. The first piece I lifted had a huge silver tabletop food warmer. The contents were spilled out on the floor. Steam vented into the chilled night. The next torn section revealed one of the Sudanese chefs. His contents spilled out on the floor. Steam vented into the chilled night.

'I would stick with the goat's brain curry instead, fella.'

'Blister,' I shrieked.

Jumping the smouldering parts, I then gave him a bear hug. He kept his muscular arms by his side.

'You really ought to stop that homosexual play. You know buggery is a criminal offence in the British Army, punished by the firing squad.'

'Unless you're German,' I said.

'Oh yes, then it's down to Private Johnny Vince to kill them, like you did Wilhelm Angern and his lover, Bruce.'

'That's not funny, Mark,' I retorted.

'Oh, sorry, I forgot we had to keep it quiet,' he said sarcastically.

'No, not that, you keep calling me "Private". We've left that joke on the Somme. Now where are the others?'

'Titan has gone back to the casualty clearing station, whilst…'

'I told you to start shortening…' I stopped as Blister had sniggered. 'Your banter and wit have become annoying.'

'I've learnt a lot from you over these last months.'

'Where's the rest of the squad?' I said.

'Scrap grabbed a Vickers and a Lewis. He ordered a few new lads to carry the ammo and bipod, and then to follow him. I think Tommy is lighting some of that head-fuck stuff.'

'Which way did he go?' I said.

'Back towards the officers' billet with a trail of smoke.'

'Not Tommy. Scrap.'

Blister pointed left towards the far away dunes.

Not noticing the silence before, we were the only ones out in the open, except some of the corpses that had not been retrieved. Many armed men crouched behind sandbag reinforced bunkers, fearing what was coming. Everyone around the defended AA-guns were ready, all backed up by men with rifles ready.

'I think the toilet is going to hit the propeller,' Blister mumbled.

I went to correct him, but it seemed more appropriate. 'You've trained for ten months as a killer, now fight as a killer.'

Coming through from our right was the Pierce-Arrow armoured truck. Blister ran onto the track waving his arms whilst standing in front of a dead horse. The Arrow's lantern headlights hardly lit-up Blister as he continued to yell and wave his Enfield. The driver couldn't see properly out of the armoured shutter. Blister took aim as it hurtled towards him and eventually fired at the front 7.5 mm plate. One of the crew stood up behind the Vickers Naval 2-pounder automatic gun and screamed at the driver. The six-ton beast tried to stop on its four-spoked and rubber-tyre wheels. Blister dived for cover as the fourteen-foot wheelbase mounted the horse.

One of the three gunners climbed down to see what they had become stuck on. The driver tried to find reverse. The RMA lad's flat hat looked odd compared to the desert toupee we had to wear. Blister got up looking pleased with himself, until the co-driver got out and aimed his pistol at Blister. Quickly, I began running with my hands defensively up.

'Whoa, whoa, we're British,' I yelled.

The co-driver lowered his pistol, and Blister took his finger off his Enfield's trigger. The rest of the crew came around to see what the trouble was.

'Why the devil are you shooting at us?' the co-driver said. 'We have orders to head into the desert.'

'We could have run over you, dear boy,' the crewman said.

'I doubt it,' Blister whispered. 'You Navy boys can't even steer a boat properly.'

'What did you say?'

'He said, he was trying to warn you of the horse,' I butted in Blister's reply. 'Now you're stuck on it.'

'Oh tremendous,' the driver said.

'Right, you urgently need to get everyone out to heave the horse out the way.'

Everyone debussed and took hold of the rear legs and tail. Whilst the five-crew heaved, I nodded at Blister to get in the truck. He got the message. Machine gun fire erupted in the distance, intensifying the situation. It spurred them on with grunts and groans. The main horse's body became clear, so I snuck around the rear. Blister did not wait for the head as the four-cylinder gasoline, liquid-cooled, truck bounced over the horse. The crew shouted abuse.

'Put your fucking foot down, Blister,' I shouted.

'It only has thirty horsepower, and one less now.'

His laugh was drowned out by the noisy engine, even though we were only cruising at about twenty-five miles per hour.

Entering the dark and desolate landscape on black-light, the leaf-spring suspension did their best to stabilise. After about two klicks, I ordered Blister to stop as we had entered a large bowl-like dip in the desert. Remembering the recent vehicle training, I wound the small brass wheel to aim the main pom pom gun into the bleakness. The original crew had already fed the 40 mm loaded fabric-belt through. I had personally found out that the belt made of fabric, instead of steel, sometimes let the ammunition fall out.

Blister was now poised on the Maxim-machine gun. I wished I had some binoculars. However, there was no need as from our left front, streams of tracers streaked upwards. The wall of low descending bombers became clear by the amount of returning flames that spewed from the German gunners. They were possibly three to four thousand feet high. Why were they so low? Was it because our base had all 'lights out'? Is this why the Empire dangerously sent in their fighters to bomb first? Marking the way.

I aimed down the rear brass sight and aligned the front AA sight. I left the windage adjustment screw, but lifted the elevation adjustment to max. Keeping my face and hands away from the reciprocating side charging handle, as it could easily take them off, I gripped the small brass pistol-like handle. Flicking the safety catch, I squeezed the trigger. The power pumped out about four rounds per second. It had covered the area in cordite, and shells at my feet. It was terrifying as it shook the whole vehicle. Yet, not as petrifying for those in the wooden-framed canvas bombers. Continually firing, the heat warmed the chill. My aim was too low, so I adjusted my sights, bearing in mind the bombers were closing. Blister fired the formidable Maxim water-cooled .303 machine gun.

Again, I squeezed the trigger. The AA guns from behind fired. Bright flashes lit up the planes in formation. Some had caught fire. The bombers returned fire with their machine guns. Our side did the same. A huge explosion rocked the earth to the left. Most probably a pilot letting go of his load before crashing. The cloud spread high into the air.

Heightened by the excitement, I reached down for the ammo box to replace the empty one sat on the side-plate. I was hauled backwards and then thrown out. Finding my breath, Blister stood with his hands raised. The out of breath co-driver lowered his pistol and then climbed aboard, as did the rest of the angry crew.

The armoured truck screamed up the slight incline and then it carried on towards the incoming bombers that were almost overhead. For us to run back to our AA guns and camp would be desperate, but to stay here with falling parts and their bomb load was as suicidal. Fuck.

With machine gun fire directly above, I grabbed Blister down from the edge. We tucked ourselves into a tight ball. Everything from the wreckage, fire, and rounds seem to be falling around us. The Pierce-Arrow that had been firing at the rear of the bombers stopped. A huge explosion followed. The rumble above continued towards the base. I caught Blister's wide stare at me. Further explosions rippled to our southwest. Suddenly, a crash to our right made us flinch. Blister put his arm over me, squeezing. Heat rolled over the top. Strange noises crackled.

It wasn't until everything had gone quiet that Blister released his hold. I let go of his jacket. Still curled up, he started to giggle.

'What's so fucking funny?' I whispered.

'Do you reckon Titan was standing up again with that hunting gun?' Blister started to laugh. Imagining Titan, I joined in.

'Perhaps Sikes was waving his cudgel.'

'This fuckery stops now,' Blister impersonated.

It took a little time before we both stopped the camaraderie. Gingerly turning over, we were covered head to toe in sand. Ash was still falling like snow.

'I do believe we're both going to get thrashed by Sikes,' Blister said.

'Why?'

'Because we've both left our rifles in the Pierce-Arrow.'

'Oh Shit,' I said.

Blister walked up to the rim, dusting his uniform. 'Perhaps we should go and find the…'

'What's up?'

He didn't finish his previous sentence, but just stood on the flats. I ran up the tracks that had been left by the Arrow and joined him. Small fires were littered as far as the eye could see, like that at a concert when everyone waves their illuminated phone screens. Stunned, I slowly spun around in a 360-rotation. Close to us was a smouldering timber wreckage. The pilot and crew had possibly jumped to their death rather than to go down in the flames; hopefully, shot dead first. I turned back towards our base. Blister was still looking east.

'I would say that it was luck that those Royal Marines kicked us out,' he said solemnly.

I looked east. Quite a way back was the upside-down burning twisted wreck of the Arrow—I had nothing to add.

After making ourselves a bit more respectful for meeting Sikes, we started to trudge back. The carnage was spread wide. The fires were dying out. It was hard to distinguish plane parts from dead humans, horses, or camels. From time to time I would look up at the beautiful star-filled sky, fooling myself that a plane had shot by.

As we neared our camp, the lights started to return to normal. We were still going around huge bomb craters. Silhouetted forms cared for people on stretchers. Some were re-stocking ammo. Sikes was yelling. It was good to know he was alive.

On the outskirts, we came across a three-man defence pit. The sandbags had been blown away; three soldiers shredded beyond the debris. We still checked to see if they were alive. As I got to my feet, Tommy's Rottweiler, Baka, was standing and eying me. He showed his teeth.

'Take,' Tommy said to Blister.

Blister snatched the Enfield from Tommy without thanking him and then went over to the Vizsla, Rudi. Blister stroked the mutt. Tommy walked over to me and held out another weapon. I took it by the lug on the wooden heel of the pistol.

'*Lange Pistole*,' he said. '*Pilóta. Német.*'

I frowned, perplexed.

Tommy ran around with his arms out like a plane. '*Bombázó.*'

The mutts began chasing him, enjoying it. A waft of Tommy's perfume hit my nostrils. Tommy fell to the floor and pretended to die. Blister shook his head and tutted. The mutts licked Tommy's face—revolting.

'*Pilóta*,' Tommy said to me.

I studied the seven to eight-inch barrel and was curious about the black round magazine at the bottom. 'Luger?' I said. 'German Pilot?' I pointed in the air.

Tommy frowned and pointed at the Luger's magazine. '*Harminckét golyók.*'

I shrugged.

Tommy held up three fingers, then two. '*Harminckét.*'

As an educated guess, Tommy was trying to tell me it held thirty-two rounds. Blister abruptly held up two fingers and swore. Tommy innocently smiled.

'I'm off to find my best mate Titan,' Blister said.

'I thought I was your best,' I said sarcastically.

'Bollocks. You and Tommy can fight over Sikes when he drops the soap in the shower.'

I had taught him too much banter of our era.

Trying to keep my hands away from Tommy's growling mutts, I gesticulated and told Tommy to get these dead men back to the base. It took a few goes for him to understand.

Tommy was in Captain Don Wade's squad. Strangely, Tommy was Hungarian: Tamas 'Tommy' Sandor Ungvari. He was an infantryman from the common Hungarian Army; well, that's what we could glean. Tommy hardly spoke any English, mainly what he had picked up from this base. He would always pronounce things wrong. None of us could speak his language. Our squad constantly took the piss, and he always laughed along with the banter. Or was it just at us? He also appeared very spiritual and did not have any real fighting skills. We named him 'Tommy', being nothing like us British soldiers. Tommy had been a dog handler. His two faithful mutts were here with him. One, a muscular Hungarian Vizsla. The other, a stocky and mean Rottweiler. I hated them. They loathed me. In fact, the only person to get on with the mutts was Blister. But, he disliked Tommy. What a mess.

Three hours later, the first shift had dug a huge pit. After deciphering humans from animals, the remains and dead were buried. Where possible, each soldier, chef, and nurse had their pay book and dog-tag removed. The only padre on the base was remarkably busy, as well as emotionally overwhelmed.

The fantastic news: I had bumped into Titan, keeping our celebration down to a minimum handshake. Many others had lost their mates. The unwelcome news: we had lost another squad member. Captain Don Wade had been trampled to death trying to put out the fire at his stables—irony.

Captain Don Wade, VC, 1st Division Australian Imperial Force. Captain Wade, as he had to be addressed, was a tall, tanned, blunt, and a tough officer. Respectfully to his credit, he had survived Deville Wood and Gallipoli. He would ride in on his huge horse and order us to clean up the shit. I didn't get along with him too well, and was still waiting for him to ask me to pick up the dung. That would have gone down like a senior detective being thrown a huge surprise party, an ultimate insult.

Guilt came over me as I looked down at my blood-stained shins. It had been so hectic that I had forgotten about Lance Corporal Andrew 'Scouse' Price. No way was I going to join the squads of Sikes or Tommy and his mutts.

We left Blister to re-defence the artillery cannons and AA-guns. Titan told of the many that he had tried to save at the CCS. And, those he could not. Roll call in the morning would identify those that had not survived the unforeseen night air raid, a costly mistake on our part. Daylight would also show the extent of the bombing to our base.

I walked alone back to my tepee to gather my thoughts. With the new shift starting, I made sure my feet were healthy and then climbed into my cold bed. A simple nod to Blister and Titan as they entered was enough to show we understood how we felt. I shook the grit from my pillow and laid my head. My mind played the night's battle. An exhausted Seagal and Tommy poked their heads in to see if we were in bed.

A little while later, Werner came in limping, and then went out. I closed my eyes again and tried to shut out the battle sounds. I wondered if the other squad members, Matilda, and Khalida, were OK. Any negative that Scrap wasn't, I blocked. He had to be fine, being he was on stag or sleeping off his hangover on the ridge.

'That was some Saturday night bash,' Titan said.

A small chuckle resounded between us.

'Bloody hell, Tommy, if your dogs are going to have flatulence tonight, can you throw them outside,' Blister said.

Me and Titan laughed when we heard another fart from the opposite tepee.

'*Van a szép almákban is vannak savanyuk,*' Tommy shouted back.

After a light momentarily lit up the side of the tarpaulin, a wonderful incense captured me. Tommy began to mumble a prayer. Someone's deep breathing added to the hypnotic state.

CHAPTER THREE

It wasn't till I opened my crusty eyes to sounds of planes flying over and shouting, that I realised I wasn't dreaming about last night. I sat up at the same time as Blister. He looked fearful. The sun was just rising, adding a warming glow through the tarpaulin. I guessed the time to be 06:00 hours.

Quickly checking my boots for any nasty critters, I slung them on without doing up the laces and then grabbed my rifle. Scrap's bed was still empty, but I had no time for dread. I was closely followed out by Titan and Blister.

The planes were diving. Weirdly, no heavy machine guns or explosions echoed. Strangely, our men were cheering. I held the flap open to the neighbouring tepee to see Werner and Tommy still racing to get ready. Sikes wasn't in there.

'You lot should be fucking ready for action,' I reprimanded.

Blister and Titan smirked. Werner and Tommy frowned as if to say that I wasn't either. It would take a little time for them to understand me. Seagal stepped over a guide rope. He was fully kitted, and his puffy eyes showed he had not had much sleep. I had been told recently he was leaving the camp in the early hours of the morning.

'No one likes a show-off,' I said.

Private Michael Sorahan was 13th Division Royal Warwickshire Regiment. Michael's nickname 'Mick' was too obvious, so I changed it to 'Seagal'. Scrap had agreed with me that Sorahan resembled the actor and martial arts expert Steven Seagal. Our Seagal couldn't speak. He would intently listen, read books, make notes, and keep fit. It was fortunate that he could read and write. Many here couldn't. On the first few days of his arrival, a few soldiers had taken the piss whilst he did his martial arts workout. However, that stopped when word had got out that he was a crack-shot with any weapon, and that he oversaw the firing squad.

Seagal had been assigned to this mission whilst touring many French ladies' bedrooms whilst on R&R. Rumours were that he is larger endowed than Titan. His apparent skill was to take on his surroundings, blending in wherever he was sent, and to take out key people. He had also been ordered to pick men to join him in the firing squad. No one wanted that task. The only downside to his constant exercise routines and weapons training, was he would not workout with our squad. On occasions he would disappear off camp. Even those I had asked to tail him, had lost him. I was concerned he wasn't a team player, but at least he had stopped shaving and tanned himself like our squad.

Instinctively, Werner leapt to the ground on another low flyby. He would, they were the British B.E.2c, nicknamed 'Stability Jane'. It boosted us all. I knew the RFC had flown from their aerodrome based in Ujret el Zol, near El Arish. If only they had been alerted earlier before the night raid.

The two-seater B.E.2c fighter pilots did one more sweep. More silhouettes came out of the shadows and crazily waved at the planes that headed back off into the dusky-blue sky. A silence enveloped the camp as the tiny specks disappeared. I reckoned we all had mindfully wished them good luck.

'Get a brew on, Werner,' I said vacantly.

Werner shrugged his shoulders at me.

'*Holen Sie sich ein Gebräu auf,*' I repeated to him. '*Ja, ich habe Deutsch gelernt.*' I smugly nodded.

'Yes, our little Kaiser friend, we know a few phrases. Don't we, Blister,' Titan added.

'I would rather not speak to the fucking Jerry. At all,' Blister said, lip rising.

Werner mumbled something and then frostily opened the tepee flap to go in. Seagal held up his rifle and mimicked shooting Werner in the back. As we smirked, Tommy stood there grinning like a cat, even though it was in plain sight that Tommy hadn't a clue.

Wade's last squad member was Werner Löwenhardt, a German prisoner of war. He was a young pilot in the Deutsche Luftstreitkräfte who had deserted the frontline and landed on the French coast. His English was worse than Tommy's. Werner had no humour and kept his distance from everyone. Blister loathed him. Everyone kept a beady eye on Werner, especially when he was armed. We didn't have a nickname for him, other than derogatory words. I objected to him being on the mission. Yet,

Rowe had told me to shut up and get on with it. How Rowe got to find Werner and why the German was here was anyone's guess.

'We need a nickname for Werner,' I said. 'And to cut him some slack.'

'Why?' Blister asked.

'It's easier than pronouncing his real name Werner Löwenhardt.'

'I meant, why do we have to cut the Jerry some slack?' Blister said.

'Like Tommy, Werner has defected and could be an asset. I'd rather have him accepted into the mission, than an outcast.'

'Bollocks. I'm never going to accept…'

'I hope you've brought that shiny armoured vest with you, pal,' Titan interrupted Blister, 'as Werner may turn his weapon on your back.'

Blister rubbed his old back injury from the Somme, looking distant.

'Werner, come here,' I shouted. '*Komm her.*'

Werner came out, dubious as to why we were all eying him.

'I know you understand English more than you let on. All Germans were taught it,' I said.

'A little,' he said.

'Good…*gute.*' I held my hand out—someone tutted.

Werner looked at the others, possibly contemplating this was a trick. Perhaps Sikes had headbutted him. I prompted Werner's hand, and he nervously shook mine.

'Welcome into the squad,' I said.

Werner nodded the acceptance.

'Not in our squad,' Blister muttered. 'He can stay in Wade's. Perhaps he should have died instead of Wade.'

Titan put his huge hand out. And so, it went around until it came to Blister. I knew this would be challenging.

'Shake it, Blister,' I ordered.

Blister kept his hand on his rifle.

'Respect is not imposed nor begged, Blister. It's earned *and* offered,' I said.

Werner, staring passively into Blister's harsh gaze, prompted the handshake. '*Genosse.*'

None of us had any idea, until Tommy said, 'He say, *Elvtárs*…err… comrade…friend.'

Blister lent his rifle against himself and gave Werner a firm but short shake. Tommy sighed in happiness.

'Right, Werner, we need a nickname for you as your real name is shit,' I said.

'*Scheiße?*' he replied incredulously.

'How about deserter?' Blister said.

Werner hadn't understood that remark.

'You're literally too dumb to insult, Mark. Stay out of it,' I said.

'*Dunai svábok*,' Tommy said.

'Speak English, Tommy, for fuck's sake,' I said.

'*Dunai svábok is* Hungarian for *Donauschwaben*,' Werner translated. 'Means Danube Swabians in *Englisch*. German-speaking people of south-eastern Europe, big in the Danube River valley…err…ethnic German…'

'Yeah, all right, Werner,' I interrupted, 'I don't want a fucking history lesson. Just a bloody nickname for fuck's sake.'

Everyone found it amusing. Well, except Werner and Tommy.

Shouting from the main camp stopped any more amusement. The voices were becoming heightened. Others joined in, the loudest and angriest being Sikes. Now who was he upsetting? A single shot fired. Like the start of a race, we all jumped the white wooden pegs holding the guide ropes and ran towards the trouble. At the bottom of the dune in the dusk was a large group of RFC servicemen and pilots. All were jostling with Sikes. Army lads like us were running over to the base of the slope. A fist was thrown and then all hell broke loose. I gave strict instructions to our squad to only pull them apart.

Titan had picked up most of the scrawnier blokes and carried them away. A few RFC officers still held down Sikes. The rest of our squad formed a line between the divisions with arms out to calm it all down. I spotted a German pilot on his back. His uniform was torn, and he had a bullet hole in his forehead. The sand soaked up the red mist. I narrowed my eyes at Sikes who still held his pistol in his restricted movement.

A furious officer came charging through the restless crowd.

'This is not how we do things,' he said. 'Move aside. I am Squadron Commander Geoff Williams.'

I couldn't think of any excuses for Sikes' crazy actions. It didn't help when Williams saw me scoff at his thigh length putties and wing-like trousers that stuck out a good ten inches. The widest I had seen so far. Werner emotionally stood over the dead German pilot.

'We have a chivalrous conduct between us and the German pilots,' Williams said. 'If this ruddy well gets out, they will slaughter any of our chaps that are found.'

'What do you mean?' I said.

'We give them the finest hospitality and hand them back unharmed. Occasionally, we trade them for our captured pilots.'

'It's a bit different from what we're used to on the Somme,' I said.

'We hardly have any pilots and planes as it is,' Williams retorted.

'You could always fly your trousers,' I muttered.

'I beg your pardon?'

'I said, you could always buy some Howitzers.'

'Listen in, young man, we are still the gentlemanly type here, and take to the skies. Now, you play by my...'

'We're just gentlemen playing the thugs game,' I butted in.

'By Jove, that sort of behaviour can get you into hot water.'

'Tell your men to release our sergeant,' I ordered.

'Young man, he has just shot...'

'Do it now, or you'll have a fucking bloodbath on your hands.'

Williams' large moustache twitched; his monocle dropped. The officer took off his peaked cap. Was he gearing up for a fight?

'Werner, take the German's tags and pay book,' I said.

Werner understood the importance and started searching.

'Who is your superior?' Williams asked, frustrated.

'You lads just gawping,' I said to the army lads, 'pick up the corpse and take him over to the burial ground before he attracts any further flies in your breakfast.'

'You have not heard the last of this...'

'It's Johnny Vince,' I filled in Williams' pause. 'And yes, I've heard the last. Including any more of your threats. Now fuck off.'

I turned and took hold of one of the RFC blokes. Twisting his hand around, he released his grip on Sikes. I carried on turning it. He yelled. There was a stalemate as I held it. The RFC lads started to circle me. Tommy held his mutts at bay on leads. With minimal commands, they started to growl.

'Your chap won't fly much with a broken arm, fella,' Blister said to Williams.

'Oh, I have forgotten my first aid if it snaps,' Titan added.

'Release the sergeant,' Williams said.

I let go of the hand and took a step back. The six blokes got off Sikes.

'Titan, get a brew on for us,' I ordered.

'But you asked Werner...'

'Add a bit of rum in Werner's whilst you make him one,' I interrupted Titan.

Titan frowned. I nodded at a tearful Werner as he fumbled through the dead pilot's photos and papers.

'Two sugars in mine,' Blister said smugly.

'And you can get the Sudanese chefs to make us a *special* breakfast, Blister,' I ordered.

'Plenty of salt on mine,' Titan added.

With the crowd dispersing, Tommy kept Baka and Rudi close to Sikes. Sikes had now sat up with his arms around his knees, staring into nothing.

'Leave us, Tommy,' I said.

Tommy looked at me for more translation.

'Go. Take your mutts and leave us.' I pointed.

Tommy smiled; the dogs growled.

Turning back to Sikes, he was reloading his pistol. I handed him a reassuring hand to get up. He got onto his knees by pushing on his cudgel, so I pulled in my offer.

'Fucking traitors,' he hissed.

I wasn't sure if he had meant the German pilot, the RFC, or both. 'You didn't have to kill him.'

'You missed the roll call. I could have you in front of Private Sorahan. Make sure you're at the next stand-to, Corporal Hurst.'

I frustratingly sighed. 'How many men have we lost?'

'Twenty-three army, six flying corps, two nurses, four cooks, seven horses, four camels, all two Pierce-Arrows, six RM, one truck, two motorbikes, and a lot of equipment.' Sikes came in close to my face, eyes maddened. 'Do you still question why I shot the Hun?'

'Have you seen Georges?'

'Who, laddie?' he grumbled.

'You know who I mean.'

I stared hard into his cold eyes. His expression remained dead-pan. Sick of his games, I took back my own personal space. Sikes looked me up and down in my vest, shorts, and undone bootlaces. He then pushed me aside with his club and began to trudge back to camp.

'You need to get your shambles sorted,' he said.

'We leave tonight.'

'Good.'

I was not expecting him to agree so easily. Yet, there was something malevolent growing in him. Worse than it already was.

With my hand shielding the rising sun, I looked across at the high dunes to where Scrap had apparently set up his fire-position. There were quite a lot of unidentified objects still scattered about. I scratched my bites and pondered whether to venture out to search, but decided I first had to get kitted. It added to the tension of finding him alive.

On the way back to camp, most of the carnage had been cleared, except the flies that swarmed on the raked sand. I pictured Blister running over the horse before it was pulled out. It was morbid, but it lifted me.

A new marquee had been erected. The smell of cooking wafted in. Seagal came out and handed me a steaming billy can of stewed meat in a sauce with naan bread on top.

'Bit early for a curry. What happened to a bully beef and egg sandwich?' I said, hoping he might just speak.

Seagal nodded once and then walked away.

Titan came over and placed a mug at my feet. 'Here you go, pal.'

I spat the hot food back in the billy can. 'Shit. That's hot.'

Titan pulled a disgusted face. 'Your etiquette is that of a Bedouin.'

'Well, we all look like them now.'

I pulled at his beard. The naan fell onto the floor; also spilling my tea.

'You do that again, pal, and I'll shave your tiny beard off with a blunt bone-saw,' he said.

Savouring the last of the black tea, I said, 'Where's the goat milk?'

Titan tapped the mess tin in my hand and said, 'Poor old Billy Goat Gruff had to be sacrificed. But we've still got two of them back at the bridge.'

'That's fucking dark, Titan.'

'Not as dark as the curry for supper, and it's not Bloodstone they're using.' He smiled.

'What's "Bloodstone"?'

'Came second at the 1912 Grand National. My father won a grand on that horse.'

'What's that got to do with dinner?'

'You said the goat meat was dark. Well, dinner will be an Australian Waler horse. Possibly Captain Wade's.' Titan walked back to the mess marquee.

I lowered my food tin and said, 'I meant your *humour* was dark. You've changed, Jason.'

'Taught by the best.' He bellowed a laugh.

Next to come up to me was Tommy with his mutts off the lead. Rudi munched frantically at the naan bread. Could it get any worse? I gulped back the unwelcome black tea to wash down the spicy curried goat. My hand jolted, and I looked down to see Baka was licking at the billy can whilst Rudi enviously looked on. I shook my head. Baka looked up with a 'what you gonna do about it' look. I dropped the tin in dismay.

'What do you want, Tommy?' I snapped.

Tommy pointed to the ADS and said, '*Fémhulladék.*'

'Right now, Tommy, I haven't got the fucking time. I need to find Scrap.'

He grabbed my arm and thrust his pointing. '*Igen,*' he shrieked. 'Yes. Scrap…Scrap.'

'Is he OK?'

'Huh?'

I grabbed both his shoulders; the mutts throatily growled. 'Is he dead or alive?'

'Err…yes…*diákok, segítsen neki.*'

'"*Diákok*"?' I repeated. 'D for dead? Yes?'

'*Igen…*yes…*diákok.*'

Sprinting back to my tent, I ignored Tommy's shouting. I tried to block the thoughts of Georges being dead, but it was impossible. Perhaps this meant he would wake up in the tomb. Maybe he would wake me up. Did I want to wake up now? Before the mission. Leave my squad to do it without me.

Inside our humid tepee, I whipped on my uniform and then properly did up my boots. Finally adjusting my hat, I slipped on my watch. Blister walked casualty in. He rubbed his belly and then belched.

'How was the breakfast? *Special* enough for you?' he said flippantly.

'Was that your idea?'

'We don't want goats sniffing out the Special Forces. Remember those stories you told us.'

'Blister, round the whole squad up. We're leaving this evening. Meet me at the main hangar for a briefing at 09:00 hours. On the dot. Bring my kit.'

'What's up? You look flustered. Where're you going?'

I didn't want to lower his morale about the death of Georges, so I said, 'Just do as you've been ordered. And get Sikes there.'

Knowing where they were parked, I ran across the main area to the RFC officers' tents and found one of the six aligned Triumph Model-H. As always, I knew it would not start straight off. I had to get the starting procedure correct or I would have to dry out the spark plug before trying again. There were seven controls, plus the manual oil pump. Remembering my recent training, I set the gear lever to the neutral position. As the bike was cold, I gave three full pumps of oil and then screwed it clockwise to close the pump. A few soldiers walked by, inquisitively muttering. Yet, I had to concentrate on getting the thing started.

I opened the decompression lever on the crankcase and slightly held back the ignition lever. Voices had started inside the tent next to me. I quickly fully closed the air valve. My sweat landed on the green-beige coloured tank. After turning the fuel tank on, I pulled out the kick-start lever. I gave it a thrust down, one…two…three.

'Excuse me, Corporal, what are you doing?'

Ignoring the RFC private holding a load of used billy cans next to me, I set the air lever to normal, about one third open. I then moved the throttle to about one eighth open.

'You know these are the officers' motorbikes, do you not?' he asked.

With a brisk kick, I started the motorbike. The distinctive sound and smell of the engine revved as if waking the whole of Egypt. This was not the stealthiest of 'borrows' I had done.

'I am off to find Squadron Commander Williams,' the stroppy lad blurted.

Oh shit, I am already in his disciplinary book. I had to keep the lad and engine sweet, but at the same time, get the hell out of here.

'Hop on. I've received direct orders from Williams to deliver this bike to the Shepheard's Hotel in Cairo,' I lied.

'That is eighty miles away.'

'When you're having champagne with Colonel Thomas Lawrence, you do as you're told.'

'My gosh. Hold on, I will get my cap,' he said enthusiastically.

'Don't forget your rifle, or Lawrence of Arabia will have your guts for garters,' I said, impersonating a fine Rupert.

I fiddled all the controls to normal running and closed off the air decompression as he sprinted off with joy. By now the stand had sunk into the sand. I rolled the bike forward and then fastened the stand to the rear mudguard. The seat springs squeaked under the large brown leather saddle. One legged, I pushed it out onto the main track. At last, I selected first gear with the side lever. I still smirked at the time it had taken, even though I was frantic to get to the hospital. Setting off, I clunked it into second gear, wobbling as I did. The lad came out of his tent at the end of the track.

'Wanker,' I shouted.

The undulating ground bounced me out of the seat. At the same time, I tried to avoid missing the oncoming patrols and horses. I did not appear to be flavour of the month as I sped by causing a mini dust storm. One of last night's attacks had obviously got close, I thought, skirting around the huge crater. If Trish hadn't gone back and made sure all the inside and outside lights had been turned off, I wonder if a catastrophic direct hit would have been made on the hospital.

Pulling the break lever well in advance was something I had learnt, having previously crashed into one of our trucks on a training exercise, much to the amusement of my squad. I cut the engine and leant the bike against a high sandbagged wall. I couldn't be arsed to find some hard ground to set the stand. Blinking the grit from my eyes and dusting myself down, I mentally laughed at the rigmarole of using the Triumph Trusty compared to the well-advanced and kitted quads we had used in Afghanistan. It was a brief enjoyment; my thoughts had turned to Georges. Yes, we had lost two of the mission's great men last night. However, to lose a mate, someone who I could talk to about my world and them utterly understanding, was sickening. I took in a large breath, psyching myself up for what Tommy had told me.

CHAPTER FOUR

Quickly entering the rear of the main tent, I bumped into Matron Law carrying a load of bandages. She had flecks of blood on her normally pristine white uniform. Obviously from the lack of torso stains, she had worn an apron. I went to go around her, but she firmly held my arm.

'Good morning, Corporal Jim Hurst. What brings you over to the real battle?'

'Not now, Becky, I need to find Georges Demblon. I've heard he's dead.'

'It is Rebecca. And you address me as Matron Law. Also, we have not had a Private Georges Demblon in, dead or injured.'

I relaxed.

'But we had Private William Hewitt stretchered in last night.'

I sighed. 'You know Georges is his real name. Forget what Sikes says.'

'I am sorry, Corporal Jim Hurst, but rules when addressing soldiers must be up-held. Especially the undaunted Sergeant Sean Rowe. And it is about time you and your men stopped looking like filthy Arabs.'

I frustratingly edged forwards and looked along the many perfectly aligned cane camp beds.

'Where's Scrap? Is he dead?'

'As soon as you stop using nicknames, the...'

'Listen, Matron, I've had a really fucking pissy morning. I've just found out my mate is...'

'Vinnie.'

My heart jumped knowing the voice. I then spotted the big arm that was waving through a group of soldiers who were surrounding him at the side of the marquee.

'Georges,' I yelled excitedly.

Matron Law let my arm go. I sifted through the male and female medical staff wearing white head and face cloths. The boards on the floor were covered loosely in desert sand. I wondered if it was blown in or laid purposely to soak up the mess. It stunk of all sorts in here.

The soldiers moved slightly back. I didn't recognise their uniform and insignia. Georges swung his legs over the bed. His trust-up nightgown bared his uninjured legs. He managed to stand, although with a little trouble. We were both really pleased to see each other, and I gave him a hug. His huge hands slapped my back. As we parted, the men around seemed a little unsure.

'*Aweh, my bru*,' he said. 'It is *befok* to see you are OK.'

'Scrap, I've told you about using that Africana shit. What happened…'

I stopped as my shoulder was abruptly turned, just after I had studied Scrap's awkward look. The tanned and rugged brute soldier still had his hand on me. His mates also seemed irritated.

'These are my brothers from the first South African Infantry,' Georges said, concerned.

I looked at the animal head with horns over the infantry unit name badge on this soldier's collar, and then to his stare. He squeezed my shoulder.

'They are from the Cape Regiment. They have been asking loads of questions about me, but I cannot remember as I am concussed,' Georges said, overdoing it.

I realised why Georges was lying, and half-smiled at the soldier. I sensed more had stood close behind me, energising the tension.

'Scrap, ask him if he speaks English,' I facetiously said.

'*Hier kom Groot Kak*,' another soldier said.

'What did the prick behind me say?' I said, taking the hand off my shoulder. 'Get your shit together, Scrap. We're heading out tonight.'

'Hey,' someone shouted. 'If you boys are here for a cough and drop, then follow me.'

Trish barged her way in and stood between us. She held up a large pair of blooded forceps and then leant towards the soldier still defiantly standing in front of me. Her beady eyes provoked his.

'I will yank yours so hard, that they will spring back up and sit on your chest like a row of medals,' she sinisterly whispered.

'Best do what the fucking crazy surgeon says, boys,' I said.

'This is far from over, Georges. I am off to find Company Sergeant Major Laver,' the leader said.

'Yeah, I know him. Give him my regards,' Scrap said—it was too false.

With Trish snapping the forceps together, the group quickly followed the main man towards the exit.

'Ready for your examination before we leave?' she said to me.

'I think my balls went into hiding as quick as Scrap's. And what do you mean, "before we leave"?'

'I would suggest you get out of bed earlier,' Trish said, 'instead of playing with your penis. Half the camp is moving out towards Tel el Sheria after our bombing raid blew the shit out of them. Orders from General Rowe.'

I took my cold stare back from an injured soldier who had obviously found Trish's penis remark funny. 'General Rowe is here?'

Georges started getting hurriedly changed.

'Yes, and Albert was *very* kind to me,' she coyly said.

'You never,' I said. 'Did you?'

Trish smiled and tapped her nose. 'I see you never denied playing with your penis.'

The injured soldier was now laughing in his pillow.

'Oh fuck off, Trish, before I speak to Matron.'

Trish snapped the forceps together once more, smiled, and walked off.

I turned to Scrap who was almost dressed and grinning stupidly at me. 'What?'

'You. "Before I speak to Matron",' he said in a girly voice.

'What did your mate say? The one from the South African infantry you belonged to in World War One,' I said facetiously.

'"Here comes the big shit", I think. I am glad you came as I had no idea about this era and the South African Army. It was getting heated.'

'What's happened to you?' I asked.

'Last night, taking up a position on the outer dunes, I was giving the Lewis gun everything. The next thing, I awoke here in bed. Smith and Bell carried me back.'

'I meant, what's happened to you, as in, you lost your bottle to fend off a few pansy South African Infantry.'

Scrap stood up in urgency, but closed his mouth. He then relaxed having seen me try to hide my smirk.

'Did you come on the Trusty Triumph?' he said.

'Yes. Get your kit ready and meet me in the hangar at 09:00 hours.'

He started hobbling and over-doing his acting. 'What about my lift, my *bru*?'

'It's not designed for your weight.'

I went through a shorter starting procedure, being easier as it was warm. As Scrap got to within a few metres, I rode off towards the hangar. The noise drowned out his swearing, and I gave him the middle finger.

On the way, I noticed the camp being dismantled. I had previously thought it was being rebuilt after last night's raid. I will be bending Tommy's scrotum with a harsh chat, the ear not being enough. Although elated that Scrap wasn't dead, I had this horrible feeling. It was like a depression hanging over me, growing as the day went on.

Once a decent track was found, I operated the Sturmey-Archer three-speed countershaft gearbox lever into third and opened up this 499-cc air-cooled four-stroke single-cylinder Trusty. The hangar destination was right on the outskirts of the main village. The idea being it was easier to get the stock off the train and stored away. In the hangar was the kit and trucks I had requested off General Rowe. I smirked thinking of Trish's wind-up about sleeping with him. Well, I hoped it was.

There still had been no word of Matilda and Khalida since last night. Why had Sikes ordered Khalida along? She was the last in Sikes' squad. A Bedouin. This was all the information we were given at the briefing. She stood away from the men. Many lads chatted about what was beneath her flowing silky clothes. No one even came close to choosing a nickname for her. Although her eyes were beautiful and sultry under her silk maroon mask, like Batman's mask, I did not trust her. At all. For all I knew he-she could have a beard and carrying an RPG and AK47; it was known in Afghan—I chuckled. Let's hope Khalida bottled it last night and rode off on a camel into the sunset: missing in action.

With the large double hangars in sight, I passed two empty AA-gunnery positions. I became annoyed that they were unmanned. On my first day here, I had compiled a whole restructure of the security defence, being previously none. Eventually, having gone through the correct channels, Sikes and his uncle had cleared my requests. Barbed wire fences had been erected around the perimeter. A secondary one a few metres inside that. Although a little crude, four timber and high sentry-posts had been erected. All had communications through high cables; HMGs, ammo, flares, and binos. The last bit of kit took some time because of the reluctance of the Marine lads. The searchlight was to create artificial moonlight to enhance opportunities for night attacks by reflecting searchlight beams off the bottoms of clouds. A gantry was built onto each side of the hangar to support the weight. Each stag would only last four hours with enough water and food. Smoking was strictly forbidden.

As I reached the choked checkpoint, I started braking in advance and slowing with the gears. The other sentry was still hunkered behind his Lewis. The first guard slung his weapon over his shoulder and approached me. I gave him my papers, even though he knew who I was. Whilst he checked, I wiped the water and dust mix from my eyes and then double-checked the sentry towers were manned—they were. He handed back my papers.

'Why aren't the fucking AA guns manned back there, Smudge?' I said.

'Sergeant Rowe ordered the gunners to help dismantle the ones in the base, Vinnie.'

What the fuck, I thought. 'Oh, great, let's hope today you don't get any Germans flying over.'

'Unless they are putting on an acrobat show. Take away the boredom,' Foxy said.

I looked across at the gunner, his silver and greasy hair glistening in the sun. 'Be careful what you wish for, Foxy. And put your bloody helmet on.'

'Nice bike,' Smudge said. 'Looks like Squadron Commander Williams'.'

He tapped the small black identification plate over the front mudguard. Oh fuck, I was now scribbled out of the 'disciplinary book', and now in the 'face the firing squad book'. An idea came to mind. I leant to my side and opened the rear attached side canvas satchel, hoping to find a bribe.

'To kill two birds with one stone, lads,' I said, 'how about you both never saw me on this bike.'

Smudge exaggerated sucking air through his teeth.

I pulled out a box of cigars and handed them over to Smudge. 'And to help take away the boredom, you make sure you keep back Blister, Titan, and Scrap for a strip search.'

Foxy came around and peered into the box at the same time as Smudge. I delved back deeper and pulled some photos. The first black and white photo was of a woman with her long dress pulled up, showing her bare legs. The next was of an Asian woman in a headdress and veil, her robe pulled open. A Tribal like necklace hung between her bare breasts. Just as I looked at the third fully naked lady posing with her bare back and bum tattoos, Foxy grabbed the lot.

'Pornography. Bloody tremendous,' he said.

Almost dropping the cigars, Smudge snatched one. 'Always thought the windy ones were worse than us.'

'The what?' I said.

'The officers. They talk flatulence.'

'So, we have a deal?' I said.

They nodded and waved me on, still looking through the wad of photos. No use asking them to keep their eyes peeled for the enemy.

A section of railway with a weight on one end was lifted by an armed guard. Behind him was a larger sheltered bunker with two HMGs facing front and rear. He looked at me inquisitively. Was it because he wanted a gift?

Slowly stopping the motorbike with the help of my feet up to the newly built underground bunker, I got off and wheeled it backwards to under the corrugated roofed entrance. Hopefully, this would hide it from prying eyes. Time check: 07:59 hours. The temperature was warming nicely. Possibly twelve degrees. It may have been higher as I had acclimatised well, being out here for eight months. The tan was also doing great.

Before I went into the door-less front hangar, I decided to walk around the perimeter and check the barbed wire. I shouted and waved to each sentry, expecting the muffled banter that came back. It was me that had drawn-up the stag rota, but it was Sikes who would choose the men he had found slacking in duties. However, I found the men of this era more disciplined, even the new recruits. I think Sikes just picked anyone because of their face or accent that annoyed him that day.

On the north side, a pile of junk sat. It had accumulated in size since my last visit a week ago. Were they parts of the German bombers that sat on top from last night's raid? It wasn't just metal sheets, wheels, and vehicle parts, but timber, canvas, and glass. You would think it was run by Gypsies. Yet, the man in charge of his engineers, mechanics, and technicians, was a bloke called Second Lieutenant Peter Brightley. He spoke like Jacob Rees-Mogg. You couldn't get any further from a pikey.

Peter Brightley was from the Royal Flying Corps. I had given him the name 'Flash-heart' after seeing him for the first time in his flying outfit whilst he tinkered with a 'Stability Jane'. He reminded me of Wing Commander Lord Flash-heart from *Blackadder*. Obviously, no one else understood the nickname. But, it stuck, much to Peter's protest.

Flash-heart had been grounded for the last month after coming in from a mission. He was involved in a dog-fight. Although his gunner had been killed, Flash-heart managed to get back on fumes. However, he made a bit of a messy landing. Even whilst getting his legs attended in the ADS, he couldn't stop speaking about planes. Flash-heart would tinker with any medical equipment left lying around. I think it was Matron Law who gave him a quick medical discharge to return to work. However, he was still not permitted to fly.

After sifting through the junk pile to see if I could use any of the new stuff, I headed back to the hangar. The familiar garage smells were evident. Yet, a little stronger than normal when our squad would visit the makeshift gym constructed by Flash-heart and his team. I shouldn't call it makeshift as he had done a decent job making it to my requirements of a gym of my era.

'Flash-heart?' I shouted, my voice echoing off the skylighted high roof.

With no answer, I checked the office area. I then decided to search the hangar next door. I smiled seeing the other team members: two Dennis trucks converted to my spec. Where was the third one? Perhaps Flash-heart had taken it out for a spin. Like the programme *Top Gear*, the whole team had bolted the North America shipped twelve-millimetre aluminium plates down the sides of the lorry. Oblong two-inch by five-inch cross slits had been cut in every metre. A sewn together skirt made from the tank crewmen's tan leather jerkins could be rolled down from the inside to cover the sixteen inches of remaining gap to the ground.

I strolled around the front, happy with small holes drilled for ventilation to the front twenty-millimetre armour plate on the radiator. The main problem was the truck's weight. Everything that could be taken off, had been. This included the main half-timber doors, wooden B-pillar panels, four mudguards, original green tarpaulin cab and rear cover, lights, and mirrors. It became an obsession: the horn, towing hook, nuts and bolts, and storage boxes. Even the side Lewis' had their bi-pods removed. The swivel joint was then bolted directly to the vehicle. We had exchanged the original heavier metal pole frame for lighter cane and then stitched on a further canvas sheet to the original material roof. The front iron bar that held the canvas straps was removed; instead, the original straps lengthened. It was the same type of cover that had been fitted to the rear of the truck, the identical material used on the planes. It was my idea to paint it beige with a pink tinge. Whilst wet with glue, we had stretched it out in the sun and caused a mini sandstorm. Once dry, we tested the camouflage from a far distance, looking like the desert we were in. With the correct colour shade chosen, everything on the truck was painted; including, anything that was added.

Becoming bored with waiting, I sauntered to the rear of the hangar.

I was pleased to see the other members: three Trusty motorbikes. All had been painted the same pinky-beige colour. A last-minute design had been added: a Bakelite fairing that shielded the engine. The main reason was to keep as much sand out of the engine parts. The holes made in the faring were covered in a fine mesh. Easy to clean if clogged. Canvas side satchels were fitted on both sides to carry extra provisions. One Trusty had a sidecar fitted that supported an HMG. Unlike the other modifications we had done, this had been shipped over as standard. But, I would have thought of it.

No kit had been loaded yet as the original mission's start date wasn't until next week. The pile of equipment wasn't huge. I wondered if my calculations were correct. We were already on the bare minimum for fuel, drinking water, and food rations. After a little persuasion from Sikes, I had agreed we took horses. However, due to the amount of provisions to keep for them, he had agreed to my negotiation that one horse to each squad.

'Johnny.'

I turned to see Flash-heart limping over. He was covered in oil and paint, including his face where he had not had a wash and shave, always leaving a blond moustache. His blond hair was scruffier than normal, appearing wild.

'Where have you been?' I asked.

'Grabbing a few winks, but not forty. Not enough time, chap.'

'Where's the third truck?'

Honk…honk…honk!

An old type of hand-squeezed horn had interrupted Flash-heart. Coming into the hangar was a beautiful dark-green car with polished brass fittings. Who was that? Oh shit, I bet that's General Rowe. To my surprise, I clocked Seagal through its half-window screen. He was beaming with joy, until he saw me. He was probably expecting it to be a mechanic. I signalled for him to stop. Reluctantly, he got out. I spotted an exceptionally large trunk sat bulkily across the rear leather seats.

'Where did you get this?' I asked.

Seagal guiltily looked at Flash-heart.

Wiping the sandy residue off its curved wing, I walked around the rear and pulled at the trunk. Seagal harshly grabbed my arm.

'Don't fucking touch me again, Seagal, unless you've got something to say.'

'That's my equipment,' he grumbled.

I was stunned. Five weeks he had been here, and not a word said.

We all looked to the raised voices coming from the main security gate.

'Flash-heart, please help me off with the trunk,' Seagal said urgently. 'I need to back slang it. And I need to hide this car.'

Going along with the haste, I helped untie the canvas straps to the material roof-liner and then pulled it back. We rapidly manhandled out the substantially heavy trunk. Seagal was unhappy that we had not taken much care as we had dropped it. Seagal speedily drove the car out the rear and turned sharply right. Flash-heart tried to wave the exhaust fumes away as a motorbike and sidecar came driving from the main gate. Two dogs followed in the background.

'Do not mention the Crossley, Johnny,' Flash-heart whispered.

'You knew that Seagal could speak.'

The motorbike went into the adjacent hangar. Perhaps we were silhouetted because it was bright outside. Two men laden with gear followed the same path. Who were they dressed in a dusky-blue uniform?

'We'll discuss this later, Flash-heart,' I sternly said. 'But for now, follow me.'

Deciding to go out the back way, we then come in the rear of the other hangar. Sikes was in discussion with Tommy who was fully kitted in his Hungarian uniform and knee-high grey suede boots and putties. Even more surprising to me, Werner was dressed in his German pilots' uniform. Werner took off his full-length brown leather coat and threw it on the large pile of kit, showing off his tightly-fitted uniform. General Rowe spotted us and came away from the gym equipment.

'By Jove, Corporal Hurst, you have changed since I last inspected you in London,' General Rowe said.

'A-plus athlete now; fit as fuck,' I boasted.

Again, Sikes looked raged and came marching over with his club in hand. Rowe held up his hand to his nephew's threat.

'I meant your down-right shabby Arab appearance. Make sure you are spick and span before you head out tonight. You are supposed to be representing the finest British Army.'

'Like Werner and Tommy,' I said flippantly.

Rowe glowered. 'May I remind you that you are only second in command, and Sean here is first.'

'Oi, Vinnie, was that your fucking idea back there?'

Cringing, I turned to see Blister blinking fast to get accustomed to the gloom. Blister stopped suddenly and dropped everything he was holding. He saluted. Titan bumped hard into Blister. Seeing General Rowe, Titan did the same salute—it was a Laurel and Hardy moment. To make things even worse, Scrap strolled in and stood holding a load of kit. His untucked shirt was over his hips. Scrap looked at Titan and Blister and then dropped his stuff. He then incorrectly saluted. I shook my head in dismay. Rowe lowered his salute and headed over to them. Rowe prodded at Titan's huge bicep with his whip, and then nodded at Scrap to tuck himself in.

'My God, what are they feeding you riffraff?' Rowe asked.

'Goats and…'

'And Australian horses, sir,' Blister interrupted Titan.

'Private Hewitt, not seen a shiny-green Crossley Model-15, have you?' Rowe insinuated.

I turned sharply to Flash-heart; my eyes ablaze. I then glared at Seagal who had crept in.

'No, sir, don't even know what one of those is?' Scrap answered, sounding guilty.

'Where did you leave it, sir?' Titan said, his voice sounding posher than normal.

'Stolen outside the Savoy Hotel in Cairo. Back seat full of the finest Cognac and cigars.'

'Jolly bad luck. "Finest Cognac and cigars", you say,' Blister said.

'I request my car returns with the gifts. If you hear anything, that is,' Rowe insinuated, again.

The three of them took on a shade of guilt. Rowe whipped Blister on the chest with a horsewhip, and then pointed the whip at me.

'Including you, Corporal Hurst, I do not want you all to resemble disgusting Arabs. You will all be clean shaven, haircut decent, and looking respectful. If not, you will be placed in front of the firing squad. We do not want the Turks and Germans to think we have no discipline.'

'Sir, that means you'll have to find someone else to replace Private Sorahan in the firing squad. Isn't that right, Seagal,' Blister said, and nodded over my shoulder.

Rowe swivelled around and clapped eyes on Seagal who looked as shabby as us. He then sharply turned to Sikes.

'Sean, what the devil has happened to this unit?' Rowe said.

'I will…'

'You unquestionably will get this rabble sorted.'

With the tension building, Baka squatted and took a big shit. I wanted the ground to swallow me up. What else could go wrong? Rudi started to smell the large turd. For reasons unknown to me, Rudi started to eat it. Tommy broke line and went over and yanked at the lead. Tommy was trying to keep his anger to a mumble, but he slid momentarily in the shit. Blister tried to keep his laugh in but couldn't. Rudi decided it was his turn to leave a deposit. I'm not sure who was going to explode first, Rowe, Sikes, or me slotting the mutts? Give me a break, I thought, like my neck.

Beep…beep!

An ambulance was driving towards our hangar. It reduced the fits of giggles, but not taking away the awful smell of shite. What the fuck had Tommy been feeding those two? Then I remembered the billy can of goat curry and spicy naan bread.

Matron and Trish got out, and from around the rear came Matilda.

'Nice to have you back, Corporal Davies,' Sikes said. 'Good to bring some real order to this mission.'

Sikes looked at me in disgust. Matilda wryly smiled. That's all we needed, more ammo for Matilda, I thought.

The other Australian to Captain Wade was Corporal Malcolm 'Matilda' Davies. He was originally from the 1st Light Horse Brigade, now called the Anzac Mounted Division. Davies had a way of getting under your skin. He would go on about his kind being superior in the Egyptian Expeditionary Force, us Brits being nothing but pathetic foot soldiers or dunny cleaners. His favourite story was to tell us the word 'Poms', as he called us, came from his forefathers in the Australian Cavalry in the Boer War. Us British couldn't ride properly without hanging onto our standard tall saddle pommel. Many times, I could have put him on his back. Yet, I was remembering when it was necessary to flick the aggressive switch. To keep the peace, I called him Matilda. He hated it.

'Sean, get this lot in the briefing room,' Rowe said. 'I just want a quick chat with Sister Spiga.'

Sikes never said a word. His revolted glare at us said it all. One by one we headed into the briefing room. I held back Tommy and Seagal.

'Tommy, why did you say Scrap was dead?' I asked.

Tommy looked dumbfounded.

I pointed at the ambulance and then in the direction of the hospital. 'You said dealock…dead.'

'Dealock? Oh…*diákok*,' he said. 'Yes, *diákok, diákok segítsen neki*.'

Seagal tried to hide his smirk.

I sharply pointed for Tommy to go into the briefing room.

Seagal leant over and whispered, 'Tommy said, "Students help him", as in Scrap. *Diákok* means students, not dead.'

'Not only do you now miraculously speak, but you can fucking translate Hungarian.'

Time check: 09:00 hours.

CHAPTER FIVE

Like that of Operation Poppy Pride, in the briefing room the lads sat on chairs in front of desks. With Blister on one side and Titan on the other, they whispered about the strip search hassle they had with the guards. Sat in front of them, I played ignorant. Scrap whacked the back of my head with something and cursed me for not giving him a lift from the hospital. The others sniggered. This class was getting out of hand.

Sikes and Rowe put a stop to the silliness by handing out pencils and papers. With a huge blackboard, Sikes started discussing the details of the intended Target-1: the railway station at Deir el Belah, southwest of Gaza.

Target-2 was a fortified aerodrome at Beersheba, southeast of Gaza. Different maps of the area were shown. Yet, he did not mention anything about friendly villages, areas for food and water supplies, and enemy numbers. However, our squad had done all our homework over the last ten months, even asking the locals at Cairo and Ismailia. It was an extremely poor briefing from Sikes. I have had more instructions from a microwave meal.

Titan tried to hide his yawn as Rowe took over. Blister showed me a drawing of a cock and balls on his paper.

'Why are you not making notes?' Rowe asked.

Sikes came over and held up my blank sheet.

'Do you even know what the ruddy date is, Hurst?' Rowe said.

'Yeah, it's the twenty-fifth of March...' I paused, realising the significance of the date. 'I need some fresh air,' I rambled.

Under the shade of the furthest sentry tower, I sat and thought back of the dread that seemed to be clouding over me. I had been wrong; this wasn't trepidation but nostalgia. The date of this mission was exactly the date we had been inserted into Afghanistan 2013 in Operation Blue Halo. In fact, by the time I had planned to leave the safety of this base tonight, it would be about the same time that we had hit the LZ at the forest. How fucking weird. Pure coincidence?

Thinking back of the challenges on that mission and a couple since, I had never really relaxed on tour. I would always be anxious and in the fear-zone. Is this why I have been on such a journey since that helicopter crash? Is that why I returned to D-day in 1944 and 1916 at the Somme? And now here? Because now, I feel the most relaxed in a long time, even though this challenge was far greater. I have also learnt it is OK to enter the fear-zone if you can come out when you want. My anger is now more controlled. God, how many people have I told to bottle it and use it when the time arises? What a dumb thing to have said, especially if you have bottled it for too long. Losing control can get you or your mates killed. Fuck, how long have I bottled my problems? Ending up trying to blow my brains out, being an alcoholic and a tramp, or attempting to cut my climbing rope. However, now I was in the right place with a better positive mindset. I now could see clearer and was in charge of my emotions, nothing like after that deadly helicopter crash. It's OK to fail if you can get up and keep trying. I am even starting to think does it matter if I do not return to 2013 as I have got new squad mates. Conceivably a new career. Possibly an innovative and less lethal challenge could be on the cards. A family for instance. Maybe there is a life for me after this Operation Exploit. What a fucking shit name.

'Are you all right, Johnny?' Titan asked.

'Fucking ace.'

'Rowe and Sikes want a word,' Blister said.

'So do I. Fucking ammo up, lads.'

I took Scrap's hand to help me up—their grins electrifying.

Walking back in with greater confidence, the lads carried on into the next hanger. Rowe and Sikes were chatting with Tommy, Werner, and Matilda. The ambulance had gone.

'Sorry for interrupting, but you wanted to see me, sir,' I said, professional-like.

'That's better, Corporal Hurst,' Rowe said.

Sikes' eyes narrowed.

'I'm sorry about earlier,' I continued. 'I just needed some fresh air to get my head clear. I hope you both are not offended.'

'I am glad your fuckery has stopped, Hurst,' Sikes said.

'It has, Sergeant Rowe. And I am deeply sorry for any insubordination I have shown you.'

Sikes acknowledged my apology.

'Listen,' I hushed, 'one of the lads has told me in the strictest confidence that your car is being held by the chief elder of Ismailia. Worryingly, your champagne and cigars are being used to bribe the locals for sex.'

'What?' Sikes growled.

'What man told you?' Rowe snapped.

'I'm not going to say because it will destroy their trust in me as a leader. Then this mission Operation Exploit, that you brilliantly named, will fail.'

'Where is this elder?'

'I have no idea,' I said. 'Sergeant Rowe, why don't you take your uncle and help him find the town hall or the prime house. Or even the largest compound. That's where I would start. We can manage here.'

'Magnificent idea, Jim,' General Rowe said.

'You had better be ready on my return, Hurst,' Sikes said, his beery breath in my face.

'Of course.'

Once the motorbike started, I looked at my watch: 09:48 hours. As they reached the gate, I gave them the middle finger and then pointed at Tommy, Werner, and Matilda.

'Right, you fucking bellends, get fucking around there and load-up. No slacking.'

Werner kind of got the message and followed the resentful Matilda. Tommy sheepishly followed Werner. Once they were out of sight, I faced Flash-heart.

'Where's Truck-3?' I asked.

'Someone checked it out last night.'

'Who?'

'The point is, Johnny, it caught fire before the attack.'

'Was that the explosion in the heart of the camp? The truck everyone was trying to put out.' I didn't let him answer. 'Fuck me.'

'All that work,' he said sorrowfully.

I put my hand on his shoulder. 'Yeah, Truck-3 is a big loss, but we'll manage.'

'You will need another team member and squad member. How about I drive the Crossley? It will not take me and the boys long to adapt it.'

'No. This is a ground offensive, not air.'

'Exactly, I am grounded.' Flash-heart smiled.

'I can't, it's too dangerous, and…'

'I am missing the action. Missing being involved. I want to kill the enemy.'

'Hmm?'

'Please, Johnny, I beg you.'

'If you're ready to do whatever I say and without hesitation. Put your life on the line for us, like we will you…'

'I will get that car around and get it ready,' he interrupted. 'But what about Sergeant Rowe?'

'Fuck him. Leave him to me.'

The excitement was written all over Flash-heart's oily and paint-splattered face.

Before I helped get stuck into the car, I went through to the other hangar. My squad was already loading up our truck with provisions that we had sorted ages ago. Everything had been checked and double-checked and was now being crossed off the load manifest.

Matilda started raising his voice at Seagal. Seagal put down the load he was carrying and folded his arms. I went over to stop the disruption; it's not what we needed before any mission. I let the same old shit elapse about the Aussies being better than us Brits, including that Sikes had said it was good that only Matilda had brought real order to this mission. Matilda then explained that he didn't want the "dumb mute" to load up his truck. And "why was Private Sorahan here anyway? Not as if he can relay messages.".

'Right, Seagal, leave this squad to sort their own truck out,' I said, releasing my fists.

I nodded at Seagal to follow me. As soon as we were out of earshot, I told Seagal that he was our eyes and ears. The mole. I also let him know that there were further revelations to why he now had no Truck-3 to go in.

With the help from the mechanics and engineers, me, Seagal, and Flash-heart stripped back the Crossley. Away went the material convertible roof, front screen, brass lights, mirrors, horn, and the rear leather bench seat. The side attached spare wheel had been left. The tasks had only taken four hours.

We stopped for a lunch of bread and Miris: a Sudanese stew made from sheep's fat, onions, and dried okra. Straight back to work, an air-vented thick aluminium plate was being bodged to protect the radiator. My squad had finished loading up our truck, and were complaining how much they had eaten. Seeing the work being speedily but professionally carried out on the Crossley, enthusiastically they wanted to get stuck in.

'No,' I said, 'because I reckon you had something to do with stealing it and the loot. I'm going to give you the punishment that is required.'

'But we don't know where Seagal stole...'

Titan elbowed Scrap to shut his gob any further.

'I fucking knew it,' I ranted. 'Grab your main weapons, a Lewis, and the Stokes mortar. Then find something to make some targets way over the rear desert. Now.'

The worry went to excitement, and they patted each other on the back.

'Make sure you let the sentries know,' I said.

A thumbs-up was given as they legged it out the front.

Over the next two hours, we loaded some of Truck-3's supplies in the car's rear compartment. We finally covered them in an off-cut of canvas. We then strapped water cans and a wooden chest with ammo to the sides. Lastly, we had painted the Crossley the same colour as our trucks. The best part, although the paint was tacky, was we had bolted a Vickers to the bulkhead.

Once finished, the mechanics had given us a run-down of the basic maintenance. Finally, we tied down the folded modified and portable squared fishing net over the lift-up bonnet side panels. The net had been camouflaged with dyed raffia, canvas strips, and sparse plantation to match the desert.

We all took a step back, silently welcoming the new member. Leaving their weapons at the entrance, my squad then came and joined us. To me, the modified Crossley looked like a World War Two LRDG jeep that the SAS had used. I was as proud as a lion amongst the pride.

'Vinnie, I need to ask you a question,' Titan whispered.

'Sure.'

Titan nodded our squad to head a little way back from the others who were now tidying up.

'Why are the vehicles a slight shade of pink?' he meekly asked.

'Because during many campaigns in the desert, it was seen to be highly effective as camouflage. Although, I have toned it down from a straight pink.'

'Were you Special Forces all homosexuals?' Blister asked.

'It was called Mountbatten Pink, after Lord Mountbatten, used by the Royal Navy in...'

'Oh, definitely homo then,' Blister interrupted my nerdy outburst.

Scrap let out a held back snigger.

'Have you also brought your *Le Bon March* lacy knickers?' Titan said, like a giggly girl.

'Whatever,' I said, and left them.

'Shit himself in no man's land,' Titan just managed to say.

'Shredded them,' Scrap said.

'Blew them to smithereens,' Blister added—all three of them hysterical.

I strutted back to them and said, 'You ever dis those original SAS again, and you'll see a fucking ugly side of me you've not seen before. I've lost too many good friends that followed in the original shoes. You can strip all your weapons down and clean them. Twats.'

The silliness had stopped.

Seagal shut the lid on his huge trunk as he saw me coming, and then he sat on it.

'Missed your coach?' I joked.

Seagal first looked over my shoulder and then quietly said, 'Looks like I am going to miss this benjo without Truck-3.'

'First you don't speak, and now you talk shit that I don't understand, like Tommy and Werner.'

'Benjo means a riotous holiday.'

'I can't believe Truck-3 was taken out last night,' I said.

'Like it was set alight to show our position.'

'Did you see who lit it before the attack?'

'Only a shadow lighting a rag in the fuel tank.'

'I'll find out who checked it out. What's in the trunk?'

'Is that an order for me to show you?'

I nodded.

'Can you give me your word you will not tell a soul of the contents? Do not sell me a dog.'

'You would have my word if I were a Brummie.'

'A what? "Brummie"?'

'Birmingham, where your slight accent is from.'

'Ah, Brummagem, historically also Bromichan and Bremicham.'

Fiddling with the old lock, Seagal then lifted the huge lid. Looking across the hanger, he then averted his eyes to me. Seagal slightly lowered the lid.

'*A szavát adja?*' he said.

'Is that Hungarian?'

'Yes, for, do I have your word?'

I shook my head in disbelief that he could have helped with translating Tommy.

Seagal closed the lid.

'No, I was shaking my head in…look, you have my word.'

Excited, but a little dubious of something macabre that I might find, I lifted the top. A waft of must and glue entered my nostrils. I flinched after seeing four heads facing me, but then realised they were life-like painted papier-mâché. I picked up the hollow head by the stick protruding at the neck and studied the model.

'Mastered the sniper lure technique,' he said. 'If you place a tin hat on it, it becomes your 'mate'. Also, to make it convincing at night, you can smoke a cigarette from your mate's sauce box with a rubber tube when hidden in the trench.'

'What do you mean, "sauce box"?'

'Mouth. You and the others should read Victorian books. You can pick up some delightful sayings.'

'You should stop using such antiquated nonsensical words, you bellend,' I retorted, and grinned.

Seagal pondered, and then continued, 'When a German sniper has been taking out your side, I would choose an obvious hiding place opposite to him. Somewhere the enemy sniper would expect. Then, I would stealthily push two stakes into our parapet until only about a foot of them remained above. To these I would secure a board on which it shaped a groove, exactly fitting the handle fixed to your mate. This stick was inserted in the groove, and your mate slowly pushed up above our parapet.'

I passed the head over to show me how.

'If the enemy sniper fired and hit your mate, the entry and exit of the bullet made two holes. One in the front, and one in the back. Your mate, immediately on the impact, was pulled down in a natural ducking manner. The handle on which your mate was mounted was then replaced in the groove, precisely at the elevation between the two periscope glasses. All that remained was to place the top periscope to the rear hole, align with the front hole, and investigate the lower part of the periscope below the parapet. Taking the trajectory of the bullet, this would spot the hidden sniper. It was better than the turnips they used.'

'Brilliant idea for this era,' I said.

'Thank you.'

'Your invention?'

'Yes, you have to be a thinking man's soldier. You say, "brilliant idea for this era". Era?'

'Forget that, I'm here now.'

Seagal took the three 'mates' off me. I delved in to see what else was in the trunk. The huge rifle was colossal, guessing the weight to be fifteen kilograms.

'Holy fuck,' I said. 'I want one of these beasts.'

'German T-Gewehr anti-tank rifle. Take your mate's head clean off.'

'No added scope then,' I said, seeing if he had any more ideas.

'If you cannot see the maximum firing range of seventy yards, then you should not be on the battlefield.'

'Yeah, I knew its range,' I lied.

I pulled out a worn rifle with what appeared to be an unorthodox thick telescope fitted, including an eye relief coupling. The inscription read 'John Rigby & Company'. Seagal said the hunting rifle fired a .406 cartridge. Further in the treasure trove were folded clothes. As I lifted them, Seagal told me to be careful. Gently, I unravelled the exact military boiler suit as we had sourced in England. This had also been dyed black from the original white, previously used for winter months. It also had pads sewn into the elbows and knees, like ours.

Next, I held up a hessian hood with local plantation attached, along with a *shemagh* and *dishdasha*, strips of hessian, and empty sandbags. The last was a suit made from hessian with sand glued between parts of dried grass.

'You've been a busy lad,' I said. 'Is this where you have been disappearing to?'

'Amongst physical training, I have been studying books and maps. That is my version of the Symien sniper suit. I am going to shake a flannin. Sorry, that means, going to fight. And I am not taking prisoners.'

I started to search underneath the respirator, standard kit, specialised ammo, a periscope, and coloured paints presumably for the face and hands. The last piece of kit was a Bergmann MP-18, not yet put into action. Our squad had the rights for testing the German submachine gun. My curiosity heightened to suspicion when it had an officers' leather trench cylindrical torch taped to the underside of the holed barrel. The sling lug had been removed and the white metal was blacked out. Also like our squad's, the standard 'British Made' and 'TEC' oval stamp were filed away. The only problem with our design was that it stuck out about seventy millimetres past the end of the barrel. However, even though the torch was forty millimetres in diameter, with a little training it was like the underslung grenade launcher of my day. I turned the torch on and off.

'Where did you get this sub?' I insinuated.

'I have a stock of batteries and bulbs.'

I half-smiled as he had avoided the question. 'Go and ask Flash-heart to fit a stronger bulb and magnified lens cover on the end. It makes the beam more powerful.'

'Knowledge can disperse fear. Knowing your enemies' equipment is less effective than yours, can be the difference between life and death.'

I lowered the trench-knife with a knuckle duster incorporated in the handle and studied his face to try to see if he was the link to get back to 2013. He was not your regular soldier: an advanced thinking and forward planner before his time. I had never heard of his surname, and he did not resemble anyone from my era.

'What?' he asked.

'Have you been to a secret temple in Indonesia recently and met an old man? Are you stuck in a tomb?' I gauged the littlest inclination that he knew.

Seagal frowned, perplexed. 'I silently observe a lot of people from all social classes and occupations. I find you remarkably interesting, unconventional, and complex. But, I have not figured out when you are being jovial, serious, or simply arfarfan'arf.'

'Dare I fucking ask what that means?'

'Surely you have heard of the saying arfarfan'arf?' Meaning he has had many 'arfs'. You know, half-pints of stout.'

'Us ladies drink pints where I'm from,' I joked. 'Now stop your Queen Victoria shit sayings and pass me the gear back.' Bollocks, I thought he was my ticket back to 2013.

Placing the first of the kit back as he handed them to me, I noticed a small wooden chest. I grabbed the mahogany jewellery-like box and lifted the lid.

'Put that back,' Seagal snapped.

'There are no secrets from each other on this mission. We need to get to know how we tick. Got it.'

Seagal sighed.

The smell was rotten. A huge wad of coloured pieces of cloth about six inches square were piled. All were stained with holes in them. I picked the top one out and turned it over to see what was safety-pinned to the other side: a tatty and red stained piece of paper had a name written in pencil: Private Christopher Webster. 24th February 1917.

'My first desertion here,' Seagal admitted. 'The young lad had been caught twice in Cairo visiting the ladies of the night. And I do not mean for a cough and drop. Typical TA: Saturday night soldiers queuing at a brothel. He had only been in the TA for two weeks.'

I remembered Bruce telling me about pieces of cloth placed over the heart as a target for the firing party to aim at. My lip curled as I put it back.

'I need to put each one in the box,' he said. 'It's where I lock the images away to stop the nightmares.'

With everything back, I called Flash-heart over and told him to go and find Scrap, Titan, and Blister. When they were all in front, I gave them a grilling about keeping the stolen car a secret. Whether they were involved or not, it could have compromised this mission. OK, it had worked out that we could now use the Crossley as one truck had been destroyed. I told them to handover the cognac and cigars to Flash-heart's exhausted team who stood there waiting to be dismissed. Then, a line would be drawn under it. Lastly, I ordered them to round up everyone and meet me in the briefing room. It was my turn to give the task details now that both Rowes weren't here. Time check: 17:07 hours.

CHAPTER SIX

Flash-heart handed me a mug of coffee. Sitting on a thick timber desk with my feet on a chair, I waited for the lads to settle. Less than thirty seconds later, the class went quiet.

'Before we start, let's get the serious stuff out of the way,' I said. 'We need a nickname for Werner.'

Werner uncomfortably looked around.

'Alleyman,' Matilda blurted.

'Why?' I asked.

'It's what the piliknins name us Germans,' Werner said spitefully.

'What is "piliknins"?' I dreaded asking.

'It is what the bare prive calls us superior Aussies,' Matilda said. 'It means tan men.'

Matilda continued his disgusted stare. Werner aggressively stood from his chair, as did Matilda.

'Sit the fuck down, children,' Titan yelled. 'Show some respect.'

'How about Bratwurst? After those horrendous German sausages,' Scrap said, and grinned.

'Better than English sausage,' Werner said.

'Well, as you're related to a German sausage and you've been acting like a typically badly-behaved child: Brat,' I said.

A chuckle went around. Well, except Werner.

'Right, let's get down to the fun stuff,' I said.

Opening my satchel, each person got the same aerial black and white photographs, maps, compasses, scaled rulers, and notes I had made. Although I knew my squad was up to speed since we left England, they still received the items. Just as I was about to start, Khalida, Rowe, and Sikes entered. Law and Trish sheepishly followed and then stood in the corner. Khalida pulled her chair away from the lads. Sikes slumped in the chair; Rowe sat next to him.

'Carry on,' Rowe said.

'Why are Law and Trish here?' I said.

'Because, Corporal…Hist…we need…a medoc,' Sikes slurred.

'You're out of your mind. And pissed,' I raged.

Rowe placed a hand on Sikes' shoulder to stop him getting up. 'Now listen here, Hurst. What goes on at the officers' mess has nothing to do with you.'

'But this mission does.'

'And it is me who sanctioned Operation Exploit and authorised all your equipment and men. My orders are that you have a mobile dressing station.'

'And if they come under…'

'It is quite simple,' he stopped me, 'you agree, or be detained for disobeying my orders.'

In front of the silence, I felt as small as the hairs on a hamster's scrotum. I sighed. 'That's a brilliant idea. Please, Matron and Sister, take a seat. We leave in about one hour. Why don't you, sir, take your nephew and get him…*ready* for duty.'

Rowe looked at Sikes, knowing what I had meant. 'Yes, as there are not enough seats for the women.'

I waited till they had left, then said, 'Fucktards.'

I handed out Captain Wade's and Scouse's briefing pack to the medics. I then gave Khalida hers and bollocked her for being late. I then returned to the front.

'We're not here to stop the war or to overthrow the Empire. Simply, to hit both targets,' I said. 'The job will be done with minimum fuss. Swift and silent. Yet, we use controlled extreme-killer aggression if necessary. And only if it's necessary. Our only objectives are to destroy the railway system and aerodrome. If you can save a life, do it. Once each task is completed, get the fuck out and back to safety. With the overwhelming odds of the enemy in this hostile and unforgiving land, it will be the ultimate test of courage and skill. Perhaps your survival. There will be times when you must improvise. Perhaps in a tactical situation. Let your training and skills take over. Be in the autopilot-zone. Don't be worried about being scared. Use your fear.'

I took a sip of the sweet coffee whilst eyeing them: Trish appeared out of her depth. Werner and Tommy looked a little lost. Maybe I should ask Seagal to translate? If I let the others know he could speak, would the ones I did not trust speak freely in front of him? I contemplated the pros and cons.

'OK, we've not got much intelligence, but get your first photo out of the railway station and the map,' I said. 'This is Target-1: the railway station at Deir el Belah, southwest of Gaza. It's one hundred and twenty miles away. Converting to one hundred and ninety-three klicks, and that's not as the crow would fly.'

With all the information I had requested and studied, I continued to discuss the direction we were going to take, the possible terrain, likely weather, and the time and place I wanted to reach our first ERL. Again, like at the Somme, Blister answered what ERL had meant: Emergency Rendezvous Location. I told them that two point-men would recce ahead on a Trusty. Explaining further, I wanted the ERL to be where the mobile dressing station became a permanent position. I ignored Trish's objections of it being permanent. Once she had shut up, I informed the group of approximately where the next LUP would be. And, the OP where we would have eyes on through the daylight. Once strategically set before dawn, there was to be total silence and minimal movement from everyone, even when using the prearranged hand signals. I waited whilst they all looked at the notes.

I then informed them that those on stag could grab some sleep after their set time. Nevertheless, everyone must be ready for any threat. Anyone caught sleeping on sentry duty would be in serious shit. After daylight had passed, we would meet at the LUP to discuss notes, and then plan an assault that evening, including a defended withdrawal.

'Questions?' I said.

'General Albert Rowe's and Sergeant Sean Rowe's orders were that we had to be on this operation,' Matron Law said.

'You are, Beccy,' I said. 'Next question.'

Apart from Law being anal again about not using the correct name procedure, no one else said a word. I continued with the next part of the mission: once Target-1 had been successful, we would lay low throughout daylight. As the sun went down, we would send back any injured or dead to the ERL where Law and Trish would take care of. We would then silently pack up and move out to the next job: Target-2, the fortified aerodrome at Beersheba, southeast of Gaza. Target-2 was forty-eight kilometres from Target-1 as the crow would fly. I showed them the second photo, distance on the map, and the proposed LUP and OP. I then discussed what we would be expected to find. And, perhaps the unexpected.

'I want all insignia stripped from your uniforms. No ID or pay-books are to be taken,' I ordered. 'I want you sterile. The medics will always keep their British Cross markings on. Finally, I want all the vehicles looked after, as if your best mate and an extension of your kit. Any questions?'

'What is Squad-3 going to do without a truck?' Matilda asked. 'Who is going to bite the dust and have this squad?'

'Oh shit, I forgot to mention. That's not your truck, but Sikes',' I said smugly.

'But we loaded it,' he said. 'Ah bollocks, ya bott.'

'A what?' I said, thinking of Ocker's Australian slang.

'A useless person.'

'I've heard a lot worse than that, but you're heading in the same direction as Ocker. You sure you're not related to the Australian pikey Tommy White?'

Matilda appeared shocked, the stupid grin disappearing.

'What are the new squads, Vinnie?' Scrap blurted.

I took my inquisitive stare from Matilda's worried look and said, 'Tommy and Matilda are now joining Squad-2: Sikes and Seagal. I'm moving Khalida to the ambulance with Matron Law and Sister Spiga, until they have set up the ERL. Khalida can then join us later on horseback, being she loves horses more than men. Lastly, Brat will join the patrol squad in the pinky with Flash-heart, being German and English pilots have a gentlemanly understanding.'

'My Baka and Rudi?' Tommy asked.

'Take them, but the welfare is down to you alone,' I said.

'That answer is a lemon, mate,' Matilda muttered.

He was starting to batter my bollocks. 'Speak English, or not the fuck at all.'

'Just saying that your answer is less to his foolish question.'

'You didn't say it, but fucking mumbled it,' I said.

'Yes, no?' Tommy said.

I stuck my thumb up at him. 'Everyone done?'

'We need a nickname for the nurses and Khalida,' Blister said.

'We already have Trish,' I said. 'Hmm, Matron Law?'

Law cast her beady eye at me.

I pondered, thinking back of Matron Frosty Knickers in 1944. 'Matron.' I had bottled it. 'Lastly, Khalida.'

A murmur went around us men. Titan looked down at his notes. She stared meaningfully deep through her facemask, disturbing my soul. I imagined her sliding her dagger out of the sheath and slitting my throat whilst I slept.

'Batgirl,' I said.

'Good one,' Scrap said.

'Batgirl?' Titan quizzed.

'I'll tell you later…'

'Don't you mean Batman?' Matilda interrupted me.

Me and Scrap looked at him. Did Scrap also wonder how Matilda knew about Batman of our time.

'You know…the Aussie saying for 'officer's servant'.'

'Right, briefing closed,' I said. 'You have about two hours to revise everything. None of the documents are to be brought with you. Also, in your break, I want you to grab as much food and rehydrate as you can. No alcohol. Matilda, I want you to sort two of your best horses with all that they need to survive.'

'How long?' Matilda asked.

I mentally heard my old CO banging on why every desert mission is set for four weeks. I smirked.

'Well?' he asked.

'Twenty-eight days,' I lied.

'Twenty-eight bloody days. I have not got enough Anzac wafers.'

'Stop your fucking moaning, Matilda, and get it done,' Titan said.

'I want you all back here dead on 20:00 hours. Dismissed, except Matron and Trish.'

My squad patted me on the back and remarked that it was a good briefing. With both medics only in the room, I folded my arms.

'You know I am against you coming on this mission,' I bluntly said. 'It's a ludicrous idea from Sikes and Rowe.'

'Well, you are not in…'

'Not only could you get killed or injured because of your lack of fighting and weapons drills,' I interrupted Matron, 'but what would the Bedouin, Turks, Arabs, or Germans do if they took you prisoner? Hand you back over like the RFC. Torture you for information. Or sexually abuse, just for fun.'

'Well, we are going. And you can address me as Matron Law.' She sharply left.

I sighed.

Trish patted me on the back. 'Don't worry, Johnny, I've got time to sew my vagina up.'

'You'll need a lot of rope,' I shouted after her. 'Make sure you sort all your own medical equipment out.'

'Yes, sir, Corporal Jim Hurst, sir,' she yelled back.

I smirked. Bitch, I thought.

Seagal and Tommy were unloading Squad-2's truck. Why? I poked my head in the back, disheartened to see it had been poorly loaded. Seagal looked as unimpressed with Matilda's leadership as me. I apologised to Seagal that he had to be with Squad-2. Tommy hadn't understood what I had said. As much as I wanted Sikes to load his own stuff because he had got drunk instead, I did not want to delay the start. I ordered them to properly load Sikes' kit. Brat came around the corner and started taking his gear, retracing his steps after. I followed. Flash-heart was helping Brat load the pinky, getting along with the language barrier.

I finished going through my gear and checking all the ammo, and then put my weapons and grenades in the front cab. I took the keys, knowing there would be a race to sit in the seat. I had lost on many other earlier missions.

Before these Dennis trucks were delivered, General Rowe had ordered the Guildford depot to fit them all with a more powerful engine. Just meeting the shipping deadline, each truck had a high-speed White and Poppe V6 petrol engine. This mod easily drove this standard three-tonne truck up a one-in-six gradient. The whiniest vehicle was the ambulance. Again, I began to wish I had never agreed to them coming, but my hands were tied.

Getting changed into my knee-padded trousers and shirt, I then put my head back. I closed my eyes and memorised the maps, photos, and the plan.

★

It had been eight weeks away with the successful Operation Blue Halo, including a two-week piss-up with the SAS and SBS squads in Cyprus. However, I was desperate to get home.

Riding my pushbike back from the SBS base, I was excited to see Ella. I knew she would pull back the curtains and then greet me with hugs and kisses. I skipped her offer of a meal and went straight to bed, as you do. I then took her out to dinner, both getting blissfully drunk. I told her I wanted kids and would leave the British Army. Staggering home, we crashed out on the sofa—what a lovely day.

Further on in my well-earned R&R, we travelled down to Newquay to visit her parents. Although awkwardly frosty, I told them about me leaving the army to get a new job. This meant less trouble in their eyes.

Capping that, we told them that we were going to start a family here in Newquay. It seemed to break the ice wall between us.

We invited all our friends and family to the pub and told them all of our plans. My parents and brother were overwhelmed. I spent most of that evening with my dad, mentioning how I had let the black dogs cripple me before Operation Edge. One thing I did make sure of was that we staggered home together, making sure he properly crossed the road. It was a fabulous start to my new life.

A crash alerted me from my dream. I thought about when I had been under the sentry tower. How could I have pondered about not returning to my life in 2013? Guilt followed, but it was interrupted by mutts barking. I sat up and rubbed my eyes. Tommy was yanking the leads. If any of those mutts compromise us, like the fucking goats had, I would get them on Blister's special breakfast menu, I thought.

Shadows came from the dark into the hangar's lowlights. Seeing Sikes, I jumped down and made my way over to him and the following lads. Sikes looked like a bag of shite, not even dressed smartly. He grumbled at everyone to fall into line.

Once we had, he lifted his cudgel and his bloodshot eyes narrowed.

'Fear becomes spineless when one extracts oneself from obligations,' he said flatly. 'You kill every ghastly Boche, Turk, and any filth that tries to halt us. You respect my orders.'

There were some stunned faces. Sikes turned around and whistled with his fingers. The mutts started to bounce about. From the gloom, a wiry man in a suit, tin hat, and attached respirator walked in carrying his camera. I recognised the same press photographer from the Somme.

'Good evening. I am Mr Pickard from the Daily Chronicle. Please watch the camera and stay perfectly still.'

After the flash, I had remorse that Scouse and Wade were not in the photo.

I eyed our squad as Sikes strutted by to his truck. They in turn had the same look of discontent as me: we did not want Sikes on this mission.

With everyone dismissed to their vehicles, I jerked my head for my squad to follow me. Out of earshot of the others, I asked them to huddle in.

'We're going to have to keep a 360-degree watch on this lot,' I whispered.

'Can't we send them all the wrong way,' Scrap said.

'For once, I like your rhetorical question,' I replied. 'Seagal is on our Elite level, but…'

'How do you know that?' Titan butted in.

We could not have secrets between us, I thought. 'He told me,' I said, waiting for the backlash.

They nodded.

'You lot fucking knew, didn't you,' I said.

'For once, I *don't* like your rhetorical question,' Scrap said.

'You mean about Seagal's sniper and soldiering ways?' Blister said— Titan nudged him.

'You're not supposed to keep any secrets,' I reprimanded.

'Oh. Well then, you best know about these,' Titan said, and his huge hands delved into his medic satchel.

'Why the fuck have you got five RFC pay books on you? You're fucking supposed to be sterile. Where did you get them?'

'I got them from under Scouse's bed. His idea was for us to have them in case we were captured by the Kaiser. So they would return us.'

'Do we fucking look like pilots?' I fumed.

'Another rhetorical…'

'Shut up, Georges,' I interrupted.

'Oh, back to first names, chaps,' Titan said.

'Any more to bring to the table, guys?'

I individually eyed them. Scrap dropped his haversack and reached in. He reluctantly showed me a brass trench-lighter.

'Scouse had this stashed as well.'

I tutted. 'That's not what I meant, Georges. From now on, we tell each other the truth and everything that is going on. OK?'

'OK, boss,' Blister said. 'Like you told us about you killing Bruce and his lover, Wilhelm Angern.'

'Yet, you really liked Bruce,' Titan added.

'They deserved to die,' I said.

'I am sure you have said on a couple of occasions, "if you can save a life, do it",' Scrap said.

'I wonder what was said when they found their bodies. Strange how it has not been reported,' Blister said.

I became slightly flustered, rapidly thinking of a convincing answer.

'We know you're lethal,' Blister said, 'but you've a non-predigest outlook to coloured chaps, homosexuals, religion…'

'And you told us about you not killing a German boy in an underground communications bunker in the next big war,' Titan interrupted.

I had to bluff my way out, I thought.

'We know you never shot them,' Scrap blurted. 'We are not stupid.'

'Fucking ammo up,' Blister said.

All three went by and patted me on the back.

'Get your own fucking saying, Blister,' I said.

Once everyone was in their vehicles, I went to each member and wished them good luck. By strength and guile. Sikes and Batgirl never even acknowledged me.

I climbed aboard my truck. Although a weight had been lifted about Bruce and Wilhelm, Titan sat next to me overdoing a smug grin. His tight-fitted flying goggles made him look even more stupid, but what could I say.

Time check: 20:05 hours. The hangar was filled with exhaust fumes and testosterone. Blister and Scrap came to the front on the Trusty motorbikes. It came to me how we all got on so well: Blister was like Shrek. Titan was comparable to Planet. Seagal was similar to Fish. And lastly, Scrap was a little like Rabbit. Was it supposed to be like this? The problem was, I loved this squad. I wanted it to continue, but I was now torn to returning to 2013. I knew that if I could convert all my Elite skills learnt on operations with this era mission, it would be a success. Just like before Operation Blue Halo, I was nervous, excited, and proud all at the same time. This was it.

Ten klicks from Katia, forty-eight klicks northeast from our base at Ismailia, I spotted both Trusty motorbikes up ahead. As instructed, Seagal was the driver of Truck-2. Seagal's vehicle was alongside the ambulance, driven by Trish. As I was the lead vehicle, I stopped. Trish came alongside and pulled her goggles over her dusty, black hair. She put her thumb up, and I nodded at her. Matilda drew alongside, his horse frothing at the mouth. Stopping on the other side of the ambulance was Seagal. Sikes was waking up in the passenger seat. To my left was the pinky, closely followed by the motorbike and sidecar driven by Tommy. Strangely, both mutts in the sidecar wore a black headscarf and goggles. I noted a Wallace and Gromit joke for later.

Killing the engine, I hand signalled for all to do the same. Tinkering filled the quietness. Time check: 22:26 hours. Batgirl tied her horse to the side of my truck. I noticed the horse had no saddle. Jumping down, as the step had been removed for weight reduction, I ordered Matilda to make sure the horses got the rations they needed. Tommy was already giving the mutts a drink from his water bottle. I hoped Tommy had cleaned Rudi's teeth after eating Baka's shit. Seagal was making his way over. Sikes pulled up a brown blanket over himself.

'Titan, keep an eye on Sikes,' I said.

'Sure, boss.'

Blister and Scrap had finished cleaning the fairing filters, and were now dusting themselves down. I unwrapped my *shemagh*, and then asked certain squad members to follow me to the top of one of the dunes. In a dip on my knees, I unfolded the map. As the lads circled it, I turned on the torch. It was a little chilled after coming away from the warmth of the truck's engine. I guessed it to be ten degrees Celsius. Taking on some water, Scrap was the first to check the map with his compass.

'Everyone OK?' I asked. 'Trusty-1 and two OK?'

Scrap and Blister nodded.

'What's the sitrep?' I said.

'Boss, we have done a recce of these sand dunes,' Scrap said, pointing on the map. 'They are too soft, even for our motorbikes. They will slow our time to reach an ERL.'

'What's the best route?' I said.

'Directly twelve klicks east is Mageibra. There is not much going on in a small village. They do have a few dogs chained up, and worse, goats.'

'Fuck me, let's call in an airstrike,' Blister said—I laughed. 'Further east about twenty-four klicks is a settlement called Bir el Ganadil. The inhabitants were sitting and dancing around large fires.'

'Drunk?' I said.

'Who wouldn't be in this shithole?'

'More like opium,' Seagal added.

'I noticed quite a few camels and horses,' Scrap said.

'Weapons? Vehicles?'

'No vehicles, boss. But unsure of concealed weapons,' Blister said.

'Possible Bedouin threat, chaps?' Seagal asked.

'Thirty per cent,' Scrap said.

Seagal unfolded a different map from ours and placed it over the top of the existing. Under torchlight, Blister turned the page in his own diary.

'Looking at the railway to the left, there are villages dotted along its length: Oghratina and Salmana. Before the wadi is Bir el Mazar,' Blister said.

'How far is the wadi from the last village Bir el Mazar?'

'Forty-eight klicks, boss. On the other side of the wadi is El Arish.'

'The British Empire destroyed a lot of resistance when the sappers built the railway,' Seagal said. 'Last December at El Arish, the Turks fled the Desert Column attack.'

'You read a lot like an old friend of mine,' I reminisced.

'Fish?' Blister said.

I nodded. 'So like in Afghan, some of the locals have lost friends and family, and would seek the chance of revenge. There could be a dicker in any of those towns.'

'"Dicker"?' Seagal questioned.

'A low grade scrote who reports on movements. Basically, the enemy,' I said.

'I reckon there will also be pockets of Turks and Germans setting up for a counter,' Scrap added.

'Last thing they ever fucking do,' Blister grumbled.

'I would rather make the ERL with as many men and ammo as possible,' I said. 'I've told this to Titan, but be vigilant of Brat.'

'I fucking always have been,' Blister said menacingly.

'What's the new intel on Brat?' Scrap said.

'Let me find out first if what I heard from Foxy and Smudge is true. Right, orders: Blister and Scrap refuel and head east to the wadi. Make sure you travel dead centre of the villages. It should give you about six klicks each side. Stay back from the wadi about five-hundred yards till we arrive. You know the drill if you meet any trouble along the way. Fucking ammo up.'

Packing our kit, I found out from Seagal that Sikes had been drinking whisky. That's probably why he hadn't noticed the pinky was the Crossley.

Hearing the motorbikes head off into the blackness, I did a quick check on Truck-1. I asked the others to attend theirs, making the priority to have everything that could rattle was re-tied.

Back in formation at a lower speed, we drove past Mageibra on our right. It was approximately five klicks away. Even with the stars and moon lighting our path, I could not see any sign of a village on the horizon. Perhaps the weird contours of the dunes were shadowing the village. With just a low hum and no lights, there was no way they could see us, till close. By then, if a threat, they would have been challenged and dealt with.

We drove very slowly past the next settlement with bonfires, Bir el Ganadil, on our right. I then steadily gained speed to the max, continuing east from a compass bearing that Titan navigated. I was accustomed to the monotony of long distances across the desert. Whether tabbing or in a vehicle, you had to be careful that the boredom did not get you wishing for action.

'What are we going to do about Sikes when we hit Target-1?' Titan unexpectedly asked.

'It's been on my mind as well,' I said.

'Guess he's let the black panthers in.'

'You mean black dogs.'

'No, panthers, as they are bigger and scarier.'

'No, you're missing the point. It's not the size…'

'My father said he saw one in Africa,' Titan interrupted.

'Was that with the Zulu tribe?' I jested.

'No, that was later.'

It had killed the piss-take. 'I know why he didn't kill it,' I continued.

'Why's that?'

'Because of that tiny shitty shotgun he owned.'

Titan pulled it from under his robe and placed it on his lap, the barrel facing me. 'Remember that time you were taking a shit in no man's land. The Kaiser couldn't scope your tiny bollocks. I won't miss.'

I smirked. 'Could you say in a Scottish accent, fuck ye, I'll twist ye fuckin' balls off when we get back,' I said in the best impersonation of Planet.

'Why did you say that in a Sikh accent?'

'Oh piss off.'

'I'm not going to have your mate Planet's nickname, so stop asking.'

We were making good ground. Since leaving the dunes we had been travelling for two hours and forty-five minutes. Stretching my numb arse, Matilda came alongside and signalled that the horses needed a rest. Pulling into the base of some low dunes to our right, I began to summarise where we were on the map: slightly southeast of Bir el Mazar. Approximately seventy kilometres since our first stop at Katia.

Everyone was now out and stretching. The mutts had another turd. I was about to call everyone in for a sitrep when Sikes came thundering over. He was more malignant than back in the trenches. After a bit of an argument, he saw right that we had to stop for a few hours for the tired horses. Yeah, his fucking idea to bring them. He brashly ordered the women to cook a meal whilst the men took a worthy rest as they had a battle to attend to. I was speechless by my anger.

Once he had disappeared over the grassy mound to take watch, I motioned everyone in for a chat.

'Put that fucking cigarette out, Matilda,' I said—he did after a little backchat. 'You have two hours to eat, sleep, sort the animals and your own kit, and the team member's maintenance. All as silently as possible. No fires and no smoking. We're only sixteen klicks from the nearest town. And, we've passed over many trails.'

Tommy and Brat tried to help each other with the translation. It was silly enough that I had to change my terminology from talking to our squad to these regulars, let alone try my limited German and non-Hungarian.

'Trish, help the two foreigners understand what I just said.' I winked at her.

'Don't you mean five,' she replied, thumbing at Batgirl and Matilda, then herself.

'Four and a half. You're not all Italian,' Blister quipped.

She wound her middle finger up at him.

Blister looked at me, knowing who she had learnt it from.

'I would rather eat with an Abdul than you Andy McNoon's,' Matilda said.

I had heard from Captain Wade that an "Abdul" was Australian slang for a Turk.

'Who "Andy McNoon"?' Tommy asked.

'Means, unqualified idiots. And that's the lot of you.'

I sighed.

'Don't worry, Johnny, I'll squat in his tea,' Trish whispered.

'Flash-heart, on the next leg of the journey, swap drivers and get some sleep,' I ordered. 'In fact, that goes for all of you. Titan, take stag to the front of the dunes. I'll take the south.'

Whilst taking the bully beef out from the indestructible biscuit sandwich, I scanned the area from behind the Lewis. I had looked at my watch countless times, knowing that we still had to set up an ERL for Matron and Trish. I also had that sixth sense that something out there was watching us.

The noise from the camp was too loud, but I didn't want to leave my post. I started on the sweet dates, having given up on the biscuits. All went quiet behind me. Hopefully, no one would snore. Looking through the latest British stamped French high-grade prismatic binoculars showed nothing but the eerie night. I remembered everyone but me getting excited about the 6 x 30 view. Perhaps Seagal had invented some night vision goggles, I thought, and smirked.

Five minutes before the stand down, I went around and woke everyone up. I told each member to silently collect all their waste in an empty sandbag, remove any sign we had been here, and to quietly load their vehicles. I didn't have to wake Sikes; he was already sitting in the driver's seat. I was still sceptical as to why he was letting me lead the convoy. Maybe he saw these as little duties beneath him.

Brat took the pinky driver's seat. Trish swapped with Matron in the ambulance. Khalida and Matilda would not swap their jockey positions. Even though I had trained hard, horses weren't my thing. Reluctantly, I let the tired Tommy sit next to the driver, Titan, of Truck-1. That meant me in the Trusty and sidecar. Time check: 03:24 hours.

The dust thrown up from the other vehicles, and my jolting spine, were not the problem. It was the constant growling and teeth showing from Baka and Rudi. If I could have turned the fixed Lewis around and let rip, I would have.

After what seemed hours, I had learnt that it was only when I turned to my side to look at them, or the bike had hit a bump, that they would growl. It came to me just as I thought about unbolting the sidecar: the indestructible biscuit. Slowly, like on a covert plain-clothes mission, I slid my hand inside my robe. The growling intensified. Fuck, these guys were good. Perhaps some interrogation techniques, I thought. I continued playing the bad guy in an exact impersonation of Ant. Yelling, cursing, holding the biscuit out and then taking it away. I told the captives that I knew who they were and where their LUP kennel was, and I had details on their breeders. I finished by saying that I would torture them if they did not tell me who their pack leader was.

Then the good guy, Steve Steve, came in. Soft voiced. Cool. Offering them each the biscuit. Rudi and Baka were still silent. Their eyes were submissive, and they took the bait. The next time with my hand in my pocket, I pushed the last biscuit hard against my chest. The snap caught the prisoners' attention. It was time to ask the questions: how many were in the pack? Who was your leader? Still, they stayed quiet, only licking their dry lips. Was that fear? With no information, should I bring back the bad guy, Ant? Maybe some stress positions and constant cats meowing would break them. Perhaps we should bring out Sikes on a lead to bark at them whilst still in stress positions with hoods on. Sikes could even have a little nibble.

The ambulance to my front left began bellowing out steam from the engine's side cover grills. It had brought me out from the interrogation. Pushing the throttle lever, I caught up with Sikes and waved at him to stop, but he did not even acknowledge me. Annoyed, I gestured at Trish to stop. I then sped alongside Seagal and yelled at him to get Sikes to stop. Seagal lowered his binos and pointed ahead. I wiped my goggles but couldn't see anything. Facing him, he did a curved gesture with one hand, back and forth. The wadi was ahead. I did the 'OK' sign and then slowed up to turn back, the brakes as non-responsive as ever.

Reaching the ambulance, Titan was ordering everyone into a defensive position. Flash-heart had the triangular front-pointed bonnet off. The mutts had made their escape from prison and now joined their CO in the back of my truck. Tommy was rolling up part of the canvas, sitting behind the fixed pivotal Lewis. Brat had moved the pinky to the other defensive side and was now manning the Vickers. Titan had just finished giving Trish and Matron a rifle who were under the safety of the truck's side armour. Titan looked at me. In that glance, he appeared spooked. Looking in the direction we had travelled, Matilda had found a ditch running parallel to the track. His head was just above the ridge. I couldn't see Batgirl. Yet, her horse snorted from far away. Then, everything went still and quiet.

'Can you fix it?' I whispered to Flash-heart.

'Ruddy pipe split. Lost all the water from the radiator.'

'Can you fix it?' I asked again.

'We have no spare steel pipe. I could take off the rubber air-filter hose, slide it over, and then put a metal band around each side.'

A breeze blew across the desert, whipping the steam away. Flash-heart took his head out and looked the way it had quickly come and gone. The atmosphere turned eerie, as if something was looming.

'What the fuck are you waiting for?' I whispered. 'The OK?'

'Right away, Vinnie.' He made his way over to the pinky for spares.

'Flash-heart.'

He stopped and faced me.

'How long?' I said.

'Half-hour.'

'Fucking longer than you would without your rifle,' I said.

He came running back to his weapon leaning against the wheel, and said, 'Sorry.'

'You will be, travelling in the back of this fucking ambulance. Do not fucking leave your weapon out of reach again. You have twenty minutes to get this fucking thing repaired.'

'Bit harsh the word, "thing",' he said.

'It's not won my respect like the other members. Get on with it.'

'I am going to have to use the drinking water.'

'Use the horse piss if you have to.'

Flash-heart grimaced.

Stealthily joining Titan in a shallow dip on a small mound, I settled in behind my rifle. I had set the ammo and grenades to how I preferred.

'You feel it too,' Titan hushed.

'Yes.'

'Who do you reckon?'

'We're not leaving much of a trail…'

'Except horse shit,' Titan butted in.

'Fucking stupid idea to bring them. And the dogs.'

'Oh, at least they've gone from "mutts" to "dogs".'

'They're not like the highly-trained dogs of my time,' I said.

'Including the owner, but at least Tommy is picking up the turds.'

I scoffed. 'Could be Bedouin following us.'

Titan sniggered.

'What?'

'Did you know that Batgirl rode all this way without a saddle?' Titan was now holding back his laugh.

'Yeah. And?'

Titan leant over and whispered, 'Reckon she has a fanny like a headlock, without a head.'

The vision cracked me up. He put his face into his arm, his laugh muffled. I tried to stop laughing.

'A headlock that of the circus strongman, Author Saxton, that you wanted to be nicknamed after,' I added.

Trying to catch his breath, he said, 'I'm going to piss myself.'

Bang…**bang**!

CHAPTER EIGHT

Matilda had fired his Martini-Henry rifle. All hell broke loose with Tommy on the Lewis. Me and Titan scanned our arcs but didn't report any PIDs. The dogs were going berserk. Matilda's horse reared up as Matilda had fired another shot. A small explosion erupted directly ahead. Another short sharp breeze brought the odours in. Titan was slowly swinging the Lewis side to side. I still had my finger on the outside of the trigger guard. Calm but ready to react.

'What the fuck are they firing at?' Titan said.

'No idea. Let your training take over.'

Tommy's Lewis stopped at last. Baka and Rudi went sprinting and barking into the desert. A horse to my right galloped by. I swung my sights around and caressed the trigger. I saw Batgirl with a merciless half-sword wielded in her right hand. Losing sight of her in the abyss, strange yells bounced from all over the place like Sioux Indians. Looking quickly behind, Brat was bursting off the Vickers towards the wadi. Fuck, we were going to have blue on blue if Sikes and Seagal were heading back for support.

Flash-heart was frantically still repairing the ambulance, his rifle two metres away on the ground.

The last burst was from Brat. The wind stopped. Silence fell for the first time. I tuned in, not realising my heart was beating fast. With a sharp 'psst' to each person, I gestured to them to stand down. Titan swung his Lewis; I then faintly heard an engine to the north. I tapped his shoulder, letting him know I had his back.

Out of the gloom came an object. I placed my finger on the trigger. Two barely visible red low-lit lights jolted around. They then stopped moving. Titan unclipped his breast body red-filtered torch and flicked the switch three times. We waited.

Three short bursts came from both lights. I relaxed my shoulders.

Titan breathed out. Time check: 04:25 hours. Fuck, the sun would be rising from the east at 05:55 hours.

'Go and tell the others that Scrap and Blister are coming in,' I ordered. 'But they are to remain effective. I'll go and meet them.'

Titan patted me on the shoulder and then headed back.

The lads walked the bikes in. My anger was still simmering at the shit firing drills. I brashly told Flash-heart he was on his final warning for leaving his weapon, and then ordered him to hurry finishing the ambulance. I calmly told Titan, Blister, and Scrap to set up a defensive OP on the mound we had just left. Seagal walked in with his rifle above his head. Brat lowered his sights at Seagal's red body light. I ordered Seagal to take Matron and Trish in my truck to the wadi. I followed up with an abrupt bark and gesture for Tommy to follow on the motorbike and sidecar. He didn't object about leaving his dogs as I had thought he would. Perhaps he knew I was not in the fucking mood for him. Matilda stopped his drivel as soon as I had told him to shut the fuck up. I ordered him to keep rear guard on the route the others were heading. Whilst Flash-heart kept his head low in the engine bay, I filled the motorbikes and pinky with fuel. On the way back to the ambulance, I gave Brat a dirty look for his firing madness. Reaching Flash-heart, I nudged him with two water containers and then placed them at his feet.

'Get a move on,' I said.

I felt the enemy attack had not happened; all having been a release of nerves. Moronic soldiers following each other. I called back Titan, Blister, and Scrap and ordered them to pick up as many empty shells and other evidence that we had been here. Leaning in the back of the ambulance, I checked the map with a compass and ruler: in a direct line, the railway station was fifty-six klicks away. I wanted the ERL to be set back a minimum of ten klicks from Target-1. If we could find a crossing over the wadi and the direct route was straightforward, we could make the ERL before dawn. Yet, to set up the casualty clearing station was going to be as tight as a super model's thong on an elephant.

'Finished, Vinnie,' Flash-heart said.

'Well done, but we'll talk later about your shit soldiering. Drive it east to the wadi. Titan.'

'Yes, boss.'

'Be the gunner on the Ambulance. Scrap, Blister, escort them on the Trusty.'

'Yes, boss.'

I strolled over to the pinky and sat in the driver's seat. 'We need a little chat,' I sternly said.

Brat looked concerned.

Once the area was devoid of life, I faced Brat who was reloading the Vickers. Rather than talk about his dangerous actions, repeating myself when I was going to discuss at camp to those about their horrendous basic drills, I started the pinky. Crawling along in first gear and making sure we had no unwelcome followers, I then went straight for the jugular.

'Why the fuck did you take Truck-3 out of the hangar the other night?'

Second gear…

'Erm…'

Third gear…

'Do you want me to fucking ask in German?'

Brat put his hand to his right and said, '*Ich kann nicht sagen.*'

Fourth gear…

I put my foot down. 'What do you mean, "You cannot say"?'

The popper clicked on his holster.

Slamming the brakes on, I rapidly drew my pistol from under my *dishdasha*. At his temple, I pressed it hard.

'Two choices,' I said. 'You take your hand off your pistol and tell me why. Or, you don't…live.'

He slowly put his hands on the dash and said, 'My orders to drive truck.'

'Why?'

'I was asked to *laufwerk* to *lager*. I not know why.'

'Who asked you to "drive to camp"?'

He stayed silent.

I grabbed him around the throat. 'Who asked you to keep quiet?'

'Sergeant Rowe,' he blurted.

'Was it you who set the Truck-3 alight?'

'*Nein.*'

'Get out the jeep,' I ordered. 'Leave your pistol on the seat. One wrong move and I'll slot you and leave you for the Egyptian vultures. You don't deserve to wear that German Flying Ace uniform.'

I didn't care if he hadn't understood as I would eagerly squeeze the trigger against this twice traitor. Brat lethargically climbed out and chucked the pistol on the seat. I told him to walk ahead. As he started to, I revved the pinky so he would move quicker.

Over the next five hundred metres, I had thought about whether to continue tonight if the wadi gave us a great LUP. I decided I would put it to vote to either move out in the remaining light, or to stay until dusk the following evening. Everyone would have to consider the time we had left to find a decent ERL and set up the CCS for Matron and Trish. If we did find a position before dawn, there was no way we could travel the next ten klicks to find an LUP nearer to Target-1 in the daylight.

Ten metres from the edge of the wadi, I ordered Brat to stop. The dwindling twilight from the stars and moon made it almost impossible to see the wadi's other side. Seagal stood up twenty metres to my right. I had not seen him, or his hessian wrapped rifle. With my pistol aimed at Brat's back, I debussed. Brat raised his hands. I didn't even have to nod at Seagal as he had read the situation, having his sniper rifle raised.

Holstering my semi-auto Webley and removing my *dishdasha*, I yanked down Brat's right wrist behind him, and then his left. Reaching to my belt, I unclipped the heavy steel Hiaat Darby handcuffs, like those in the late 1800s. I clamped his wrists. There was no adjustment. From my top shirt pocket, I retrieved the key and locked them.

'Keep him away from the others. Especially Sikes,' I said.

'Yes, boss,' Seagal said. 'He can dig me a new pit. With his fucking teeth.'

Brat sharply turned his head, shocked that Seagal could speak.

Seagal winked and shouldered his weapon, exchanging for the same type of pistol as mine. Keeping the correct distance, Seagal ordered Brat to move back to where his hide was. I didn't have to tell Seagal he could shoot Brat if he tried to escape. Brat also knew even if he got past Seagal's martial arts, Seagal was a cracking shot.

I was still pissed off with the uncontrolled firepower and the unleashed barking dogs. Batgirl was also MIA. Worst was the revelation about Sikes and Brat destroying the beloved Truck-3. I will call a meeting after we have set up our LUP.

Cheering me up was seeing that the bank had been shovelled away to a low-gradient slope. The four steel-reinforced timber planks that had been stored under the trucks had been used. We had previously tested different ideas until a set hadn't snapped.

Sikes was huskily ordering to lay the nets with poles over the vehicles. Even though the bodywork and tyres had been camouflaged, the nets would break up any forming shadows. It would also give us some shade and let us walk freely about. Also, the ambulance would not now stick out like a rhino dung in a fruit bowl—one of Scrap's sayings.

'Where the fuck have you been, laddie?'

'I could say the same for you, Sikes?' I muttered.

'Pardon,' he throatily said.

'I see you have decided we'll stay here today.' There goes the Chinese parliament between us, I thought.

'Problem with that, private? No, I thought not. Were you there at the Siege of Mafeking in the Boer? No, so stop fucking bleating and help Sister Spiga make the sandbags, Hurst.'

'Yes, Sarge,' I said. Anything to get away from you, I thought.

Rowe smacked the end of his club down and then stomped off.

I held open a hessian bag and Trish began to fill it.

'Sikes seems to prevaricate when you speak to him,' Trish whispered.

'What does "prevaricate" mean?'

'Speak or act in an evasive way.'

Rowe was now bending Blister's ear about setting up HMG posts at each end.

'Yeah, very indirect,' I said sarcastically. Somehow, I had to get the lads together without Sikes, I thought.

Dawn broke, causing a desolated scene across the desert. There were some tired people sleeping in the wadi, including Matilda's horse. Rudi and Baka were nowhere to be seen. I decided to do a perimeter check. Blister was sat at the far end behind the HMG defence, just inside the netting shade and facing north. He had at least three-hundred yards before the wadi cornered out of sight. The south end mirrored, but with Scrap taking sentry. Standing on the sandbag steps, I raised the net six inches. At ground level, the desert-coloured camouflaged canvas was pegged over a small wall of sandbags. I knew Titan would have his hessian wrapped Lewis' barrel resting on the double-layered wall facing west, the way we had travelled. I walked across the crusted bed to the other side that was about seven metres apart. I then stepped up on the step. Seagal's easterly defence aspect mirror-imaged Titan's. Dawn and dusk were the main times an enemy would attack. Another reason I did not believe the attack last night happened.

Kneeling close to Matron who was half-under the ambulance, I gently shook her. She was startled. I reassuringly smiled and asked her to softly wake the others for a briefing. I then went to find Sikes, the above netting making weird patterns on my shirt.

Having a feeling where he would be, I looked under the Truck-2's rear canvas. Yet, I was surprised to see him sprawled out instead of shaving from a billy can. Just as I was about to wake him, I pulled my hand back. It was easier to leave him be.

Hitching up onto the front radiator's armour and avoiding sitting on the filler cap, the squads went quiet. Without holding in the expletives, I quietly reprimanded the group for their poor soldiering drills last night at the dunes. I gave each of the guilty a short lesson of how they should have reacted to a possible sighting, likely threat, or contact. It was also imperative they should not be worried if they unintentionally made a quiet false alarm call; there will be no ridicule.

After I let their thinking subside, I asked what they had all seen: perhaps shadows. Possibly black horses. Maybe men dressed in dark robes and turbans. Again, I bollocked them for not positively identifying before laying down their incorrect firepower. Also, I told them about Brat's lunacy on the Vickers towards Seagal and Sikes at the wadi.

'Where's Brat and Batgirl?' Matilda asked.

'Brat is on sentry duty with Seagal,' I said. 'I'm not sure where Batgirl rode off to.'

'Shall we not look for her? She could be injured,' Matron said.

'No,' I said. 'I want you all to stay under this netting. I will sort out a patrol.'

'Rudi and Baka?' Tommy said, upset.

'I'm sure they will be back, Tommy,' I said sympathetically.

Matron put her arm around him.

'Right, moving on from the balls-up last night. First, let's all synchronise our watches.' I counted down the seconds to 06:20 hours. 'We have twelve hours of daylight left before we pack up silently and head out to the ERL. At the ERL we'll set up a casualty clearing station. Yes, a CCS before you interrupt, Trish. Make tea from each squad's trench stove and kettle kit. No bucket or log fires. No cooking food. Only rat packs. You ration your amount as per your drills. I want no obvious signs that we've been here when we leave tonight. Between you, I want a rota quickly drawn up for sentry duty. It must include two hours on and four hours off. If you're not on stag, get some rationed scoff and water, and then sleep. But you sleep ready for immediate action. If I catch anyone sleeping, smoking, or even lighting their fucking joss-sticks on stag, you will be RTU'd.'

'What does that mean?' Flash-heart asked.

'Returned to your unit. And I don't mean catch a train from 'platform four'. You can fucking walk back.'

'But the base has moved,' Matron said.

'Exactly. Do not sleep or smoke on stag.'

I then reminded them that paratyphoid and dysentery could easily break out in an environment where water and sanitation were basic, at best. Swarms of flies carried infection from refuse, latrines, and food being uneaten in unwashed billy cans. All faeces, including animal, had to be immediately 'bagged' in grease-proof baking-paper that had been supplied. It then had to be buried to a minimum depth of three feet, and hands sanitised after. All food remains had to be addressed in the same manner. You had to mark your pit with a simple marker, such as a stone. Again, all tell-tail signs had to be removed on leaving. Disease was just as much a threat to the troops as the enemy was.

Carrying on with the disease threat aspect, I went over the need for self-hygiene. But strictly no perfumed soaps. I instructed them to especially look after the feet, being as important out here as your rifle. Matilda and Flash-heart looked baffled.

'Yes, your feet,' I said. 'Imagine your vehicle breaks down or your horse dies, and your feet are in a shit condition. Now think about trudging back to a friendly civilization. Let alone a British base over a hundred miles away. We're in the middle of fucking nowhere.'

Everyone nodded at the basic rule, as if new—how worrying.

'Visualise infected feet caused by uncared blisters,' I continued, 'or skin that's been worn off by tiny granules of sand. Now envisage running from many enemies. So, constantly change your sweaty socks. Wash and dry them if you can. Clean and dry your feet properly. Empty the sand from your boots. Find the correct time to let your feet breathe. Make sure your boots are not loose. I hope you all wore-in your boots before you came.'

'Is it true you Poms piss in yours to make them supple?' Matilda said.

I smirked. 'See the medics on treating blisters and athletes' foot. Whilst we're on hygiene, check your bollocks, arse-crack, and armpits for sweat rashes.'

'I am happy to check the privates,' Trish said, looking at Tommy's groin.

'That's all ranks,' I bantered. 'Right, first stag at 08:00 hours. Any questions?

'Yes, Corporal Jim Hurst,' Matron said. 'Why do we not have proper names and ranks? It will cause susceptibility and lead to disorder.'

'Very simple, Matron. If any of us are captured, not only will you put yourself in danger, but a squad member as well. Especially if the interrogators know what the higher and lower ranks are. Also, I don't want members in the squads thinking they are far superior to the next. It can be demoralising or will not let that person have their say, especially if they have something important or critical to add. Of course, I am the DS, but you have a right to put an objection across or add to my plans. However, the final decision is mine. So, nicknames it is.'

'The others call you "boss". Surely that would give it away to the enemy,' Matilda smugly said.

'No, because my squad are highly trained to resist interrogation and call me by my nickname, Vinnie, when the time is right.'

His arrogant face dropped.

'From now on, you call me Vinnie, or boss.'

'What about Sergeant Sean Rowe?' Matron said.

'Sikes? He's our CO. If you have an issue with him, come to me. For your own health and safety, I would address him by his rank and surname. Right, dismissed.'

The tin kettle steamed. I lifted the hot handle with a cloth and extinguished the flame ring. The compartment underneath had to be either lit by oil, kerosene, or fuel blocks. If desperate, you could use animal fat to light. If gagging for tea, a small amount of hessian soaked in petrol could be used.

I poured out two mugs, refilled the kettle, and then took the third mug off my personal Tommy-cooker. I had learnt first to bind string around the mug's metal handle, as it got very hot. Adding another mug back to the stove, those ready I stirred in powdered milk from a Ministry of Food tin. I then added two sugar lumps in each from a Henry & Tate tin. Not a bad brew for the Sinai Desert in 1917.

The first to receive their well-earned drink was Scrap. He also received the dreadful Huntley & Palmers rock hard biscuit and then a small string-tied grease-paper parcel of dates. He welcomed the hotel room service and the news he would be relieved at 08:00 hours.

'What the fuck went on last night?' he asked.

'I'll give the low-down later.'

I headed over to Blister. He was as happy as Scrap for the exact breakfast. Blister asked me if I wanted to join his morning glory. I declined.

'What the fuck went on last night?' he asked.

'I'll update our squad later.'

Steadying myself up the ramps, I kept as low as possible towards Titan's dugout. Whispering it was me with his five-star meal, his large hand came out from the pegged down canvas and took the mug of tea. I handed him the biscuits and dates, but he gave back the Huntley & Palmers.

'Cheers,' he said.

'Aren't you going to ask what went on last night?' I asked.

'You got yourself stuck in her headlock.'

'That's fucking grim,' I said. 'I thought you northern posh boys from a privileged background didn't get to see any muff. Just cock.'

'Do not fucking take the piss out of my heritage, you fucking softy southerner,' he said.

'Let me know when you can grow a proper beard like we do across the divide.'

'Fuck ye, I'll twist ye fuckin' balls off when we get back,' he said, impersonating Planet.

At last, I thought, I had been asking him for ten months, and it was near spot on. 'I'm going now.'

'Good.'

'To ask Tommy if he can do a better impersonation as yours was fucking shit.'

Repeating making the fourth mug, I then walked over to the ladder against the wadi wall. Precariously climbing it, I crouched over to Seagal's large dugout.

'Tea up,' I whispered.

The canvas slowly unravelled. Seagal and Brat squinted. I handed Seagal the tea and dates, and then a water bottle to give to Brat. I told Seagal that the stag was to end at 08:00 hours. He then was to secure Brat in the back of our truck until I decided how to handle the situation with him and Sikes when I returned from a patrol. Lastly, I gave Seagal the handcuff key.

CHAPTER NINE

After discussing with the squad that I was going to search for Batgirl and the dogs, I unloaded most of the rear pinky whilst the sentry handover took place. I then added my kit I wanted to take on patrol, and checked my ammo was secure under my *dishdasha*. Seagal manhandled Brat to the rear of Truck-1. Titan assisted lifting Brat into the back. With the help from the rest of the squad, except Sikes, they guided me driving up the ramps.

Up top, Tommy sat in the passenger seat before Scrap had. I tried reasoning and then ordering Tommy to get out. Yet, Tommy had a determined look to stay put. He was heavily loaded with weapons and ammo.

'How long?' Scrap asked.

'Two hours,' I said.

'Do we send out a search party if you're not back?'

'No, finish the objectives.'

'Oh *lekker*, I get to spend time with Sikes.'

'So, it's "great" to spend time with your mate Sikes, but not worry where your best *bru* is,' I joked.

'*Yebbo*,' he said enthusiastically.

'Give Tommy your *dishdasha* and *shemagh*. His Hungarian uniform and hat stick out like a doctor with full blown herpes.'

Scrap moodily took it off and threw it in Tommy's lap. 'Do not get it all smelling of perfume, Tommy.'

Tommy half-smiled.

'No one leaves the LUP,' I said.

'Sure, boss,' Scrap said.

'And no teaching them your shit lingo, Scrap,' I said.

Driving slowly back to the dunes, a stone hit the back of the pinky and flew over the front. I smiled thinking of Scrap having thrown it.

In the far distance, the vast open flats were surrounded with different spectacular shaped rock summits. Green vegetation widely grew in clusters in the different gradients of sand. I followed the faint tyre grooves; the sand being whipped across the desert floor from a northwesterly direction. The breeze slightly diminished the morning's warmth of about twelve degrees Celsius. Although the visibility was a clear five klicks, I knew our patrol's camouflage would be almost impossible to distinguish. My low-speed dust trail would blend in with the swirls already. Even though there were only two of us, if compromised we had enough firepower to engage.

Tommy had not taken his resolute stare from the front. When I was back at base, I had done a little homework with some of the British soldiers. The Hungarian troops fought faithfully and intrepidly, being one of the causes of their high losses. Yet, I couldn't see this in Tommy.

As we drew alongside the dunes, approximately five hundred metres from the LUP, from the rear I grabbed my sack and slowly walked up the mound. At eye level, I peeked over. The little thickets slightly rustled. As Tommy joined me, I signalled for him to follow me down into the shallow dip that me and Titan had sat in during the early hours of this morning. On our bellies and side by side, I lifted my binoculars. Tommy pushed them down. I turned to him as he delved back into his kit bag. He then handed me a pair of his binos. I frowned at why. He tapped the lens.

'*Magnézium-fluorid.*'

'Magnesium fluoride?'

'Yes,' Tommy said exuberantly, happy because I had understood him.

I looked at the lens coating in the sunlight. 'Anti-reflective? In this era?'

'*Német*…German. Tommy are *baromság*.' He laughed.

'What's "*baromság*"?'

Tommy suddenly rolled me onto my side and pointed at my groin. '*Baromság…baromság.*'

'English binos are "bollocks",' I translated. 'Oh well, I'll have to keep your German ones then.'

Focusing to my left, I spotted the ditch running parallel to the track where Matilda had fired from. Panning across to the featureless plain I saw something abnormal. Again, like when spotting Gavin's remains in Sumatra, I lowered and checked with the mark-one eyeball. Focusing back through his binos, my heart gave a little flutter. However, I was too late to stop Tommy viewing through mine. Shit. For ten seconds or more he just stared. I placed a hand on his shoulder. Suddenly, venting in Hungarian, he jumped to his feet and bolted across the mound. I called as loud as I dared for him to come back. By the side of me was his Mannlicher rifle, binos, and kit bag.

Tommy was halfway across to Rudi. The dog lay a hundred and fifty metres away, covered by a thin layer of sand. Tommy stripped off his *dishdasha* and *shemagh* whilst still running. Standing a few strides back from his companion, Tommy looked down at the body. First, Tommy's shoulders began to shake. Then, with his hands to his face, he sank to his knees. I felt for him, knowing what it was like to lose a trusted friend on the battlefield.

Not wanting to see anymore and to give him some dignity, I moved the binos east towards El Arish. It was too far to identify anything with these, especially with the heat effect off the damp sand. At least there were no enemies waiting, I thought. Our LUP was impossible to locate at first. We did an amazing job, and I made a mental note to give praise on our return.

From the peace, a new noise filtered in. I switched the view to Tommy: he was leaning over embracing Rudi. Searching without the binos, I squinted at an almost obscured object in the haze. I speedily refocused the dial. Fuck. Friend or foe? If there's doubt, there is no doubt. With galloping noises from the two horses at the distance of about three hundred metres, whoever they were wouldn't have heard me shout for Tommy. However, Tommy did not move.

Sliding back his rifle action-bolt, I laid it next to me. I then readied mine.

Two hundred metres…

I looked through the binos: both horses were beige. The riders were in yellow and white robes…

Hundred and fifty metres…

Shit. Both riders had spears…

Hundred metres…

No saddles but a rug: Bedouin. Look up, Tommy…

Fifty metres…

I dropped the binos and sighted the closest rider, swivelling as I followed.

Unexpectedly, Tommy sprung up and sprinted towards them. He shrieked and hollered in different pitches and waved his arms. Has he gone crazy? My finger caressed the trigger even more to squeeze off a round. My mind flashed to pull immediately back on the action-bolt to take the second shot.

The furthest horse reared as Tommy closed in, still yelling. I couldn't take the shot as Tommy had run through the middle of them. The first spear barely missed him. As both riders pulled on the reins to turn, I sighted one. Tommy turned and fled back towards them. Grabbing the grounded spear, he snapped it on his knee—idiot. Each time I went to take a shot as they circled him, Tommy got in the way. Another spear came in, sticking into the sand. The horses started to gain speed. The riders realised they had managed to keep him in the death ring. Worryingly, the spear was trampled. Even worse, the Bedouin had both drawn Sabre swords.

I had to get a cleaner shot, so I ran with both rifles down the mound.

Bang…bang…bang…bang!

The first horse buckled to the ground. As the Bedouin had sprawled out face first, Tommy then shot the rider, twice. I knelt and took aim, slowing my breathing and steadying my hand. Just as the other rider took a swing at him, Tommy ducked and grabbed the other sword from the floor.

Bang!

I had missed, but quickly cocked it.

Tommy, with a charging yell, swung at the horse's rear leg, slicing it off above the knee. A weird scream followed. The rider went to the ground. The horse frantically tried to get up, its legs all over the place. Tommy's blade reflecting off the sun took my eyes off the grisly scene, only to see it come down. The impact was out of view behind the horse. Tommy stood up with the pistol and shot the physically jerking horse through its head, twice.

Standing up, I checked in a complete circle that we had no more threats. Lowering my Enfield, I ran over. Aiming at the first rider, his head wounds were being soaked up by the rider's *keffiyeh* and the sand. I wished I hadn't followed SOP to check the other rider as he had been decapitated. The first horse was barely breathing. Tommy came over to it and knelt on one knee. Putting his face up to the horse's ear, he whispered something. After stroking it, he put it out of its misery. The last shot echoed across the quiet desert. I panned around.

Tommy's mumbling got me back to the situation. He was cross-legged, praying with his eyes shut.

In anger, I kicked the sand and said, 'Fuck. This carnage is going to compromise us. We need to hide it all or break cover and move out. Yet, more than likely we'll be seen by a search party. Bollocks.'

It wasn't blame; Tommy had reacted with pure killer-controlled aggression to save himself. It was a him or them situation. In fact, it quite shocked me. Not the blood and gore, but that he had it in him. Many would have frozen, run, or not had it in them to finish the job. He had gone up in my estimation.

I walked over to Tommy and placed my hand on his trembling shoulder.

'It for Rudi,' he sobbed.

I guessed "it" had meant revenge. 'Tommy, listen, pick up Rudi and head back in the pinky to the wadi.'

I did the steering wheel action and then pointed to the wadi. Tommy wiped away the tears and nodded.

'Tell Scrap and Titan to bring some rope.'

Tommy frowned.

I went over to the thin rope attached around the horse's gut. 'Rope. Titan and Scrap bring it here. OK?'

Picking up Tommy's compact pistol, I brushed the sand off its gunmetal coloured body. It revealed a motif on the screwed-on brown handle plate. He took my stretched-out hand and stood up. The grit had stuck to the blood splats. He took back his pistol.

'*Frommer Stop Pisztoly*,' he said. 'English Tommy *Pisztoly* bollocks.'

'Get moving, Tommy, I need to clear up your shit.' I smiled.

I started mopping up, one of Lieutenant James Mullen's sayings in Operation Poppy Pride. Each Bedouin had an ivory-handle curved dagger in a sheath. The sheath was bound by a green cloth around their waste. There were no more weapons under their robes, only a loin cloth covering the sweaty and dirty bodies.

At the same time as keeping a watch of the battlefield, I fastidiously collected each 7.65 cartridge. Eight in total. Picking up the other strewn weapons, I placed them in a pile. A squawk above alerted me. Circling high were four long-winged birds. Shit, this would cause more vultures to follow, warning any scavengers or curious locals. Word would spread to the Bedouin and the enemy.

Two sharp hooked and yellow beaked vultures landed ten metres from me. The breeze ruffled their beige, white, and black features. They weren't the only visitors: flies started buzzing. For a split-second, I thought about chasing off the ravenous birds, but it was better they were grounded. Come on lads, I thought.

Backing away from the scene towards the mound, I picked up Tommy's clothes and my cartridge. As I reached the top of the dunes, I cleared any trace we had been there. The pinky was heading towards my position at full speed. Scrap had his Enfield aimed at me. He then lowered it. I signalled them to where I wanted them to head, and then ran down the soft slope. The edgy flock of eight took to the sky. Titan slowed up and I jumped on the rear side.

'South African AA at your service,' Scrap said, as a lady-like receptionist. 'Where's your broken-down car?'

'What's that?' Titan said.

'As we are recovering a stranded…'

'No, that,' Titan exclaimed.

'Fuck. We need a horsebox trailer,' Scrap said.

I let the banter continue whilst both horses were tied to the rear of the pinky. However, it was obvious they were too heavy. Guessing each weighed around five-hundred kilograms, we untied one. We then placed its rider on top of the tied horse. Titan made a joke about himself not winning a horse bet of a grand this time. He had changed since I had first met him at the Somme. This time, the pertinacious pinky managed the new weight.

In a shallow dip, me and Scrap lay with our weapons facing in opposite directions. I told him what had happened. He was as surprised as me about Tommy's aggressive counterattack. It wasn't long before the insults came in about me not even being able to hit a Bedouin, let alone a horse.

We hitched up the last horse and jockey. They had been on the tasting menu for the vultures. On the way back to the wadi, I let them know about Brat and Sikes. It stopped the mockery. I ordered them to covertly tell Seagal, Blister, and Trish about Truck-3. We unanimously agreed not to tell the others.

Back at the LUP, Blister had already taken charge by getting everyone to dig a huge pit. Fortunately, the sand underneath the crusty top was very soft. Tommy was helping dig the pit, leaving his lost friend under a grey blanket. The itchy type in the trenches.

Just after the sixteen-metre square pit had been dug, we stood back and took on much needed water. The rations were depleting at a rapid rate. Our squad and Seagal were the only ones to have worn thin leather gloves, knowing the weapons and tools you used out here became hot. The others looked at their sores. Blister made a pun about needing the action as the trip was getting boring. I snapped at him to shut the fuck up and to be careful what he wished for.

Back filling the almost five feet deep pit, Sikes wandered aimlessly over. He was scruffy with bloodshot eyes. Sikes pushed me out of the way, looking at the earth covering the dead. The shovelling stopped.

'What's going on, laddie?' he said, croaky.

'Sergeant, two enemies were taken out trying to attack us,' I said.

'Bedouin. Who fucking ordered to open fire?'

'No one. It was a surprise attack,' I said.

Seething, he growled and raised his club. He then pointed it at everyone in a sweeping circle.

'This fuckery stops now. I own this hundred metre trench.'

For a second, there was a group look of confusion. Then, a look of displeasure. Sikes came closer to me. I didn't get the smell of alcohol.

'Who killed them?' Sikes asked, in his London growl.

'I did. I had to make a…'

Sucking in air, I took a few steps back. I raised my hand at Blister who started to raise his shovel to attack him. Sikes stepped into my space again.

'Do you understand what you have started with the Bedouin? One more disobeyed order, and I'll fucking have you shot at dawn, Hurst. You ought to be dead already, laddie. Now get this camp cleared up. We move out in two hours.'

'In the daylight, sir?' Trish asked.

'Do not fucking call me "sir". Where is Lieutenant Löwenhardt and Khalida?'

'They've both headed north up the wadi on a foot patrol,' I lied.

Sikes nodded, about turned, and marched off towards the back of his truck.

'And get that fucking dead dog in the pit,' he yelled.

I cringed, hoping Tommy hadn't understood.

From the constant negativity from Sikes, the morale was low when shovelling the piled sand. Something had to change with him before something big was going to happen. I needed an excuse for the squad not to head out in the daylight. Instead, to wait for dusk.

Taking a midday break, I saw Sikes dressed in full kit heading north up the wadi. The group's self-esteem was still low as we all took shade on sentry duty or under the trucks. Again, our lunch consisted of warm Fray Bentos tinned corned beef. The worst, almost vile, was a warm tin of Maconochie's meat and veg stew. I soaked my hard biscuit into the mix to absorb the fats that were melting in the near twenty-five degrees heat. Matron and Trish boasted how they had brought their own tin of ox tongue in brine. I threw some walnuts and dates in to experiment if it tasted better—failed. Scrap looked as dismayed as me as he came and joined me. He mentioned he could do a mean spit-roast if we uncovered one of the horses—for a second, I contemplated it. Me and Scrap seemed the only ones to not accept the rations.

Having squeezed down my lunch, I individually told everyone that they had done a brilliant job of setting up this LUP and for the challenging work of burying the horses and riders. Tommy wasn't eating. By choice of having buried his mate on his own, he had the thousand-yard stare.

Finishing off my coffee and tidying my mess away in my sandbag, I asked Scrap if he would head down the wadi with me in the other direction. My plan was, once Sikes had returned, he would not leave without me and Scrap—I hoped. Gently waking Trish, I told her our plans and asked her to tell the others on handover. Getting closer, I whispered in her ear for her to feed Brat who was in the back of my truck.

'I thought you were going to kiss me,' she said.

'After going with General Rowe?' I joked, and pulled a disgusted face.

She gave me the wanker sign.

CHAPTER TEN

Scrap had grown into the forward planner role by double-checking both motorbikes had a full tank, and each carried a spare fuel container as there was no reserve tank. He now fastidiously made sure we had enough water, ammo, and a rolled-up netted sheet. I retracted the stand from the aluminium base plate and fastened it to the mudguard. I then tapped the tank. Time check: 12:32 hours.

Letting the bike tick-over, I studied the map and took a bearing of where we were camped and the direction I wanted to head. I knew the Trusty had a range of 95 to 112 klicks per 1.5-gallon tank. I reminded Scrap that Flash-heart had said the front fork spring was prone to breaking over rough ground. Smugly, Scrap pointed at the front of my bike. A thick leather belt was wrapped around mine, including one around his forks. A forward planning precaution, I thought.

We rode south down the wadi. The banks kept the noise and dust down, diminishing the risks of riding in the daylight. The situation was like in Afghan when on a quad bike.

After approximately ten klicks, the ground had become softer. I squeezed the front stirrup brake. With insignificant effect again, I used the rear to assist. Leaning the bike against the bank, Scrap did the same on the opposite. I took a piss, the colour dehydrated. A goat bleated. I almost stopped mid-flow. Pushing it out, I watched the bank's edge where the noise had filtered from. Scrap had finished and was quietly engaging his rifle action-bolt. He then got a foothold in the collapsed bank.

Moving slightly to his left, I eased my head up to the ridge. Sand granules bounced off my goggles. Fifty metres away were six goats of all sizes feeding on sporadic clumps of vegetation. One had strayed, nourishing only five metres from us. About ten metres from the main herd was the herder. An Arab boy of about ten years old with pineapple designed hair. The boy was making patterns in the sand with a stick, oblivious to the dangers he could be in. Scrap quietly tapped my arm with his binos. I shook my head and retrieved mine. He frowned. I whispered mine were better than his shit ones as his had no anti-reflection on.

Further south, about eight hundred metres was a village. I murmured what I saw: several single-story and round-shaped mud huts with stones protruding through from the seasonal rains. Each dwelling had hessian, probably stolen from the armies. Palm-leaves were laid over as a roof with timbers ends protruding. Scrap raised his binos and I stopped relaying.

Closest to the wadi's edge was a large and odd-shaped mud building. It was as if it had many extensions terribly added over the years. Each one appeared older than the other. The palm roofing was bulkily layered. People were walking around carrying objects. Too far to tell gender and what. Scrap nudged me. I turned back to see he had ducked and was frantically pointing at the bank. Fuck, the goat had wandered closer this way. This was all too familiar to Andy McNab's *Bravo Two Zero*. I knew the herder would come to the edge. I didn't want to make the right decision to shoot the kid if he ran. Or, the wrong decision not to. Both would get our unit compromised. I hushed in Scrap's ear that we were to run the bikes further down the wadi. Fucking goats, I thought.

We had quietly pushed the bikes close to the bank over the four hundred metre dash. The ground had become softer the further we had travelled. We were breathing heavily. Yet, we were supposed to be super-fit. Our direction had banked left, hiding us from where we had sprinted from. I sunk back into the wall with the bike. Scrap left his bike and lay prone behind his rifle, trying to slow his breathing.

I knew it must have been clear as his face dropped into the sand. The tyre groove I had left started to fill with water. The flow ran south, the way we were heading. My thirst took a grip, so I took a few large gulps of water. Warm, but ever so refreshing. Scrap came alongside and took a well-earned drink. He wiped the sweat as if the drink had poured straight from him.

'Those goats aren't giving chase in a Pierce-Arrow, then,' I said.

'I doubt it, we ate Billy the driver for breakfast...' Scrap lowered his *shemagh* and ruffled his matted hair. 'Fuck, when was that?'

'Yesterday morning, I think. Seems like a lifetime ago.'

'Talking of the Pierce-Arrow, did you know that it was us South Africans that invented the words pom pom for the guns?'

'Really?' I said lamely.

'Yeah.'

'I meant, really, as your knowledge is as lame as Rabbit's.'

'Piss off.'

Standing on the saddle, I first checked for the herder. The herd had disappeared with the mere boy who could alert any enemy or a local. Or, even a religious fundamentalist pent up with revenge. I shook McNab's book from my thoughts.

Panning the binos, we were about four hundred metres from the village. Next to the largest and ugliest building were five donkeys. All were under the shade of sewn together animal skins held up by sticks and rope. Behind the main building was a cultivated tree plantation with irrigation. In the centre of the village was a stone-built circled wall. My educated guess was that it was a water-well into the watercourse level. That's why there were palm trees and inhabitants settled here, relying on it when the wadi dried up.

Women were dressed in black robes with the uniquely and strange pineapple design hair. Some had shawls, and a few were carrying what looked like baskets of fruit. My mouth watered. I smirked; having thought of the crazy woman I had stolen from at the Afghan farm.

Scrap moved to the bend where the wadi turned right towards the village.

'Boss, there's a cutout in the left bank, big enough for our bikes to go up.'

'How far?'

'Fifty metres. We could head east into the dunes and check the area.'

I thought about whether to turn back and listen to Sikes ordering me to pack up and move out in broad daylight, or risk going up top through the gap in the wall. A dog barking disturbed my thought, not that it was a difficult choice to make. I lifted the binos in the direction it was coming from: the village.

'Baka,' I muttered.

'Are you sure?'

'I've been barked and growled by that bloody Rottweiler for the last month.'

'Do we head through the gap or turn back to that psychotic sergeant?'

'We don't go back to the base till dusk,' I said.

'Good.'

'But we'll return in the dark to rescue Baka.'

'What? Why risk it for a dog?'

'Would you turn back for me, Scrap?'

'Yes.'

'End of discussion.'

We covertly wheeled the bikes to the bank's cut-out. I was surprised to see it wasn't a slope leading up to the desert. Instead, it was a ditch big enough for one person to ride down. The risk was starting our motorbikes here. On a countdown, we simultaneously started. Under low revs we followed the ditch. The further we travelled; the ground became wetter.

I reckoned we had ridden about ten klicks when a fork in the direction was presented. I stopped the Trusty; the ground seeped the water. Leaning back to my side satchel, Scrap lifted his goggles. He was covered in wet sand. I sneered at the state of him.

'Left, or right?' I asked.

'Left appears to level out, rather than head down. The left route also seems more man-made, like an escape route. It's also dryer. I am sick of you covering me in shit where you can't ride properly.'

'I'm a fucking good rider,' I snapped.

Pulling down his goggles, he said, 'Yeah, like your shooting.'

'You need to take some fucking Canesten. You're becoming as irritating as Rabbit was.'

I tried not to make the left turn manoeuvre an ordeal, knowing Scrap was beaming. A few metres in, I became aware of fresh hoof prints. I killed the engine. Sliding around my rifle, I pulled the bayonet from its fixed sheath and secured it.

Ahead was a pile of horse shit. Scrap shuffled by. On one knee, he picked it up and smelt it. He then squeezed the moisture.

'It's not even a day old,' he said quietly.

'Horse, donkey, or camel?'

'Definitely horse.'

Leaning my bike on the wall, I cautiously stood on the saddle and slowly raised to ground level. The north side was bleak, except for a large mass of dunes two hundred metres away. With Scrap keeping watch both ways of the ditch, I swivelled west—barren. Facing south had endless miles of featureless desert, except the mountains in the furthest background. I checked east towards the 'Turco-Egyptian Frontline' and viewed many peaks of the Arizona Desert. I whispered that we would push the bikes up the incline where we should start them and head over to the dunes.

After being in the comfort of the ditch and wadi for so long, up top I was feeling vulnerable. Keeping a beady eye out for anything that looked remotely abnormal, we raced across until I found a large depression in the ground. Unclipping the new quick-release mudguard with the engine running, I crouched behind it. I waved Scrap on towards the dunes. Lying prone at the edge, I scanned my arcs. Scrap entered the dunes on foot. I apprehensively waited.

Three minutes later, his hand came up above a grass mound and signalled he had seen one person. I killed the purring engine and then tapped the saddle.

'I'll be back soon,' I muttered.

Squat running the last twenty metres, I wondered who this one person was. A Bedouin? A Turk or German? If so, why only one? Perhaps it was a herder.

Creeping over the edge, I pulled myself up to Scrap who was peering through his binos. Seeing his Enfield next to him, I assumed it wasn't a threat he was viewing. Keeping the grassy thicket in front, I parted my own view east. Being positioned five metres off ground level gave me good eyes on the stunning scenery. Panning down the ancient carved sides of the eroded landscape was a horse tied to a boulder. It was situated under an overhang, like a shallow cave. I recognised the horse as Batgirl's. Its front upper leg was bandaged, the blood staining the white shin.

Even from this height, it was impossible to see the bottom of this sixty-metre diameter sinkhole. Perhaps Batgirl had fallen to her death last night. Maybe she was lying injured on the precarious path that helter-skeltered around the edge.

'There's nothing in the surrounding area to challenge us to have a look,' Scrap said.

'Best entry point?'

'There's a few footprints leading over the edge.'

There was nothing I could pinpoint. 'What are you, some sort of Aboriginal tracker?' I jested.

'I wouldn't say "Aboriginal", but more Terry Grant.'

'Who?'

'North America's best tracker.'

'Is that because South Africans have no tracking skills,' I bantered.

'What the fuck is it with you with my roots, Johnny?'

'Getting a bit prickly, Georges.'

'Always looking down your...'

'Not now,' I interrupted.

Before I slid down the slope, I unfixed the bayonet from the rifle.

Squat running over to the sinkhole's edge, I checked for trip hazards. On my stomach and inching towards the edge, the view was spectacular. This dream-like oasis had palm trees surrounding a large and beautiful blue pool at the bottom. The main ditch that we had left now trickled water over the edge, adding years of attrition carved into the precipice. Bushes sat around the edges of the rocks and boulders at the base. The main path that led from here circled down anticlockwise to the tied horse. From there, only a thin trail led to the bottom.

'Are you seeing what I'm seeing?' Scrap said, heightened.

I thought of a Batgirl dead at the bottom. I looked at him and then followed his binocular direction without mine. By the tranquil water's edge and under the shade of a large boulder was Batgirl on her back, naked. I pulled around my binos to see if she had fallen to her death—she hadn't.

'I didn't know they have alpaca out here?' he whispered.

'Huh?'

'Her tuft is like the top of an alpaca's head.'

'Oh my days,' I said, quietly laughing, the binos shaking. 'It's no landing strip, I grant you that.'

'Worse than that pigmy midget's hairpiece we saw in the jungle,' he said, then joined in the silent hysterics.

'You can't say "midget",' I said. 'It's not PC. Must be, vertically challenged, or small person.'

'Bollocks.'

Once the giggling died down to the odd smirk, the warm sun on my back lessened into a chill. The dense grey clouds were forming, and the breeze had picked up.

'How are we going to alert her?' I asked.

'I think the chill has.'

I pulled his binos down. 'Forget the nipples and switch on. We need a plan as we can't just go down there with her naked.'

'Why not?' he asked.

'Because you must respect her religious beliefs. We're in her country.'

Scrap crawled back a metre. Looking around first, he then stood up bold as brass. 'Hey, Johnny,' he yelled. 'Let's recce the oasis over there.'

Fuck. I stared back at her. Batgirl had looked up. I scurried backwards and stood, giving Scrap a dirty look.

'Come on, Johnny, let's head down this path,' he shouted.

I shook my head at his shit acting.

Holding back his arm, I looked at the time: 14:08 hours. Once a few minutes had gone by, I led down the path. Shingle fell thirty metres as I watched my step. How the fuck had she ridden down here? The rain began to lightly moisten the dusty trail. Ripples formed in the pool. As the path levelled out, the shower became heavier. The horse nodded; perhaps enjoying the heat respite as much as me.

Batgirl had begun to climb the huge boulder. As she reached her horse, I called out for her. Suddenly, Batgirl turned around and pulled out the large sword that had been attached to her horse. She also had a dagger in the other hand, like that of the Bedouin Tommy had killed. I raised my hands at the same time as Scrap. She took a threatening step forward, her eyes intent under her mask. I raised my rifle and took aim.

Even though she now had two trained weapons on her centre mass, it didn't look like she was going to back down. There was no way we could talk our way out of the stalemate because of the language barrier. So, like in Anoosha's house in Afghan, I smiled and then lowered my rifle.

'Lower your weapon, Scrap,' I ordered.

'Yes, boss,' he said reluctantly.

'Peace,' I said to her, then remembered my Arabic. '*Al-sallam*,' I repeated.

'Your alpaca is not under threat,' Scrap said, barely audible.

I gave a little shake of the head to Scrap.

'*Al-sallam*,' Scrap said.

Batgirl stood resolute. I thought about the translation that we could help her horse; perhaps winning her over.

'*Nahin nesade hessank*,' I tried—nothing. 'Scrap is a veterinary surgeon. Erm…' Fuck, how do I translate that?

'*Tabib alpitri*, you say,' she said. 'You, Johnny, follow me.' She lowered her weapons and began to head down the trail.

'I have no idea how to treat a horse,' Scrap whispered.

'I'm not even going to mention your roots about fixing up zebras as I don't want you getting all prickly again. But try to remember your Terry Grant skills.'

'Piss off.'

With the rain pouring, I gingerly followed her down to the bottom of the oasis. I kept my distance because she still had her sword and dagger. Sliding down the last wet boulder, her prints led around the pool and then through some plush-green thickets. Cautiously, I checked around the last palm tree. She was sitting in a cave, embers glowing and the ash floating up with the slight wind. I looked back at Scrap who was trying to reassure the horse. His four-legged friend was not happy.

To appear unconcerned by Batgirl, even though I really was, I boldly walked in. I dumped my wet *shemagh* and kit, but I had left the Enfield within reach. She had done the same with her weapons. A roll of thunder echoed around the walls, adding to the mistrust. Batgirl put dried palm leaves on the fire whilst I sat down. The smoke obscured my view for a few seconds. When it had cleared, she was staring at me. A lightning strike lit up the dark atmosphere. Slowly, I leant into my bag and retrieved the dates. She eyed me as I unwrapped them.

'*Rajaa*,' I said, holding the packet out to her. 'Please.'

Batgirl vigilantly came forward on her hands and knees. Her silky robes were a little too close to the fire for my liking. She then took one. I noticed her elegant hands, but quickly remembered that she was lethal. I nodded for her to take the lot, but she only took one more. Her eyes narrowed as if she was thinking. Popping one in my mouth, I started chewing the delight. Perhaps trusting that they weren't poisoned, she ate one. I smiled.

Surprisingly, she lifted off her black headgear and purple mask. Her sultry eyes matched her stunning beauty. I sensed the trust was growing between us. I shook my captivated eyes, averting them to the fire. Yet, I was drawn back. She smiled and popped another date in her mouth. I caught a better view of her perfect white teeth. She licked the sticky residue off her delicate lips. Her exquisiteness matched that of Haleema.

'Fucking pissing it down,' Scrap blurted. 'Budge up, *bru*.'

He took the remaining dates, and the ambiance. Batgirl had placed on her mask; also, putting the sword on her lap.

Not only was Scrap dampening the mood, but the hammering rain had also not relented. However, being like most practical South Africans, he made a small sand berm to stop the water coming in. Whilst he collected more palm leaves and bark, I pondered how much rainfall it would take to fill this oasis. It was trying its best.

Me and Scrap shared out the dates, biscuits, and mints. After a few hours, the conversation had been about the shit weather and this stunning oasis. The chat had now dried out, like the fire had us. Eventually, Batgirl asked how her horse, Imam, was doing. It was named after Batgirl's dead Bedouin husband. After Scrap had consoled her, she revealed how she had been captured by the British Army after they killed her husband. General Rowe had offered her safety and wealth, but only if she joined this mission. Her role was to keep any Bedouin tribes happy that we might meet. Me and Scrap looked at each other, both reading each other's minds not to mention the two Tommy had killed.

The night was drawing in. The storm overhead lit up the oasis on each strike, bringing an eerie atmosphere outside. At least the cave still had an ember glow. Batgirl removed her headgear and mask. I had to forcibly nudge Scrap to stop stupidly ogling, more than once. After offering us nuts, she then handed over camel biltong. It tasted rich compared to our army rations.

Her version of what happened last night was vague. She said in the confusion that Imam had taken a British bullet to his leg. She was even more ambiguous about what everyone had been firing at. She also didn't answer why she had stayed here rather than return.

I didn't want the mistrust to return, so I started the discussion about when to head back to the LUP. In the Chinese parliament, it was agreed it was too dangerous at night to return to the top on the slippery trail; especially as it was still raining. The plan: at dawn, we would head back to the village where Batgirl would negotiate the return of Baka. I was sure our unit would be OK for at least a night, except for the ear bashing from Sikes.

We had not only successfully found Batgirl, but also Baka. Our mission was only a day behind. Positively, we had found an oasis where we could return to re-stock water. This place could also make an emergency rendezvoused if the mission went tits-up. There was good cover from the desert's weather, enemy troops, and planes.

Batgirl passed around a billy can of steaming liquid, resembling a strong mulled wine. It warmed me and Scrap. Scrap said I should take the first stag on the path. Gazing between the flames at her, I quickly overruled that.

Lying on my side, I became mellow and enriched by the beauty of Batgirl. Or was it the drink? Had she spiked it? Was she going to slit my throat? Looking at the embers, I drifted off.

CHAPTER ELEVEN

Two fucking days of non-stop heavy rain had passed. In that numbing time, on the first day we had managed to climb the slippery boulders to reach the horse. The path had started to crumble under the amount of water cascading. Imam was in a sorrowful state. Blood had stained the rockface. Clinging onto the precipice, Batgirl untied the rope and carefully manoeuvred him around in the shallow rockface. Once facing correctly, she yelled and slapped its arse. Forearm out trying to stop the slicing rain, she followed. Just as I pulled up Scrap from the boulder below, part of the path fell away. Imam with it. Underneath the landslide, the horse didn't move. We rapidly slid down and frantically tried to dig him out with our hands. There was no point, it was nearly dead from its injuries. We left Batgirl to stop Imam's suffering with my pistol.

That same evening, we had managed to stay warm by huddling close to the embers using the dried leaves. The embracing wasn't just for warmth, mainly for a sobbing Batgirl for losing Imam, her faithful friend. To cheer her up, Scrap had secretly handed her an oblong tin. It had been Scrap's secret until she had offered me the pre-melted hard mass of Cadbury's chocolate.

The next morning, the rations had run out. The clouds hadn't. By midday, a mist had rolled in. From our leaking cave, you couldn't even see the outside. Batgirl said it was the strangest weather she had ever seen for this time of year, blaming someone for upsetting her God. Scrap muttered he was going to kill Tommy.

Just before dusk, our defensive sand berm was deteriorating. Perhaps we should have made our escape. Yet, it would have been the blind leading the blind in the mist and lashing rain. The evening was the worst: water had flowed in, extinguishing what little heat remained. Holding onto each other, we formed a line and waded through the water. I tried to remember where the deep pool was. The pounding rain and the slapping waterfall disorientated me. Through the fog and no light, I was also guessing where the large boulder was.

Eventually, I found it. Just as well as the water level was above my knees. In complete darkness, we bunched together on top of the rock and held on tight to stop the shivering. What a terrible night with no sleep and horrible thoughts of drowning.

I hadn't realised I had fallen asleep until Scrap shook my head that was nestled on Batgirl. Opening my puffy eyes revealed a wonderful sight: no rain. The sun's rays were coming through the clouds and bouncing off the edge behind us. It caused a shadow across the waterlogged bottom. This all made last night's angry waterfall now look majestically calm. The water level was almost over the boulder. Imam was floating by the flooded cave. Blue sky was coming through the patchy clouds. It was like the dawn of man, until a flock of vultures circled. We're not fucking dead, I thought.

Soaked through and cold, I needed that sun. Clinging onto the rock face with the other hand, I decided to hitch up first. I tried not to knock the others in from our tight saviour. Leaning down, I lifted her. Scrap pushed from below. With her next to me, we carefully heaved up Scrap.

Evaluating the ground as I shuffled along, I came to the section that had taken Imam. The gap was about five feet across. I could jump it, but there was nothing to hold onto the other side. Also, I wasn't sure how stable the higher-level landing would be. Looking at the crystal water below, sharp edges of rocks were barely submerged. I began to doubt the jump.

The safest way across was to use the remaining ten-inch edge that concaved with the shape of the shallow cave. Swapping my gear and rifle strap to the front, the others copied. Scrap held my wrist with a fireman's grip. Remembering all the feats I had accomplished; I took a deep breath to draw as much psyched up strength as possible. Inch by inch, I shuffled sideways with my back against the uneven surface. Looking straight ahead, I focused positively that I would easily make it. Scrap had to release his grip at arm's length. Parts of the edges crumbled into the water below.

Reaching relative safety, I then beckoned Scrap. Concern was written on his face. Even though the remaining ledge looked worse on Batgirl's go, she didn't appear worried. She ignored Scrap's hand and told us to move away. She made that leap of faith, making the jump. Feeling a little inferior, I nearly asked her to lead.

At times, the path fell away after the last person. After half an hour of going around what felt like a spiral staircase, we lay sprawled out in the sun. Half-dry, I rolled onto my front and took off the watch's leather cap. Time check: 09:13 hours.

As we lay motionless, sleep deprivation gripped us all. Scrap began to snore. The little alarm inside my head was impossible to ignore. It came to a crescendo of Big Ben chimes: the dread that our unit had moved out from the LUP.

'Right, get up,' I groggily said. 'We've got to move. Get up.'

I moved closer to the edge and peered over. The boulder on which we had sat was now completely submerged. The vultures had found their breakfast: Imam. Grunting, Scrap stood and looked over the edge. I went over to help Batgirl up, but she shoved my hand away and did it herself.

'Fucking great idea to stay the night,' Scrap said.

'Shut up, Georges,' I retorted.

The sand was soft as we trudged back to the area where I had left the team member. At first, I couldn't see my Trusty. I stopped jogging when it had become apparent that the Trusty was lying half-sunk on its side. Scrap lamely strolled over to his bike that had fallen onto the bank. I struggled lifting mine, until Batgirl helped. Our team member looked as sorrowful as us.

After going through the rigmarole of getting it started, it still wouldn't. Scrap had managed his, the smoke very thick and spreading wide. We both scanned the horizons for unwanted guests.

Once his bike was warm, he rode over to me and made an unnecessary quip about me flooding mine. I had not, being wet from lying on its side. Now that I had a dud-bike and no tools, do we rescue Baka? Do I order Batgirl to go alone? Is it too dangerous for us to wheel my Trusty back? I couldn't just leave the member here; it was too important.

Scrap towed Batgirl across the desert using the leather strap that was initially around his forks. They left no dust trail, but the wet tracks could easily be seen. That was a negative concern when we left to find an ERL.

Lowering the binos after losing them in the mirror effect heat, I headed back to the tributary. Sat on the slope to the main ditch, I started to clean my weapons and kit. The vultures above increased, tempting me to shoot the evil birds.

With everything back in the damp kit bag, I returned to the flowing ditch. I'd had enough of water and mucky sand, but I had to balance it with fast-paced tabbing across the desert. Particularly, as I had stupidly not worn my *dishdasha*. Would wearing a *shemagh* blend me in enough? Would any enemy ground troops or planes be out this early? They were stupid questions.

To keep the paced tabbing ten klicks from becoming lonely, I thought back on the funnier banter since leaving. I smirked at Scrap's alpaca joke. Although his strong personality, banter, and quips could go over the top, we had been through so much together.

Reaching the wadi, my feet and lower trousers were drenched again. I checked how long it had taken me: two hours. It seemed longer. The temperature was the most humid so far. I sipped the last of the water-bottle as we had not filled up from the oasis pool because of the bloated horse.

Slightly revitalised but still extremely tired, I sloshed across the wadi to the far bank. Being too high for me to see over, I remembered the village was about four hundred metres the way the wadi was flowing. Trying to keep out of the centre stream, I headed to the settlement.

Reaching a crude timber jetty that was positioned parallel to the wadi, I climbed the low bank and shaded under it. The stench was awful. Tuning in, goats were bleating, and a donkey was braying. A male started shouting. I couldn't determine what was being said, as if he was hollering nonsense. The reply to the yelling was a strange mix of moaning and groaning with high-pitched bleats and loud bellows and roars. The next Arabic voice I had translated, and she was coming closer. Shit. Another male was angrily telling her to clean all the rooms. The woman was submissively agreeing. Looking above the two-inch gaps in the laid timber poles, I slowly tucked myself further into the edge. A slop in the wadi made me switch views: stodgy muck steadily disintegrating. The brown film followed the sluggish flow. The woman dressed all in black banged the wooden bucket on the edge. The stench of more shit was overpowering. Then the worst, a steady flow of piss came.

As soon as she had gone, I took my arm from my nose and decided to get out of this shithole. I found my quip a little funny, although I now knew what the unpleasant odour was when I had first crawled under.

The only exit from this bathroom was through her deposited piss. Feet first, I bulldozed the damp sand and shuffled right. I then studied the large and odd-shaped mud building directly ahead. The five donkeys that were under the shade had gone. The boy herder was picking up the dung and putting it in a wooden bucket. Fortunately, he went off skipping with the load in the direction of several single-story round-shaped mud huts. I breathed a sigh of relief.

Baka's barking alerted me to the left side of the main building, the area I had not yet explored. Spotting a new observation post, I came out from the cesspit and scurried left to the group of palm trees. I tucked in against the rough bark and stealthily nosed around: a male was feeding the camels and whipping some away. Now I understood what his untranslatable animal chanting was. The strange moaning and groaning sounds were in fact the camels.

The herder jumped the three timber-pole fence and walked to the main building. Baka came at race-speed towards him, growling and gnashing. My heart rate increased. The dirty and dusty camel herder stopped and raised his cane. Not much chance then, I thought. Baka almost did a backflip as the heavy steel chain had gone taught. Rasping, Baka scrambled to his feet. The herder whipped him. I raised my rifle. My lip curled as he continued to abuse one of the lads. Respectfully, Baka continued to attack. The herder lifted his robe and pissed in the direction of Baka. My finger came off the guard and onto the trigger. The herder kicked dust and yelled at Baka to be quiet. He then walked backwards, smiling, and nodding. Baka stopped barking and smelt the air. Baka looked my way. I hid, knowing Baka had picked up my pissy scent.

Peering around the trunk, Baka was standing and panting. His mouth and tongue were dry. His gums were sticky and his eyes sunken. Had they not fed and watered the Hungarian prisoner? Motherfuckers.

With my sharp pointing gesture, Baka surprisingly took my order and went back inside his cell. Impressed with myself, I sprinted low to the mud wall. Removing my pistol from the adapted leg holster, I quietly cocked it. Hugging the shadow of the wall, I crept silently forward to the front. The herder at the far end of the ranch was picking up a large metal bucket. Again, it was a British Army issue, like Baka's chain. Thieving bastards, I thought.

Slipping inside the gloom whilst staring down my pistol, my eyes adjusted. I had done this manoeuvre many times before, but this time I felt more relaxed. Baka came over and started licking me. The chain rattled. Bending down to see how it was connected, he started to lick my face. I hated that. Now his huge head was nudging me, and his tail madly wagged. What the fuck was he doing? Did he want water? Not liking dogs, I had not been this friendly to one.

Baka had now started to paw me. Now what? I grabbed his leg and hissed at him to stop moving as the chain was clanging. His muscular frame stood to attention. I started to undo his thick leather collar, when the light in the door aperture flickered. Someone had walked by. Me and Baka were locked in a stare. His brown eyes widened and then narrowed. What was he thinking?

At last, the collar came undone. I picked up the pistol. Placing it to my lips, I made the shh sound. Baka whined slightly and then cocked his head. Not fluent in Rottweiler or Hungarian, I patted him on the back and nodded. Suddenly, he bolted outside. Fuck. What had I ordered? I rapidly leant against the door frame. He was charging over to the guard carrying a bucket of water. Baka had bounded at the back of his tormentor and knocked the man to the floor. The herder's cane and screaming were pathetic in comparison to Baka unleashing his weapon: his teeth.

I ran back to the wadi and remembered Tommy using his fingers to do a sharp whistle. I gave it ago. It had worked, but I had a weird and sickly-sweet taste in my mouth. I looked at my blooded fingers and then spat the taste. Landing in the soft sand, I sprinted north up the wadi. I visualised the mauled herder, and I was invigorated that I had released one of the lads. Baka came alongside doing a strange bound, as if playing and showing off. What the fuck? I ordered him to switch on.

Once out of the danger-zone, I stopped as Baka had slowed up. The wadi had become as dehydrated as him. Why wasn't he drinking the wadi? Had he seen what had been deposited in there? Facing the way that we had escaped from, I pulled around the reserve water bottle and lifted it at the same time as Baka's head. I gently poured it so he would not bulk it back up. I noticed lacerations on his torso and legs. When I stopped pouring, Baka did a different whine, so I let it run until it was empty. He needed it more than me.

'I haven't forgotten all the times you growled at me,' I said. 'And for stealing my goat curry.'

Baka turned his head on the side and stared aimlessly at me.

'Don't you make out you don't understand English. Right, get your shit together and let's head back to the LUP.'

His tail did a slight wag. Hidden, but I had noticed it.

Numerous times I scaled the bank to check the plains in a 360-degree rotation with the binos. Every time, Baka lifted his head and sniffed. Knowing that we were near, I kicked a hole in the steep bank and lifted my eyes just above the ridgeline. After a prolonged period of scrutinising,

I worked out the netting was about three hundred metres away. Coming down, I pulled my rifle off my shoulder. Baka was moaning. He would look forwards and then back at me, rocking slightly as if wanting to take off.

'Listen, Baka, I'm afraid your best mate has been killed in action. I'm sorry. Go.'

Like a Formula-1 car, he sped off. On the limit of adhesion, he hit the first bend and was gone.

I was plodding in the last hundred metres with my *shemagh* pulled down and my rifle above my head. But then, I was tanned, bearded, and with scruffy hair. I kept an eye on the shaded machine gun nest.

The next ten metres passed. I was becoming a little apprehensive, even though I knew the sentry would have binoculars. A thud behind me made me look behind: Titan. He grinned and lowered his Enfield. Titan then sent the signal to the camp that it was OK. Dropping my aching arms, I became enormously heavy. My legs became jellified. Titan strode over and bear-hugged me. I could have fallen asleep. Titan kept his arm around me, supporting my trudge.

'The army is my life, boss. But so is this squad. So don't fucking disappear again.'

'We're not just in the British Army,' I croaked, 'we're the Regiment. Above all else. The Elite.'

'By the way, you stink of piss,' he said.

Ten metres to go, something was different about the camp. Yet, I was disturbed in thought by all the lads running down to us, except Sikes, Tommy, and obviously Brat. First to embrace me was an overjoyed Matron. The delight, back slapping, and kind words continued from the rest of them. It boosted my energy tenfold, and I made my own way unaided.

An evil odour whacked my nostrils. The lads parted to the sides. A mound of sand had formed. Batgirl gave me a dirty stare from under her mask. Blister explained that the heavy rains had lifted the horses, and for three days the sand had to be kept piled on to stop the corpses coming to the top. No one wanted to dig a new pit further away. Who could blame them? Instead, they moved the rear south half of the camp to the front north.

Treading around the grim grave, I entered the base. Tommy got up from sitting with Baka. Teary, he came over. On one knee he bowed his head, and with his right hand touched his forehead.

'*Apja*,' he said. '*Fia…szent…*'

'Yeah, all right, Tommy,' I interrupted. 'I'm not the bloody messiah out of *Life of Brian*.'

He touched his right shoulder and continued, '*Szellem*.'

I mentally heard Shrek doing his impersonation of Brian's mother, *He's not the messiah. He's a very naughty boy. Now go away.*

After a little more handshaking from Tommy, he embraced me tight. His unique hippy-perfumed smell overpowered my body odour. I ordered him to leave me alone. Baka looked on from his bowls of indestructible biscuits and water. He was lying on a brown blanket and his wounds had a sort of Vaseline on. Perhaps Bipp, like Titan used in the CCS at the Somme.

Although exhausted, I called everyone in for a briefing. It felt we were safe enough to leave the sentry positions unguarded. Sat back on my faithful truck's radiator, they all crowded around, including Baka. Trish handed me a mug of tea and a few dates. The sugar helped with my over-tiredness.

'Someone get Sikes and Brat please,' I said reluctantly.

A look of discomfort went around.

'What's happened?' I said.

Blister abruptly shoved Seagal forward, denying him slipping backwards after.

'Sikes has gone, boss,' Seagal said meekly—no one batted an eye that Seagal had spoken.

'Gone? Where?' I said.

'He was livid when he found you had led a patrol,' Seagal said. 'He ensued by aggressively ordering everyone to pack up. I tried to reason with him, but he was bang up to the elephant.'

'I'm too tired to work that out,' I said. 'Someone translate.'

'Unapproachable,' Flash-heart said.

'I tried to keep him away from the back of the Dennis as he wanted to load it,' Seagal continued. 'But he must have sensed something was untoward. He barged me aside and found Brat.'

'He went fucking nuts, boss,' Blister said.

'He ordered your arrest when you returned,' Flash-heart said. 'And to face the firing squad immediately.'

'We slowly packed up whilst he drank the whisky,' Trish added.

'Yeah, the bottle you gave him, Trish,' Titan said. 'Telling him to "Toodle-pip and calm himself".'

'It worked long enough for you to head a munity,' she retorted.

'We didn't have to though,' he said. 'I was checking on him under his truck when I saw an empty packet of cocaine tooth drops. Searching the back of the lorry, I found opium and morphine. I just made sure that when he had stirred, he got some of the old magic medicine.'

I remembered the heroin filled syringe and large needle from the Somme. 'So, what happened?'

'After you pissed off to paradise and left us to deal with the floods,' Blister said, 'he woke up last night and started pacing up and down. He was pulling at his hair and mumbling to himself. We were all too exhausted to deal with him.'

'He bullied me and Brat to get the motorbike and sidecar up the ramps,' Flash-heart said. 'Once we had achieved this, Sikes left with Brat. I am sorry, Vinnie.'

'I would say he had a dose of the funks,' Matron said.

'I am no coward,' Flash-heart snapped.

'Matron meant Sikes, Flash-heart. Not you,' Titan said.

'Oh, I apologise.'

I itched the bites under my beard and contemplated what had happened. I was pissed off that Sikes had abducted a team member: Trusty-3. The others looked on, perhaps waiting for my outburst. Time check: 14:05 hours.

'How much supplies did they take?' I asked.

'The motorbike was full of fuel and had ammo for the attached Lewis. Apart from his club, personal weapons, and ammo, he took no extra,' Flash-heart said.

'And Brat?'

'Nothing, Vinnie.'

'Water and food?'

'Just a half-empty jar of rum between them, Vinnie.'

'Cheers, Flash-heart,' I said.

I knew that Trusty-3 had enough range to make the ERL. Yet, I had doubts that's where they were going, dreading they were heading to Target-1. If they attacked it alone, that would be the end of the mission. Looking around, it was like the lads could read my mind. Even Baka looked distressed.

'Right, get back to your duties. At dusk, we quietly pack and leave for the ERL,' I said. 'I'm taking a nap. Whilst I'm in the land of paradise again, Blister, I want you all to think of a decent mission name. Not the wanky Operation Exploit.'

'Yes, boss,' they all said, except Matilda who had stayed quiet the whole briefing.

I jumped down. An excited buzz went around, or that's how I perceived it. I waited till they started to leave and then held Matilda's shirt back.

'Something on your mind, Matilda?'

'There's something you need to…'

'Go and sort the horse out, Matilda,' Scrap moodily interrupted. 'And take this *choty goty* with you.'

'A what?' Matilda said.

'The beautiful girl Batgirl. You want to brush up on your lingo, *bru*.'

That's twice that Scrap had weirdly interrupted Matilda, but I couldn't be bothered with them. Instead, I slogged to the back of my truck and patted the wooden side. I spotted a string tied to it and Truck-2. Matron caught me up.

'Can I wash and dry your uniform?' she asked.

'Are you brown nosing me?'

'I am not sure what that means.'

'Licking my arse. Making up for all the harsh shit you have given me,' I said lamely.

'Oh good God, no. You just smell horrendous, boss.'

After slowly stripping off naked, I made a big effort to climb into the back of my home. I slumped on an itchy brown blanket and pulled one over me. Lifting the watch cover, I wound the watch and studied the seconds hand move for twenty seconds…

CHAPTER TWELVE

As I lay snuggled up, Ella elbowed me to stop snoring. I opened my eyes, alerted to the hairy body and smell of paraffin.

'I know you think we're blood brothers because I've tasted yours, but I've not shared mine in a pact. And won't be,' I said.

He licked my face, again.

'Get off, Baka. You may now be a part of the Elite, and we're supposed to do everything with your main oppo, but find your own fucking bed. I'd rather sleep with the hairy Batgirl, thanks.'

Baka farted.

'Johnny, the sun has gone down.'

I looked up to see Batgirl holding a corner of the flap. I went embarrassingly red from my rude comment and Baka's smell. Batgirl's nose twitched and then she looked at my naked body sleeping with Baka. It made the awkwardness a million times worse. She dropped the flap.

'Thanks, Baka,' I said. 'Twat.'

Kicking Baka out first, I then opened the flap. The unit was standing there. I covered my indecency and wondered how long I had been asleep. Yet, I dared not look at my watch. Trish's grin was enormous.

'Operation Well Endowed,' Trish said.

'That's nothing,' Titan added.

'If you can't come up with a serious mission name, just keep quiet,' I said. 'You're as bad as Ant.'

Matron pulled down my clothes off the string and held them to me, but out of reach. After seeing my dissatisfied look, she smiled and went to hand them. Then she paused and pulled away—why was everyone suddenly a fucking comedian? Once she had handed them amongst the sniggers, I shut the flap.

Adding a bit of Keating's Powder to my inner thighs and bollocks in case Baka carried some nasty fleas from the camel ranch, I then swapped the tin for some British Army Foot Powder. Fully dressed, I jumped down to wolf whistles. Matron was taking down the washing line in the fading daylight. I was just about to have a rant about waking me up late, when I noticed everything had been cleared and packed. I looked at my watch: 18:34 hours. I ruffled my beard and hair, perplexed at how I could have been asleep that long and without being awoken by the lads.

'Have you…'

'Swept the perimeter?' Blister interrupted. 'Yes, boss. And filled in the bank to make it look like a natural collapse. And even emptied the sandbags and spread the remains. We can't all sleep when there's work to be done.'

'Bollocks,' I said. 'And the graves?'

'Yep, flattened them. Even the mutt's,' Scrap said.

'You mean the hero Rudi,' I retorted.

Scrap looked at Tommy and acknowledged his own mistake.

Seagal passed me my kit bag and said, 'What are the orders, boss?'

'First, let's synchronise.' I counted down to 18:37 hours and then continued, 'With three down…'

'Four,' Batgirl butted in.

'Sorry, four members down, I want Flash-heart to drive the pinky with Titan as shotgun. Not that shitty peashooter,' I said—a laugh simmered amongst everyone but Titan. 'Batgirl, you drive Truck-2 with Tommy and Baka as…'

'Give your fanny a rest, Batgirl,' Titan blurted—no one laughed.

'It's OK, it's cushioned well,' Scrap whispered to Titan.

I scoffed. 'Blister and Scrap, you take a Trusty each. Matilda, you're on your horse.'

'His name is Trumper, after Victor Thomas Trumper. The most stylish and versatile Australian batsman…'

'You're boring me now, Matilda,' I over spoke. 'Matron and Trish, you take the Ambulance. That leaves you, Seagal, with me.'

'Are you sure you don't want me up front with you, boss,' Trish said flirtatiously.

'Definitely. Same formation, lads. Right, get your maps out.'

After a quick briefing of the direction and distance, I finished by reminding them of the attack and defensive drills they should have at least learnt. With the help of everyone pushing and pulling with the motorbikes, I drove my truck up the newly ramped cutout on the opposite bank. It was great to be behind the wheel again.

Once all the vehicles were up, I ordered Scrap and Blister to go scout. Thirty minutes later after putting the ramps away and making the bank look a bit less man-made, we set off. To make the time go quicker on the journey, I started to tell Seagal about the recent patrol saga. I had just finished the part about deciding to head left or right at the fork in the ditch when he interrupted.

'A fork?'

'A metaphor based on a literal expression for a determining moment in life or history. When a major choice of options is required,' I smugly said.

Just as I thought I had become more educated than him, he looked at me and then coughed. I turned to him.

'You mean, Crossing the Rubicon,' he said.

'What the actual fuck?'

'It is an idiom. Meaning to pass a point of no return. It refers to Julius Caesar's armies crossing of the Rubicon River in 49 BC, which was considered an act of insurgency and treason.'

'You've been fucking reading too much.'

'Oh, by the way, Scrap has already informed me of the whole sinkhole tale. Especially highlighting you having flip-flop sex with Batgirl.'

'What? I never,' I shrieked. 'And what the hell is "flip-flop sex" supposed to be?'

'I was unsure myself, until Scrap politely explained that there was some sort of shoe-wear called a flip flop that made the sound of sex when walking in them. Apparently, it was better when starting off at a slow-paced walk, to a run.'

'Jesus,' I cringed. 'Don't let Scrap convert you.'

Just over an hour and forty-five minutes since the first truck scaled the wadi onto the desert, we had reached the railway tracks. It had been the straightest drive so far. With us parked in a row, I gave the signal to kill the engines. Seagal handed me the map and told me we had travelled forty klicks. He then left, taking his sniper rifle with him.

We were out of sight and sound of the village Rafa, nine klicks west. However, there was a wide track where we were parked. It had been compressed with many years of travel and sun. I knew there would be some sort of railway crossing point to take the traffic up to Deir el Belah, a further thirteen klicks northeast. I didn't want to sit out in the open, yet I had given orders for the scouts to meet us here.

After washing down the pre-travel meal that Matron had prepared, I jumped down and went over to Flash-heart who was refilling the ambulance radiator. Again, steam poured, and the hot water seeped into the sand. The vehicle was empty. Trish and Matron must have taken up a defensive position—both turning out to be an asset.

'The engine has got so hot, it has now sprung an oil leak,' Flash-heart whispered.

'Can you fix it?'

'No, Vinnie.'

'Shit. Will it make it another few miles?'

'With a prayer, perhaps.'

'If my old mate Blondie were here, he would be happy to help with a bible. But as he's not, get fucking praying. We can't leave it out in the open or we'll have to destroy it. As not to let it fall into enemy hands. But that would wake the whole of Egypt at night. Do I make myself clear, Peter?'

'Yes, Vinnie, I will get praying.'

Everyone was in their defensive positions. I walked across the railway with Baka beside me. Standing on top of an incline, I was unsure of the light that spread out across the desert in the far distance. It was like a searchlight. I then realised it was far too big, even for a ship. It was in fact the moon reflecting off the Mediterranean Sea. It was a stark difference from seeing nothing but sand. Baka lifted his nose and sniffed the air. My nose was unable to smell the salty sea approximately five klicks north. Or hear it, as Baka's ears twitched.

Without warning, Baka stood and faced west. His body went rigid, and his firm tail pointed horizontal. On one knee I aimed down my sight, unsure of what was coming. Baka growled low. I strained my eyes for the littlest signal and the slightest reflection off the moon. Baka stopped his warning and relaxed. Ten seconds later, I heard bikes on the limit of my hearing. Did the enemy have their own bikes? Or worse, stolen the lads' motorbikes? Baka glanced at me and made a groaning noise as if sighing. He then laid down and crossed his front feet.

Out of the blackness came the red lights. Three flashes in total. I did the same back. Baka looked at me, again.

'Yeah, all right, so you knew first. But no one likes a show-off. We should have a nickname for you. How about Bagpuss? Not so smart now, are you. You've not even watched it.'

He licked my hand.

Both scouts informed me that their first observation post was on the outskirts of Weli Shiekh Nuran. A massive distance of forty-five klicks northeast of our wadi LUP. Building lights glowed into the night. Farm animals were seen outside the buildings, including a few sleeping camels. After this, Blister and Scrap had headed the shorter distance of thirty klicks west to within a safe distance of Sheikh Zowaiid. They had observed for a while. But with no light or movement, they followed the railway back east to Rafa. Observing Rafa, strange shapes confused them. Having taken the calculated risk to search the buildings, they had found many headless corpses. The mud buildings had not shown any battle scars and there was no evidence of rifle shells being found. The only signs were many hoof prints in the village grounds and dung found about a kilometre away. Our educated guess was it was the Turks that had massacred the villagers.

We asked Batgirl to join us. Once we had told her the sitrep, she looked alarmed. Yet, she did not answer why, appearing to hide something. I sent her away to get everyone in. Whilst she was gone, I ordered Scrap and Blister to refuel. However, Flash-heart was already on it. Instead, I told both to ride ahead and find a decent ERL halfway between our position and Target-1. Also, making sure it was on the beach side of the track.

With the point-men going off into the distance, I went briefly over the sitrep with the rest of the lads. I praised Flash-heart for the ambulance effort and then ordered Tommy to drive Truck-2, and Seagal to swap with Batgirl. I wanted to quiz her about why she was so concerned. That had been twice that she had remained tight-lipped about the Bedouin or Turks.

After making sure any signs here were removed, I checked the time: 21:22 hours. The ambulance led over the track first, but it got stuck. I asked Batgirl to push the ambulance over with our truck. Making it across, the ambulance's front wheels were at an odd angle. I had never accepted this team member to be up to the task.

We had only been travelling for about a kilometre. Batgirl had confided in me about a dark and mysterious force at night. Suddenly, two red lights were waving left to right ahead. The signal had been a warning. Matilda rode ahead, his Martini-Henry rifle raised. Everyone was scanning.

Matilda returned at a higher speed than he had left.

'Bloody bastard has killed the Alleyman with a bullet to the head,' he said.

'Fuck,' I said.

I followed on foot behind his horse with Batgirl behind me. I slowed up when I saw the body lying in front of the motorbike wheel. Brat's red piping uniform was covered in blood. The entry and exit wound had been from the side, as if Sikes had done it whilst driving along. Brat's wrists were still cuffed. The dragging marks in the sand were a couple of metres long. Brat's decision to follow Sikes' direct order to drive Truck-3 out had ended up dead. But perhaps if Brat had said no, he would have been shot anyway. Sikes must have known Brat was an easy target.

'You two go ahead,' I said. 'We'll bury him.'

'I never trusted Brat anyway,' Blister said.

Blister and Scrap wheeled their bikes around and set off. Weirdly, Batgirl started to check Brat's pockets. When I had asked what she was looking for, she just looked at me and then took a few steps back—tight-lipped, again.

As soon as Matron had said the Lord's prayer, I ran back to the truck as I was itching to move out of the area. Before I set off, I made a small mark on the map signifying where Werner was buried to tell General Rowe to inform Werner's family. If Rowe wouldn't, I am sure a slip of what his nephew had done to jeopardise this mission, would persuade him.

It was refreshing to see the beach, reminding me of home. Something I desperately wanted. Yet at the same time, I wanted to stay with the lads in this era. Scrap returned on his own. He put me at ease that Blister was keeping guard at the proposed site.

Slowing the speed of the convoy, we followed the Trusty along the coastline, keeping the water's edge to our left. Baka was running in the waves, jumping, and eating the breaks. A large part of me wanted that. I caught Batgirl looking sympathetically at me, the moon catching her amazing eyes. She pulled across her veil.

Blister stood in front of the barbed wire that stretched fifty metres from the water into the desert. A clunking from behind sounded. Scrap and Titan came to the front, each holding a ramp. They laid them over the wire and waved me forwards. Just before I drove across, they adjusted the ramps with their feet. Blister ran in front and parked me slightly left and facing south across the desert.

Once we were all stationary inside, I quietly called over Matron, Blister, and Scrap.

'Scrap, get a defensive ring set up,' I said.

'Yes, boss.'

'Blister, where's the best place for Matron and Trish to set up?' I said.

'Follow me. We've searched this old trench system, but it has been smashed up from artillery.' He climbed down the strewn sandbags into a fortified trench. 'Don't worry, Matron, we found no bodies.'

Matron swiftly took her hand back from Blister's helping hand and said, 'Listen, boy, I have seen thousands of ghastly injured, sufficient dead, and dismembered body parts undreamt of.'

I grinned. 'Shut you the fuck up, Blister.'

The trench to our left ended as it was completely covered in sand and damaged corrugated sheets. Battered timbers were poking out. The floor was strewn with spent cartridges. Blister led us up the trench to a set of steps made from railway sleepers. In the darkness, I put my hand back for Matron. Her stern look made me whip it back—tough old bird.

Feeling the sandbagged walls, we came to the top of a large and flat semicircle area. The eight-foot-high sandbagged defence had been broken in the middle. Blister showed us some marks on the ground.

'Used to be an artillery position here,' he said. 'And over there an AA-gun.'

'All taken through the gap in the wall.'

'You're learning, boss,' he said.

'So, the plan is, smart arse?' I said.

'We drive the ambulance around the front and park it in here,' Matron answered for him. 'And with the corrugated sheets and material, we erect a shelter to hide from the sun and any planes. We should lay a netting over it to break up the shape.'

'Fuck me,' I said. 'I think Blister should stay here with Trish, and you come with us, Matron.'

Matron smiled.

Blister gave me the middle finger.

'Right, Matron, go and show Flash-heart, Titan, and Matilda where you want the ambulance parked,' I said. 'Then get them building.'

'Yes, boss,' she said enthusiastically.

'Blister, follow me,' I said.

Walking through the breach, we did a perimeter check of the barbed wire.

'I want you to make sure all this wire is fixed,' I ordered. 'Then set up the mortars and two HMG posts.'

'Are we not heading to the LUP?'

'If we get time.'

'I'm not going on a raid just before dawn,' he said. 'We won't live till sunrise, let alone the next stars over our heads.'

'Be serious.'

'I was.'

'There's no way that ambulance can make it back to our base. It's here to stay.'

'It was a load of old donkey anyway,' he said in a terrible London accent.

'That's pony, you dickhead.'

'Oh.'

'On a more serious note, I need some advice,' I said.

'Go on.'

'I'm now doubting myself if the fracas on the dunes was just nerves, but it had been an attack. OK, the firing drills were a bag of shite, but Batgirl fears something.'

'What?'

'I've not yet found out. I don't want to leave Matron and Trish here.'

'What vehicle are they going to take to get back to base?'

I smirked.

'No, not the two invaluable motorbikes.'

I shook my head and eyed him.

'You mean, take them both with us?' Blister rubbed his beard and then took a sharp intake, slowly blowing it out. 'On paper and in a briefing room, I would have said no way. Yet, they have been damn good.'

'Well?'

'They would be safer with us, but they don't go on the raid.'

'Thanks, Blister.' I patted his shoulder. 'Now fucking get back to work. Make sure those fucking mortar distances are correct.'

'Such unsuitable language,' he said.

'What, swearing?'

'No, you telling me how to do my job. I am Bombardier Morrison.'

I had taken a gamble by removing everyone but Seagal and Baka away from their posts. With all hands-on-deck, it had helped with the scavenging to build a half-decent ERL. I asked Trish to make a hot meal inside the new building. I was banking on the northerly breeze blowing through the front slits and taking the cooking smells out the rear door aperture to sea.

Whilst all seemed quiet with no threat, I ordered half the men to go down to the shore with one guard. The lads needed a damn good wash. It was Trish who stood guard of their clothes and weapons—had to be.

Once they had returned, Matron and Batgirl wandered down. We ate hot bully beef and vegetable stew, dipped with very salty bread. We waited for the rest to come back and finish their main meal, then we had hot Christmas pudding and jam. Baka had the same dessert. Trumper easily munched on the indestructible biscuits and dried oat mix.

Returning to work, we all had an extra vigour about us, even though the morale was already up when Sikes had left. It was like a wanker of a boss leaving the workplace. I didn't want to admit it to the others, but a part of me felt sorry as the black dogs had not only got in for Sikes but were eating him. He had lost all his credibility of what a hard bastard hero he had been. Yet, I had to put the rest of us first. If I could reach him in time, I would make sure he gets home and receives the right treatment. He had fought too many battles not to.

The last of the canvas and nets were placed over the vehicles and weapons. Time check: 04:36 hours. After quick praises for all the successful arduous work, I gave the orders we were back on hard routine. And the sentry and sleep rota would start where it left off in the wadi, right through till dusk this evening. Anything suspicious must be reported. Only my squad and Seagal had the rules to engage, unless critical. Tonight, we would all travel to the next LUP. Matron and Trish were relieved. It had obviously been playing on their mind.

CHAPTER THIRTEEN

Dusk turned into day in the blink of an eye, but at least the camp was ready. Under the canvas sheet, I relieved Matilda of duty and told him to get himself breakfast. Then, he was to visit Trumper who was in a shelter at the back with Baka.

I raised the Lewis up to the height I preferred and then took off the top round mag. Blowing it out, I then slapped it back on.

'Go,' I said.

Shiftily, he looked around and sighed before grabbing his kit and rubbish bag.

'What's up, Matilda?' I asked.

'I know we don't see eye to eye, but now that ante-Christ on tin wheels has disappeared, I need to tell ya something.'

'Yeah, like what is a "Ante-Christ on tin wheels" meant to be?'

'That pompous and self-sufficient Sergeant Rowe and his APM uncle.'

I sighed. 'If you don't stop using Aussie expressions that I don't understand, then it will be your turn for stag again.'

'APM means a permanent malingerer.'

'Get on with whatever you need to say,' I said.

'There's a reward for the capture of a traitor who has defected. You mentioned Tommy White, and I wondered if you were here in secret as well to find him.'

'Tell me more about this Tommy White and the reward,' I sternly said. 'We don't fucking have secrets in this unit that affect us.'

I continued to glower. Matilda went red in the cheeks, knowing he had just thrown the grenade amongst the terrorists.

'Well?' I said.

'General Rowe offered me a reward of a hundred and twenty pounds to capture or kill Lieutenant Thomas White.'

'You're putting your life on the line for that much?'

'Sarcasm. Christ. I could buy half of Sydney for eight hundred and sixty dollars.'

'What's this British lieutenant done for such a bounty on his head?' I mocked.

'British? You think I would be chasing a Pom across Egypt. Not for all the beer-ups in the world. And that means drunken orgies to you, Pom. He's Australian.'

'What's he done wrong?'

'Making some nasty gas agent and smuggling Egyptian gold.'

'Thanks for the heads-up. You can go now.'

'Oh. And what does "heads-up" mean?'

'One last question, Matilda. Who else is on this?'

'Sikes, Brat, and that blow-hole Scouse. But they're not so boshter now. I'm not sure about your squad and the rest. We could split the reward, mate.'

'Fuck off now, Matilda.'

I worked out the date to be Friday 30th March. We were behind schedule. It didn't take me long to go back to what Matilda had said. The lure of money and gold can make people turn evil, taking a hundred per cent concentration off the job we had to do. Trust can all be ruined. Is this why a different mixture of soldiers was brought in? A pilot for a getaway? A dog trainer to sniff out? An Australian to befriend Thomas White? Sikes the hardman doing it alone? Scouse the thief and locksmith? A Bedouin woman who knows the lie of the land, her people, and the locals? I doubt Flash-heart is in on it as it was me who had asked him to join. Could the Hungarian Tommy really speak English? Even good German?

Taking a sip of coffee, I looked across the desert with the binos for any sign of our sniper. Has Seagal been hired? He could blend in anywhere undercover and had exceptional skills for this era. Even though I squashed Trish and Matron, why were they asked in at the last minute? Was this the norm to have all these stay-awake and knock-out drugs on a mission? What would happen if we assaulted Lieutenant White's position? Would it be a mad rush to take him down first, ignoring the plan? Would everyone turn on each other and those not involved just for the bounty or gold?

I had let the paranoia get in. So, I asked myself three main questions. One, why was I asked to head the mission? Two, had any of my squad been approached? And lastly, what was this deadly gas agent? Was it like the reported weapons of mass destruction in Iraq? Perhaps it was a ruse to get the gold. If it was some sort of nerve agent, then we had no protection against it.

As my stag continued, I mulled it over. I mentally wrote down questions for the lads. It wasn't the boredom that made me start to wish for action, or at least something to see. I wanted to take my mind off the constant inferior motives behind Operation Exploit.

A new sound from the east filtered through my machine gun emplacement. I scanned the desert. Dots high in the blue sky caught my attention. Trying to find them again with the binos was difficult. Eventually, I focused on four planes. I wasn't sure if friend or foe. Yet, coming from the east, I would put money on the enemy. They were too far away for any threat. However, it ensured that it was too deadly to move through the day. Perhaps when we had been out on patrol looking for Batgirl, the storm moving from the east had grounded them. Very lucky for us.

Suddenly, a fleet of planes came across directly above. I waited for the explosions, but they soared off into the background. A horn began to wind up. Who the fuck was setting that off? The area to the netted sheet was exposed, so I couldn't run across to stop it as I could be spotted if more were heading our way. Crashing and banging made the horn weirdly die out. I still had my face arching out the slit when two more whizzed across less than two hundred metres off the ground. Back behind the Lewis, I waited, and waited, but the wind returned across the desert.

With changeover, Tommy took my position. He appeared very sheepish, not even making eye contact. In the main hub, I began to feast on warm tinned rations, dried fruit, and warm tea. I left the biscuit for my new mate, Baka. But, for some bizarre reason, he began to roll his back on top of it.

The hub was clean and tidy. Titan, Matron, and Seagal walked in and put the timber board back across the rear door aperture. I gave Matron a pile of spare haversacks and then handed her a wad of sketches. I asked her to put her surgeon skills to the test by making what was on the paper.

Flash-heart moodily entered and threw his kit down. He then slammed back the board.

'Ruddy, Tommy. Damn fool could have got us killed,' Flash-heart said.

'What's up?' I asked.

'He sounded the ruddy klaxon for the incoming German Albatross-DIII.'

Titan lightly laughed. 'Flash-heart beat me to him and smashed the fucker with a hammer.'

'What, Tommy?' I jested.

'What is it you say?' Flash-heart asked. 'Oh yes…Tommy is a bellend.'

It made humour of the situation, but it could have been a lot worse.

I found a place with no stones and laid out a brown blanket. Getting comfortable, I pulled over a grey one. I received some incredulous stares as if jinxing myself having used a grey one like at the Somme. I wasn't superstitious.

'Seagal, before you get some scoff and sleep, what's the definition of exploit?' I asked.

'Exploit is to make use of a situation in a way considered unfair or underhand.'

That fitted the mission named by General Rowe, I thought.

We had no more visitors from the sky or ground, so our camouflage had worked. Again, we went through the laborious stag and off duty boredom. Luckily, Matron had brought her new board game. However, there's only so many times you can play a game called *Suffragetto*. Instead, Seagal taught Trish a card game he had learnt in the French brothels: strip poker. She always lost, getting down to her underwear. Perhaps on purpose or by Seagal being too sharp.

After feeding Baka, I took myself away and studied maps and notes. I even started to draw what I thought the railway station and trains would look like. In the back of my mind, I knew the hour was approaching to pack up and move.

As if turning on a wind machine, dark ominous clouds raced across the sky. With the sun going down, it made them look even more sinister. For a moment, we all stopped taking the flapping netting down and looked up. Fuck, it was like a fireman's high-pressure hose was jetted into the wind machine. Matron and Trish had the innovative idea of bringing out as many containers as possible to collect the rain.

Again, I was getting drenched by re-fastening the rippling netting. I was becoming negative. It was a situation you had to pull yourself out of. Not just for your own sake, but not to bring down anyone else. Everyone started making for cover, except Baka who was strangely trying to catch the rain in his mouth. I ran over to Blister who was pushing up the canvas sheet to release the weight of the pooled water. Sitting on his ammo crate, I ordered him out as I was taking stag first—he didn't argue.

Alone and battling the elements, I checked the time under my torch:

18:36 hours. The rain patting was driving me mad, and there are only so many times you can check your HMG. I even played out scenarios that I'd had in Afghan when I had manned the Browning 50. Cal. The sea crashing behind me reminded me of home. At times, though, I did wonder if the original engineers had thought about sea defences. Of all times to have another downpour. Hopefully, it will die out soon.

It hadn't. Just over eleven hours later, the sun came up at 05:46 hours and the rain eased off for the first time. With any luck, it was going to be a good start to the weekend.

Once the stand-to had passed, I took another risk for a meeting in the hub. The only two lads who had stayed dry were Baka and Trumper under their lean-to. We were all damp. The roof still dripped above our heads whilst the sand stuck to our feet. We were a miserable bunch, whilst Baka now seemed joyful. Perhaps it was because we had formed a bond.

With the hot coffee going around, Matron offered me a tin of Huntley & Palmers biscuits.

'Ooooo, Matron, please. I'm not that kind of doctor,' I said, impersonating Kenneth Williams from *Carry on Matron*.

Everyone stopped and stared.

'Right, I have a new name for the mission,' I boasted.

A low cheer bounced back.

'Operation Baka.'

Baka's ears pricked up.

'But you hated the mutt,' Blister said.

'No I never,' I lied.

'Yes, you did,' Titan added. 'And why not Operation Titan?'

I stopped all the children adding their own name and then said, 'Right, we move at dusk.'

'Even if it rains?' Blister said.

'Flash-heart, will these dependable vehicles make it?' I said.

'Even with lowering the tyre pressures on the Crossley, it would be difficult in the softer sand. Yes, the Dennis has the power with the new engines, but it has solid tyres. The Trusty would, but the cam wheels for the inlet and exhaust valve would have to stay clean and dry, along with the chain drive.'

'A fucking simple yes or no would have been sufficing, Flash-heart,' I said.

A few sniggers went around.

'I suppose it's all on Trumper,' Matilda said proudly.

'Oh, shit, we ate him last night,' Blister said.

Laughter replaced the sniggering. Well, except Matilda.

'What about if we stay on the main track?' Titan asked.

'The suspension will not last on the vehicles,' Flash-heart said.

'Not the railway track, you dick. The road,' Titan retorted.

Flash-heart went red whilst he flattened his blond moustache.

'It's a ballsy move as we look different from military vehicles,' I said.

'And we're supposed to be audacious,' Blister added.

'Yeah, but not lunatics like you, Blister,' Scrap said. 'It's madness to go by daylight with the enemy planes, ground troops, and Bedouin. We will be compromised before we even set up the LUP. Let alone the OP. One dicker, and bang goes the element of surprise.'

'Great input, Scrap. Right, let's take a vote. Those who say we pack up now and head to the LUP.'

No one put a hand up. The unity between us was still strong.

'Right, before your next holiday in the sun, two things,' I said. 'Trish, you need to get rid of the lily-white complexion.'

'Hey, fuck you, I'm Italian and not British,' she said.

Got her, I thought, and gestured I was reeling her in.

'What's that sign?' Trish asked.

'Fucking reeled you in. Don't worry if you can't sun yourself, there might be a spray tan studio on the way.'

'A what?'

Scrap, being the only one who had found it amusing, said, 'Trish, at least your Arab beard is better than Titan's.'

'Bollocks,' Titan said, and slapped Scrap's grip off his beard.

Trish rubbed her chin and then gave Scrap the wanger sign. I let the jokes continue for a bit, then blurted, 'Who's here for the money reward and gold?'

I glared at them one by one. The camaraderie fizzled out. Matilda looked at his bare feet.

'What gold?' Blister asked.

'Money reward?' Titan added.

'Are you paying us extra, boss?' Seagal asked.

'Well?' I said to Tommy, Matilda, and Batgirl who had stayed at the back, silent.

Everyone parted aside, leaving the culprits. Instead of causing a rift, I explained to the others that the guilty trio had been under General Rowe's direct orders. I lied that each had come to me privately to express their concerns. With the little info I had, I told them of Sikes' and Rowe's deception to path the way across the border, taking out two targets. Perhaps with only a handful of us left, their main objective was to find the gold and Lieutenant White. I was sceptical of any new weapons being built and the new revelation of nerve gas production.

After telling them I was only going to hit Target-1 and Target-2, I gave them their choices: Option-1, to take Truck-2 with enough ammo and rations for one week and fuck off now to Akaba where the suspected weapons are being built. Then, find this allusive Lieutenant Thomas White, the gold, and grab the bounty reward after. Or, Option-2, forget anything to do with Option-1, and instead hit the two targets and then return home.

Giving them a brief time to think, I then asked those who wanted Option-1 to step forward. They all stepped forwards. Fuck. Then one laugh started the others off—it must have been the look on my face.

With time pressing on, I asked if anyone had anything constructive to add. Batgirl squeezed through from the back and stood next to me. She removed her headgear and mask. A low gasp went around from those who had not seen her beauty.

'At night, evil spirits in black robes and no face ride on black ghost horses,' she said.

'Utter bollocks the Bedouin talks,' Blister said.

Batgirl pulled out her dagger.

Blister cocked his pistol, stopping her coming closer.

'The L-khaba-a will take your head off. Eat your brain,' she seethed.

'The what?' I exclaimed, going cold. 'Say that name again.'

'L-khaba-a,' she repeated. 'They known as the…'

'Hidden,' I interrupted. 'Elkhaba.' The hairs on my neck raised. I staggered back against the sandbags.

'You come across them in battle?' Batgirl asked.

'Not in this era, but the same modern-day Vikings of my era,' I mumbled.

'I told you I saw something on the dunes, but you all jested me,' Matilda said.

'I hear…erm…how you say?' Tommy said.

'Voices in your head,' Scrap joked.

'Yes…in ears…strange talk on wind.'

'Fuck me, Tommy's turned into Little Big Chief,' Titan added.

'It's true,' Seagal said. 'There was something out there that night.

They moved like shadows, making weird calls to each other. I hit one of the horses.'

Batgirl nodded at Seagal for backing her. 'It's who beheaded the people of Rafa.'

'Did the horse bleed, Seagal?' I asked.

'I did not see any from the impact, but it wailed.'

'Should have used my Nitro Express rifle,' Titan said.

'I doubt you could…'

'I want everyone to be extra vigil today,' I butted in.

'What's up, boss?' Flash-heart asked. 'You've gone as white as a ghost.'

'We've been over the border far too long,' I said. 'No matter if a snow blizzard hits, we are moving out at dusk. Back to your posts.'

This time there was no chance of being bored as I tried to find things to do to take my mind off the Elkhaba. Matron was putting the finishing sewing touches on my design. I asked her and Trish to separate what they believed as important medical kit to leave in case one or more had to head back here seriously injured. I also wanted them to take provisions for the remainder of the mission, including the long journey back to Ismailia. Against them also was the extra space for them and their kit—not an easy task.

At 16:47 hours, I was getting excited that the clouds had not rolled in. I Enfield sighted Seagal's low running from the craggy rocks which were two hundred metres in front of our wire. He was wearing his effective camo suit and had an array of weapons and kit. In the direct sun's heat of about twenty-five degrees, he must have already been as sweaty as Cyril Smith on a kid's bouncy castle. It must have been urgent to leave his post. I dreaded what he had to say, not wanting to spend another night and further day here.

Pulling back the wood panel, I let him in the hub. He put down his kit, breathing heavily. I handed him a water bottle and waited till he finished. Up close, he whispered that he had just seen an army of heavily armed Bedouin on camels heading east about thirty metres from his hide. When I asked to define "army" as in numbers, he told me between fifty and eighty. He went onto say that "heavily armed" had meant rifles, swords, and a team of horses pulling a Gatling-gun and another a cannon. I told him it was just part of the challenge. He should also let the others know what he has seen, and what the Bedouin would be up against if they took us on—bravado, of course.

Just as the sun was setting, we had almost packed up. The animal containers and radiators had been topped up with the collected rainwater. Flash-heart had worked tirelessly to make sure all the vehicles were maintained. It was now his responsibility to make sure the ambulance would never be driven again, even if the enemy fixed the pipe. He filled the engine up with wet sand and cut all the electrical cables—he was a brilliant asset.

With the side section rolled up on each truck and a gunner behind the Lewis, I drove over the ramps that were laid on the barbed wire. I then waited for everyone to catch up. This time I asked Matilda to be point-man as I wanted more firepower in our convoy. He set off into the hornets' nest. We, however, followed at a slower pace to keep the noise at minimum. Stealth was now key.

After travelling about two-hundred metres away from our ERL defences, I noticed a gap in the bank in the distance that must lead down to the beach. I signalled to Blister to go ahead and recce. We slowed down to a first gear crawl. Just as we reached the gap, Blister was coming up the soft incline. I stopped, something I didn't enjoy doing in a convoy, but needs must. Blister lifted his goggles and lowered his *shemagh*. He told me it was the perfect route as the waves would deaden the engines and the bank was as tall as the trucks. He also said there were fresh prints from a single horse, reckoning it was Matilda. At last, a break in our fortune.

Driving on the beach, it was easy to be distracted by Egypt's coastline beauty. The shimmering sea and white waves were emphasised by the vast stars and the brightness of the moon, all entwined with its hypnotic rhythm. However, we had to stay switched on as the distance from our ERL to Target-1 was eight klicks east. Deir el Belah was less than three klicks northeast and on the coastline. I had ordered our LUP to be approximately five hundred metres from a suitable OP. From there we could watch the station.

Matilda urgently returned and said that a heavily armed camp was situated one mile ahead and overlooking the beach, and we had to take the next culvert off the beach. Batgirl explained the layout of the Deir el Belah with its stone wall structures, temples, and religious beliefs. The locals would die to protect this.

'Right, Batgirl, I want you to swap with Matilda and then head towards Target-1. You need to find an LUP around five hundred metres before it.'

'You're giving it to this bag,' Matilda said. 'Why?'

'Because she knows more about this area than any of us. Now do it.'

Matilda got off in a strop and removed his kit and weapons. Batgirl took off Matilda's horse saddle.

'She has a superior headlock to you anyway, Matilda,' Titan whispered in his ear.

'I am known for my wrestling in Australia, ya bludger.'

Titan laughed as Matilda hadn't got the crude 'headlock' joke. Matilda squared up to Titan; well, to his huge chest.

'Wrestle away, you little Aussie dick.'

Matilda took a step back and looked at us all. I was mentally saying, 'go on then, pick a fight with Titan.'

With the spat over and everyone back in a defensive role, I waited half an hour before re-starting and then headed off. Time check: 20:10 hours.

The slope leading to the top of the cliff had been full of noisy revving. On the flats, I kept it down to a second gear crawl. The desert sand soon changed to a rock formation. We bumped over the different crumbling edges, holding on tight whilst being jolted around. Everyone had lifted their goggles. It got to the stage where I had to order the two superior motorbikes to lead us through. However, it wasn't long before both riders braked suddenly. Peering down, they then turned ninety degrees to whatever had stopped them. Looking over the drop to the abyss below was a close call, but in the darkness and uneven surface was another challenge.

Eventually, we returned to the sand. On the slope down to the next plateau, it was very soft. I became stuck half-way by the side plates and the narrow wheels. Fuck. Slightly hitting the incline further east at a different angle, almost side on, was Truck-2 driven by Scrap. He completed the forty-metre slope. There was no point me revving the nuts out of the truck, digging deeper in the shit I was already going to be in. I knew the mud was going to come my way. To make things worse, Matron made it easy in the pinky with Trish next to her. Trish gave me the reeling gesture that I had done to her. It wasn't the correct meaning, even though I was stuck and needed a tow. Baka got out from next to me. Deserter, I thought.

Flash-heart, Matilda, and Seagal returned to me with a large coil of rope. Nothing was said about being stuck. I slightly relaxed. It had been an easy mistake to make. With the three ropes secured to my truck, they attached each one to the remaining vehicles. I slipped it into first and then let the clutch out as the arm signal went down. The revving increased. I didn't appear to be moving. I became worried about the noise and the consequences of leaving a team member. Those who weren't driving grabbed the ropes, looking as concerned as me. With a bit of rocking, they pulled me free, and I drove through the exhaust smoke. Very quickly, the ropes were unhooked at each end simultaneously. Not even being coiled up properly, they were chucked in the back of Truck-2.

Driving alone and leading, Seagal was on the side's HMG. Baka sat back with his CO, Tommy, me having been demoted. I stopped in a large depression and jumped down. Up on the ridge, I went to view my binos but heard the thumping of a horse. I swung around my rifle but relaxed seeing Trumper. Fuck, where was Batgirl? Matilda managed to stop his comrade, almost getting kicked as it reared up. Seagal ran up alongside me and viewed through his sniper rifle. With the horse snorting and still bucking, I went back to the centre and told Matilda to shut Trumper up.

'Right, listen in,' I whispered. 'This is now our LUP. We're low enough in the depression to be hidden. We've a complete circle view of the area. The same drills as before at the first LUP. The importance of being silent and alert is critical. We're right in their backyard.'

'Where is Khalida?' Matron asked.

'Get to it,' I ordered, and walked back to Seagal. 'See anything?'

'No, boss.'

I searched through my binos, defiant that she would be walking in. I pointed to the large single rock pillar left by many years of erosion.

'Seagal, take your special kit and find a way up that stack to keep watch.'

'You are jesting me.'

'Do I fucking look like I'm fooling around?' I said.

'It is April Fool's Day tomorrow. In 1539, Flemish poet Eduard de Dene wrote of a nobleman...'

'You're now in charge of D-squadron Mountain Troop,' I interjected.

Seagal frowned and looked around. 'What mountain squadron?'

'Just you.'

'It is a bit of a mean feat to climb.'

'You're fucking lucky it's not as bitterly icy as what D and G Squadron had to endure in the Falklands. Now get your shit together and fucking ammo up before I demote you to your former unit.'

'Yes, boss.'

'Take enough hard routine for twenty-four hours.'

'I'll cut off a horse's leg to share with the mountain troop,' he said sarcastically.

'Once we've finished setting up here, I'm taking one man to set up an OP. It might go noisy, so be ready.'

Seagal slipped back down the bank. 'Oh, by the way, on the way to your OP, do not get fucking stuck in the sand.'

I cringed.

CHAPTER FOURTEEN

I quietly called everyone in for a quick briefing. First, I made everyone individually repeat what their role was in this LUP and what was expected if it went noisy.

'Questions?' I whispered.

'Do you think Batgirl has been captured or is dead?'

'No, Matron, or the enemy would have sent out a patrol.'

'What do we do if Sikes returns, boss?' Titan asked.

'Restrain him and then drug him.'

'Fucking pleasure,' Blister added.

'I have come up with another new mission name, boss,' Trish said.

'Oh God, what?'

'Operation Shit Driver.'

The whole unit tried to hold in their amusement.

'Wankers,' I said. 'I'm wrapping this briefing up.'

Loaded up with surveillance equipment and enough rations for twenty-four hours, me and Flash-heart slung on our modern style Bergan. Matron had managed to finish my design from the spare haversacks I had loaded before we had left. I told her how good they were.

Tabbing a good pace slightly left and downhill towards the mountain stack, I tried to spot Seagal on the jutted ledges, but couldn't. I scanned the cliff's rockface which sat forty metres back. Again, I couldn't see anything out of the ordinary. So far, our sniper has been brilliant. I hoped he lived up to his firing attributes.

Upping the speed as we crossed the railway tracks at the bottom of the canyon, I stopped in the precipice's shadow. When Flash-heart had joined me, I signalled him to keep watch northeast of the tracks. Unzipping my sandy-coloured boiler suit, I pulled out the new map and cupped my hand holding a torch. With a pinhole cover over the lens, I studied our position, making sure no light escaped.

Packing the items away, I then leant over to Flash-heart's standard issue balaclava.

'Are you OK?' I barely whispered.

Flash-heart turned, only his eyes showing through his blacked-out face. 'I would rather be up in a plane.'

'Forget all that numpty flying shit. We're the SBS now. The SR role.'

'What is that supposed to mean?'

'SR? Special reconnaissance.'

'No, your strange saying, "numpty". And the Royal Flying Corps is far superior to whatever the SBS is.'

'Special Boat Service, or Severely Best Soldier. Which is better than what poor old Seagal joined: the SAS. Slightly Average Soldier.' I sneered.

'Your abbreviations are doing my fucking head in. You talk so much shit, I should have brought more Kitchener posters for you to wipe on.'

I was shocked at him sounding nothing like his normal Jacob Rees-Mogg, but then it dawned.

'Blister told you to say it.'

He nodded and smiled.

'Right, switch on,' I said.

For a further two hundred metres of tabbing, the bottom of the canyon began to incline to the level with the cliff edge. Hiding in the last of the shadows, I faced the way we had come and tried to spot our LUP. It was invisible. Hopefully the same in the daylight. Flash-heart caught me up. He quietly moaned that his legs were playing him up. I knew it was a risk bringing him. Yet, he had the best knowledge of the railway machinery. Our squad had done a recce of the train station at Ismailia. When the station was closed, we practised our simulated building and carriage entry; also, how to best place the explosives. However, we didn't fully know the best position to lay them to cause maximum damage and to prevent anything getting a quick repair. Therefore, I had decided to ask the amazing mechanic and engineer Flash-heart to advise.

Reaching the brow, I stopped. On one knee, I scanned the carnage spread over a fifty-metre radius. Flash-heart moved a further five metres into a shallow scrape. I signalled to Flash-heart to remain whilst I patrolled the area. Before I moved, I checked the cliff edge and surrounding desert for any HMG nests, thinking this was what had caused the deaths.

Heading in closer, seven camels had been killed. One breath husked into the cool night. Creeping low to the first camel with its legs facing me, I tucked into the body for concealment—it stunk. I felt its matted body for puncture wounds and blood—nothing. On my stomach, I shimmied around to the head, stopping at the amount of blood that had flowed from its neck. I touched it—lukewarm. Lifting slowly above the clumpy mound, a human form lay crumpled a few metres away behind a solitary sunken boulder. I looked back at Flash-heart, making sure he had my back.

Rapidly, I squatted over to the boulder and rolled the man over. I quickly turned away after seeing he had lost his head. The blood and gore stark on his yellow *dishdasha*. Looking down my sights, I crept up to the next camel. The rider was half under it. Both had come to the same fate. The recent camel that had been rasping, stopped.

There were no weapons lying around. Each Bedouin had lost their head. Some even a limb. Every camel's throat had been slit. Perhaps so the Bedouin tribe couldn't have any further stock. Was this the hands of the Turks? But why no gunshot wounds? Had these dead been part of the colony that Seagal had seen? I checked for wheel tracks. Why cut the head off each rider and take it? Fuck, the Elkhaba. What about Batgirl? I had seen enough.

Finding the perfect OP, I concealed myself behind the craggy rock. Flash-heart eventually reached me, breathing hard and sweating. He handed me a black piece of cloth and then slumped to the ground holding his thighs. The black material was a wet shirt cuff. I detected blood on my gloves. Flash-heart told me he had left behind the glove as it still had the hand in it. Flash-heart began to wretch. Silently, I told him.

So, these mysterious evil spirits that rode on black ghost horses were a load of bollocks. They bleed. I knew I had to kill the whole Elkhaba tribe. That meant they would never travel to Afghanistan and start eradicating the Taliban in 2011. But then, would Operation Blue Halo have ever taken place? Was this why I was here?

Through the binos, I scanned the station. We were eight metres left of the main railway track. Directly in front but slightly offset was a large building approximately seventy metres away. Its outer structure was made of heavy natural stone that held a tiled apex roof. More modern than the station at Ismailia. A corrugated roof on timber pillars almost spanned across the sandy platform. A five-foot wall of sandbags sat between the pillars with one opening. White edging stones separated the platform from the tracks. There were two sets of railway tracks: one going past us and the other veering southeast into the desert. Further back on this track was an intersection which headed into a storage area. Two large timber sheds stood, like the hangars at our base but smaller. I finished writing the notes.

'Are you better now?' I whispered.

'Those scenes were frightful.'

'I meant your legs.'

'Oh. Yes, I have taken morphine.'

'I hope a little as I need you to stay awake.'

He nodded—not convincingly.

'Right, you have decent eyes on this main area here,' I said. 'As silently as possible, we need to dig in under that rock slab and make a slit just enough for you to view. We're slightly higher than ground level, so we need to pull over a net and surround you with grassy thickets.'

'Where are you going?'

'I want to take a closer look around and then set up another OP to the rear.'

'Leave me here on my own for the entire watch?'

'Remember, you're not in the RFC but in the SBS on a special reconnaissance,' I said, and grinned.

'I would rather be in the SAS, whatever that was. I loathe you.' He tried not to smirk, but his big blond moustache twitched.

'Right, synchronise to dead on 12:10 hours in five…four…three… two…one…now.'

Pinning the net, I then placed the grass around the sandbagged entrance. I peered into his one-man pit. It was just large enough to store his kit and weapons. Importantly, he had room to have a toilet; although, cramped and making it awkward bagging it. I was hoping when the sun rose that the sand that was left over from digging the pit would dry out where we had scattered it. I instructed Flash-heart there was no reason for him to come out till the next evening when I returned. If I did not return by an hour after dusk at 19:15 hours, then he was to head back to the LUP. It was crucial that he made sure he was not followed or left any obvious signs he was here. Once at camp, he would discuss all his notes with the lads. Titan would take leadership if I did not return. Flash-heart looked concerned.

Making sure all my kit was tight, I headed towards the rear of the sheds. Reaching the railway curve that led south, I laid behind the track and viewed through the binos. There was quite a lot of debris discarded: a buckled bike, motorbike wheels, smashed empty wooden crates, remnants of charcoal and campfires, and general rubbish. Whoever was in charge needed a kick up the arse.

Two interjections went into each shed. In front of the furthest was an empty single push-along loading tram on the track. Movement to my right caught my attention. Immediately, I aimed at the long and greasy-black rat. It was different to what we'd had in the trenches. I thought of the London Dogs cooking and eating them—grim.

Staying at a furtive pace, I sucked into the first timber wall. I spotted the high telegraph pole not only had wires traipsing to others heading east, but each one had a lamp on. Why weren't they lit? At head height on the corner of the shed was the dreaded klaxon. Keeping out of the view of the main building's windows across the station, I crept around the back and came across the rear door. My mind flashed with the images of the cowshed in Operation Poppy Pride—I didn't want that episode again.

The smell of oil hit me as I gently pulled back the door. From the skylight's beams, I made out a steam locomotive. It was too much of a risk to search the building. I decided to move onto the next shed, making mental notes of all the security horns and lights so far.

The next shed was also dark inside. In one corner was a large control box with levers and dials. A cough nearby made me freeze for a second. I slid inside and softly closed the door. Out came my dagger. A shadow stood outside the door. The light through the crack moved. I had one hand on the door, ready to bash it back if he came through. Then, the footsteps continued by.

Relaxing, I continued with the job. Spread on the nearby floor were tools. Inspection pits disappeared into the dark. Should I make the hazardous sneak to the large timber doors? Would they creak if I opened them on the raid? Too risky.

Following the guard's route, I reached the corner of the building and watched him open the main building's door. A light shone out, showing his uniform and rifle. A mutt greeted him. Thank fuck the guard wasn't on patrol with it. The door was shut, and I made a mental note of the patrol time.

Double backing, I came to a stack of empty crates. I couldn't translate the inscription on the side. The gothic-like black cross had to be German. The timber lid underneath had a Turkish flag stencilled. I didn't recognise the next symbol of a black phoenix with two heads and talons holding something. Like at our base, there was a scrapheap. Concerningly, it also held British parts.

To the east side of the main station, set back about a hundred metres, was a different type of building. Instinctively it shouted fortification. The walls were made of the same stone as the station building. Only, this was a single storey. One oblong stone in the wall had been taken out every two metres. Perhaps firing positions. The fortification appeared to have poles vertically erected on the roof. Objects were set in front, but I couldn't make out what. Next to the oblong fortress was a stone wall structure. Round and about ten metres in diameter. I should find out what these were. Do I take the risk?

Heading east into a ditch, I became aware of the crusty feeling underfoot. The stench was putrid. A ditch of shit like in Haleema's village. I laid on the bank thinking back of the goats that had nearly compromised me. Suddenly, a mutt barked from the main platform.

'Fuck,' I muttered.

A light lit up the guard's face for a few seconds. Most probably a match. That's why I had put a ban on smoking and Tommy's joss-sticks. How far can dogs smell other dogs? Would Baka start to bark? Has Tommy trained him well? At least my own smell was masked by hundreds of years of turds. It was time for me to get the hell out and find a decent OP, so I decided I would search a hundred metres behind the fortification. I waited for the end of the fag's glow to head behind the sheds and then I sprinted low across the tracks.

With luck on my side, for once, I found a mound of dunes like the one me and Titan had sat in laughing about the headlock joke. The downside was that it was set back at a hundred and fifty metres, but it would have to do.

Keeping all movement down to slow and minimal, I dug the pit. Next, I filled the sandbags and then made a double-layered rim around my OP. On my stomach, I pegged across the canvas camouflage and finely spread the sand on top. The top of the mound already had living and dead vegetation. The rest of the piled sand, I discarded down the rear slope.

Once inside, I placed all my weapons and then pulled out my pad and pencil. After a rationed amount of water and dates, I pulled away the main stick. The flap closed. Under a torch, I made notes on all that I had seen. Time check: 03:17 hours.

I was awake before the sun rose, thinking back on my recent dream about taking out specific targets on Operation Blue Halo with originally assigned SAS and SBS squads. Was I having these dreams because this mission was very similar to the Afghan mission? Including when I had returned to find Haleema? I shook my head at the car bomb images. Perhaps soon I would find the link to get back to 2013. Then a small memory popped up: Scrap dropping the modern-day shell which the temple's old man had given him. Why would he have been given Ocker's cartridge? Surely this criminal Lieutenant Thomas White couldn't be related to Tommy White, aka Ocker, of my era. Could they? They were both Australian.

I thought about the SS badge and the World War One pistol that were either placed in the tomb or on you. Was Scrap sent back to find Lieutenant White? But why? The answer smacked me: to get revenge on Ocker for his tribal killings. Killing Lieutenant White in 1917 would mean Ocker would never be born. Fuck. Would Scrap do this? I knew he loathed Ocker. He had said the rescued tribal woman spoke broken English to him. And yet, she didn't me. Why would he come back just to do that? Had he been told about the gold? Is this why Scrap had interrupted Matilda twice? To keep it from me.

A whistle blowing brought me back to what I was supposed to be doing. I lifted the stick just enough to see out the canvas. The warming sun was appearing behind the white clouds. Resting Tommy's binos on the sandbag between the grass, I was shocked at how close I was to an artillery cannon emplacement. My OP was slightly behind this defensive position. The emplacement was hidden behind trees and bushes. It had two cannons, each having a tall and wide cupboard leaning back at a 45-degree angle. The doors were latched shut. The protective perimeter wall was made up of different sized stones. At the back was a stack of empty brass shells that were ineffectively covered and glinting off the sun.

Through the binos, I watched the first sleepy group of five soldiers leave the round fortification. They plodded their way towards me. My heart sank. Four of them had red material bands around their waist and over their beige desert uniform. They wore beige hats with the sides and back pulled down to protect from the sun. The soldier that led them had a dusky-blue hat. Their rifles were slung over their shoulders.

Two more soldiers headed to the left and reached a raised mound. They pulled back the canvas sheet and settled behind a HMG. Although they had the same idea as our squad, they had lazily strolled to it in broad daylight. It also had not been manned at night.

By the time the five soldiers had reached the artillery cannons, another two HMG nests with double crews had been set up. Furthest away was a twin crew for a mortar outpost. I had not seen any of these defences at night. I quickly drew them on my sketch.

The cannon crew sat around eating, drinking, and smoking. One took a shit no more than eight metres from me—grim. It was made worse as he didn't wipe and didn't bury it.

Between the top of the shed roofs was a water tower. A soldier in a dark uniform climbed the side ladder. On top he was doing something at his feet, until another man stood with a rifle. I had not seen the tower or the sniper guard last night. He must have been asleep. A further two sharpshooters set up positions on the apex roof where it met a gully. They were not blended into the colour of the tiles, and without any shade—they were going to cook.

Back at the fortification, more people left. All twenty were wearing boiler suits. On top of this solid structure, four men started to use a pulley system to haul something up. Tarpaulin was taken off two heavy-calibre pom pom guns. They were now being maintained by a crew of eight.

In the very far distance, I couldn't work out two objects due to being partly obscured by the fortress and the scrapheap. The heat mirage and useless binocular range didn't help.

3 Snipers. 5 artillerymen. 6 HMG gunners. 2 mortar team. 24 armed workers. 8 pom pom crew. 1 mutt.

Time dragged on, except when the artillery squad opened the cabinets and did a drill with the used shells. There was no soldier change over. A group of four women dressed in French black robes and headscarves with white veils came up to each defensive position with water and food. The clothes were the same as the women from Ismailia, importing them from Paris. Why was everyone so laid back? Perhaps because it was a Sunday. Perhaps the Gods were looking down on me. I mean, there were no goats here. It was a stupid thought, but it kept my mind active from boredom.

I was just counting my chickens, thinking how shabby this defence was, when there was buzz from the east. A loud whistle followed. The counted chickens scattered—never underestimate the enemy. A formation of six German fighters flew over. Everyone waved as they split. I didn't bother making a mental note of the markings as I am sure Flash-heart was.

Panning back with the binos towards the steam train, between the smoke that chugged out were two men in dark uniforms standing behind the main cab. As it neared, the brakes started to squeal. Right at the front was a HMG with four barrels poking out from behind a metal guard. The turret scanned its arcs. Was this a show of strength to those on top of the fortress?

Four German soldiers stood up on the front and waved at the Turk soldiers on top of the building. On the front carriage was a huge spotting light. The open top carriage was full of heads, some poking their rifles out of the steel sheet slits. As it rolled into the station, behind the cab where two officers stood, was a flat bed of four objects covered in dirty beige tarpaulins. The outline was very noticeable: tanks. Fuck.

Mirroring the front was the back. Four gunners stood up and waved. With just the front and rear ends showing past the building, I wondered what was going on. I hoped Flash-heart could see and was making notes; also, holding his nerve.

Each plane landed safely in the far background that was left of the sheds. There must have been a man-made runway built; although, I had heard stories that these pilots could land anywhere in the desert.

Everyone left their positions, except from behind the AA guns. I took my time to stretch. Doing so prompted a piss, so I did in my spare bottle. Why was I now getting the urge to dump? Having a quick look out the front, I unravelled my sweaty boiler suit and started to ceremonially go above the grease-proof paper. Just as I was wrapping it up, goats started bleating close by. Are you fucking joking? I quickly folded that in a cloth and rapidly shoved it inside a sandbag that had sand at the bottom. Scraping the ground, I added more inside the hessian sack and placed the bag and bottle in my Bergan.

One of the goats was munching grass right outside the front slit. You couldn't have made this up—why now? An Arab boy herder walked by and realised one in his flock wasn't following. He stopped and turned around. I drew my knife. He shouted for the goat to follow, but it continued to chew whilst staring at me. The boy threw a stone and it bounced on my canvas roof. He inquisitively looked and began to walk back. Fuck.

Fifteen metres…

I hushed the goat to fuck off…

Thirteen metres…

The goat started bleating. I wanted to grab it and slit it…

Ten metres…

The boy started hollering…

Nine metres…

The artillery crew began to return from the station. I gripped my rifle…

The lad was still shouting…

Six metres…

The crew on the building swung the AA gun. I held my breath…

The train's whistle and chugging steam stopped the herder. The goat looked up. The boy turned and ran towards the moving train. The artillery crew shouted something in Turkish and then laughed at all the goats chasing him, including the one that nearly compromised me—I wanted a genocide of all goats.

The locomotive followed the tracks southeast, with the tanks still onboard. The rear compartment of troops had debussed. Shit. To make things worse, four Alsatians and twelve soldiers were heading towards the fortress. One mutt had a baby goat in its jaws.

The train's steam soon disappeared. Everyone was back on duty. The herder and goats headed in the direction of our LUP. I made more notes and sketches, keeping my mind off the negative worry that the squad of trained goats and their CO would sniff out Flash-heart or the lads at the LUP. Would any of them be able to kill the lad if he spotted them? Or would our unit let him flee to alert everyone? Would Baka go crazy seeing the enemy goats?

As soon as the sunset was in its last stages, the defensive positions were abandoned. A sumptuous waft of cooking smells roamed across the desert. I wanted some of that barbecued goat. The only sentry that was left was the sniper on the water-tower. Very quietly, I packed up all my gear.

When it was dark, I crawled out from my hide and rolled up the canvas. I then stashed it away with the pegs. Making sure I wasn't silhouetted against the top of the mound, I bulldozered as much sand back as I could and then loosely spread my prints around with my hands. Hopefully, Flash-heart was doing the exact same as I had instructed.

Weirdly, there were hardly any stars in the sky and the moon was very thin. The blackest night I had seen since being here. Realising I didn't have long to get to the first OP, I set off. I wasn't concerned about the sniper as visibility was down to a few metres. Yet, I was concerned about the Elkhaba.

It was difficult to find the first OP because the light was very poor. To avoid the station, I took a different route.

'Halt. Who goes there?' Flash-heart whispered.

'Vinnie,' I whispered.

Flash-heart got up from the slab of rock and came down to meet me.

'By Jove, you smell unpleasant.'

It still amazes me that men of this era didn't give a man hug or a slap on the back. My squad had taken time to adapt, even though the gay banter still happened. Perhaps a fist-bump should have to be taught.

We re-traced the exact route through the canyon. The pace was slow due to his aching legs. Facing the stack, Flash-heart flashed the red filtered torch three times. The same dim signal came back from up high. We wearily made our way back to the LUP with the red glow out in front. The first sentry came streaking out, but Baka's snarl turned to a joyful bound and flappy grin. I went to stop him licking Flash-heart, but Flash-heart was enjoying it more than he had my embrace. Baka rolled on his back with his legs spread wide. What was he saying? Has someone died? He whined as I left him there.

Seagal returned and was hand-shaken by Flash-heart. My bear hug was pushed away. Seagal sharply told Baka to get his front paws off him. I waited half an hour before individually calling everyone in. Titan told me I stunk. Baka stood guard facing the station. Matilda had his head bowed with his peaked cap hiding his face. There was an edgy atmosphere, so I asked what was troubling. It transpired that Matilda had started taking the piss out of us 'Poms' at the Somme. It led onto a story about two Cardiff brothers, Second Lieutenant Leonard Tregaskis, and his brother Lieutenant Arthur Tregaskis. Both were killed within fifty metres of each other at Mametz Wood last July. One brother left his post to save the brother's life, and they died in each other's arms.

In the end, Blister lost control and violently attacked Matilda. Titan and Tommy had to leave their positions to drag Blister off—very dangerous. I couldn't blame Blister as he had lost two brothers. Yet, I warned him if he lost control of his killer aggression again, he would be out. The same that I was warned about in the Paras. I also told Matilda that if he had one more piss-take about us Tommy and Poms being worse than him, his horse would be the next target practice. Also, Matilda would wear the cloth over his heart and sit on Trumper.

With us all huddled under the truck's armour, it was pleasing to know they had not seen the herder and his posse. I went over my notes and sketches, asking everyone to copy them onto their own stationery. I was keen to hear Flash-heart's notes. However, I was shocked to find out that he had moved position further south following the track. I gave him a roasting for moving and possibly jeopardising the mission. I slightly relinquished as he spoke about what he had seen there: two two-manned HMG posts. One two-manned mortar post. One five-manned artillery post. And one sniper on top of a stable containing six horses. All were set more than a hundred and fifty metres to the south of the sheds. Set back behind the stables was a round building where all the enemy stayed.

4 Snipers. 10 artilleries. 9 HMG gunners. 4 mortar teams. 24 armed workers. 8 pom pom crew. 5 mutts. 6 cavalrymen. 12 German infantryman.

Flash-heart told us the best place to set each charge. It excited us. Although we had more targets than we had expected, we opted not to attack the mortar encampment and stables at the south. Instead, keep the remaining ammunition back for the aerodrome. We were to detonate the two HMG nests, the cannon, and locomotive in the shed. Flash-heart still tried to reason again about us not using the RFC Spencer Bomb as well, but it was pointless.

At the end of the briefing, I knew there was something on Seagal's mind. I asked him to speak up, which got a bit of piss-taking from the others.

'What about the Bedouin massacre?' he asked.

'I want everyone on high alert tonight, especially with the visibility so poor. However, we will be more invisible to them. Only unleash hell if it's necessary as your muzzle flash will be seen.'

'I have invented a flash-hider for each of my weapons,' Seagal said, and showed the new rifle adaptation.

'Can you fit one of each to my weapons?' Titan asked.

'No, not that pea-shooter shotgun.' He winked.

'How does it work?' Blister asked.

'It moves some of the flash of hot gas and combustion out of the enemy's sightline. Also increasing the mixing of those gases with the air. Both...'

'You're fucking boring me now,' Blister interrupted, and fist-bumped Titan.

'What was that hand sign?' Flash-heart asked.

'I'll teach you that later,' I said. 'Listen in, lads. The Elkhaba do not use rifles but swords and spears. Use your grenades to try not to compromise yourself. They take the heads of those they have killed.'

'What?' Tommy said.

'Batgirl said they eat the brains, so you'll be fine,' Titan said. 'Oh, not sure about that hideous ponytail.'

Scrap tugged at Tommy's hair tail.

'OK, switch on,' I said. 'Tonight, we hit Target-1. Study your notes and then dispose of them. Scrap, Titan, Blister, you're coming with me. Seagal, I want you to have eyes on those sniper positions. The rest of you know what role you have and the different scenario drills. Synchronise your watches to 19:50 hours…now. Fucking ammo up.'

From each truck, the special raiding party pulled down six wooden crates and then jimmied the lids. From the first three, we each loaded up with three steel Bangalore Torpedoes. Although recently invented in 1912 by Captain McClintock of the British Indian Army in Bangalore, they were very effective at clearing mines and barbed wire fences. However, after testing them, we wanted more destructive power. We also thought they were too cumbersome. We had pre-cut ours down to five hundred millimetres, and then we packed with a new double mixture of Amatol: ammonium nitrate and toluene: TNT. At one end, the nose sleeve was pre-fitted. The other had a non-electric blast cap. We had opted for the non-electric cap and time blasting fuse on this raid. The other method of wires and plunge detonator was too heavy, and dangerous if wires had tangled.

The other benefiting experiment had been an old locomotive funnel where we had tested a tailfin-less 20lb Spencer Bomb attached to the Torpedo. The result found the 'danger close' blast range had to be a greater distance when ignited, which ruled out carrying reels of longer det-wire. It would also mean putting more men in the field to detonate, possibly resulting in one of the SRP being wounded or killed. It had been a thrilling day of blowing shit up in the desert.

With the other crates opened, we packed the rest of the bomb kit in our packs. This was it: Target-1.

CHAPTER FIFTEEN

Everyone patted Seagal on his Bergan as he was to set off first. Tommy gave him some aqua-coloured stones. Seagal raised his eyes at me. Seagal was wearing his own camouflaged suit and armed with his John Rigby 406. hunting rifle, and Bergmann MP. He didn't believe in carrying a pistol as he was not in close quarters. He had also left his papier-mâché mates behind as the night was too dark.

After Blister made sure everything was tight and secure on Seagal, Trish lifted the net. Seagal had soon disappeared into the abyss. The atmosphere became strange. Disquietly portentous. How weird. Was this how it felt to my family and friends when I went on ops?

All geared-up in our new black-ops boiler suits, balaclavas, and cam-cream faces, we tested our adapted torches on the unclassified Bergmann MP-18. Blister and I took the Enfield rifle with scope. Titan carried his Nitro Express. Scrap had opted for the heavy Lewis and three spare magazines as his physique and fitness could easily warrant it. We all had opted for the unofficial M1911A1 Colt 45. automatic pistol with a holster modified to our thigh. Our squad had assessed it. Liked them. Had them. It was that simple. At our base, we binned the metal plate armour vest we had made. It was too cumbersome and heavy. The vest material would split, thus falling out.

Securing my adapted ammo pouch vest, I made sure my dagger was at the front. No one said a word. The task ahead was electrifying, nothing like on the lads we had left behind as we headed out to Target-1.

Distancing ourselves, I led as point-man in a direct route to just before the recent first OP. I was mentally studying what I had seen before, knowing the others would be thinking of where to lay their explosives.

Hunkered behind the slab of rock which overhung OP-1, Titan tapped me on my shoulder. Scrap was the next in and made himself known to Titan. With Blister carrying up the rear, we huddled together. With four sets of eyes above the ridgeline, I was shocked to see the station had its telegraph pole lamplights lit. Bollocks.

'This is going to make it fun,' Blister excitedly whispered.

'Just like Shrek,' I implied—Blister grinned.

'This is what I signed up for,' Titan muttered.

'I should have called you Planet,' I hushed. 'Right, you know the objectives. Meet back…'

'Why don't we leave the Lewis here, just in case,' Scrap interrupted. 'Make this the RV.'

'Can't the little man mountain carry it,' Titan chipped in.

Scrap grabbed Titan by his straps. 'Little mountain?' Scrap hissed. 'Better than being a fucking mole hill.'

'And now we have Rabbit for fuck's sake,' I muttered. 'We've a fucking job to do. Save your girly squabble for later. And Scrap, it's a great idea to set up the Lewis.'

Titan huffed.

Scrap silently made the HMG ready. After piling extra mags next to it, he pegged down a hessian sheet across it.

Checking the synchronisation, Titan then crept in a wide arc towards my original OP-2 near the artillery encampment. Within ten metres, his bulking frame had disappeared. Scrap squatted low with minimal movement and made his way south to head back in an arc to the horse shed area. As he crossed the railway tracks, he sank into the night. I held back Blister.

'No lunacy. Stealth is key,' I whispered close.

'I'm not here to catch the Jerries with a fucking butterfly net.'

I went to give him some strong advice, but he stood up and started walking as bold as brass the seventy metres towards the main station's building. I didn't have the time to cover his brazen and stupid ways as I had my own set of objectives to complete by zero hour. I trusted Seagal was in a great position to take out the enemy snipers.

Like the black rat I had seen here before, I lurked across the open towards the curve in the railway that headed southeast. Heart racing but excited at the same time, I studied the sheds before sneaking off to the side. Against the timber wall, I tuned in. From the shadows, I gauged the station building. The station's lights weren't bright, but the dimness was enough for me to see a black shape quickly scale the five feet wall of sandbags and then into the corrugated roofed porch.

Lowering my weapon, I slung the sling over my shoulder and took out the spanner from under my wrist cuff. I let the string unravel. It had been added to make sure the spanner didn't hit the floor if dropped.

Scurrying along the structure, I had to come out into the lamplight. At head height, I wound the adjustable spanner to fit the nut and started to undo it. It was seized. Bollocks. With both hands, I pulled down on the spanner. The nut creaked as it released. I looked around. Letting go of my breath, I rapidly wound the nut off. Once it became free, I stole the operating handle.

Quickly slipping back into the shadows, I spotted movement from the sandbagged entrance. It had only been for a split-second, and it had disappeared as quickly. The klaxon handle on the main platform had been removed. Blister's first set explosive charge was the most dangerous to lay, but he had volunteered.

Two more klaxon to disable. Time was ticking for me to lay my explosives with the right delay fuse. I snuck around the rear and gently pulled open the door. The familiar smell of oil hit me as I entered. Weapon tucked firmly in my shoulder, I scanned the dark with the beam. I let the door close quietly with my foot. Many rats scarpered. A few of the huge rats just stared. Maybe they thought I was a ginormous black rat, part of the British Desert Rats. I smirked.

I made sure I didn't kick any tins of paint, tools, or metal parts. At the same time, I scanned every inch of the building. I went up to the imposing steam locomotive. The main body had been painted beige, leaving parts of the shutters the original dusky-blue. A shit job compared to what we had done with our vehicles. However, feeling the large rivet heads as I made my way along the front, I realised they had fitted heavy armour to every part of it. In my beam, I studied the pom pom barrels that poked out of the cylinder turret at the front.

Switching off the weapon's light contrasted me into complete blackness; also, darkening the mood. Quietly, I slung off my Bergan and unzipped my suit pocket to bring out a torch. With the light in my teeth, I carefully pulled out the first torpedo and bomb. Then, the rest of the kit to arm it. Winding the coiled wire around the tube and bomb, I connected them together. With extreme caution, I placed the blast cap on the end. I smelt that strange chemical odour again. Ever so slowly, I inserted the thirty-minute fuse, designated with a stripe. My mind flashed back to the task at the bomb dump in Operation Poppy Pride. I had one minute to lay the device and start the fuse.

Unlatching the cab's heavy steel door, I carefully pulled it open. The creaking resounded off the timber walls. Did they not have WD40 out here? A low growl stopped my heart. I switched off the torch and carefully placed the device on the floor of the cab. An inaudible German voice came from the rear of the building. It was coming in the same direction as the last guard. They had changed their patrol times. Stealthily, I tip-toed back towards the door, but knocked a tin over. Fuck. The growl heightened. The guard ordered the mutt to "go see". Years of training kicked in, masking the urge to take flight. Instead, to use fear as a lethal force, in the zone.

As if I had the leisure to plan the move, I picked up a tin of grease and made my way to the door quicker than the imminent threat. Knowing the swing arc of the door, I shook the tin of the smelly grease just beyond this. The outside shadow stopped. I painstakingly gradually slid out my knife. The dog sniffed at the door gap. I held every muscle and my breath, mentally telling them to move on. The metal door swung open. I held the timber framework on the door against my body. The guard ordered the first enemy in. I let the door go as the opponent smelt the grease. The growl and the dim light through the skylights reflected in the killer's eyes. I reacted at super-speed by grabbing the target around its scrawny neck and twisted the young attacker down on top of me. On my back, I thrust the knife in and pulled it up and to the side. As the target jerked and whined, I held its jaw shut.

Pushing and sliding with my feet in the grease and wetness, I slid back to the inner wall. The door swung open, and the guard called out for his companion. I was on my feet. A lighter's flame gradually came in first in his left hand, followed by the right hand holding the infamous Lugar. He was shaking. As soon as I spotted the target's hair, I sharply kicked the door against him. The shock sent him sprawling to his side and the grease caught alight. The target was still in shock as he half sat up. He began to pat his putties that had caught fire. It was too late; his eyes had lifted to see the black shadow moving in. I kicked him in his head and followed him up with my knife to the heart. A few seconds later, I dragged him through the dwindling fire and dumped him in the pit under the train. I quickly trailed him with the skinny mutt.

Back at the door in almost complete darkness, I intently listened to see if anyone had heard the commotion. Especially when I had knocked over further items when dragging them away. Yet, I couldn't remember any noise in the two attacks.

I couldn't wait here; I was now behind time. Backing away from the door with my sub aimed at it, I blindly felt the cold steel with my blooded and greasy hands. The rats came out of hiding and scurried to the pit. With the weapon slung back, I hitched up under the trembling torchlight and carefully picked up the device. Making sure the coal Furness was cold, I then placed the explosive inside. Before I let the timer-plunger go, I checked the time and waited for the second hand to hit the twelve. Time: 21:33 hours. First detonation armed.

Trying not to slip in the mess but move quickly and quietly to make up for three minutes, I reached the door and checked both ways outside before hurrying along the back of Shed-1. Reaching the corner, I frugally looked at the high water-tower. With any luck, the sniper would be dozing.

I glanced south across the desert but could see jack shit. Darting low to shed-2, I imagined Scrap laying the first explosives on the HMG emplacements. I hope he did not run into any trouble like I had. I gently pulled open the rear door with my sub raised. At the far end, the huge oak doors were open. The outside lamp lights filtered part way in. Silently closing the door behind me, I stepped over each object and turned my underslung light off as I didn't want to alert anyone who could see in the gap. Again, rats scattered, except those that were scrapping over bones.

Moving around a large bowser, I peered around the oak door. To my right was the single-storey stone-walled heavy fortification. I checked the round building next to it, visualising the number of enemies inside. The tarpaulin was not covering the two AA guns this time. Why?

Sinking back, I realised the bowser was sitting on a single push-along loading tram. The same empty tram that had lain previously on the tracks outside. Wiping a film of dust off it revealed words I couldn't translate, along with the recurring symbol of a black phoenix with two heads with talons holding something. I rubbed some more off and recognised the German black cross. Worryingly, also a skull and crossbones.

I backed up towards the large control box, feeling vulnerable in the open gloom.

Swinging the Bergan around with minimal movement, I meticulously set the next explosive. I then correctly fitted the twenty-five-minute delay fuse, noticing my blooded hands and cuffs. I checked the time: two minutes behind time. Placing the device on the pull-out levers, I thought about the bowser behind me. It must have been unloaded off the armoured train. What kind of liquid did it hold? Petrol perhaps. Second detonation armed.

Checking for miscellaneous tools on the floor, I slowly made my way to the rear. Weapon firmly in hand, I exited and turned left towards the scrapheap. The concern of the enemy patrol soldier and mutt missing was growing. I was also still two minutes late till zero hour.

Being still positively focused on the job, I tried to make out any sign of life to the south. Nothing but the eerie black reflected. Just as I was about to head to the next destination, a white bent sign caught my eye on top of the pile of crates. I couldn't ignore what I thought I had seen and reached up to retrieve it. I had correctly seen it: skull and crossbones. Bending the metal back, it read in German: *Gefahr Minen*— Danger Mines. I assumed the other Turkish dialect was the same: *Tehlike Mayınları*. Immediately, I checked the ground in the direction I was heading. But then, I had already been this way on my recce. Perhaps a pure fluke. I tried to see if I could see my prints. I knew in this era they used anti-tank mines. But what about personnel mines? Would my combined weight with Bergan trigger a tank mine? I mentally cursed for not doing my homework thoroughly enough.

Leaving the shadows, I gingerly headed to the ditch. I was very uneasy at every step. Before I entered, I contemplated if the enemy would have laid IEDs in it. Sliding down, I was directly opposite the partly lit fortification. It appeared more intimidatingly grandiose. Perhaps because the structure was lit by a lamplight. Making matters worse, the putrid ditch had fresh excrement in. Could the night get any more problematic?

A shout came from the station. I mentally cursed my stupid thoughts and lowered my eyeline. The stench dissipated. One of the guards was sitting on the white edging platform stones. He lit a cigarette. Surely if he had come through the main building's door, he would have seen Blister's explosive charge. He repeated the two German names and even looked my way. My hand slid onto the stock of my Enfield that was slung on my shoulder. How long is he going to stay patient and not go looking for his comrades? I mentally urged him to finish his cigarette. But then, would he go back to the front entrance? I had to set the last explosive; time was ticking.

Ten seconds…

He inhaled and blew the smoke…

Twenty seconds…

He shouted again…

Thirty seconds…

The guard stood up and flicked his fag out…

Thirty-five seconds…

The guard turned and headed back towards the sandbags but stopped at the klaxon…

Fuck…

Forty seconds…

I laid on the bank and took aim…

Dismissing the missing handle, he went through the sandbag aperture. I held my breath waiting for a commotion of finding Blister's device. My mind raced for the E&E from the hordes of soldiers alerted in the fortress. Like before, a light shone from the open door before it was closed. I relaxed, and the evil smell returned.

I didn't have time to answer my racing questions about why the guard had not found the explosives as I was back to being at least three minutes behind schedule. Scrambling up, I ran to the tracks. Lying between the furthest rails that headed west, I got a whiff of shit and grease. The rails had retained the heat. I went through the same motions but quicker in setting up the last explosive. I ignored the negative thoughts a train could come along, or the soldiers would stroll out of the building opposite. I didn't bother checking the time, clawing back as many precious seconds as I could. I started the twenty-minute delay fuse. Third detonation armed.

Reaching the fortress wall, the night was getting warmer. Or was it just me? Ducking under the first window, laughter came from inside. I kept going until I passed the main door and squatted under the next window. The light through the nets caused weird shapes on the sandy ground. At the corner's edge, my chest was fluttering. I was breathing heavier than I should be. I needed to get it under control, but my heart sank as I went to slip out the spanner. It wasn't there, only the sting remained. Stupidly, I even checked the other wrist and returned to the original. In desperation, I tried the nut with my fingers, just for that miracle chance it was loose—it wasn't. Bollocks. I searched the ground for something to use—nothing.

With no other option than to leave it, I dodged the pile of pallets and headed to the rear. Suddenly, a beam blinded me, but switched off as I got down on one knee and drew my pistol.

'Where the fuck have you been?' Blister hushed.

'Are all your objectives done?'

'Yes, and on time. You look and smell shite.'

'How come the guard never found the one at the station?' I whispered.

'I hid it in a chest that contained a shovel and bucket.'

'Right, on me.'

'I'm not doing piggybacks with you in that state,' he said.

Ignoring his humour in the serious situation, he followed me up the hill that was slightly right of my previous OP-2.

Energised that I had completed my objectives as well as Blister, I made easy work of the hundred and fifty metres of the soft sanded slight incline. Nearing the dunes, we stopped and flashed our breast torches. A red light came back. Almost bounding up the slope in two leaps, I reached Titan.

'You made that slope better than your driving, pal,' he said.

'Yes, but he smells as shit as his driving,' Blister added.

'Are all your objectives done?' I asked.

Titan unclipped the leather cover and pulled his watch in close to his eye. 'We'll find out in thirty-seconds.'

'What?' I hissed, and quickly looked at the 45-degree angle cupboards.

Titan sniggered.

'Now's not the time, Jason,' I retorted.

'Sorry, fella, but your jokes are as shit as you smell,' Blister said to Titan. 'What the fuck have you two been doing? Rolling in shit.'

'I've trod in some rank donkey shit,' Titan replied.

I remembered watching one of the Turks taking a dump. It was too tempting not to join in. 'That's proper Turk shit.'

'Proper medal of honour for his meritorious conduct,' Blister added.

'Right, let's get back to the RV and pick up the Lewis before we're blown to dust,' I ordered.

We started tabbing back towards the RV, keeping in mind the possible threat of snipers and zero hour. Within approximately ten metres of the RV, we stopped and quickly flashed our chest torches. A very dimmed one came back. It didn't make sense. Was Scrap lying on the floor behind something? Shit, was he injured? We all must have sensed something as we walked in. The dim red light was slightly flickering. I caressed the trigger.

'Psst. Scrap?' I hissed.

'It's Seagal.'

Blister sighed and went to go check, but I held up my fist to stop him.

'Are you alone?' I whispered.

'No, I've got a couple of French whores with me.' I joined in the amusement.

Seagal had made use of the soft sand and dried grass from my first OP, re-digging and now commandeering it as his. We had not even realised he had built this when we had sat behind the rocks. Titan put away the hessian sheet and pegs and then hunkered behind the Lewis that was on top of the rock platform.

'Where's Scrap?' I asked.

'I have not seen him since he left,' Seagal said, and scanned south with the binos.

'Amazing hide, Seagal,' Blister said.

'That was mine,' I said defensively.

'That is a bit butter upon bacon,' Seagal said.

'Oh here we go, more shit from Queen Victoria,' I said.

'It means extravagant,' Titan whispered. 'Everyone knows that saying.'

'Maybe from your posh neck of the woods.'

'Piss off,' Titan said.

I covered my hands around the torch and checked the time.

'Come on Scrap, where the fuck are you?' I muttered. 'Seven minutes to zero hour.'

'We need to head back to the LUP,' Blister whispered—the others stared at me.

'No, we don't leave a man behind,' I said.

'You said this RV was danger close,' Titan said. 'Shall we go look for him?'

'No.'

What seemed ages went by. But in truth, it must have been a few minutes.

'Right, pack up. Let's head over to the south...'

An echoing rumble of a machine gun firing stopped my order. An air-raid klaxon to the south started to whir, killing the silence that prevailed. I didn't have to say anything as we had all got into our defensive positions. Through my binos, I watched the station. Blister scanned south, muttering for Scrap to return. Out of the fortress, a half-lit silhouette ran to the klaxon, the one I didn't disarm. He set it off, and all five lights went out. Fuck.

CHAPTER SIXTEEN

A bright light flashed, followed by a small explosion.

'That's the mortar crew frazzled. I accidentally left a phos-grenade on a trip wire,' Titan said. 'We best fuck off now.'

'Wait, I see someone running from the south,' Blister said.

Everyone turned their binos whilst Seagal sighted the person. The familiar 'plop' sound resonated, followed by a whistle. We all laid low and covered our heads. Fortunately, the impact didn't explode near us. Then, another one was fired.

'Scrap has just got up. The fat bastard is sprinting this way,' Titan said.

BOOOM!

Again, the explosion was well away from us, but the smoke it had left covered Scrap's sprint. I held my breath, but then he appeared.

'Light the fuckers up,' I ordered.

'But zero hour is…'

'Do it,' I snapped.

Whilst the others retrieved their flare-guns, Seagal fired a flare high above the station and sat back behind his rifle.

Bang!

'Sniper on the tower dropped,' he said.

Blister fired another flare towards the horse sheds. Groups of soldiers that lit up from the trailing light started to run down the main platform and up the incline to the HMG nests.

'Hold your fire, Titan,' I said.

Bang!

'Sniper on the roof dropped,' Seagal calmly said. 'Someone put up another Very-light.'

Blister did. The familiar sounds started to whizz nearer and stronger, almost turning into a storm of lead.

'Did you not set the timers on the heavy machine…'

BOOOM…BOOOM!
I shielded my eyes from the north's HMG nests.
BOOOM!
'There goes their artillery,' Titan boasted.
I crawled back due to the ferocity and the sonic wave blowing up the sand.
BOOOM…BOOOM…BOOOM!
Even Blister had started to withdraw. His explosives had detonated in concession, blowing the AA guns and half the main building.
BOOOM…BOOOM…BOOOM!
'That's the south side,' Seagal said.
Large chunks of metal and rubble started landing close.
'Move further back,' I said.

Forty metres back, I ordered everyone to stop and take a defensive role. Still bits of debris landed very close. I was amazed at how it would just thud between us or roll past, but I didn't want to say anything to jinx us.
Bang…bang…bang!
Seagal was having fun from his hide. Heart pumping but calmly in control, I started taking shots at those who were still alive from the horrendous explosions. The aftermath dust cloud had started to form over the station, making it difficult to see. Bodies lay littered in the light from the fire that now raged.
'Contact,' Titan said.
I glanced at who Titan had seen. Scrap was facing the way he had run from and was now suppressing the south. Titan opened up on the Lewis. The incoming rounds began to increase, mainly from the rear of the sheds. Blister let us know he was reloading a mag.
'Johnny, how many did you fucking count?' Titan asked.
'About sixty-eight men, and…'
'I meant the fucking explosives. You only had three to…'
'Contact: dogs,' Blister interrupted.
'Contact: cavalry,' Scrap shouted, and let off a flare.
BOOOM…BOOOM…BOOOM!
A huge mushroom fireball filled with strange colours, dust, and debris rose high into the air.
'What the fuck? Incoming,' Blister shouted.
I squeezed tight to his curled body as the thuds not only rained in, but strange sounds whizzed close overhead. I put my arm over him as

sand and debris started to fill the gaps. Our coughing was taken away by the wind.

Once the main barrage had died down, I opened my eyes, as did Blister. Like before after our near-death experience in the bombing raid, he started to laugh.

'What's so fucking funny?' I whispered.

'Do you reckon Titan was standing up again with that hunting gun?'

'Oi, homosexuals, you best take a fucking look,' Titan said.

Titan was standing with the end of the Nitro Express pointing towards the station. Releasing Blister, sand fell from his balaclava and suit. Titan nodded forward towards Target-1. Getting to my feet, shaking the shit from me, I was shocked at the destruction. The fire in the main station, along with most of the structure, had been blown away, including the sheds. Between the vast array of strewn debris and small fires, some of the animals and men that had survived started to choke. One soldier shot himself in the head. I recalled the bowser that I'd laid the explosives on.

'Gas,' I bawled. 'Fucking Gas. Retreat.'

Making sure I was the last man, I sprinted after them. We had about four hundred metres to reach the camp to get our respirators, and to warn the others. Any enemy that was left would die. Even with us fully loaded, if anyone fell or slowed up, he was quickly reminded to get a move on.

Nearing where I expected the LUP to be, I ordered everyone to turn on the breast torches and not to stop. Baka came charging from the abyss, stupidly happy. I only heard Trumper and Matilda from the left in the last seconds. Matilda lowered his rifle and almost turned on the spot. He galloped back to the LUP. I hoped he had heard me shout the gas warning.

By the time we had made it, the net was already lifted. Titan fell down the slope, causing Blister to fall over him. Scrap shouted the gas alert as he helped them both up. There was a scurry of bodies to reach their personal respirators. Matilda was tightening the respirator's leather straps to Trumper's head. Finally, his own.

After fitting mine, I jumped down from the truck and headed back to the broken net. I stopped when I saw Baka being fitted with a paper fibre-gauze mask. Tommy had a cloth around the lower part of his face. Rapidly, I went to the back of Truck-2 and rummaged till I found Sikes'. Returning, I hit Tommy on the head with it.

Titan and Scrap were repairing the net. Seagal's muffled orders were getting everyone else into position. Grabbing my arm, Blister asked me to be his number-two mortar man. Within three minutes all was deathly quiet, except the breathing from your own mask. A weird glow lit up the night in the far distance.

About an hour had gone painfully by, but at least there had been no counterattack. Something was bothering me about the gas. I then remembered there had not been an 'H S' stamped on the bowser, known at first as 'Hun Stuff' by the British. Later it was called mustard gas because of the yellow cloud. When the enemy had been consumed by it, there had been no yellow cloud. I left Blister and went over to Titan who was manning a Lewis.

'Sitrep?' I asked.

'Nothing. It's too quiet. Something isn't right,' he said, sounding deeper with his respirator on.

'What do you mean?'

'Normally with mustard gas, not only would you hear a different type of landing with the mortar, but there was no cloud. Not even a haze.'

Shit, I had to tell him. 'In Shed-2, there was a bowser painted with skull and crossbones and a German cross. There was Turkish or the Empire war symbol.'

'And it blew up with your bomb. Fuck. But as evil and barbaric as mustard is, you wouldn't drop to the ground and suffocate within seconds. Why didn't the horses and dogs scarper? Or the men run or get their respirators out?'

Titan looked at the ends of his finger poking through his gloves.

'What is it?' I said.

'I've treated many after a gas attack. Some visited me within an hour. If not, a day later with red spots forming on their skin that rapidly turned into painful blisters. Many complained of feeling pain and swelling in the nose and throat where the blisters can develop. Restricting or permanently closing off the airwaves. Yet, I feel fine.'

'A new nerve agent?'

Titan nodded. 'Perhaps the explosion burnt most of it away?'

'Right, get everyone into the middle.'

Once everyone had joined, I let Titan explain the symptoms of mustard gas. He then asked if anyone was feeling sick, had spots, sore throats, etcetera. Yet, everyone seemed fine. He also said anyone who started to get abdominal pains, diarrhoea, fever, nausea, and vomiting should immediately see a medic. Banter or persecution should be upheld.

I took over the conversation telling them about the nerve agent that had been destroyed in the blast, rendering anything in the vicinity dead within thirty seconds. Even with the moisture in the glass lenses, you could see fear in the eyes.

The area is too contaminated, I continued, and ordered an immediate evacuation. All skin must be covered up, borrowing, or improvising with what you could. Trish said she had some Hydrargyri Chloridum Corrosivum already mixed to disinfect the skin, a fantastic input. Wrapping the meeting up, I reminded them that everything had to be done quickly but as silently as possible. Main weapons had to be to hand, putting away the HMGs last.

Within record time we had packed away. I still checked for any sign that we had been here. It seemed stupid to the others because of the carnage we had left. There wasn't one of us that was not steamed up, especially us SRP who still wore the balaclavas. I showed each of them the next LUP on their maps. It made Tommy and Matilda laugh as I had shown Baka and Trumper. We needed a bit of light relief. Time check: 01:11 hours. I was drained.

I led the way up the slope. My fingers were mentally crossed that I would make it up the sandy slope this time. Matilda followed and then both motorbikes trailed. With Truck-2 easily clearing the ridge, we formed a tight convoy. It was against SOP, but with it so dark I didn't want anyone straying off course. I also took the educated guess there would be no more enemy to deal with, unless from the air. Yet, they had no stars and moon to navigate by. I signalled Blister to lead the way.

Coming near to the top of the canyon slope, Blister stopped and then looked back at me. I briskly signalled him to head right, knowing he had seen the beheaded Bedouin and slit camels. We weaved through the bloated bodies to the cliff edge that formed a ground level upland. Blister headed right, looking left across the open desert. What was left of Target-1 shocked me. Perhaps my eyes deceived me because it was dark. A few fires glowed. It added to the creepy unidentifiable structures, mounds, and parts scattered everywhere.

Travelling further south, Blister changed direction slightly southeast as instructed. He stopped. Setting his stand, he returned and picked two items up on the way.

'Why have you stopped in the danger-zone?' I asked.

'There are loads of shrapnel. It's too much of a risk of getting a puncture.' He showed me the jagged lump of steel and then peculiarly a blooded hoof. 'Good luck this. Well, not for the horse.'

I got out the map and studied it under the breast torch. 'Tell Matilda to lead. Scrap, Trish, and Titan are to follow me in the Truck-2 as we're on solid tyres. Meet here by this mass of dunes.'

Whilst Blister went to the convoy to relay my messages, I looked in the direction where Scrap had laid his explosives. It mirror-imaged that of the station and surrounding area. Target-1 had been annihilated.

0 Snipers. 0 artillery. 0 HMG gunners. 0 mortar teams. 0 armed workers. 0 pom pom crew. 0 dogs. 0 cavalrymen. 0 German infantrymen. All shot, gassed, burnt, shredded, or vaporised.

Baka and Tommy were getting some sleep in the back as we headed south, keeping the train track to our left. I glanced at Matron who just stared forwards.

'Are you OK?' I asked.

'Nothing but a cup of tea in the finest crockery would sort.'

'You said to Blister you had seen "thousands of ghastly injured, sufficient dead, and dismembered body parts". On the Somme?'

'I had a nursing station on the RMS *Titanic*. That unsinkable ship,' she said.

'Are you kidding me?'

'No. What soul would lie about that? Quite an ordeal for a twenty-five-year young woman?'

'You're only twen…' I stopped, not opening my big mouth for once. I smirked at her word "ordeal".

'There was worse to come after extraordinarily seeing hundreds of people drown,' she continued. 'I was sent to work on the HMHS *Britannic*. The next unsinkable ship. Yes, quite. We had already saved around twelve-thousand wounded British soldiers. On our fifth trip leaving Southampton, I had a peculiar feeling about that voyage to pick up the wounded from Gallipoli.'

'Wasn't it torpedoed sixty miles off an island?'

'Kia island. We sailed by Port Moudros. Brat had informed me the Germans had not torpedoed it as according to our press, but Captain Edward J. Smith had hit a mine. I remember the ship shaking and an unnatural silence after. We were ordered to head to our posts. An orderly said there had been a message to abandon ship. It struck me how we were not lowered into the ocean whilst the ship took an acute angle. I clutched my bible. The real order was given to abandon ship. In the red water and amongst the mutilated limbs, we busied ourselves attending active persons who had been chopped by the propellers.'

'Jesus. You survived two tragedies and…'

'I am stronger than two unsinkable ships,' she interrupted.

'Why did you come to Egypt? I would have taken some R&R, forever.'

'Patriotism. To save our allies. However, I opted not to join HMHS *Donegal*. I left my friends and work colleagues to duty on that ship as I was rather cynical of ships. I boarded a battleship to Port Said, another six hundred and thirty miles to dry land.'

'I was here before you?' I asked.

'I was Matron on the fourteenth of December.'

Not missing a chance, I said, 'Don't you mean Matron *Rebecca Law*?' She didn't reply.

'How many have you saved?' I asked, wishing I hadn't.

'You have your skills and faults. I have mine.'

She had been through the mill, back, and again. That's why she looked forty going on fifty. I could understand why she was so strong and resilient, but had those horrific scenes not got to her? What the fuck was she made of that I wasn't? For the rest of the journey, we remained silent.

A sight loomed from the bleak desert night: a bridge spanning a gorge. I halted and pulled out my binos. It was difficult to view because of the respirator. As if reading my mind, Matron took hers off, took a deep breath, and exhaled.

'Ironic if the air killed me now,' she said, 'rather than drowning.'

Not finding the humour funny as she deserved to live to a grand old age, I removed mine and the sweaty balaclava. Jumping down, I gave the order to Trish in the pinky to kill the engine. They appeared dubious to take off their respirators. I told them to get everyone to my Truck. Baka and Tommy jumped down, already not wearing their protective equipment. I ruffled Baka's head. Weirdly, Tommy did the same to me.

Under red light with the map spread on the floor, the bridge wasn't marked. I knew we had travelled about twenty klicks, half the distance to Target-2. Time check: 02:27 hours. Eventually, everyone removed their head gear. The SRP faces looked funny with the oval camo. Had they waited to see if me and Matron would die first? I ordered Blister and Scrap to head across the bridge to recce the area; also, being mindful of potential mines. Matilda was to search the gorge. As for the rest of us, we would form a defensive circle. We were only to drink fresh water and eat unopened rations using utensils rather than our hands.

Half an hour later, my head kept drooping behind the truck's onboard Lewis. A faint sound alerted me. Seeing the red flashes, I lethargically did the same. I was shattered. Sitrep: a mass of dunes was set sixty metres further southwest, right of the bridge. Blister said it was a brilliant position for an LUP. That last piece of information had been overstated; I knew they were as exhausted as me to rest up.

Matilda came galloping in without the safety drill which could have got him shot. He apologised, saying he had forgotten. It was unequivocally time to stop before any further mistakes happened. Matilda said a small stream ran at the bottom of the gorge and was easily accessible from the other side as a path had already been formed.

The LUP was indeed brilliant. With a crater in the dunes, it gave us a ridgeline to observe from. And, if necessary, to take fire from in a 360-degree advance. It had also made fitting the camouflage netting easier. The only concern was how long it had taken. The whole squad had become agitated with each other. Even I had I bollocked them for the noise levels.

Leaving the rest behind to disinfect the vehicles and weapons, I took Tommy, Flash-heart, and Titan back to the gorge. Baka followed. We carried seven long timber poles, rope, two buckets, and soap. I disregarded Tommy's and Flash-heart's mumbling moans.

Carefully manoeuvring down the path, leaving Tommy up top to keep guard, Titan placed the poles down. He then took the buckets off Flash-heart and made a sarcastic quip about how heavy they were. Me and Titan fixed a tripod with rope at each end and then placed the final pole across. Flash-heart had finished making holes in the bottom of one bucket, so we fixed it to the centre. I ordered Flash-heart to fetch some water with the other bucket. Quickly, I unholstered my pistol and aimed it at the back of his head. I coughed to get his attention. He rapidly returned and picked up his forgotten rifle, fumbling with the soap.

'I'm not picking the soap up,' Titan whispered. 'Not after you told me what they did to you in prison. Does Flash-heart know your little game?'

'Ha, ha, piss off,' I said.

All of us stripped off, Flash-heart appearing very embarrassed. I took the first refreshingly cold shower with a bar of Sunlight Soap. Titan told me that recently in 1915, the Sunlight Soap Company declared us Tommy's to be the cleanest fighters in the world. The Wirral-based company had offered a thousand-pounds money guarantee of purity in every bar. Even being able to wash the tough, filthy, brave miners after tunnelling mines into position.

Once I was done and the shower refilled, I washed my boots, boiler suit, and underwear in the stream that ran around a bridge arch, one of six. Finally, I made a joke about how tiny Titan's dick was due to the cold water. He hated that more than his posh heritage being slated, saying his was bigger than the poles put together. Flash-heart found our laddish behaviour and nakedness all too incomprehensible. Instead, he kept his back to us as he showered. The three of us kept watch whilst Tommy and Baka took their turn, both having fun with the water and suds.

Back at the LUP, me and Titan wore just our pants. Flash-heart had opted to get fully dressed, whereas we had to ask Tommy to put trousers on as he didn't wear gruds. I ordered the rest to go shower. Whilst they were gone, we took the piss out of Tommy's frizzy black and silver-streaked hair as he had taken it out of his ponytail. He made out he couldn't understand, but he could. The banter continued, even from Tommy and Flash-heart. It was much needed relief. Suddenly, a train whistled from far southeast. Fuck.

CHAPTER SEVENTEEN

I scrambled to get my uniform on, the tiredness vanishing. Flash-heart lowered his binos.

'Flash-heart, how far away is it?'

'I cannot see it or the smoke,' he said, heightened.

'How far, Flash-heart?' I barked.

'Three to five minutes, depending on the speed.'

I thought back to the weapons and soldiers aboard the armoured train that I'd seen. Once the enemy has seen the destruction at the station, they would surely get a message to the aerodrome that we were in the area and the enemy would come searching for us.

'We have to stop it reaching Target-1, or our surprise attack on Target-2 will be compromised,' I said.

'With its heavy armour and firepower, how?' Flash-heart squeaked.

'Who dares win,' Titan said.

I looked behind to see Titan holding a Bangalore torpedo, Spencer bomb, and kit.

'Give it here,' I ordered.

'No fucking way. My explosives were all almost simultaneous. Whereas yours were fucking late.'

'Mine was the biggest explosion,' I countered.

'Yes, you nearly fucking gassed us all.'

'Now, Jason.'

'You can't even take a handle off a klaxon, let alone…'

'*Gyereknek, a mozdony jön*,' Tommy shouted.

'What?' we both said.

'He said, "Children, the locomotive is coming",' Seagal translated.

I grabbed the explosive devices from Titan. 'Right, you two get on your high-calibre weapons and take out the armoured turret.'

'But the weapon's range is only seventy yards. We're beyond the maximum,' Seagal said.

'Well fucking move closer,' I snapped.

'I see the smoke,' Flash-heart said.

'How long do I have, Flash-heart?'

'About three minutes, but it won't stop for anything. You need to slow it down.'

'Like how? There's no time. You and Tommy man a Lewis each,' I said.

It was the fastest sixty metre sprint I had ever done, spurred on by the chugging getting closer. I didn't have my rifle or sub due to the load I was carrying against the time. Running along the left of the track, I was thankful there was a steel handrail to stop me from falling over. Half-way across, I eventually found a spot. Lying down, I rapidly wound the copper wire around the torpedo and bomb. Quickly peering up in the direction of the train, I pulled out the fuse. Fuck, I only had a five-minute fuse. I carefully inserted it. My hands were shaking, and the rails vibrated. Again, I looked up. I was totally perplexed as to why Trish and Matron were running towards me. They ran past me, naked. What the actual fuck?

A round was fired, then another. A large spotlight went on. Further shots were fired. A small explosion followed as I sprinted back to the LUP. The brakes squealed; the spotlight faced forwards at me. I immediately jumped over the rusty handrail at the end and fell down the embankment, smashing my body on the rocks. For a moment, I lay hurt and dizzy from hitting my head. I tried to suck in the air, and to suck up the pain.

The ground trembled as the huge beam cast the shadow of the bridge. Crawling out for the light, I tucked into the stone-bridge arch. My uniform was ripped. The screeching intensified as the train hit the bridge, plunging me back into darkness as the light went past. The beast stopped, as well as my heart. I thought of the soldiers disembarking. Had they seen the device? I knew I only had a couple of minutes to escape.

As I got to my sore knees, a door creaked open like the train cab I had opened in the shed. German voices started shouting, and boots thumped. I slid back to the shadows knowing I couldn't make a run for it. However, I couldn't stay here as I had about sixty seconds.

BOOOM!

The air ripped out of me, my body rippling in pressure. Cracks of weapons firing echoed with the aftermath. Between the high-pitched ringing and dizziness, strange creaking filtered in. It was the last thing I heard before blacking out.

★

Rabbit took my orders from the satcom and aborted the Chinook extraction. Under the bright stars in the dip in the featureless desert, I called the curious lads over to the Supacat HMT400. Planet threw his Elkhaba prisoner to the floor, as did Shrek. Both captives were face planting the desert with their hands tied behind their backs.

'What's spooked ye?' Planet asked.

'This goat fucking scumbag has laid a trap for us,' I said.

I harshly rolled the leader over. He was shocked at my revelation, and he scrambled to his feet. He grabbed my rifle that I had stupidly left leaning against the vehicle. Before I had the chance to work out how he had slipped the cable ties, he shot Fish in the head, and then Shrek. Planet raised his weapon. I went for my pistol. Planet's head sprayed the red mist, taking my concentration away from me drawing and firing. He raised my rifle at me, smiling in his white *dishdasha* and black turban. I knew I had seen this expression: *déjà vu*. Again, I studied the gaps in his blackened-toothed smile and the scars on his face. His piercing eyes penetrated my soul. He squeezed the trigger.

'Nooooo,' I cried out.

'Easy, boss, easy,' Titan said.

Titan came into focus; his hand was holding down my chest. I coughed up a load of gunge after being jolted around in the blackness. Titan turned on two more hung torches.

'What the fuck happened?' I croaked. 'Where are we?'

'You're safe. We're in the back of Truck-1.'

'Have you been crying?'

Titan sniffed. 'No.'

'What happened? Why are we on the move?'

'We needed to leave the fucking mess you left.'

I looked down at my shredded uniform. Frightening sounds and terrifying blurry images came back. I took a long sip of water and then rinsed the blood out of my mouth.

'Are you going to fill in the missing blanks?' I asked.

'Ten seconds after you left with *my* device, the rest of the unit came running into camp. Obviously, less frightened than you.'

'Are you going to be a wanker all night? Just tell me what the fuck actually happened.'

'Flash-heart kept bleating on about slowing the train, so Matilda sped off on his horse to see if he could. Trish said she had an idea and then whispered to Matron. Both her and Matron were already scantily dressed in their underwear. They both stripped naked and ran across the bridge. It was horrific.'

'What, seeing them naked?'

'No, you bellend, the train toppling over the edge with you somewhere underneath.'

'Hold on, rewind a bit.'

'We watched you lay the bomb and thought you weren't going to get off the bridge in time. We saw you jump over the edge. You cut that fine. The locomotive had stopped once they had seen Trish and Matron waving in the search light. Who wouldn't? They both ran for their lives back into the desert. The main engine was now directly over the bomb. As soon as the dozen or so Kaiser got out, Blister shot out the main light and then Seagal shot the bomb.'

'Fuck me,' I muttered. 'That could have destroyed me. What about Trish and Matron?'

Our truck stopped and Titan turned off one of the torches.

'Well?' I asked.

'At first, we weren't sure as we continued to suppress the side of the locomotive. The front tipped over the edge and brought the rest down like a snake. Once the dust settled, we started…'

'What about the Trish and Matron?' I interrupted.

The rear flap was lifted. I arched my neck to see Trish and Matron. Blister joined them.

'Thought you would have at least chased me,' Trish said.

'He must be batting for the other side,' Blister said.

'The what?' Matron said.

'At least we now have a better driver that won't get stuck on a little incline,' Flash-heart added—surprisingly.

Baka put his paws up on the end. He cocked his head at me and whined. Was he wondering like me how I hadn't ended up with a train on my head or at least blown to bits?

Scrap was giving orders to those that had left me to now set up an LUP. Titan checked my pulse, and I rested my head back.

'Where's Matilda?' I asked.

Titan placed the brown blanket over me and then checked my pulse, again.

'Well?' I said.

'Rest whilst we set up, boss.'

'I know when you're hiding something by now, Jason.'

He sighed. 'I'm afraid Matilda's in a bad way. Trumper didn't make it. We had to drag him over the gorge as we didn't have time to bury him with the fire going on.'

'Matilda?'

'No, the horse. Now rest, Johnny.'

'No, I need to see Matilda.'

'Matilda has taken a bullet to the thigh and one to the chest. Matron has done an amazing job, but I don't think he'll make it. Shall I give him the magic…'

'No.'

Groaning, I shimmied along and then dropped delicately to the floor. I gritted my teeth at the stinging abrasions. Trish came over with a pair of crutches and joked about me being an old man. We were positioned in another large bowl feature. The largest so far. Yet, I had my concerns with this LUP. Yes, we were hidden, but there was too much room between the camouflage and the slope to the ridge.

On the back of Truck-2, I lifted the flap. Matilda was on a stretcher. The familiar smells of the CCS at the Somme flooded me with bad memories. The hanging red lights reminded me of the scene in the back of the Chinook on the way back to Camp Bastion—memories I didn't want. I chucked in the crutches and painfully hitched up.

'How is he?' I asked.

'Wrenched from the jaws of death,' Matron replied. 'What my eyes beheld; you should be dead.'

'Oh cheers.'

'I am glad you are not, Johnny.'

'I feel dead.'

Around me were different surgical equipment, bottles, and used swabs and bandages poking out the top of a sandbag. I checked Matilda's pulse against my watch—barely noticeable. I lifted back the brown itchy blanket, revealing his trouser leg had been cut away and the blood still on his boot. The thigh was heavily bandaged. I could smell the chemicals used to clean. Matilda's bare upper torso was blood stained. Matron was cleaning it above and below the bandage that had been wrapped around his chest. Matilda's breathing was shallow.

'I have removed the bullet and femur fragments from his thigh,' she said. 'Brave soul as we couldn't sedate him.'

'Because of his chest wound.'

'Yes. The entry wound was high in the chest, with a neat exit in the lower back.'

'But his lungs are minced from the shockwave. How have you treated it?' I said.

Matron looked at me with displeasure.

'I'm a trained medic,' I appeased, not boasting.

'And I am a surgeon.'

I nodded. 'Continue.'

'I had cleaned the wounds extensively. With the blood that trickled out, I sealed the front and back wounds with grease proof paper to stop the sucking.'

'Excellent, but don't be going to have a shit without enough bagging paper,' I jested.

With her beady stare, she said, 'He is now sedated with morphine.'

'You know he won't make it without a medivac.'

Matron pondered, before saying, 'Yes, he needs a hospital, or he will not last a few days in the desert. If he gets gangrene, I have no instruments here to remove.'

What she had just said had galvanised my thoughts about her being here. Matron handed over a frayed white cotton belt.

'He asked me to give you these.'

Heavier than I expected, I first felt the objects inside. Under the light, I popped out a gold coin from the slit.

'Where did he get these?' I said.

'Sikes and Rowe had issued them to him. The impetus in bribing the Bedouin to not torture but to return each person unharmed. Matilda, Brat, and Batgirl each had a belt of fifty gold sovereigns. They are the going rate set by the Bedouin.'

That's why Batgirl had been nervous in the cave and why she had been searching Brat when we found him dead. Sikes must have stolen the coins first.

Back outside, I hobbled away from Seagal after our quick chat.

With only one crutch for bravado, I continued over to the pinky where Flash-heart was tinkering with the Vickers. His rifle was slung over his shoulder—at last.

'Flash-heart,' I said.

He went for a hug, but indecisively he pulled back. 'Yes, boss.'

'Clear the supplies from the back. Take everything off but two fuel cans.'

'But why?'

'Is the fuel tank topped up?'

'Of course. But why am I stripping the supplies out?'

'Leave the Vickers and spare ammo as well.'

'Why are you ignoring…'

'Just do it.'

'Yes, boss.'

'By the way, I'm gonna have to teach you the less stressful fist-bump,' I added.

I made a fist, but I spotted Scrap carrying the mortar.

'Later, Flash-heart,' I said. 'Scrap, come here.'

'Glad to see you are on your feet,' he said.

'New objective for you: I want you to get Matilda loaded on the back of this pinky with a makeshift canopy.'

'*Yebbo*, sure.'

'Matron is going to take him back to Ismailia as I doubt the main camp has totally gone. You're going to ride gunner.'

'What?' he exclaimed. 'Why me?'

'Because I ordered you to.'

'Well, *fokkoff*. I am here for Target-2.'

I stood away from the pinky and said, 'You mean to kill Lieutenant Thomas White.'

'What the fuck are you on about? Have you gone *mal*?'

'That's why you carry Ocker's cartridge from the temple's old man. You're here to get revenge on White, so Ocker is never born.'

'I am not going back to Ismailia.'

Scrap pushed me back. I quickly stood back into his space, my injury pains disappearing.

'Are you disobeying my order?'

'What the fuck are you about it, cripple?'

'I don't have to fight you because I would beat you to a mess, but I could place a piece of cloth on your heart. Isn't that right, Seagal.'

Seagal pulled back on the action bolt. He had been standing behind Scrap and watching like I had asked him to. Scrap turned back to me.

'Is this what it has come down to? All this time...'

'The emotional blackmail shit doesn't work on me,' I interrupted. 'Save that for your zebra.'

Scrap grabbed my shirt and spun me around, my back now facing Seagal—the plan had worked. I sharply brought my knee up to his bollocks. It shocked him into bending over. Twisting Scrap's arms over to break the grip, I followed up with a hard blow to his kidney and then a sharp knee to his chest. As he sucked in air, I foot swiped his unsteady foot, sending him to the dust. I raised the wooden crutch to smash his face.

'That's enough, Johnny,' Titan shouted.

I stopped and looked up at the faces; I had lost control. My squad knew it. Lowering the crutch, Baka trotted off with disgust. Taking a step back, I held out my hand to Scrap.

'Get your shit together, Georges.'

He slapped my hand away.

Less than an hour later, Blister and Tommy had returned from the bridge. They had gone not only to recce the destruction fifteen klicks north, but to retrieve the wooden poles for a makeshift canopy on the pinky; Flash-heart's design. Luckily, the shower frame had sat in the water whilst all the timber on the twisted metal train was cindered.

With the canopy constructed, I told Matilda what a great squad member he was and how he had saved us. I then said my heartfelt goodbyes and luck. He barely opened his eyes. Taking a few steps away, everyone else did the same to him.

'See you soon,' Matron said to me.

'You're the most courageous and strong woman I've ever met. Now go and start a family, so you can have more kids like you.'

I gave her a holding embrace and kissed her cheek. Matron was redder than the Egyptian sunset.

'I will be back.'

'I'll look forward to your shit bedside manner, Beccy.' I winked—she sighed.

Scrap sheepishly came over to me. I nodded at him to come away a few metres. Titan was warily watching me.

'Make sure Matron doesn't return,' I whispered.

Scrap looked horrified.

'No, not slot her, but resupply her space in the pinky,' I corrected. 'She's been through enough in her career. Do you understand?'

'You want me to "resupply", meaning you want me to return as well, then.'

'Of course I fucking do. I need you on Target-2. Are you sure you want to return?'

'Yes, I love this unit.'

I held out my hand, and he shook it. Time check: 05:18 hours.

'Good,' I said. 'You have until ten PM tonight to return. And don't come within fifty metres of the camp until we have guided you in.'

'Where will you be if I am late?'

'Alive, I hope. Don't be late.'

With the net pegged down, the sound of the pinky disappeared. In a selfish way, it was sad seeing the resilient vehicle with them gone. Blister and Titan came over. The warming sun was starting to rise, and the clouds were beautifully illuminated as if last night's carnage had never happened.

'Are you OK, pal?' Titan asked.

'No, I'm fucking not,' I snapped. 'Who the fuck chose this LUP?'

'Should have fucking shot him instead of the bomb, Titan,' Blister said.

Titan elbowed him hard and then raised his eyes.

'Oh, Titan, tut tut. Fancy lying that Seagal had taken the shot,' I said. 'Looks like you're going to be my bitch this morning.'

Blister smiled.

'And you can be his bitch,' I said to Blister.

Titan smiled.

'Right, with three down we need to set up an extra defence before sunset, in case the Elkhaba motherfuckers decide they want to attack our *large* LUP.'

'But it's daylight,' Titan said.

'You two get Flash-heart and meet me by my truck.'

'That cripple has changed,' Blister mumbled to Titan.

'Yes, but Flash-heart is getting better,' I said.

'I meant you.'

It had been dangerous, almost crazy, to come out of the LUP. Yet, with the dusk's mist that had rolled across the desert, the four of us had set up a wired IED perimeter with the coiled copper-wire roll. The first had been set thirty metres out from our ridge. Using the empty fuel and drinking containers, we had cut the tops off and set them below the sand. Inside we placed spent cartridges, nails, and screws. Using a cut down wooden pole, we held up the tripwire. Everything had been quickly painted. A stick in the shape of a crucifix had been placed next to each container. Then, a No. 36M Mills Bomb was placed on the horizontal piece of cross. This explosive had been specially designed and waterproofed with shellac and was excellent in the desert climate. Very carefully, the pin had been tied with the copper wire to the stick. The idea was that the partly removed pin would be pulled by the cable, priming the grenade, and would fall into the container.

The remaining task, the deadly part, had been trying not to move the sand or the trip wire whilst we poured the petrol into the buried can. Knowing the sun would do its best to evaporate, the can was filled to the top. Each wire now had an IED at each end. If an enemy tripped it, four seconds later the blast radius would light their position at night and ignite them. If they survived the shrapnel, that is. Each IED had been staggered back from each other in a circle pattern, as not to try to set off a chain reaction. A section at the rear of the camp had been left. One: Scrap to drive the pinky through. Two: if we needed to escape.

Last of all, a painted steel loop had been dug into each compass ridge. The sand had been dug away from the front slit with the edge at ground level with sandbags. Each sentry position had a canvas sheet to protect the view from the planes and the harsh sun. If the clouds dispersed, that is.

With everything set, I called everyone in. I sat on my office chair: Truck-1's radiator. First, I made sure everyone was all right after the attack on Target-1, both mentally and physically. I told them to keep an eye on their own stress and trauma levels, making sure they spoke freely. They were also to observe anyone that seemed different from who they normally are; quiet, distant, angry outbursts, restless, trembling, crying, loss of appetite, etcetera. Sit with that person and share their grief or inform another squad member. Be tactile. Lastly, there is no shame, we are at the harsh shitty end of the razor-sharp pointed stick.

With less staff, the stag was increased to four hours on, four hours off; also, back to hard routine. Trish, Seagal, Baka, and I took up each compass point on the ridge. Baka's senses were far greater than ours, and he had been trained to wake Tommy in any event.

On the map set out in my digs, I worked out that our camp's position was further south. Blister had taken us away from the aerodrome at Beersheba towards Khalasa. His thought had been that we would be out of any direct flight path and advancing ground troops. Khalasa was about the same distance back to the bridge, about fifteen klicks. We agreed it must be hostile, given that we were balls deep in their backyard. Beersheba was now thirty-five klicks east.

Time check: 09:16 hours. As I checked the area around the aerodrome on the map, a faint buzz came from the east. Through the binos, I counted eight tiny dots: a squadron of planes; I doubted they were friendly.

CHAPTER EIGHTEEN

I was slightly anxious because the planes had not returned after three hours, guessing they had landed by the station and the pilots and crew were scouring the area.

The outside temperature was creeping up to the mid-twenties, magnified here by the canvas above. I wiped the sweat again from my brow. I had nearly drunk my water and eaten all my warm and fatty bully beef. This was a cruel environment.

I began to get restless wondering what the link was to get me back to 2013. Perhaps it was yet to come after Target-2. Was this infamous Lieutenant Thomas White the link? Even if I did meet the link to get back, how would it happen? Did I have to save someone? Perhaps I had to die.

Suddenly, after hearing the buzz at the last second, a two-man German fighter had flown low and directly above. It was now climbing. A waft of exhaust entered my hide as I sighted it in the Lewis. Surprisingly, the pilot had not set off an IED. Further planes directly in front whizzed over. The lads held their nerve. The initial plane turned and headed back directly at us and dived. My finger poised. An object was thrown, the smoke trailed. I was about to shout incoming when the engine was cut.

'Do not fire,' Flash-heart yelled.

The plane banked and restarted whilst the other planes were doing the same actions across the sky. The bombs that had landed smoked furiously in the desert. Was it some sort of gas?

With the eight planes heading back east, I slid out and crawled back under the net. Tommy was manning the other HMG with Baka by his side. Trish and Blister were crouched behind the truck with rifles ready. Flash-heart was the first to come over, holding a pair of binos. He brushed back his wild blond hair.

'What was that all about? Should we grab our respirators?' I said hurriedly.

'The smoke bomb and cutting the engine at a thousand feet drill was to notify that they were not engaging but dropping a message. Most probably in a leather satchel.'

'Are you sure?'

'You are in the RFC now, not the SBS,' he countered. 'They have scattered them far and wide for us to find.'

'So, they haven't spotted us?'

He pulled an astounded face—it had been a daft question. 'And I doubt the German pilots of those Halberstadt D.III and the Bull-nosed Albatross are going to be so gentlemanly after your guys destroyed their station and bridge.'

'Oh, it's my guys now, is it?'

'If I am kidnapped on this atrocious mission, yes,' he jested.

'Wasn't it you, a member of the SR squad, who sat in the first OP over the station.'

'No, I've always been in the RFC. That was someone else.' He grinned.

'With that kind of blond mop and facial hair, I fucking doubt it.'

Taking the binos from him, I stood on the truck and peered through the netting. The smoke bomb had almost fizzled out. I scanned the surrounding area—nothing.

'Inform everyone about this, and that at 13:00 hours you will be heading out to collect the closest message,' I ordered.

'Me?'

'As you're Second Lieutenant Peter Brightley, RFC, you must lead by example.' I grinned. 'Perhaps like Flash-heart would have.' I pretended to barge open double doors and then stood with my hands on my hips. 'Hi, it's me,' I said in a gruff, boasting, and arrogant voice. 'Flash by name, Flash by nature.'

Baka tilted his head and whined in Flash-heart's stunned expression.

'Oh piss off. Get up to speed with *Blackadder*.'

Dead on stag handover, I ordered everyone to stay in position. Flash-heart slid down the front slope on his belly to the left of my hide. I called his name, and he half-twisted around. His thick blond facial hair poked out from his *shemagh*.

'Don't get your *dishdasha* caught on the trip wire,' I said.

His head focused forwards and then back at me.

'And don't vibrate the sand,' I added.

As carefully as you could have, he had crossed the IED perimeter. Any ballerina would have been proud of his moves. Instead of running, he casually strolled along with a cane that he had pulled out from under his robe. He continued to make patterns in the ground and whipped it around like the boy header had. It's a shame he never had any goats to go with the acting. I grimaced at my thought.

A hundred metres later, he picked up an object off the ground and then went through the same herding routine as he headed back. Instead of coming over the wire, he veered in a large arc to the rear and out of my sight. I waited, watching. Five minutes later, there was a whisper that he was back.

Under the main netting, I ordered for the change-over. The new stags were disappointed as they wanted to know what was in the satchel. Flash-heart had stripped off and was now taking on large gulps of water. His skinny body trembled. I proudly back slapped him.

'That was the most frightful thing I have ever done,' he said, even posher.

'Well done, but no medals for that, Mogg,' I said.

'Who is this Jacob Rees-Mogg you keep referring to?'

'Put it this way, with your build and voice, if you shaved your blond hair and moustache and wore some round glasses, you could fit straight into British politics.'

'How cretinous of you.'

'Exactly.'

Flash-heart undone the satchel and pulled out the paper. I had to wait whilst he read it all first.

'It is not very good English,' he said, 'but I will translate to the best of my ability. Invading Tommy. We Germans fear nobody in the world, and we will soon conquer Europe, Great Britain, and the world. Victory will be ours.'

'Some big-headed nob wrote it, then,' I interrupted.

'Do you mind.'

'Sorry.'

'Tommy and your allies, how badly you fight. Your Empire is hungry and thirsty. We have wine, sausage, and fruit. Give up. Hand yourselves in and join the German Empire. Do not let yourself be deceived. We will be victorious. The Germans have defeated Russia and France.'

He handed it to me. I scanned it and then ripped it up.

'They're scared of the force that is coming,' I said. 'But they will also be extra manned at Target-2. We must be even more vigil from now on.'

My four-hour sleep went quickly. Like at the first LUP, I pushed

Baka off me. I made everyone a cup of tea and handed around Matilda's and Matron's rations. Seagal and Trish were curious as to why I was dishing out Matron's rations, so I was up-front with them about her not returning. Seagal translated it for Tommy, who looked teary and began to pray. Trish put up fierce objections to her not returning. I waited for her speedy ranting to finish, including a few Italian words thrown in, and then I ordered the new rota to get on stag with me.

In my new westerly facing sentry pit, I laughed at the stinking turd wrapped in grease-proof paper at the top of my Bergan. It had to be Blister or Titan as I had told them stories of old.

I was bored of nothing to spot. The temperature had been the hottest so far. Perhaps thirty degrees Celsius. I had taken on extra water as we were nine lads down: the ambulance, Trusty and sidecar, Sikes, Brat, Batgirl, Matilda, Trumper, Rudi, and Matron. That's not including Captain Wade and Scouse. I desperately wanted the pinky and Scrap to return so we could move to the next objective. Guilt followed from our fall out. Thinking on, Scrap had never denied he was here only to kill Thomas White.

As much as Matilda got under my skin at times, he was a fine soldier. I really hope he recovers. In fact, having looked at my watch, they should be there by now, covering about two hundred klicks by the shortest drivable route.

Eating some nuts, I wondered if Batgirl and Sikes were alive. If captured by the enemy or even the Bedouin, would they be tortured or killed? How far had Sikes made it? Would his lucky streak finally end? His own doing. And, what about the flashbacks I keep having about Operation Blue Halo? Perhaps premonitions for when I returned to 2013. Was all this nostalgia to make me decide whether to stay in this era with the lads or return to my other friends and family? It was becoming harder to make the decision.

Coming out and casualty stretching, the sun was in the last stages of going down. I strolled back under the net. With no rush, I washed my mug out and then sorted my rubbish. The others came back from stag and were concerned that everyone was still sleeping. I told them to chill out and then gave Baka the left-over indestructible biscuit.

Gently, I woke Tommy. He had his crystals around him. I then shook Titan who was snoring, and then Flash-heart who was cuddling his rifle. Lastly, Blister, who had a grenade in his hand. I threw the wrapped turd on him.

'Nice prank, but ancient.'

'What the fuck?' he said. 'It's not mine. Or human.'

'Baka's,' I said.

'Perhaps Tommy ran out of crystals for you.'

'Bury it.'

'Tommy?'

I chuckled under my breath.

Needing sleep, I crawled under the safety of my faithful truck. Watching the shadows go past the slits in the aluminium, I left my weapons within reach. Pulling the grey blanket over, I settled down. I began reliving the successful assault on Target-1 and the bridge. Well, apart from Matilda being either brave or stupid trying to slow the train. I shut my eyes. Baka came in beside me, my loyal friend.

'I hope that's your rifle poking in me.'

Shocked, I lifted and banged my head. 'Trish, I thought you were Baka.'

'Oh, thanks.'

'What do you want?'

'Perhaps a treat like Baka gets,' she whispered.

Baka started low growling on the other side of the plate.

'No, Trish, not on tour. And now you've upset Baka.'

I tried to stop her hands coming in by holding her wrists. She tried to kiss me. Baka's low growl became throaty, then he sniffed the air.

'Something's wrong,' I said.

'Tell me about it.'

'No, something has spooked Baka.' I grabbed my weapons and scrambled out.

'You fancy that dog more than me, now,' Trish immaturely said.

'What do you mean, "now"?'

'Fine. I'll go with Titan,' she sulked.

'Good luck with that. Titan is as trained as me to resist. Especially Italians.'

Baka stared at me with his lip raising over his teeth. I wasn't sure if it was in contempt of me or something had alerted him.

'What's up?' I whispered.

Baka bolted up to the southerly ridge next to Seagal's sentry hide and sniffed. He looked back at me and then south again. He went rigid, tail pointing straight behind. Trish came alongside doing up her shirt.

'Wake everyone up quickly and silently,' I ordered. 'Tell them to be hyperalert.'

With the moon and stars hiding behind the clouds, I couldn't see beyond the perimeter, let alone the IEDs. Baka twitched his head right, sniffed, and went solid. He then did the same actions left. Ok, there was more than one. Well done, Baka, I thought. Tommy came up first and patted his dog. In his other hand he had a sharpened pole.

'I ought to shove that up your arse for the shit prank,' I said quietly.

Tommy's eyes glazed over as he shrugged. He was rubbish at lying.

'New plan,' I said. 'Get everyone out from their sentry pits and arm only with grenades, knives, and bayonets. Spears if they must. Sling the main weapons over the shoulder.'

'What? Have you gone nuts?' Trish asked.

'If it's the Elkhaba, we don't know how many there are. Perhaps up to thirty,' Titan said. 'One muzzle-flash would give away our position.'

'What's if it's the Germans or Turks?' Flash-heart asked.

'I doubt it's them or the Bedouin. If they have decided for a night ground offensive, we wait till the defences light them up. Then we hit them with the HMG nests,' I said. 'Remember your fucking drills. Right, two men to each side. We always stay inside the LUP. The rear north is the weak point. Guard that with your life, Titan.'

'Yes, boss.'

The adrenaline was pumping through me in bucket loads.

The same Indian sounds as before at the dunes chanted. The Elkhaba are here. They were trying to spook us, tempt us to open fire to reveal our position. They had not seen us yet, scouring the land until they found their prey.

The grenade had become sweaty in my hand. Keeping the tribal hollering in earshot, I crept low to the west side. All went quiet. I strained my senses—nothing. Baka remained ridged and growling low. Thank fuck he was here. We could have done with Rudi as well.

'You'll get your revenge for Rudi,' I muttered in Baka's ear. 'I want revenge for Haleema.'

Baka licked his chops.

A few times, Baka whined and wanted to set off. This time I was very careful not to give him the wrong command. Eventually, after what seemed an eternity, Baka sniffed the air and crossed his feet, panting. He was drained. My mouth was also as dry as the sand we laid on. Just to be sure, I instructed Baka to sniff each side of the LUP's facing desert. I couldn't believe he had taken his orders. Tommy gave him a huge amount of affection. Probably because Tommy had already lost a faithful companion.

I began to tremble slightly with the comedown. Covering my watch, I lifted the leather cap and shone the red light. Time check: 20:59 hours. I signalled for Flash-heart to join me. He looked fearful of something. Perhaps of what I was going to say, so I thought I would play along.

'I want you to go out there and count the amount of horse shit so we can ascertain how many Elkhaba there were,' I whispered close.

Flash-heart put his thumb up and started to crawl over the lip. I held his leg, shaking my head at him and raising my eyes.

'Was that a joke?' he asked.

'Even the brave SBS wouldn't have done that.'

'Oh. Maybe the braver SAS would have.'

'Bloody would have as well,' I muttered. 'Keep an eye out for Scrap returning in the pinky.'

Back under the truck, I couldn't sleep. I sneered thinking back of Trish. She was undoubtedly one of the lads. However, it was my strict protocol for no one to have sex on tour.

Turning on each side trying to get comfortable, I tried to work out what day it was. I finally calculated that it was Monday 2nd April. We were into our ninth long night. It seemed a shit load longer. I shut my eyes again and wondered what it would have been like to have all the lads from Operation Poppy Pride here. I added my old SBS squad and Rabbit here as well. I opened my eyes thinking of Ant leading our 'Crazy Bastard Elite Platoon'. I smiled. Shutting my eyes, hopefully for the last time, I thought of maid Tina Dobson.

Something pulled at my boots, disturbing my enjoyable dream. Baka growled. Groggy from a great sleep, I grabbed my weapon.

BOOOM!

CHAPTER NINETEEN

Abnormal shrills resounded between the swarm of moving flames, leaving the larger concentrated horde screaming off into the black desert. The human thrashing and weird noises on the ground came to a final mass. Facing south, Trish was the first to throw a grenade at the smouldering mass.

BOOOM!

Horses neighed; the tribal yelling was mixed with bawling pain.

BOOOM!

To the east, another defence had been triggered. The single horse and its rider were now engulfed, the animal reflecting the ball of swishing flames off its black armour. Another galloped this way. I quickly tore off a grenade, priming the pin automatically, and lobbed it high. Following the projectile, another one landed first.

BOOOM!

The horse buckled, still alight.

BOOOM!

The blast and debris extinguished the fire.

We had plunged back into the dark. Thuds raced at speed. I spotted a glint reflecting off the partially clouded moon. Shit, we needed the dense cloud. I pointed Trish in the direction. Fuck, it had found a way in and was charging to our camp. A smaller explosion threw up the sand, followed by a violent iridescent cloud of light and gases. The target continued through the thrown phos grenade. I didn't have enough time to run to the east rim and throw a grenade. A shadow emerged over the ridge heading towards the closing target. Like a samurai against a US 7th Cavalry Regiment horse, both went into battle. At the maximum of my sight, an array of shadows fought in the night. The horse groaned; the remaining form stood up.

BOOOM!

The light from slightly north of the east ridge illuminated the burning enemy. Tommy was sprinting back with his spear. Another target smashed over the fleeing fireball from the initial explosion and then jumped the withering lit body. Swirls of smoke followed the thundering horse as it was gaining on Tommy. I checked to see what Titan was doing. A huge figure stood, but instead of throwing a grenade, a silhouette of his weapon faced out. I went to shout the order not to fire, but that would also give our position away.

Bang...**bang**!

Each flash had momentarily lit up Titan with the cordite evaporating. Both targets laid yards apart. Silence fell.

Scanning my arcs, I tuned in. Only the crackling and smouldering of death remained. We were compromised.

'Trish,' I whispered, 'you and Flash-heart get the trucks set up in a V-formation facing slightly sideways on the southeast and southwest.'

She tapped my shoulder and sprinted away as I pulled around my rifle. Two minutes went by, and I knew the enemy was reforming. We were now sitting targets, but we had decent firepower. Where the fuck was Scrap? We could do with the Vickers. Why was the enemy taking so long to attack?

A large thud next to me boosted my morale.

'Sorry, boss, it was the only option,' Titan said quietly.

'At least you hit something with that shitty shotgun for a change.'

'Bollocks.'

Both trucks revved into position having ripped away part of the netting in their rush, but it was a tiny problem compared. Titan had moved position and was now covering with the Lewis.

'Well done, lads,' I softly spoke. 'Trish, get under the truck's side plating. Use the slits...'

'Fuck off, sir,' she quietly interrupted.

Hugging into the truck's side, she then entered the rear.

'I've not held something this big in ages,' she said from inside.

I smirked. 'Fucking switch on.'

The enemy were probably guessing what we were up to because it was almost pitch-black. I told Trish not to lift the side until my order. Where had the brave new Flash-heart gone? I saw his rifle poking out from under the armour of another truck. He was so inconsistent. Sneaking around the back, I met Blister. He grinned and moved his eyebrows up and down—I dreaded it.

'What now?' I said.

'Seagal passed on a message that he had gone slightly northwest to cover that side with his fancy weapons. On my signal, we mallet the motherfuckers.'

He walked away with an arsenal of weapons.

'Blister,' I hissed. 'Mark.'

Fuck, now what was the nutter up to? Trying not to get entangled in the netting, I ran over to Tommy and Baka. Tommy was pushing a steak into the ground. A lead from this was attached to Baka's new collar. Next to Tommy was his Mannlicher rifle, Frommer-Stop pistol, a new spear, and grenades. He shook his head at me, so I closed my mouth. There was no point asking Tommy to move from this position. Instead, I warned him of no more lunatic hand-to-hand combat missions.

This left me and Titan. I knew that Titan wasn't going to give up his Nitro Express and Lewis, so I ordered him to watch the rear west side. He did—at last, someone had taken their orders.

Cutting a hole in Truck-2's canvas, I peered through—bleakness. I drew my eyes back to the slightly smouldering bodies and then scanned my southwesterly arcs—silence. Perhaps they've had enough. I scoffed; this was the renowned Elkhaba. A slight breeze rippled the canvas bringing a low hum of inaudible sounds. My sixth sense told me that it was coming. Goosebumps rose.

'On my signal only,' I said.

One muffled voice below and one from the other truck acknowledged.

The only sound was of my own breathing. Weirdly, I thought something hugely ominous was out there, like a giant. Suddenly, I clapped eyes on a white horse slowly walking directly in front. I raised my binos through the slit. The horse had no plating at the front. It stopped; the low rumble in the distance ceased.

'Wait,' I said—the horse's ears moved.

The rider appeared out of the inky-black dressed all in white with a black turban: the leader. In one hand he held the reins. In the other a staff with a nasty looking sabre on the end. Through his *dishdasha* his eyes scoured the ground below.

'Wait,' I said, again.

The leader looked up and searched our area.

I calmly released my breath and mumbled, 'Off you fuck.'

Unwrapping his *shemagh* he stroked his black beard. Perhaps pondering whether to come and have a look.

'Do not fire,' I hissed.

His right leg nudged the horse's gut but didn't pull on the reins to turn back.

Pop...whoosh!

Who the fuck fired that?

The leader watched the flare float down.

Pop...whoosh!

'Oh my fucking days,' I muttered, at what the flare exposed.

Creeping back behind the Lewis, I held the rope firmly and watched through the jagged oblong gap. I was ready for the onslaught of hundreds of enemies on horseback aligned in rows. The second flare lit the rear of the army, another nightmare of foot soldiers carrying spears. I gulped hard.

'Hold your...'

The leader held his side, interrupting my order. He then slipped to the floor. A crack of a weapon echoed. The front line took off. Their hollering and chanting flicked the killing switch to pull the rope.

'Fire,' I yelled.

BOOOM...BOOOM!

The IEDs fireball lit up the other targets that galloped in. Swords flashed high. Trish was firing the Lewis fully open, but at least mowing them down. As soon as she had finished, I yelled for her to control her fire otherwise it would overheat. I continued to burst my trigger, lighting up the stack of round mags piled next to me. Those that had managed to get up from the crashing horses quickly slumped to the floor holding their chests. Red mist exploded out from the mashed heads that had kept charging. The powerful Nitro resounded whilst I changed the mag. Trish was squeezing the trigger in short bursts—good girl. Flash-heart was taking controlled shots at those trying to get out from under their horses—good man. Some of the crawling targets were trampled as another wave came in.

Replacing another mag, out of the corner of my eye an IED exploded to the west. I swivelled around and mowed the mass of charging flames. More tried to breach. Another IED went off to the east, out of my sight. The firepower increased to maximum. Calmly grabbing another mag, everything just stopped. Blindly exchanging the mag, I then wafted the cordite away. The battleground was horrific. Very close, spears were sticking out of the ground. I had not even seen the incoming.

Regulating my adrenalin, I scanned my arcs and quietly ordered everyone to stay focused. At least the wall of scattered bodies would make it harder for another foot charge, I thought.

'Everyone OK?' I asked.

'I have got a stoppage,' Trish said.

'Clear it.'

'How?'

'Fuck.'

'I will do it,' Flash-heart said.

Two lights about a hundred and twenty metres away danced on and off. Then others started to light systematically in a lengthy line till they met in the middle. I pumped my fingers in and out and took a sharp inhale and then exhaled.

'How's the stoppage?' I asked.

'Not good,' Flash-heart said.

'Can you fix it?'

'I might…'

'Can you fucking fix it? Yes, or no?'

'No.'

'Find another fucking weapon, Trish.'

You must be kidding, I thought, as I aimed at the right end of the archers. I imagined the Truck's combustible canvas catching alight with all our kit and ammo. Yet, I couldn't leave this main weapon. Fuck.

'He's fixed it,' Trish said, heightened—I'm sure I heard a kissing sound.

'One in the spout,' a voice shouted from way behind.

A mortar's familiar 'plop' sounded. I searched the ahead sky, but noticed the bows were pulled back. Arrows lit up the enemies' black masks.

BOOOM!

Tracers lit across the night and smashed into the archers. I searched west. It had to be the Scrap on the Vickers as it had been fitted with coated ammo.

'Fire,' I said.

All hell broke loose. The Vickers' sporadic firing lit up the pinky. Another weapon next to it became evident after a huge explosion, dust clouds enveloping. What the fuck was Matron doing back? And firing a cannon? My turn, I thought, and faced forwards. I mowed down those desperately trying to put the flames out.

I had lost count of the amount of mortar explosions; the battle was the most frenetic yet. Against the blackened clouds, a stream of whistling lights piled in.

'Incoming,' Titan yelled.

Suddenly, weird zipping and fizzing impacted.

'Fire…fire.'

I was going to reply to Flash-heart that I was changing a mag, but smoke wafted in. I quickly checked the canvas behind me before firing into the next wave that was heading towards the pinky and cannon. An underslung torch went on. My last mag stopped with the dreaded click. Grabbing the sub, I yelled at Trish to cease firing and then jumped down and made my way to the frontline. Side-glancing, Titan had switched his underslung light on. He stepped over the mass of bodies and fired a burst at a target on the floor. Snorting came towards me. I got down on one knee and listened to the growing thuds. Blocking out the sonic booms and Vickers to the west, I flicked the beam on. The horse reared up, losing the rider holding a sword.

Brrt…brrt…brrt!

I stepped up and forward. The next target blindly swung his weapon.

Brrt…brrt…brrt!

Still counting my rounds, I was hunched in and moving forwards. I identified anything still alive in the beam. A sub ripped to my left. Cocking my head, Blister was set slightly back twenty metres to my side. The Vickers silenced, letting me hear. To my left, Tommy was further back right of Titan, picking off anyone that flanked. I had recognised his weapon. A lone horse came charging out of the abyss. I lit it up, but it buckled fifteen metres out before I reacted. Seagal's weapon echoed. I picked up pace amongst the littered bodies, identifying the blooded white robes of the leader.

Energised by Trish breathing heavily by my side, I began jogging between the smouldering dead towards the remaining twenty or so riders who sat behind the glowing mass of dead archers. An Elkhaba jumped from a horse and turned towards Trish. I instinctively reacted with the sub. After the short burst, I was out of ammo. Trish had fallen to the ground. I ran over, dreading she had been hit. She snapped out the bipod on a bloodied horse and settled behind it.

Half the enemy began hollering and charging, zig-zagging with sabers raised.

'Bayonets,' I yelled.

On one knee, I swapped the sub for the Enfield and then fixed the bayonet. 'Charge,' I screamed.

Louder than the enemy, we charged and scaled anything in the way.

Our charge reached a clear piece of desert. Trish fired a burst from the Lewis, whizzing very close to me—perilously. Seagal was picking off the riders and horses. I dodged the first horse, but the rider turned and lifted his sword. I screamed and thrust it into his chest, the momentum pushing him to the ground. Tommy fired his pistol and a body fell on me, knocking me over. I pulled my knife and then lunged. Pushing the attacker off, I scrambled to my feet. My rifle was under the dead Elkhaba. Another horse thundered in. I took aim with my pistol, the wire pulling at my leg holster.

Bang…bang…bang!

With the last man down, the seven-remaining enemy on horseback looked at each other. Tommy led the charge, ironically with the enemy's spear. He yelled in Hungarian. Not finding my rifle, I picked up a sword and charged. I copied what Tommy had said and raced through the craters. The few Elkhaba raising their spears were taken out by someone. I didn't know who. It didn't matter. The remaining five twisted their horses and fled. The Lewis opened fire—danger close. I dived into a shell-hole, almost checking to see if I'd been hit. Trish needed a grilling.

Two horses fell with each rider taken out. Titan's Nitro hit another rider. The horse continued to gallop alongside the remaining two. Then, all went strangely quiet, except the loud ringing in my ears. Breathing hard, I started to shake. The graphic carnage was worse than that of the hundreds of Somali pirates on Hordio.

'Scrap,' I shouted. 'Scrap.'

When he acknowledged me, I first held up a thumb and then pulled up the pistol wire. Holding up the weapon, I gestured two fingers to my eyes and then pointed towards the smouldering archers. Next, I shouted at Blister to help Scrap finish off any survivors. Lastly, I ordered Titan and Tommy to keep watch.

Chucking the sword away, I returned to find my rifle. I only found the Bergmann. Cracking my neck to each side, I put the beam on and picked out Trish who had her face behind the horse. She was shaking and uncontrollably sobbing. I switched the light off and stroked the back of her hair with my gloved hand.

'It's over, Trish,' I said softly.

'I want to go home.'

'I understand. You've exceeded what I already thought highly of you.'

I lifted her chin. She sniffed and then wiped her eyes with her shaking hand, smearing the blood. A pistol being fired made her jump.

'It's just Blister trying to look brave for a change,' I joked.

She managed a half-smile.

'Tommy, get over here,' I yelled.

'Don't tell the others I cried,' she said.

'Don't be so fucking stupid. Do not bottle this. Talk about it. Except help. I expect some special banter later.'

'Yes?' Tommy said.

'Are you OK, Tommy?' I asked.

'Yes. You OK, Trash?' he said.

'It's Trish,' she said.

Tommy placed down his weapons and came in and hugged her, both sharing tears.

'Take her back, Tommy, whilst we mop up,' I whispered.

He nodded with his face still on her shoulder.

Titan and I began to withdraw. Scrap's pistol firing was pathetic to the recent crescendo. I found the leader, most definitely dead. Just as I was about to move on, the tattoo on his arm stopped me, dead. My heart fluttered. Images of the same symbol on the white Toyota and the banner above my head whilst captive came back to haunt me. Then, the face of Baha Udeen.

A gunshot snapped me out of it. I looked in the direction of the remaining two Elkhaba that had fled. If only we had killed all of them.

'Are you OK, boss?' Seagal said reservedly. 'We will not be seeing any more of the Elkhaba.'

'Perhaps not in your time,' I replied negatively.

'Johnny.'

'What?'

'I have shocking news. We have lost a chuckaboo. Sorry, I mean a close friend.'

He placed a hand on my shoulder. I turned sharply and looked at the smoke over his shoulder in the LUP.

'No, not Flash-heart?'

Seagal lowered his head and then covered his eyes with his hand.

Angered, sad, anxious, I started to sprint back. I felt sick. I didn't bother to jump the littered dead—I didn't give a fuck. An Elkhaba half-staggered to his feet. I shot him in the back—I didn't give a fuck. Reaching the smouldering net, I lifted the melted end and turned on the underslung torch. Laid next to a tipped-over Trusty was Flash-heart resting on a spear. My heart hurt. Instinctively, I shouted for a medic as I knelt by his side and checked his airwaves. Placing my hands on his blooded shirt, I started to compress his chest, but it oozed through. Holding back my emotions, I listened close to his mouth. Blood trickled down his face in my torch beam that was lying next to him.

A hand was placed on my shoulder. I released the anguish and pulled at my hair; the hand squeezed tighter.

'Fucking hell,' I said. 'Such a charismatic and good guy.'

Another hand was placed on my shoulder, pulling me away. I fought to stay.

'What a waste of life. His knowledge and skills,' I raged.

'He with God's angels now,' Tommy said softly. 'Do not suffer pain on yourself.'

I wiped my tears and sniffed. 'It was me who had agreed to him joining this mission.'

'Flash-heart told me he would rather die fighting as an infantry man than a grounded pilot,' Blister said. 'He was a brave man who would die for his country and men.'

I picked Flash-heart's lifeless hand up. Curling it into a fist, I bumped it with my other fist. Standing tall, I looked at the faces in front of me: not a dry eye.

'Before we pack up and head out, I want him buried with respect,' I ordered.

'We certainly spanked their arses,' Scrap said.

He let the mangled net go, excited at first. His shoulders sloped seeing the depressive scene. He came over and wrapped his huge arms around me without patting me on the back. Trish started to cry. Opening my eyes, into focus came a stranger. Her dyed red hair was poking from her pith helmet.

'Who's that?' I asked, frowning.

'You asked me to "resupply" Matron. This is the Jewel in the Crown, if you pardon the Egyptian pun. Signaller Julie 'Jules' Richardson from the Worcester Regiment,' Scrap said, pleased.

I shook my head at him, dismayed. 'Help get Flash-heart buried. Fetch me when it's done. I'll be in my office.'

I did not want to sit in the cab negatively reflecting that we had lost a fine man, my friend. Even when balanced with the hundreds that we had killed. In the rear of the truck, I started angrily throwing out all the spent shells and empty mags. I then began whacking back the poking through spears. Moodily aligning the ammo boxes and kit, I then jumped down and marched over to Truck-2. I caught my leg on something: Flash-heart's rifle poking out the plating's slit. He must have left it to put out the fires. Kicking the arrows that poked up out of the sand, I went around the back of the lorry and fastidiously cleaned up. After, I snapped the spears and dragged away those bodies close by, spitting my disgust. I knew I was going to lose control of my temper. I couldn't help it.

'Flash-heart ready,' Tommy meekly said.

'Second Lieutenant Peter Brightley, you mean,' I barked. 'Sorry, Tommy.'

He shrugged and smiled.

Fifty metres at the rear of the base was a formation of jagged rocks standing out of the desert. It looked like a rocket facing the sky. The lads were huddled around the mound of sand. The new soldier kept back. I snapped at her to pay her respects and get used to it if she was going to be with us. Tommy showed me some joss-sticks. I relaxed and appeased him by nodding so that he could light them. Praying and mumbling in his own language amongst the crystals and perfumed smoke, I shut my eyes and mentally paid my respects and goodbyes. I was the first to leave.

Back in the main hub, I picked up the team member and brushed the sand from the mechanical parts. The ground next to it had been raked over and the spear removed. Seagal came over and helped with the stand on a plate.

'How did it happen?' I asked.

'Are you OK with it?'

I nodded.

'Flash-heart had been putting out the fires with the water, when two riders came in. I managed one kill. My second shot almost blew the horse's head off. Flash-heart had tried to hit the attacker away with the water-can as I took aim. Flash-heart turned his back and ran. The spear was thrown just before I had hit the target's torso. I tried to help Flash-heart, but he was dead by the time I got there. The spear had pierced his...'

'Mark the spot on everyone's map with the initials, PB. RFC, please,' I interrupted, and checked the time: 02:03 hours. 'You have twenty-seven minutes to get everyone ready before I head out. I'm point-man.' The pinky towing the cannon was driven over to our awaiting convey, zig-zagging the bloodshed. Under the red light in the cab, I worked out the distance of the route to take: Khalasa.

CHAPTER TWENTY

Leading the convoy at speed, I unceremoniously ran over anything that got in the way. As I spotted the spent cannon shells, I drove over the ones that had been ejected by the Vickers. There had been no point clearing away any evidence of who we were and that we had been here. Also, it would have taken days to pick up all the shells and fragments. In fact, fuck it, let them fear us coming, I thought.

Khalasa was seventeen klicks south. If the Turks, Germans, or Bedouin had besieged the town, and they were now on route to this battlefield, they would be met with the same intensity as the Elkhaba. My anger and revenge hadn't left my system.

I was an exhausted wreck running on fumes. Leaning over, I poured the remaining water into Baka's mouth. I opted that he sat up front with me as I wanted to talk and not listen. Baka certainly listened to my woes. The recruit, Jules, was in the back with the side still rolled up. She must have thought I was mad as I had answered Baka's facial questions.

'Did you even get off your lead and kill any threats?' I asked him, and then slammed the brakes on. 'Shit, I've not had the gaming voice *'Threat neutralised'* after every confirmed kill I had made on this mission so far. Why, Baka?'

Baka repositioned himself and growled, but a smash up the rear sent us both back. Jules yelled. Letting off the clutch before I caused any more accidents on blacklight, I sped forwards. Baka appeared pissed off with me.

'Sorry, Baka, ignore my mood.'

Reaching the outskirts of Khalasa, I turned broadside on and then ordered Baka to take watch up ahead. The vehicles behind spread out. Still stiff, I jumped down and headed through the dust cloud. Titan jumped from the truck and stretched it out.

'Why the fuck did you slam the anchors on?' Titan whispered.

'You should have stopped in time.'

'At your speed. Why were you going so quickly?'

Irritated but ignoring, I achingly managed to sit in a dip. 'Right, gather around,' I said. 'I'm exhausted, as you are. Let's have no pretence about what we have achieved so far, and what lies ahead. If anyone wants to leave, now is the time to raise your hand.'

Trish welled up and slightly raised hers. The others appeared shocked.

'I want no recrimination for those who admit they're at their level. None whatsoever.'

They nodded. Trish lowered her hand and smiled.

'New plan details,' I said. 'I will take Tommy and Baka into the town, and...'

'I want to come,' Blister butted in—the squad agreed they should all go.

'As I said, I will take Tommy and Baka into the town to find a secure location for us to hide. Even if it means making the occupants...quiet. Once established, I will get Baka to return in two hours to lead the rest in.'

'You speak dog language now,' Blister said.

'Yes, better than your English. Being you're from Devon.'

'Piss off,' he retorted.

'Any questions?'

'What about the vehicles?' Titan asked.

'Good question. I want you and Blister to find a compound, farm building, shed, mud hut, anything with a roof. Any vehicle exposed, like in a wadi, I want you, Scrap, to untangle the netting camouflage and get everyone to help cover. These team members are as important as us. Without them, we're fucked.'

'What if it goes noisy?' Seagal asked.

'Deal with it,' I said. 'And I'm glad you're learning the proper terminology, not that Victorian shit.'

'When do I leave?' Trish asked.

'We'll stay here for three days, fooling the enemy that we have returned to base. We'll discuss everything that happened at the last LUP. I'm relying on the ground troops not expecting us to not only audaciously sit in their backyard, but in their castle as well. The importance of not being compromised is paramount. Greater than getting into a firefight. Use your hand-to-hand combat if you must. Each man brings enough hard routine and ammo for his duration. I want you all dressed as Arabs.'

'Who is taking Trish home after the three days?' Scrap asked. 'Not me again.'

'At dusk tonight, Trish, if you still feel the same, I will guide you out on foot where you can head back on a Trusty with enough provisions. OK?'

'Yes. Thanks.' She smiled.

'Right, no more questions. Fucking ammo up, Tommy, and Baka.'

My Bergan seemed the heaviest so far. Baka had a kit bag tied to his back. He led the way. Tommy followed with two haversacks, looking the fittest since I'd first met him. Baka leapt into a ditch that had been irrigated from the incline we had left. A small stream ran across the end of our ditch. I pulled my binos from under my robe. Tommy tutted. I had forgotten I still had his.

Four camels were tied up to timber rail outside the first cobbled wall. Part of the perimeter had been destroyed with a shell-hole in front. The dwellings inside were only a single storey with sloping thatched roofs. In the foreground, a group of palm trees rustled in the breeze. I leant over to Tommy and said I wasn't happy with this location, and we should head into the town. Lowering my binos, I pointed to a tall domed spire. Tommy inspected it with his binos. He tapped Baka, gesturing at the large spire, and then whispered in his ear. Baka moved out.

Having reached the first wall, a mutt barked from far away. The barking stopped. Tommy muttered Baka's name and then smiled. I was confused at first as it wasn't Baka. I then surmised that Baka somehow had got the enemy mutt to stop. From my Bergan, I handed Tommy a torch and explained to him I wanted him to use it against his knife to distract any enemy that came over too inquisitive—I think he understood. OK, we were dressed as Arabs, but carrying this amount of kit would look odd. I still had my sub hanging by my side under my robe as a last resort.

Checking we had been here for twenty minutes, I signalled that we were to go. Keeping tight against the warm walls to the opposite end of the compound, we hit our first piece of open land to the next building. Baka lay with his paws crossed, panting, and looking at us. I felt confident in his skills.

The dash across to him was fifteen metres. There was no time for pleasantries as Baka had casually got up and was leading us down a dark alleyway. I was a bit miffed he had not greeted me—moody fucker. Slightly spaced, I checked the building roofs and planked walkways that spanned the alley. Tommy just looked at Baka. My tours of Afghanistan have taught me well.

The maze continued for about a hundred and fifty metres. The side ditches stunk of shit and piss. A few times, I thought we had been the same way, a deadly labyrinth I didn't want to get lost in against the enemy. There had been quite a few straw and palm leaf thatched sheds, good enough to hide a Trusty. The size of the lorry would not be able to squeeze down the alley, let alone be pushed for quietness.

In the middle of a courtyard, a white-painted, large building imposed itself. The square building's second floor had a dome with a spire on top. The fully open courtyard had a space of about thirty metres around it with mosaic stone flooring. Positioned around the base of fruit trees were stone-set circles. My stomach rumbled. No other buildings in the vicinity were as tall. From our vantage point, the two sides we could see had ornate bars over top windows. The bottom had open wooden shutters showing more black bars. Leading up the tower was a small window on our side. On the top dome, a walkway went around with a handrail. This was perfect. I patted Baka.

Standing at the main solid wood and arched double doors, a line of bricks followed the outer frame and arch. I quietly knocked on the door and waited. Baka licked his gums. The town was creepily quiet, but it was the early hours of the morning. I knocked louder, slightly anxious that no one was home. There was no way I could force these doors or the secured windows. Perhaps there was a rear entrance on the east side. This time, I thumped the door. I cringed and looked behind: Tommy was remonstrating with his hands and mouthing something. Tucking in the shadow against the white wall, still sticking out like a pair of bull's bollocks on a pug, I gestured to Tommy what the fuck was up. He came jogging over. Instead of whispering what the problem was, he slowly turned the large door ring and pushed it open—I sighed when Baka looked at me.

Swinging my weapon's beam around, I whispered to Tommy to close the door and guard it. I first noticed how cool it was compared to the estimated fourteen degrees Celsius outside. Around the edges of the white-painted plaster walls were paintings, statues, and biblical transcripts all depicting religion. Each one was different, including some statues made of stone, gold, or painted.

Moving forward on the marble floor, I was annoyed my boots were squeaking. Baka's claws tapped over to the far end stone staircase. A sweet smell wafted from a door-less entrance, tempting me. Swinging around the aperture, a voice from the staircase sounded. I continued my turn and lit up the person. The target had a thick white beard with a brown robe and black turban. He lifted his hand up to cover the light. His other hand was carrying a candle. He said something in a language that I didn't recognise. Tommy spoke to him in the same language. Baka rolled over on his back and whined. What the fuck were all three saying? I put my finger back on the trigger guard and lowered my sub. The man bent down, knees cracking, and ruffled Baka's belly. I took off my *shemagh*.

'What did he say, Tommy?' I asked.

'It Hebrew for…erm…how you say…erm?'

'*Nahin natti fe salam*,' I interrupted, giving up on Tommy, hoping the keeper had understood Arabic for, 'we come in peace'.

'*Kel al-ha tabarkek*,' he replied in Arabic. 'All the Gods bless you,' he translated.

I nodded.

The man bowed at Tommy. '*Minden istenek áldjon meg*,' he said in Hungarian.

'Blimey, well versed in Hebrew, Arabic, English, and Hungarian,' I said.

Shouldering my weapon, I walked over and touched my heart. I then shook his hand. He pulled me in and hugged me, patting me on the back.

'*An welchen Gott glauben sie?*' he asked.

I tried to quickly translate his German, then remembered. 'I don't believe in any God.'

Tommy put his face in his hands.

I wasn't going to be bullied into believing, I thought.

'Not one?' the old man asked, slightly confused.

'How many Gods are there?' I asked.

'One for every human on earth,' he answered.

'Not *every* human, unless I'm not.' I was becoming bored of this shit, and I turned to Tommy. 'How many Gods are there?'

'Many…err…*ezer*.'

'He says, "thousands",' the religious man said.

'And how many do you believe in, Tommy?'

Tommy appeared a little unnerved. '*Kereszténység*…Christianity.'

'So, I believe in one less God than you. And you don't believe in thousands, like me.' At last, I got that off my chest, I thought.

With tensions running a little high, the religious man asked us upstairs. As he led, the candle flickered off the walls. I told Baka to get off his back and to find the lads. I then instructed Tommy to lock the main door after Baka and stay guarding it. Tommy moodily translated my orders in Hungarian to Baka. Was he pissed off that I had embarrassed him in front of the religious man?

The front door's timber planks slid across. I followed the light up the narrow walls, trying not to let my kit scrape the white paint. I stopped at the top and waited to be asked to sit. The old man lit candles. I was glad that the window's inner shutters were closed. He gestured to me to sit. Slinging my heavy Bergan on the floor, I sat on a wicker chair. I kept my Bergmann across my lap.

'What is your name?'

'Johnny Vince. And that was Tommy and Baka downstairs. And yours is?'

'Ah, Baka, meaning soldier,' he said.

'Does it?' I knew there was a good reason to name it Operation Baka, I thought.

'My name is Ra, God of sun.'

'May I take off my robe?' I asked.

'Of course.'

He went through to another room, the draped white sheet flowing back.

A little while later he came in holding a bowl of fruit and a gold chalice of something. I began to relax.

'Are you injured, Johnny?'

'Just a few grazes.'

After looking down at my torn, blooded, and filthy uniform, I then took the bowl from him. I was ecstatic at the oranges, figs, mango, and dates.

'Thank you,' I said.

He held back the chalice and said, 'Do atheists drink?'

'Not enough on this mission.'

I took it from him and then sniffed it: red wine. He disappeared back through the sheet. I had another sip—sublime. He quickly returned with a carved wooden goblet and two carafes. Sitting on another seat, he took a sip of water from his goblet. I crammed in the mango; the juice ran down my beard. I wiped the sticky juice with the back of my dirty hand, gulped, and took a large sip of wine.

'You join in this war?' he asked.

'Got into a bit of trouble with some locals,' I spluttered. 'The Elkhaba.'

'Please, say that again,' he said.

'Sorry, I've not eaten for…'

'No, not your terrible manners, the locals. Did you mean, L-khaba-a?'

'Yes, we pronounce it, Elkhaba. Meaning the…'

'Hidden,' he interrupted. 'And you three are the only survivors,' he acerbically said.

I stopped gnawing on the orange as the skin was a little too thick, like Ra's sarcasm. He narrowed his eyes.

'We've just annihilated hundreds of them,' I harshly said.

'Where?' he questioned my integrity.

'Ten miles north. Half-way between here and the bridge, which we also destroyed. Along with an armoured train,' I boasted.

I took two large gulps of wine and then shoved a handful of dates in to sweeten my mood.

Ra stroked his beard and then leant back.

'No one has ever survived a L-khaba-a attack.'

'We did,' I bragged. 'Well, except we lost one amazing soldier. A good friend.'

Ra scrutinised me as I finished off the wine. My cheeks took on a numbness. I shook the chalice for more.

'It's a fucking shame we had let two of them escape,' I said. 'I blame Titan for his shitty shotgun.'

Ra leant across, topping it up. I looked at the rich flow, wondering what percentage strength it was.

'If you know your history, I can prove it,' I said.

Placing my main weapon next to me, from inside my Bergan I rummaged until I found my diary. I slid out the pencil and drew the symbol. Determined, I thrust it towards him. After taking it, Ra went over to a large trunk with iron bands. I took another sip, tasting more mellow than the last one.

Ra sat back and undid a scroll. He compared it to my diary and then looked up, amazed. He came over and handed me the diary. Suddenly, a worrying thought came into my head. I grabbed his arm and put my pistol to his neck. Slowly standing, I then yanked down his robe on one side to check his upper arm—nothing. Twisting him around, I did the same to the other arm—nothing. Placing my pistol away, I slumped back down. Ra sat back in his seat, not asking the reason for my actions.

In the awkwardness that followed, I finished off feasting like a king. I even refilled my gold goblet.

'You have more soldiers hiding?' he asked.

'Yes,' I slightly slurred, 'they're on the way here soon. Can I trust you?'

'Yes, you are my guests.'

I brushed the mess off my lap and then took another sip of the fruity wine. From inside the Bergan, I pulled out the money belt and held it out. His eyes watered. Showing his delight, he put his hands together and bowed at me.

'This will help the good people of this village,' he said happily. 'Let me tell you a bit about me.'

I yawned, but not purposely. 'As long as it's not a boring religious lesson,' I jested.

'*Ger mouthi*,' he muttered in Arabic.

It wasn't supposed to have been "obnoxious". I went to tell him it was banter but took a drink instead.

'I, and the humble servants, accept anyone into this house of many Gods,' he forgivingly said.

'Servants?'

'Do not be concerned, Johnny. They are on pilgrimage to pray for those that died in the war at the railway station. Keeping the faith with the soldiers who they have travelled with.'

Worried we had killed all the servants, I asked, 'When did they leave?'

'Midnight. Do not worry, you are safe here.'

I relaxed back and drank some more wine.

'Al-Khalasa, its origins Hebrew,' Ra said, 'was a Palestine village founded by a nomadic tribe called the Nabeteans...'

My eyes started to droop...

'Bedouins were driven...'

'I know a Bedouin,' I blurted. 'And she was fucking hot,' I rambled, pissed. 'Her name was Bat...sorry, Khalida.'

As I poured the last of the wine, Ra attentively leant forward.

'You knew Khalida. Is she alive? I heard she was killed by the British Army with her husband, Imam.'

'Her horse and husband were, but she was in our unit. She went missing, again.'

'I hope she has found her Bedouin family.'

I finished the last of the wine and made myself comfortable, closing my eyes.

'The Bedouin were driven out by the Islamic conquest,' Ra continued. 'They are waging a war on the British Empire and Ottoman Empire. The L-khaba-a stand in their way. But now that you have crushed…'

'Whose side are you on?' I interrupted, as he was boring me.

'Over many years, this house of God has had to adapt to survive. To accept all religions, all people. It is a house of peace. A place to reflect. You are the first atheist we have…'

A guitar was filtering into my fuzzy mind, and it was playing awfully. I rolled on my side to stuff a pillow over my head. Unexpectedly, I crashed to the floor. Laughter came from opposite me. I pushed myself up to see the lads sitting around the edges of the floor and on the two remaining chairs. After telling Tommy I would shove that strange musical contraption up his arse if he didn't stop twanging the chords, I sat back properly. The sun blared through the window bars. I checked the time: 10:36 hours.

The conversation, or should I say the ridicule, was about me getting drunk and having a wonderful sleep whilst they had kept watch; of which I didn't believe—the sentry part that is. I had missed morning prayer and a Yemenite Jewish breakfast of bread, jachnun and malawach. Also, a flaky puff-pastry-like dough called ajin, and eggs, cured meats, and fruits. They had left me jack shit. Even Baka looked guiltily full. At least I had a cup of strong, green-coloured tea—yeah, great.

All morning, the front door had been repeatedly knocked. It had been locked after Ra had left, including a rear door. Ra had gone shopping at El Auja, a large market town thirty-two klicks southwest. Worryingly, he had borrowed a German troop carrier for the journey. I hoped the gold coins didn't bring us any unwanted trouble, like it had me, Rabbit, and the goat herder in Afghan.

It also transpired that both Trusty's had been hidden in a tributary ditch and then covered. The trucks and cannon had been concealed in a huge cattle-shed on the outskirts. The farming couple had been tied up by Titan. When Ra found out, he went out to compensate them.

With Trish and Jules bringing lunch, I started to discuss last night's battle. Trish gave up eating and went upstairs to a room in the top tower. Apparently, a shower room existed. It used rainwater that it collected, but at least there was soap. It emerged that it had been Seagal that had dropped the Elkhaba leader. His rational excuse was he had thought that cutting the head off the serpent would kill the snake. But, even he hadn't realised how many tenacious fighters there were. Everyone else added their own view of the battle. At the end of the discussion, I patted Baka and then gave him my leftover salami.

We then spoke about Flash-heart. Each remembered our best experience with him, adding a bit of banter and dark humour. I said it had been perfect timing when Scrap and Jules had entered the battle. If not, the possible outcome of more of us being killed would have been higher. In the quietness that followed, Scrap broke it by saying he and Matron had handed Matilda over to the British medics still at Ismailia. I felt ashamed I had forgotten to ask about both. Whilst I'd been drunkenly asleep, Scrap had told the lads of Matron surviving two maritime disasters. No one had disagreed with my decision to leave her. We all gave a low cheer for them. Scrap received praise for his part.

Scrap re-introduced us to Signaller Julie 'Jules' Richardson, and then what had happened reaching the base: General Rowe had still been stationed at Cairo, but he was visiting the hospital. Scrap had desperately tried to hide from him. Yet, Matron had shouted across the ward. Scrap had to answer all Rowe's questions about how Operation Exploit was going. Scrap told him Target-1 had been a success, including the derailment of the train. Matron had blurted out what Sergeant Rowe had done to Brat, and that he had lost his mind and deserted us. Matron and Scrap were pulled to a separate area and *advised* not to mention this trouble. Scrap said he would take a signaller to replace Matron, as a kind of barter. Rowe agreed. Matron had put up a fight to return to us–denied. General Rowe also denied our squad having reinforcements. Jules was ordered to bring Sikes back if found.

Scrap had turned up late to the battle because Jules had to pack. The resupplies that I had meant, not meaning replacing Matron with Jules, were never added. Yet at least we had a cannon and her personal kit. The Elkhaba battle had used too much ammo.

Of course, after hearing more about Jules' military and life background, the taunts came in about the size of her tits. She gave the stick back. Even Tommy joined in the filthy camaraderie. Next was her red hair: silky and clean. Apparently, it was a new dye by Eugène Schueller, named Oréale. This led to more piss-taking. Ignoring it, she went over to her kit and returned with a classy timber box—more wine inside, I thought. Disapprovingly, inside was like a comms-radio. I asked where the handheld mic was. It got a few laughs and frowns. I was re-educated that it was a Fullerphone for Morse-code. Jules had packed two but left the signalling trench lamps as Scrap had told her it wasn't that kind of mission.

Now that she had our full attention, including Baka's who had sniffed the box, she got out each part.

'Each operator has a clicker and headphones. Between the wires, which could extend twenty miles if necessary, they can communicate. It employs direct current in the line from a DC voltage…'

A few yawns came in. Baka laid down and placed his paws over his head…

'And by means of a chopping device and a filter circuit, the headphones of both transmitting and receiving Fullerphones…'

One by one, we started to fall asleep…

'Was interrupted at an audible frequency about 400 to 550 Hz…'

Snoring came in as she continued…

'Meaning that no call could be received unless the buzzer-chopper was working, and properly adjusted. Therefore, it was essential that the buzzer-chopper was always running whether transmitting or receiving…'

'Just show us how it fucking works,' Blister interrupted.

'How rude,' she snapped.

We all began to laugh.

'Can we tap it into the wires on telegraph poles?' Scrap asked.

I appreciatively nodded at his great idea.

'Yes, I suppose so if we have the right tools and connections,' Jules replied.

I thought of Flash-heart, missing his ingenious ways. 'Best get working on it, Jules.'

As much as we were enjoying Ra's hospitality, I ordered everyone to take a sentry position at a window on each side of the building. Seagal went to the walkway around the dome. Normal life continued around the town. A few locals still knocked on the front and rear door, discussing why the place was shut. I hoped we were not causing too much suspicion, but I couldn't take the risk of being found. Directly under the enemy noses, we were opposite a large compound that had been made into a barracks. Four lazy Turks guarded it. Most of the time they would be sleeping between eating. The gates to the compound were shut. Vehicle tracks led into what looked like individual timbered roofed sheds, twelve in total. The middle one had what appeared to be a lorry in, but no plating over the radiator. Adjusting the binos, the very end vehicle had heavy armour plating with large rivets on each joint. One German was fiddling with the HMG poking out the front. Fuck, a tank. Was this one of those that had been covered up on the train? How many did they have here? Where were the rest? On training or heading to the decimated station?

Whilst intelligence gathering, a German truck came into the storage area. Ra climbed down from the truck and went up to a German soldier and then placed something in his hand. Once they had shook hands, the German helped Ra load a cart that had rapidly turned up being pulled by a donkey and led by a handler. Quickly loaded, Ra sat at the front of the cart. The cart swiftly exited the row of garages, and the truck was reversed into one of the sheds.

I quickly shut the front door on Ra as he had entered. He was a little unhappy that we had kept the doors locked all day. He told us that this was a place of worship, peace, and offering. Ra waffled on that the locals always asked first if they could pick the fruits from the trees. Ra got the message that the safety of my men came first before any religion. Or figs, for that matter.

As Ra had agreed that no locals would come upstairs, I let him open the doors for his latest huge shopping trip to be stocked in the back room. I also agreed that a table could be set up outside the front door offering all sorts of goodies from food, animal provisions, medical, clothes, and jewellery. There was so much stuff, I'm not sure how the fuck one donkey pulled the load, let alone the cart not collapsing. I watched from the upper-floor window whilst Baka stood guard at the top of the stairs—who would argue.

At dusk, I pulled Trish away from her OP and took her to the top room. She lay on the sumptuous bed and placed a pillow behind her head, raising her eyebrows.

'How are you feeling?' I asked.

'Feeling like I need you,' she said.

A cough from outside filtered in. Seagal looked through the oval window, blocking out the sunset. Seagal entered the room and lifted off the white sheet he had been camouflaged in.

'Doing the bear?' he whispered.

'What does that mean?' I said.

'Courting that involves hugging.'

'Take your long one and clear off downstairs,' I ordered.

'So, you have heard,' he boasted.

'Yeah, I've heard you can't shoot shit with that long sniper rifle. Now piss off.'

Alone with Trish, I pulled the curtains and then lit two candles. She started undoing her shirt.

'What ya doing?' I asked.

'I think…'

'Tell me about the battle?' I interrupted.

She stopped undoing her shirt…

'How many did you kill?' I asked.

She started doing up the buttons…

'Can you mentally see the contorted bodies?' I said.

She shuffled away to the side of the edge of the bed…

'Head's exploding?' I continued.

She stood up, ready to leave…

'What about Flash-heart?' I finished.

Trish jerked forwards and started to shake and cry. Immediately, I got up and put my arm around her.

'He was a true gent,' she sobbed. 'Not like you ruffians, but just as brave.'

'I know, I miss him,' I said. 'But it's not your fault, this is war.'

'I had asked him to stay back and put the fires out whilst I helped you lot. I wanted to be one of the brave lads. It's my fault he…'

'Shut up, Trish,' I butted in. 'From day one, you have been more courageous than most, fitting right in with us Elite. OK, I was dubious that you and Matron were involved, but I'm so thankful you were.'

She sniffed. 'I'll be OK. Couple of glasses of wine, trust me.'

'*Trust me*, you're not. You need to talk to someone.'

'I'm fine.' She pushed me away.

'No, Patrizia, it's time you left for some rest and recuperation.'

'I'm not sure what that is, sir, but I could go on R&R though.' She smiled.

'You can fucking walk back to base if you carry on being a dick,' I bantered.

'Better than a twat, Private Hurst.'

As the hugs had gone around, every person was a little jealous that Trish was leaving. At the same time, it was very sad that she was going. Tommy was still crying. Trish said she would meet me in Cairo or back in England. Not wanting to show I wouldn't be returning, I lied by telling her she would be waiting a lifetime as she was too tanned and heavily bearded for my liking.

Scrap picked up her kit and extra rations, then led her out the main door. I had asked Scrap to accompany her on foot with another Trusty until out of earshot of the town. From there, he was to escort her to the Turco-Egyptian frontier border, thirty-two klicks directly west. Ra and Tommy prayed as the door was closed and locked. My heart felt painfully empty as she had been a great mate from the beginning.

Scrap returned safely that night. We all went back on stag, but at least the food, shower, and hospitality were five-star compared to what we had been used to.

Over the following three days, many types of planes were reported flying back and forth in the direction of Target-1. Perhaps they were still looking for us, or even dropping supplies. However, no number of materials they could relentlessly carry by ground vehicles could recover the train and rebuild the station in time. I knew the British Empire would be attacking somewhere else, putting the squeeze on. This made hitting the next target more crucial.

With no enemy returning here, we had become relaxed. The only significant sighting had been the remaining tank and lorry heading in a convoy on Thursday daytime. The German tank looked bulky, slow, and smoky. However, the armour and firepower were intimidating. I hoped we didn't come across any on the rest of this mission. Because it was heading in the same direction as us, I had told everyone we would sit tight until Saturday evening. Everyone was happy, not so much Ra.

Over the whole period, we had become so confident that we had dressed like the locals. It had let our bare feet repair and breathe. We even loitered in the town, and at times spoke a little Arabic. All the while, though, we had covertly checked on our vehicles. They were maintained in honour of Flash-heart. Blister and Titan had made friends with the old farmer couple that they had tied up.

Even though we were on a low threat level, I had still made sure everyone learnt basic Morse-code. It was also paramount to study our maps and clean their weapons. Keeping fit was done at night with the doors locked.

None of us wanted Saturday night to come, knowing we would be leaving the friendly locals, decent cuisine, and cosy sleeping. Even the toilet and cold shower that flushed out into the street somewhere would be missed.

We eventually loaded all our kit and new rations. After, I sat with Ra who had laid on a feast. Ra had even invited some of his trusty friends;

although Ra had warned them not to discuss religion and share wine with me.

Saying his goodbyes, Ra came up to Tommy and gave him a religious cross.

'May God be with you, Baka,' Ra said to Tommy, the wrong soldier.

Baka looked up—I sniggered.

Time check: 22:00 hours. It was time to recce Target-2.

CHAPTER TWENTY-ONE

Retracing our steps in pairs under the darkness of the clouds, we headed for the vehicles. The humidity had increased. Perhaps we had acclimatised too much to the cool church. I had set an RV three klicks southeast, a route going in an arch away from the track to Beersheba. It was the same direction the German tank and lorry had taken. According to Seagal's map, it was an open desert.

Reaching the farm, I let Baka search the area whilst I kept my rifle scanning my arcs of the huge, fenced area. The main building was in a poor state. The camels and cattle looked far better.

Baka chased a few goats out of the shed through the slightly open shabby doors. He hates them as much as me, I thought, and smiled. From the ditch to my left, I spotted Seagal and Titan making the OK signal. I motioned for them to go to Truck-2. Once inside the shack, I was about to go when a light came out of the farm building. Baka growled. He then trotted over and smelt the person holding the candle. Lowering my weapon, I came out of my hide and darted across the dusty area. Clunking came from where Titan and Seagal were hitching up the cannon. The elder appeared frightened of me, so I appeased him in Arabic that no harm was to come to him. The female came out, just as concerned.

Pacifying the couple, I handed them the last gold sovereign coin I had been keeping for myself for when I had returned to 2013. She hugged me, stinking as bad as her husband and animals. Seagal was now sitting in the driver's seat of Truck-2, and he tapped his watch.

Eventually, I cleared away the chicken and goat shit. I was annoyed that the seats and canvas had been chewed. Starting the engine, I thought of Flash-heart as it idled. The farmer couple opened the gates and wished us a safe journey. Leaving the fumes, I led first into the night.

'Could you not smell them two?' I asked.

Baka looked at me and his nostrils twitched.

'Oh bollocks do I smell worse, you flea ridden mutt.' I faced forward and grinned.

A little while later, a grim smell made me hold my *shemagh*. What the hell had Baka eaten?

All present at the RV, I went over to where Scrap was sitting on the Trusty. Calling everyone in for a briefing, Baka carried my small kit bag. I told him not to let rip again or he would be RTU'd. I handed out Flash-heart's new batteries for the submachine guns. Under red light, we discussed the possible LUP that had to be five hundred metres set back from the OP and looking over Target-2 at Beersheba. The black and white photos had been taken far above the aerodrome and surrounding area. They didn't relay much detail, only showing the size of the infrastructure and surrounding flat terrain. A shown track led further south towards the only place on our map: Akaba. This landmark was a hundred and ninety-three klicks from Target-2. Ten klicks northwest, a wider track headed towards a town called Irgeig. Both places we knew nothing about. I wish we had Batgirl here for her history lesson.

Like Gaza, forty-one klicks further past Irgeig on the same route, we had to expect that every location was heavily enemy occupied. These were strictly not an ERL to escape and evade if it went tits-up or being split up. If we had to safely E&E, apart from the Dead Sea some fifty-four klicks east, we had to get back west across the border to the trusted Ismailia.

Plan details agreed, I ordered Scrap to head out first to recce the area for a suitable LUP. Whilst we waited for him to get a good lead, I instructed everyone to re-check the supplies and the vehicle weapons. Time check: 23:43 hours. Sitting away from the rest of the lads, I wondered how long before someone in the village informed the enemy that we had been there. I trusted Ra, but his friends and the farmers, I wasn't so sure.

Blister was silently remonstrating with Jules whilst he was trying to paint the cannon. Titan and Seagal were touching-up the truck's scars. I thought of the RAF truck that Shrek had smashed through the pub garden. My thoughts drifted to speculating if the World War Two SRP had made it back. Has Planet met up with his girlfriend, Barbara Peet? The beautiful 1920s chic style landlady in her father's Art Deco styled pub. My heart sank when thinking of Churchill dying trying to fend off the swarm of Germans. The thought of my dad being the imposture Tim McNamara pulled me to my senses. I needed to finish this mission to get back to my family, wife, and the original SBS lads.

An hour had gone by, so I ordered everyone to bag up their unwanted shit and sweep the area. It was time to head out.

Reaching the designated area, Scrap came alongside and flagged me down. Concerned that he had not done the SOP of returning, I killed the engine. The others did the same and formed a defensive role. Scrap pulled off his head gear and shouted at Baka to get out. When Baka refused, I gave the order. Baka jumped up into the back of our truck to see Tommy.

'What's up?' I asked.

'Talk of a featureless desert,' he said.

'There must be an LUP.'

'I've scoured everywhere. There's nothing, except one close to Target-2.'

'How close?'

'About four hundred metres further south is a weird rock formation. Below is a building made of corrugated sheets, like something from the South African Boer War film, *Blood and Glory*.'

'Oh fuck, that's us finished if the South Africans are defending it,' I jested.

'I need to show you this,' he said.

Jumping down, he headed off into the desert. Catching up his fast-paced march, some ten metres, he suddenly stopped and turned. I hadn't been expecting his fist as it had made contact. I picked myself up, rubbing my aching jaw.

'That is the last time you insult my roots, Vince,' he said.

'It was a joke.'

'*Hou jou bek*,' he ranted, 'or I'll put you down again.'

My anger was rising, like it had with me and Rabbit in the desert when he had pushed my buttons too many times. I squared up, both ready to launch. Baka came running in, followed by Tommy and the rest.

'You know we're in their backyard,' Blister said. 'What the fuck is going on?'

'A misunderstanding,' I said.

Blister looked at the red mark on my face and said, 'You want to take me on, Scrap?'

Tommy stood in front of Blister and pushed him back. Titan grabbed Tommy. Baka showed his teeth. There was no time on a mission for this, we all had to get along and accept each other. It didn't matter about class, religion, roots, and views. I had to break the fuse, so I held out my hand.

'I'm sorry, Georges,' I said. 'I've been jabbing at you for too long.'

Scrap relaxed and shook my hand. Like a magic wand waved, everyone let go of their fighting pose and patted each other. At the back of my mind though, there was no way Georges would have another free hit like that again, ever.

I had not seen the film that Scrap had mentioned. Yet, the building below our rock formation was completely covered in metal corrugated sheets. The beige paint was peeling off. I hoped animals were not in there as it must have been like an oven. On the sides that we could see, two empty wooden troughs were situated on this side. A rut had been formed around the perimeter fence, like that of a captured animal would have been made at a zoo. Two rows of high fences with barbed wire surrounded the camp. Since returning to this era, it was the first time I had seen a decent fence with coiled barbed wire on top. Scrap had informed me of the troughs and razor wire gates on the other side. I guessed this either to be a storage area or a farm.

Back on ground level behind the mini mountain, I congratulated Scrap on his findings. In the relative shade from the rocks, I decided this was going to be our LUP. We were to make use of the alcoves to defensively hide the vehicles. The first stag rota was to take watch high in the peaks. I asked Seagal to advise the lads on the best stag positions to get the best all-round view and how to conceal themselves. Not only was a six hour on and off time decided, but it had to be hard routine, a horrible thought having acclimatised to Ra's hospitality.

With fewer people, but less vehicles, we had set up a good LUP under the normal expected time. With everyone in position, I set off alone to the right of the rocky hill wearing my black-ops suit and balaclava; also, using Seagal's cam-cream. Leaving my rifle behind, I checked my grenades and pistol were fastened; also, the light was working under the sub. I wasn't expecting trouble but expected to deal with it if it came. I also knew there would be at least one pair of eyes having my back.

On the edge of the last boulder, I focused on the fence. A rush of energy filled me, squashing the nerves. Keeping low, I sprinted across the soft sand to the first post. Flies in the pits swarmed amongst the excrement stench; strangely, human. Quickly and quietly, I moved around the fence to the east side. With nothing to see, I crept north to the other corner post. I stopped when I drew parallel to the building's corner. The nostalgic thoughts came of the building recce in Operation Last Assault.

Getting onto my belly, my heart rate increased. Slowly wiping away the humidity residue, I peered through the binos: one corrugated sheet door was in the centre of the building. It had an iron slide catch and padlock. Tuning in, silence prevailed. Not even a breeze. I questioned what I was doing. However, because of our LUP, I had to check this area, I argued.

Scanning past the animal troughs, I saw no evident droppings. I spotted the main gates with two padlocked chains, and a track heading north. In the background to the far left of the wire was a pile of something dark—unidentifiable. Lowering the binos to check with the mark one, I was drawn to the uneven ground to the right inside the security fence. I knew exactly what they were: graves.

Hoping they were goats or the enemy, I squat ran to the next corner. I was hyper alert to the farm building's door. Alongside me were seventeen graves. Four of the mounds were recent, the rest descending into age. Ignoring the putrid stench, I fixed the binos forwards north. A faint and fuzzy glow illuminated the night like a stadium many miles away. I tried to batter the curiosity away, but it got the better of me.

Tabbing north, I kept low. After two hundred metres, I tuned into anything else but the sound of my boots. The secure compound and mountain had disappeared. I was feeling vulnerable. Using the best of what natural light there was, I stopped and put my watch up close to my face. I made a mental note of the time, and calculated the time it would take to sprint back to the LUP's protection, if needed.

Walking another two hundred metres, the stadium glow still appeared warmly fuzzy. My boots contacted something. The stony beach noise stopped me. Drawing into a crouch, I looked around before picking up a rock. The stones led up a five-metre slope. This gradual ascending six feet berm stretched left and right as far as I could see. Shit, was there an enemy camp on the other side? Has this defence been made to alert anyone to the noise? Or prohibit vehicles? I swung my weapon forwards.

I was burning to withdraw but something inside told me to risk it. Painstakingly slowly, I started to make my way across the rocks. I noticed bits of metal, wire, bricks, and concrete mixed in. The noise seemed loud. In places, my boots sunk in. The nerves set in that I might have to either run back or take on a firefight here.

Coming closer to the ridge, I flinched after seeing a skull staring at me. Stupidly, I had still raised my weapon. Smirking, I lowered my sight, but soon went deadpan when examining the different shapes and sizes of scattered bones.

Driven forward to get off what I was on, I made the last two metres to the ridge. I was thankful no moon was up to silhouette me against the backdrop. Lying prone and ignoring the macabre, I lifted my eyeline to the glow. After three metres of descending rocks was a wide ditch. It was a metre deep and four wide. On the other side were three rows of five feet posts with four stages of barbed wire. I stared at the same danger sign that I had found at the junk heap at Target-1: Danger Mines.

Shaking my thoughts, I looked at the ground beyond. The ten-metre area was desolate and led up to an eight feet wire fence with coiled barbed wire on top. With the vision reducing, I pulled out my binos and checked the area to my left and slightly back behind me, in case I had any unwanted followers. I locked onto what looked like strange poles with mirrors on top. Objects formed out of hay and timber sheets filled the area directly in front. Suddenly, I was sprung into complete darkness. I froze. The blood pumped around my body. Even my swallowing seems loud. Why had the lights been killed? Staring back into the abyss revealed nothing.

A buzz came in from the west. Hopefully, this time the notorious planes will be on our side. I wish I had Flash-heart to tell me if British or enemy fighters. Even though in vain, I still had lifted the binos to the incoming. Why weren't the sirens going? Lights came on the strange objects from behind. I swung around my weapon. The low lights reflected off all the mirrors, appearing to be vehicles and buildings.

The planes whizzed over. Explosions rocked, momentarily lighting the desert to my left. Again, I pondered why the enemy AA guns weren't firing.

BOOOM!

The debris showered me. Not sure if it was a mortar or plane, I shook the shit and scrambled to my feet. I quickly hunkered down as machine gun fire strafed the area.

BOOOM!

The flash illuminated the skull. Using my weapon butt to steady myself, I decided to get the fuck out. Further explosions and rounds shattered the berm. The buzzing seemed lower than it had been at the night raid at our base. As soon as I reached the sand, a waft of burning straw hit me. As I continued to sprint back to the LUP, I glanced to my left: flames licked high into the black night; the British had found the deceptive enemy ruse.

Two hundred metres later, the attack stopped as quickly as it had started. However, I kept running. Reaching the corner of the compound, I controlled my breathing. The sweat ran down my body. Perhaps Squadron Commander Geoff Williams had found his stolen Trusty and ordered a raid on me. I scoffed.

A cough alerted me. I swung to the ground and searched my sights. At a range of about thirty metres, an object moving on the steel structure had caught my eye, like a lizard or snake waving its tail. Taking the binos off my rapidly moving chest, I focused in. I was shocked to see a finger poking through a hole where a bolt head was missing. It then went back in. Were they friendly? I imagined spraying the metal sheet with my sub.

The recent mound to the far left came to mind, I'm not sure why. Taking another look around, I decided I needed to check before heading back to the LUP. Weapon tucked in the shoulder without the light on, I stalked my way to it. Blocking out the images of bones on the berm, I tried to configure what it was. The first object I had identified was the tread pattern of an army boot. Coming closer showed it was a mass of uniforms of all dissimilar types. I crouched on one knee and pulled out a shirt showing a British Army insignia. Rummaging further in the pile, more types of allies appeared. I swung around and looked at the oven. How many of our side were in there? Looking at the graves, how many had not made it? Had they been shot? Or worse, died of malnutrition or disease? My lip curled.

A cough from the door sounded. Looking through my binos, a new object poked through. It was part of a British Cross flag. I acknowledged to them that I had understood, but a vehicle coming from the north stopped me thinking of a plan. The flag was rapidly withdrawn. Backing up and facing the new threat, I made my way back to the LUP.

Out of view from the approaching vehicle, I faced the rock formation and switched on my red breast light. Lightly jogging back to the boulder, I lowered my weapon from above my head once Tommy and Baka had stood down. I whispered to Titan to tell everyone we were on high alert, and only to use lethal force if fired on first. Whilst he took his orders, I climbed to the top of the rocks. Squeezing through a tight gap, I found Seagal by accident as I had trodden on him.

We waited for the vehicle to come into sight, but the sound drifted off. Lying next to his adapted Symien sniper suit, I looked at his mates set further to the left of a large rock. Seagal slowly faced me.

'Fuck me, Johnny, why does trouble always follow you?' he whispered.

'What do you mean?'

'You only went out for a quick recce of the building, but it sounded like you started a fucking war.'

'I reckon you and your muted mates have acclimatised to the church too much.'

He looked back from his models and said, 'Unlike the nose bagger you have become.' He grinned.

'I'm not even tempted to ask what the shit that means. Meet me in the hub in one hour if it's quiet.'

Halfway through the first stag, Seagal returned. I asked him to get everyone in for a briefing. Sat between the two trucks under the netting, I laid out the aerial photos and studied them under the red light. Baka came charging in and right across them. I cursed him. With everyone now around, some started yawning. I first asked Seagal to translate to Tommy. I then spoke about what I had seen at the prison camp and Target-2, including the plane attack.

'When do we all set up an OP over Target-2?' Scrap asked.

'Tonight?' Jules said enthusiastically.

'No, too risky,' I said. 'I want a four man on, four man off stag rota of three hours periodically. Those in the rocky formation, I want notes made of everything you see. Especially the prison camp below.'

A low groan went around.

'I'm going to head out on a Trusty and find a suitable OP over Target-2.'

'On own?' Tommy said, perplexed.

'Yes. If it goes noisy, you know your drills and where to head.'

Seagal continued to translate to Tommy, who then delved into his respirator satchel and handed over a blue crystal.

'*Isten sebessége,*' he said.

I raised my eyes. 'Right, let's synchronise our watches.'

Once we had, I dismissed them. Seagal stayed as the others vacated.

'Tommy called you a nose bagger,' he said.

'Oh, did he?' I said. 'That's funny as I'm sure Tommy had said, "God speed". He has said it to me before.'

'I am going to tell you then,' Seagal said. 'A nose bagger is a person who takes a day trip out, brings his own provisions, and does not contribute at all to the resort he is visiting.'

'It has been longer than a day trip. But yes, that's me,' I said.

Having deflected his "nose bagger" wind-up back to him, he walked off.

'Nob head,' he retorted.

After packing my gear, I walked over to the Trusty and patted the tank. I contemplated what the fuck I was doing. An old voice in my head said, *by strength and guile*. Taking the Trusty off the stand and clipping it back, I thought more of Ant back in the days of the selection process and further training. Oh, how I would love to have him here now.

Wheeling the loaded bike two hundred metres south, I went through the mundane process of starting it. My Bergan almost pulled me over. In idle, I sat on the warm and squeaking seat. I was about to make a mental note to Flash-heart about some oil, but then I realised. I gripped the handlebars and took a deep breath. I hoped that after all the kilometres that this Trusty had done, my teammate wouldn't let me down.

'Just you and me,' I said.

CHAPTER TWENTY-TWO

Once I had ridden a klick south, I changed direction east until I had found the track that led to Beersheba. In the other direction was Akaba. Each side of the track had stones that had obviously been flicked up by vehicles. The ringing in my ears was the only sound, as if I were the only one on the planet. The odd star twinkled between the gaps in the clouds. I could have done with the moon as the journey here had been slow, making sure I didn't get a puncture or end up in a wadi.

After taking a drink and snack, I then readjusted my black-ops suit and balaclava. This time I left off the steamed-up goggles. I set off, alert to anything out of the ordinary. Yet, I felt relaxed. I thought of the events so far of Operation Baka. I mentally laughed at Ra having called Tommy by his comrade's name Baka because it had meant soldier. Trying to work out today's date was hard as it all seemed to roll into one. After some finger arithmetic under my gloves, I worked it out: Sunday 8th April. We were way behind schedule, as I had planned for both targets to be completed within two weeks.

Apart from the death of Second Lieutenant Peter 'Flash-heart' Brightley and Pilot Werner 'Brat' Lowenhadt, the teamwork had been brilliant. I hoped Corporal Malcolm 'Matilda' Davies had survived his chest and leg wounds and would be returned to Australia with a home welcoming. I knew that the tough bird, Rebecca 'Matron' Law, would continue to do her duty until she was either dead or too old. As for Sister Patrizia 'Trish' Spiga, she was more of an infantry soldier than a medic. I don't think she gave herself enough credit for it. Perhaps the only positive aspect to the deaths of Corporal Andrew 'Scouse' Price and Captain Don Wade before this mission was having the extra recruits Trish and Matron. It's a shame that Khalida, aka Batgirl, has gone MIA. Yet, as a fighter, I predicted she was surviving her captor's torment.

The last member to enter my head was Sergeant Sean 'Sikes' Rowe.

What a shame the Boer War and Somme hero come hard-bastard warrior has not only gone off the rails, but off the bridge. I sneered at my metaphor, but then shuddered at my near-death experience. Where was he? Eaten by vultures in the desert? Captured by the enemy? God forbid anyone who tried to torture him. Had he found this Australian Thomas White and collected the bounty on him? I bet Sikes has single-handedly destroyed the secret weapons base, loaded up with the Egyptian gold, and was now heading back to his uncle. Knowing Sikes was dead, I shook my head at the stupidity of what I was thinking.

On the next stop, I had done a semicircle route and was now facing the rear of Target-2. I was about nine hundred metres away. No light glowed. Getting off the motorbike at last, I mentally praised it. I knew I was too far out for an OP but was too close to take the bike any further, even idling in gear one. However, searching the area for somewhere to hide the Trusty had proved fruitless. I was becoming a little anxious that the sunrise would be here soon. I would give it twenty minutes to continue searching or I would abort and head back under the cover of darkness.

Wheeling the bike further north and then west, I found nowhere to hide it. Ten minutes to go.

'Fuck it,' I mumbled.

The injuries from the bridge started reminding me of the fatigue and the Bergan strap sores. Hunger and thirst raged. Yet, at least I was fortunate that I'd had some R&R at Ra's. Without my decision to stay there, I'm sure we wouldn't be ready for what lies ahead. Five minutes to go.

'Why the fuck was the desert so featureless?' I whispered.

Against SOP, I slid off my heavy Bergan and then carefully laid down the bike. Retrieving the binos, I began to search as I walked in a wider circle. Not finding anything suitable, I knew zero hour was up. I walked back to the team member on its side. An image of Flash-heart painting the bike popped into my head.

'The canvas,' I whispered.

With the positivity returning in bucket loads, I undid the side satchel and pulled out the sheet. Pegging it down, I then slung on my Bergan and took a few steps back. Not satisfied, I returned and placed some sand over it. I even placed a few small rocks on top. It appeared to be a small dune or a random boulder. OK, up close it was obvious. However, when racing across the desert from the ground or air, it would fool anyone into another boring mound feature. I mentally thanked Flash-heart.

I headed to Target-2. A couple of times I glanced back from a distance, ignoring the plain obvious negative: I now had no camouflage sheet for my OP. Time check: 04:07 hours.

Eventually reaching the easterly-facing stoney berm, I decided to follow the man-made beach and search for an OP—no joy. Bollocks. I had two choices: fast tab back to the bike and race east, and then in a wide arch back to the LUP. Or, continue to search, even though dawn would be breaking. Had I been stupid like Tommy's expression had said?

Who Dares Wins.

I still checked around as the voice had been so lifelike, as if an old mate were next to me. I grew in strength, knowing what I had to do. It was audacious. Possibly lunacy. Not wanting to twist my ankle because of the extra weight, I slowly dragged my Bergan across the rocks. I stopped after it had become too loud. Once I had tuned in and was satisfied, I continued the laborious move up to the ridge. Prone, I searched the foreground. It mirror imaged what I had seen when I was on the west side. Viewing through the lenses, obscured shapes sat in the middle about two hundred metres from the high security fence: three hangars. Did they have trip wires? IEDs? Dogs? Sentries? Search lights? I'm sure they would because of the importance of this place. The threat alert must have been raised after Target-1, the train, and the Elkhaba massacre. There was nothing I could hide behind. For a moment, I considered staying here until tomorrow night—idiocy. Even a ditch full of dried shit would now do.

Just as I came level with the smouldering items from the air raid, I saw one remaining make-believe tank made from timber sheets and hay. It was also very cunningly painted. The pilots thought they could see the lights being lit, electronically controlled from a generator somewhere.

Back to searching for a closer and less dangerous OP location, I spotted a potential. Yet, it looked too dangerous to attempt. I continued to study the pile of metal with the binos, concerned at the depth of entangled junk with too many gaps.

A faint heart never fucked a pig.

'Planet,' I muttered. 'You're right.'

Crawling down the bank, my foot dragged the rucksack straps as I held onto my Bergmann in both hands. The harsh terrain eventually went soft. The sand was cool and soothing. I pulled up the Bergan with the attached Enfield and then manoeuvred it on my back with slow and minimal movement. My senses were on hyper-alert. The ditch is my saviour, I thought, and eased myself over the edge. I stopped after smelling the black tar in the bottom. The surface was littered with insects, and what looked like a bird and a rat. Not only did it ruin my safe route to the OP, but our squad's assault later by foot or vehicle.

The distance ahead to the new OP was about a hundred and fifty metres to the right. A razor wired high fence stood. I knew I had been in a similar position many times to make a brave but crazy run: Operation Blue Halo, Last Assault, Poppy Pride, and Edge. Would I be congratulating myself after? Or, running scared from the aftermath of the dreaded klaxon or searchlights?

With the sun rising behind, I gradually manipulated myself up onto my hands and knees to check the area. The once darkened objects had become clearer. The sentry towers spurred me on to move. Keeping low and gripping my sub, I hastily made my way opposite to the pile of twisted scrap now reflecting the warming sun. The scrapheap was now directly in front of me, and I congratulated myself. The celebration was short due to what lies ahead: the tar trench, three barbed fences, and a minefield. I had come too far, and I was committed.

Leaning back, I grabbed the first available stone and threw it into the middle. It took its time to sink, like the stone had in the Hordio jungle's swamp. This time I threw a larger boulder in, and it didn't go under. Keeping low in the protection of the heap, I found the largest of rocks and skulls, and then hauled them back. Making a line of stepping-stones wasn't that easy, the sound of each item splatting was making me anxious.

Eventually, I lowered one leg over and placed my boot on the first stone. It sank, the tar dripping from my sole. On the next go, I raced across, trying to let the momentum take me. Surprisingly, I made it across the homemade path.

From under the boiler suit, I unravelled the string around my wrist and pulled out the attached snippers. Remembering my previous mistake on no man's land, I held the wire with one hand. Taking the strain, I placed the cutters close to the post and held my breath.

Snip…

Gradually, I released the first wire, and my breath. I then moved for the one above…

Snip…

I hated the noise. Not wanting to risk another, and to be seen by the creeping dawn, I pulled myself under to the next fence…

Snip…

I scanned the area…

Snip…

Rapidly, I was through to the next fence…

Snip…

The next wouldn't cut. I held the cutters close to my face. The blades had notches in. Repositioning them, I gripped with both hands and with all my might.

Snip, twang!

Fuck, I mentally cursed.

The fence's attached metal sign eventually stopped flipping. Knowing I was becoming a danger of being seen, I crawled up to the minefield. I peered beyond the mass of junk at the gantry around the top of the first hangar. A soldier in a beige uniform climbed the outside steel ladder. His long rifle clanged off the rungs—I would have roasted him if he were one of my lads.

I got into a crouched position and hurried across the danger-zone. Even though I had been advised that the anti-tank mines would only be set off by a vehicle, it beggars' belief what I was doing. Reaching the fence, I was overwhelmed. But, looking back at my footprints, I became annoyed at the trail.

Mechanical noises bellowed out from the hangars. Not being able to see what they were, I quickly tried the cutters on the bulging fence where some idiot had dumped the scrap against. However, as I had struggled to cut, the pliers suddenly snapped. Bollocks. I kicked the bottom of the fence in frustration and the end flicked up the sand; a stupid mistake having not buried the fence. Taking off my Bergan and lifting the fence end, I pushed my pack under with my foot. Crawling under, I half-twisted and heaved my kit through. Once I returned the fence, I took a breather.

I tried not to let any objects fall as I pulled out the sharp angular iron. It was like a dangerous game of Kerplunk. Heaving my Bergan through the same gap that I had crawled, I had to occasionally release it of what it had become snagged on. I found a grey-coloured armoured hull with one track missing. I squeezed onto the remaining broken caterpillar track and spotted the German cross on the hull's side. Around the rim of the aperture were hundreds of holes, as if a section had been removed, perhaps a turret. Watching where I put my hands and feet as I crawled along the tracks, I made sure my head didn't knock the complexly laid objects above. The sun started to light up the front area outside the scrapheap. I tried to work out what was beyond the empty engine compartment right at the front. I summarised the thick sledge-shaped steel plate that was fixed to pistons was a mine clearing adaptation or a trench cutter. I cautiously checked inside the hull. Most of it had been robbed. There was just enough room for me and my kit.

The soldier on the rear corner gantry was covering the glinting search light with a tarpaulin. As the heat continued with the rising sun, I managed to put my Bergan and rations behind me. I left the note making items in the small gap to my side. The unenjoyable part was the odour from the trench tar and the new oil and grease I'd had to crawl through. At least if any mutts came patrolling, I would smell like the shit I was in. I was fortunate that a plane wing was directly above, giving me shade from the sun.

With tiny movements, I cleared away objects that had obscured my view. To break up the light behind me, I placed a piece of hessian at the back of my head. It had sat at the bottom of the vehicle, still damp from a down-pour. Not only was it a fantastic OP, but the effort to get here had matched it; although, slightly surreal. I mentally thanked Planet. Time check: 06:36 hours.

At the front of the base was a set of wire-meshed gates with barbed wire on top. In front of these was a lift-up security steel bar. Perhaps a railway track like the one I had planned at our base. In fact, studying the layout, it was almost identical to my design. It even had sandbagged emplacements set to each side in the foreground of the gates, and two further out in the desert. On the extremely far right of the fence were another set of unmanned gates. There were no wooden sentry towers, but I presumed there were snipers set on the roof. Beyond each berm's side that I could see, there was no way you could approach the open desert without being seen. Unless, in the pitch-black.

Every two hours, the sentry on each corner of the south side gantry had swapped duty. Both had met another two on ground level that had jogged around from the east side. Thirty minutes later, three German vehicles in similar shape to the British Pierce-Arrow came from the front of the Hangar-1. The enclosed top turret swivelled with its weapon. The front durable rubber tyres made light work of the sand due to its standard wheels having ribbed steel wheels bolted to the side like exaggerated hub caps.

Jotting notes as they split into different directions, the first one stopped, and the side hatch opened. Three of the crew got out wearing slightly different Turk uniforms to the guards. Out climbed another soldier with a broom. What were they up to?

The sweeper hurriedly began brushing the sand. Oddly, a large semi-circle, beige painted plate with oblong holes was slid around to the other half. Even more surprisingly, three soldiers quickly climbed out and jogged to the armoured car. The new crew scaled down and the steel hatch was swung back across by the sweeper. He then lightly covered the steel plate in sand.

As the vehicle's doors shut, the car did a U-turn. I panned across to the other two positions. The armoured trucks were doing the same. It was difficult to see these other underground bunkers.

Just as I was deciding what the dugouts were, the one closest started making a grating noise. From the front plate, two doors slid apart, and an object was mechanically wound out: a pom-pom AA gun. No sooner than it had stopped, it swung in a complete circle. The others did the same. Then, it was wound back in, and the hatches shut. Although impressed, I now knew what professional soldiers and weapons we would be up against.

Finishing my lunch of the original mission's shite we had started out with, I washed it down with warm water. Like the warm rations, I was beginning to cook in the confined space. I wondered if it was such a clever idea to leave Ra's generosity, especially the fruity red wine.

A roar of engines started out of my view. Smoke bellowed above the roof. I had heard that sound before, almost crossing my fingers that it wasn't. Out clunked the four superiorly heavy-armoured tanks. Large-riveted plates covered in a kaki pattern of brown and beige added to its mean look. They conformed into a convoy but stopped after a hundred metres, half the distance to the main gates. One operator came out from the guard room and wound a huge handle with both hands. A section of the tar ditch became ground level, the tar oozing off the side. The tanks moved off and each side gunner spurted a huge jet of flame.

Ten minutes after the last one had trundled across the raised platform, silence fell. It was disturbed by three large troop carriers driving to the gates. All were heavily laden with German and Turk infantry. A smaller vehicle about the size of our ambulance sped across from the hangar. It stopped and one of the Germans leant out. A chasing black mutt jumped into the covered rear. Instead of the vehicle following the dust cloud of the lorries, it turned left and headed south towards our LUP. The gates were closed, and the bridge lowered.

Except for the changeover, nothing much had happened since the whirlwind of activity. Then, I heard plane engines roar. One by one they came up from behind the hangars and headed directly north. Eight fighters in total. On the max of my eyesight, they split and started to return. I double-checked the cover above me. As they raced across my position, I thought of our LUP. A new and louder drone started. Hairs on my neck raised. Four huge bombers took off. The fighters came screaming back across and they followed close to the bombers, all heading north.

I was just finishing scribbling away all the details and times when another vehicle headed out from the hangar. The open truck was like a coal lorry. It drove across to the furthest gates. A train whistled from out of sight. Had they repaired the train bridge already? Surely, they couldn't have repaired the train that we had derailed. Three men in boiler suits debussed from the truck. Two of them started to drag a timber board. The remaining man opened the gates, and they all returned to the cab.

Almost thirty minutes boringly trickled by. I couldn't help but wish for whatever was happening, to happen. Though, I had to be careful what I wished for. Wiping my eyes, I re-focused to confirm what I thought I had seen: a small flatbed truck pulling three flatbed carriages and a small train carriage to the rear. The mini-train turned into the base and the gates were immediately shut. Out piled two of the lorry crew whilst the rear carriage debussed with four German soldiers on one side and four the other. The soldiers all took up a defensive role. The lorry's crane was manually moved to the first flatbed where the parts were attached. The scrap looked like the train parts that had nearly fallen on my head. This was repeated till the mini-train was empty, and then it silently left the base. The gates were shut, and boards covered over the rail. Time check: 17:18 hours. Good, exactly one hour to the start of sunset. I was becoming stiff and needed a toilet.

The infamous bombers began to return with the fighters flying overhead. The tanks were heading back in from the west. Suddenly, I was drawn back to the immediate threat: the flatbed lorry. It had stopped to my right. My eyes drew level with my hide's rim. I was breathing shallowly. Two armed workers disembarked and started to pull some of the objects out of the heap. The plane wing above slid down a foot. With their manual crane, they unloaded the large pieces of train. The scrapheap crunched down under the weight.

Once the main haul was unloaded, they began throwing the wheels and unidentifiable objects from the truck. They found it amusing who could throw the farthest. A couple of times the fence rattled behind me. I thought of the consequences of one landing in the minefield.

The truck started moving off, only to come to a stop directly opposite me. The driver got out with a toolbox and walked my way. I had sunk into my hide, feeling blind for my weapon.

CHAPTER TWENTY-THREE

Three shots were fired in succession. The workers continued to move objects around the front; I was in the fear-zone. The metal on metal vibrated through the main body I was sitting in. The loudest bang made me jump. Two of the workers began shouting in Turkish. I quietly cocked the pistol and went over in my mind their positions and how I would react.

Eventually, the third person calmed the other two arguing. They began doing something at the front with their tools. Why hadn't they or anyone else reacted to the three rounds that had fired from south? Surely if my squad had been compromised, the whole base here would have erupted, including our LUP. The hull I was in shook. Beads of sweat dripped from my face onto my gloves. Further grunting, groaning, and cursing followed the rhythm of the shuddering. Something heavy landed on my arched back, winding me. I screwed shut my eyes and gritted away the pain. Jubilation arose as they had removed whatever they were trying to get off. Smaller objects rained down on me as the workers heaved the item away.

Even though the truck had begun to head away to the main building, I stayed still with my weapon cocked in my hand. However, after waiting a few minutes of being entombed with the weight on my back, I stealthily raised. Upright on my shins, my head touched the wing above. More objects fell, rattling and clunking. I searched the gantry sentry and then the underground gunner crew for any signs they had heard it.

With the sun causing strange shadows as it set, I pulled around the heavy item they had thrown in: a piston ram. Carefully, I laid it on the track and rubbed my back.

Because the scrap above and around had moved and become entangled, it had taken me five minutes to stealthily get to the fence. Closing the fence down, I pulled my Bergan on and grimaced at the bruised back muscle. Some of the scrap had indeed fallen into the minefield—stupid pikeys.

My tracks were almost impossible to see as the moon was not at its brightest in the cloudless sky. I hated the thought of rushing across the minefield, but I had to urgently return to the LUP to discuss a new OP to have eyes on the inside of the hangars and the north side. Congratulating myself on my observation notes boosted the first step into the minefield, placing my feet in the footprints. Across it, I rapidly followed my trail through three cut fences. Lastly, I skipped across the almost sunk stones. Hugely relieved, I bounded up the stones and down across the other side of the ridge. As soon as I hit the sand, I turned left and tabbed at speed to the Trusty's position, passing the fake tank.

Riding a more direct route back, I was careful not to potentially get a puncture. Yet, I was excited to discuss surveillance notes with the lads.

Set back east from the LUP, I waited for the return flashes. When they did, I wheeled the bike in. Titan came jogging over as I lent the Trusty against the rocks. I quietly thanked it for getting me back. Titan gave me an embrace and slapped me hard on my backpack, adding to the already painful injury.

'Why is it when you return from a reconnaissance, you stink like shit?' he asked.

'Yeah, I'm fine. And nice to see you, too,' I said sarcastically.

He shifty looked at the ground.

'What's happened?' I asked.

'You're not going to believe this, but Captain Cock has called a halt to this mission.'

I had told him about a US Marine I named Captain Cock on the Globetrotter. Titan thumbed over his shoulder to the trucks.

'What's he doing?' I said.

'He's battering my bollocks.'

'Get your own fucking saying.'

I was shocked to see an eight group of gaunt soldiers scruffily dressed in a mismatch of uniforms. They were huddled by the German ambulance, all not under the netting. Scattered around were empty rations, and they were still feasting. I ripped off my balaclava.

'What the fuck is going on?' I loudly whispered.

A few confused faces looked up. Some were even worried.

'*Corporal* Johnny Vince,' he said, emphasising his French accent on my rank.

'Captain Cock?' I asked Titan.

Titan nodded.

I turned back to the shabby soldier coming towards me.

'You will address me as Adjutant Phillipe Clemenceau. You will salute to an officer in the French Foreign Legion.'

'Salute to a private in the Royal Fusiliers,' I said.

Captain Cock looked at his shirt insignia.

'OK, you can drop the crap French accent,' I added.

'How very dare,' he snapped. 'My men have managed to scrounge these rags from the top of the pile.'

'*British* "rags", hey,' I calmly said.

'You and your men will find our uniforms and bring them to me.'

'Oh, is that right?' I softly said. 'How's the *British* food?'

'*Dégoûtant.*'

Baka growled from the side of him.

I itched my beard, not having a clue what he had said.

'I am relieving you and your unfit men from their unwarranted duty, and confiscating your vehicles. You will return to your base in the German ambulance.'

I stared hard at him.

'You will salute me when I…'

I thumped him hard in the face and then stood over him as he went to ground. 'You can fucking slate the food and clothes, but not my lads. Titan, time for the magic medicine.'

'Pleasure, boss.'

I slung my Bergan down, leaving Titan to help Captain Cock rest his arrogant French gob.

'Right, who the fuck is next in charge?' I said.

A scrawny lad stood and gingerly came over. He reminded me a little of Sameer in Operation Last Assault. The lad wiped the sweat and food from his tanned skin. Titan came over, standing huge over the lad.

'Done, boss,' Titan said.

'Get the lads back in for a briefing,' I ordered.

'Yes, boss.'

'You kill him?' he asked in an Arabic accent.

'Probably,' I joked. 'Right, you know how to fire a weapon, so…'

'No speak English,' the lad interrupted. 'They French.'

'Fuck, you stink,' Blister said.

'With the help of this lad, Blister, get this lot to clean their shit up in our LUP. And then get them on stag,' I ordered. 'But with no weapons,' I whispered close.

'Yeah, I'm fine. Nice to see you, too,' Blister replied with sarcasm. 'What happened to the French twat?'

I left Blister and walked over to Truck-1, Baka sniffing at my odour. 'Don't you say a word, Baka.'

Snacking on rations and water, I was still annoyed at how much stock had gone from these seven Foreign Legion and one Arab boy. Also, the mess they had left. I began stripping down my weapons to clean. My unit returned as I had finished reassembling. Firstly, I asked what the hell had gone on. It transpired that Seagal had set up an OP on the east side of the prison. Titan had taken to the rocky hills. Jules had set up communication wires between both. Throughout the day, nothing had happened at the prison until the German ambulance arrived. Two Germans got out with a mutt who was then tied to the fence by a rope. After the gate was opened, one armed soldier scattered two crates of rotting fruit. The other poured a five-gallon metal urn of water into each trough.

Once the feeding had been completed, the mutt was untied but held. The other soldier had his rifle raised at the door to the prison. Unlocked, they had beckoned for the Arab boy to appear, but he hadn't. Captain Cock dragged the lad out and then went back inside, shutting the door. The lad was smacked a few times with the weapon butt, and then moved to the fence. Taking a few steps back, the German raised his rifle. The lad shut his eyes. Seagal hit a coded message through the Fullerphone. He then immediately took the shot, killing the executioner. Titan, in that split-second, killed the guard and mutt. Blister, Tommy, and Baka ran into the camp ordering the prisoners out. Whilst the prisoners scurried to put clothes on from the pile, the dead enemy were dragged inside the prison. It had been Jules who had helped the traumatised Arab lad still clinging onto the fence.

Once the compound and building were locked, the ex-prisoners were escorted around with the German ambulance. It was then that Captain Cock made himself leader. He dished out the food and water and asked many questions about our mission. Of course, he was told a pack of lies. I was more fuming that my squad let him muscle in. Lesson learnt.

The reason the lad had been facing the firing squad, like many British and French had so far, was that he had been found sneaking off at night to feed the captives extra food, water, and blankets. He would crawl under the outer fence and bend back a corner of the metal sheets—and that's the thanks he had got when Captain Cock pushed him out to the awaiting firing squad. I now knew why the enemy base had never reacted to the three shots fired, thinking it was the German firing squad. According to Blister, the French had not escaped because they thought there was no way they would make it across the desert without food and water with no weapons to take on any enemy.

The story continued that the prisoners had been captured at the base by the sea. The same one we had commandeered for ourselves and had left the ambulance at. The Foreign Legion were passing by and walked straight into a trap as the British had been killed, except a handful. They had been in the prison for two months. Those that hadn't died of starvation, dehydration, disease, or heat exhaustion, were put to work at the base. If any collapsed, they were shot at dusk.

I asked Blister to go and fetch the lad and some treats. Gingerly, the lad came into the group. Blister handed him a tin of mints and a cup of rum, the alcohol we were not allowed to drink until the return journey in friendly territory—my strict orders. Grinning like Sameer had, the boy feasted. He refused the rum. Blister went to drink it but caught my glare. The lads' mouths were open, mentally tasting it. Instead, Blister chucked the rum at the wheel. Baka sniffed it and licked it off.

'Lucky fucker,' Titan said.

'Pour some on your nob, fella,' Blister said to Titan. 'You've not had any crumpet for ages.'

'That's because you interrupted me and Chantal at the café in Rouen, you fun flannel.'

'Ah, the Marilyn Monroe lookalike,' Scrap said.

'That's a fun *sponge,* Titan,' I said.

We all sneered.

'What's your name?' I asked the lad.

'I will tell you. My name is Jamil Seif. I am nine.'

'Tuck in, Sameer.'

He frowned. 'I will tell you. My name is Jamil Seif.'

'I know, Sameer,' I said, and smiled.

The lads chuckled.

I pulled around my notes and sketches and told them in detail of everything I had seen. They all made their own records. Once they had finished, I then showed the next part of my plan: an OP on the north side. We had to see the defences on all sides and what was on the inside of the hangars. Sameer started to snigger, but he saw my glower.

'Something to add, Sameer?' I asked.

'I will tell you. Your plan camel shit. You all die.'

I snatched the mints off him, the others tried not to laugh.

'And why's that?'

'I will tell you. Tomorrow they leave and attack British with locomotive, tanks, planes, and men.'

'Fuck. Tomorrow,' I muttered. 'How can we trust you?'

'I will tell you. I come from Al-Khalasa. My…'

'Do you know Ra?' I interrupted.

'Yes.'

'Lovely geezer, and good for wine,' I reminisced.

'Hey,' Seagal blurted. 'You drank wine that evening. Yet, your strict orders were that we were not allowed alcohol on this mission.'

'Yes,' Tommy added, 'I have no wine.'

'Ah, but it was a holy night,' I said.

'But you are not religious,' Scrap snapped.

'Sorry, Sameer, you were saying before these lads rudely interrupted,' I said.

'I will tell you…'

'You don't have to fucking keep saying that at the beginning of each sentence,' Blister said.

'My father and mother killed by Germans,' Sameer continued. 'Germans save me if I come here. To work.'

I scowled at Blister whilst Titan shook his head in disbelief at him.

Blister sunk back, uncomfortable with his last remark.

'Carry on, Sameer,' I said.

'I work in camp nine months. I want to go home. My grandparents work on the farm.'

I scowled at Titan.

He sunk back, uncomfortable that he had tied them up.

Blister smugly smiled at Titan.

'Before you go home, I want to know everything about that base,' I said.

As Sameer had finished discussing everything at Target-2, I asked Seagal to give him one of the coins. Seagal tried to look innocent that he had none. I pressed harder. Begrudgingly, Seagal handed one to Sameer. Sameer cheekily held his hand out for another, like the goat herder had in Afghan when I was buying his goat. I nodded at Seagal to do so. As soon as Seagal had handed it over, Sameer sprinted off.

Inspecting my notes, I was a little apprehensive of not only what we were up against in the way of their security and defences, but also the bunk houses accommodating vast enemies. We didn't have enough explosives to hit the number of planes and tanks at the base. If Sameer was telling the truth, that is.

'So, boss, what's the plan?' Scrap asked.

'Jules, can the Fullerphone wire be fitted to a Bangalore Torpedo and then a charge sent down it?' I asked.

'Each wire that spans over…'

'Yes, or no?' I interrupted.

'Yes, if the Torpedo is fitted with an electric blasting cap.'

'Can we lay wires to multiple explosives, setting them off simultaneously from a distance?'

'If the current was wired up to multiple batteries connected to…'

'Yes, or no?'

'That would take a lot of planning,' she answered.

'What the fuck are you waiting for? Go, before the big bad wolf gets you,' I said.

She inquisitively stared.

I pulled at her red hair.

'Little Red Riding Hood was a European tale…'

'Shut fuck up, Seagal,' Tommy said—we burst into laughter.

'How are we going to get all the equipment into the base with the amount of security?' Scrap asked.

I stared at the German ambulance, and then grinned. 'The last thing they would expect.'

'You mean go in through the front door,' Blister said. 'That's fucking mental. I love it.'

'I love being in the Elite,' Titan added.

'Titan and Blister, you work with Jules to get those Torpedoes set with an electric blast cap. Seagal, Scrap, and Tommy, fucking ammo up. Baka, have a shit first this time before you sit in the ambulance.'

Once ready, we again went over the positions to set the explosives devices, three in total. After double-checking our kit, we loaded up the German ambulance. I found the next Foreign Legion soldier who could speak a little English, as Captain Cock had been bound and tied. I told him the defensive plans if he heard the shit hit the fan. I especially underlined not to fire the Lewis on us—I think he understood.

Dead on midnight we set off with Jules staying behind with the detonator in case we did not return. This was the most daring mission to date.

CHAPTER TWENTY-FOUR

The flat featureless desert helped us to lay the wires on the ground from three spools rotating on Tommy's prize Elkhaba spear situated from the back of the ambulance truck. Seagal had to keep the speed a slow place, making the mission edgier. Even Blister's eyes looked concerned against his cam-cream. We had chosen Seagal to drive as he could not only speak particularly good German, but also he looked a convincing German in the uniform we had stolen from the dead. The other German upfront was Tommy. He also looked European, but could only speak a little German. According to Sameer, the dead enemy mutt had been pinched from a local village, so I had teased Baka for looking like the stray he had to impersonate.

Turning the vehicle to face the manned gates, Scrap kept the wires apart with two canes. Once we had slowly driven forwards, he ducked back behind the tailgate and made sure the wires continued to flow from the inside drums. I was getting concerned that the speed of the ambulance was not normal.

Titan squeezed my shoulder as we drove past each sandbagged HMG emplacement in the desert. Titan then slowly breathed out. Had they even been manned? We continued in first gear through the cut out in the stony berm, and then stopped. Waiting for the bridge to raise, I kept one of the desert defences in my sights. Titan the other. Driving across the platform, the not so nostalgic smell of the tar wafted up. We drove across to the main gate.

'Both nests are manned to the left and right,' Seagal quietly said. 'Fingers crossed.'

Titan checked his Nitro Express again, and then looked at me. I pulled a crazy face at him; he and Blister smiled and shook their heads.

The fenced-off minefield area was to each side. We stopped. Titan put his thumb up. I knew we were at the steel bar barrier and sentry block.

'*İyi akşamlar,*' the guard said.

Fuck, he's a Turk.

'*Hallo. Bitte* öffnen *Sie,*' Seagal said.

Seagal had asked to open the gate, but the guard was coming closer. I raised my main weapon. Scrap withdrew his knife; we were on that edge. The guard came right up to the passenger window, Tommy's door.

'*Çirkin köpek kimin?*' the guard asked, slightly amused.

Baka growled. Tommy and Seagal remained silent.

'*Nerede diğer köpek?*' the guard asked, agitated.

I aimed at the rear of the HMG post. Titan and Blister did the other.

'Scrap, *Komm her,*' Seagal said.

There was a grunt and a scuffle. The Turk started to raise his voice. Scrap jumped out of the back. Within a couple of seconds, the guard went quiet. Dragging filled the empty void, followed by the bar raising. Titan moved to the drums and made sure the wires flowed as we drove through. The barrier went down. The mechanical winching noise told me that the gates were being opened. The tar bridge in the foreground was now being lowered.

Inside the base, I felt almost defenceless against the superpower that we were up against. Then, I remembered this is what the Elite do. Why was Scrap taking so long to close the gates? I looked at the ground. The wires were laid over the gate's steel wheel channel, something I had not calculated for. Bollocks. Had he seen the problem? If the gate closed, the wires would be damaged. If not closed, it would cause suspicion to the other security guards.

'Seagal, you and Tommy must take out the two machine gun nests. I need to make sure Scrap doesn't close the gates,' I whispered, through the bulkhead.

Seagal translated it to Tommy.

'If it goes tits-up, get this truck out and pick us up in the desert,' I hushed to Titan.

He nodded.

Tommy and Seagal walked casually past the rear with Baka leading the way. Both had fixed their bayonets. I used their cover and then darted into the guard room. Two bodies lay on the floor in the dimly lit room. One was the gate guard. Another was slumped over the HMG. Blood dripped from Scrap's knife sheath. He pointed out the small window aperture.

'I cannot close the gate on the wires,' he said.

'Brilliantly observed, Scrap,' I said. 'I'd not seen the floor channel from my OP.'

'We need to take out the two enemy positions at the front,' he said.

'I've already arranged it, that's why I'm in charge.'

'Perhaps not forever.'

I didn't like the tone he had said it in, but was more preoccupied with Baka who had entered and was sniffing each dead guard.

I asked scrap to close the gates when I had moved the wires to the centre, and then to wait for my signal to stop. Baka trotted out; I followed him back to the truck. Out in plain sight, I carefully moved the wires to the centre of the runners and then climbed back aboard. Titan was mightily relieved having waited in silence to what was happening. Scrap wound the gates closed, and I signalled for him to stop. Seagal started the engine and told me that he and Tommy had silently killed both crew, one nest at a time. Baka had been the distraction.

Scrap sprinted left, keeping tight to the inner security fence. As we drove a hundred metres in, half-way across to the hangar, I had lost sight of him. Like the rest of us, Scrap had a dangerous role in the next part of the job. I was hoping the gantry sentries couldn't see him or that the gates were slightly open.

Knowing where this ambulance would normally park, we drove into Hangar-1. The place was softly lit. Footsteps came across, and a German asked where they had been. Seagal started to reply why they were running late because of some trouble with the prisoners. Then, the conversation stopped. Tommy immediately came around the rear and nodded. I took the spear from the reels and carefully handed him a drum. Titan quietly jumped down and took the other reel from me. Baka followed Tommy who had headed out the main entrance towards Hangar-3.

Titan unravelled the wire, Seagal having his back. With Hangar-2 as their key objective, I silently climbed down whilst Blister scanned his arcs. The blood drips across the floor hadn't bothered me, but the rows and rows of pallets of aerial bombs did. Each one had the identical marks on as the bowser at the station.

Tapping Blister on the shoulder, I started wheeling the drum to the rear of the hangar, staying close to the side. Kneeling next to the dead German wearing a boiler suit, his throat was cut. I was surprised to see the inner wall was not made of the outside metal cladding, but of a heavy stone like the station's fortress at Target-1. Blister began to creep forwards with his weapon tucked in his shoulder, scanning the number of weapons and ammunition. Sameer had played this down. I knew Blister wouldn't open fire if he spotted the enemy, unless fired upon. The objective was crucial, but not paramount to our own lives. I still have to re-educate them since we have returned from the Somme.

Blister stopped. We were back-to-back. I waited. Footsteps on the gantry above walked in the direction we were heading. They headed down the stairs. Even though we were in the shadows, it was unbelievably tense having my back to it. My heart pounded, but I had to trust in Blister to deal with it if it became a threat.

My shoulders eventually relaxed as the boots squeaked off into the distance. I turned towards Blister who lowered his weapon and leant over close to my ear.

'Shrek was right in Poppy Pride,' he almost silently said. 'You can always hear the Germans.' Blister tapped the felt on his boots, nodding at my idea.

Sentimental conversation over, he continued to the target. He only stopped to move any objects that I might inadvertently knock. Reaching the mark, he silently slipped off his Bergan. He came around the front and took the drum off me. I nodded at the lights in the office in the far corner. Cigarette smoke came from the doorway.

'Klaxon,' he mouthed.

I studied the alarm and remembered the one Tommy had set off at the ERL. I rapidly undid my Bergan and took out the bomb and torpedo.

'Let's hope the Jesus Hungarian hasn't any near him when he sees the planes in Hangar-3,' Blister said facetiously.

I sharply shook my head at him, wanting him to not jinx it.

Set in a brick-built shelter was supposed to be a huge fuel tank that was used for refuelling flamethrower back-packs. At one end was a set of large tubes and valves. The front had an angle-ironed reinforced wire gate. The clasp was padlocked. Fuck. Blister grinned and then smugly took out a pair of croppers. He gave me the wanker sign and then whispered close he wouldn't lose them like I had my spanner. Not being able to verbally retaliate, I waited till he gripped the padlocked in the jaws. I signalled for him to stop and took off his balaclava. Then mine. He looked confused. I wrapped it around the cutters and lock, quickly giving him the wanker sign before tightly holding it. His half-blacked out face screwed tight. The tremors shook my hand.

Click!

The sound was worse than I had expected. We froze as someone came to the door and looked across the hangar.

'*Verdammte Ratten*,' he said.

The guard took one last look before going inside.

Together, we took away the balaclavas and made sure the padlock bits didn't fall. I looked at my watch, time was ticking for us to meet back outside. Inside was almost pitch-black. I felt blind till I touched the tank. Taking off my gloves, I placed the drum down under the supports that held up the enormous bowser. Blister came tight next to me and laid down both devices. Hunkered, I switched on the red chest torch. With us sheltering as much light as possible, Blister wound the wire around both devices. His hands were trembling. Sweat dripped from his brow onto the bomb.

Looking across at me, he nodded once at the tank above. My heart stopped when I saw the nerve agent sign that I had seen before. Turning back, Blister pulsated his hands in and out. He then engaged the wire onto the blast plug. For a moment, I imagined that Jules had left the charge on. I turned off the light, plunging us back into darkness.

Back tracking, I quietly closed the gate and then looped the chain. I pulled around my weapon, feeling relieved it was now tight in my shoulder. We traced our footsteps to the dead guard, mindful of the cable we had laid. Our felt-boots soaked up the pool of blood. With one last check of the high guard room, I moved to the ambulance and then covered Blister's move. At the rear, Blister had eyes on whilst I scurried outside of the hangar. The metal-clad sides still retained heat. Titan and Seagal were on the other side of the large entrance, blending into the night and scanning different arcs. I made a low noise to Blister, and then covered his withdrawal. Once he had reached me, we both kept watch whilst the other two came across.

Like a well-planned and rehearsed move, Seagal redressed himself and then walked around the corner. Out of sight of the low glow from the entrance, we laid down near the entrance. Blister covered all three hangars. Titan watched the gates. I kept my eyes on the hidden AA-gun area. The scrap-heap I had hid in was impossible to see, especially with the raised berm set back. I hoped Scrap had successfully wedged the tools into each sliding plate above the AA underground bunker and was now watching from the junk.

I turned my attention to Seagal who had started to climb the external ladder on the other side.

'When that Jerry had said, "*Verdammte Ratten*". Is that, fucking rat, or fucking rats?' Blister whispered.

'It's plural,' I quietly answered. 'Now switch on.'

'How fucking rude,' he mumbled. 'Did you manage to lay your explosives, Titan?'

I arched my neck to listen.

'How fucking rude,' Titan muttered, impersonating Blister. 'Of course I fucking did. There are twelve tanks in total, not six like that Arab lad had said. Fucking liar. When that store of acetylene bottles goes up, it will cause the largest explosion so far on the mission.'

I thought about the rest of the explosives, not being able to resist being drawn into the debate. 'What about Tommy's petrol bowser in the plane hangar?'

'Guys, fucking switch on,' Blister hissed. 'We're not out of the woods yet.'

'Sorry,' I whispered.

'And what about the nerve agent tank we've laid a bomb on,' Blister added, suckered in.

I cringed.

'Tell me you're fucking joking,' Titan said. 'Not again.'

Where was Baka and Tommy? I knew they had the furthest to go and had to plant the device by himself on the petrol bowser. However, they should have been out the front at least by now.

Bang…thud!

A body had dropped from the gantry.

'Contact,' Blister hissed. 'Stand down, it's Tommy and Baka.'

'Time to fuck off,' Titan said.

'Go, I'll cover them,' I said softly.

As they left, I was fearful we had been compromised. How many hundreds of soldiers were now rallying around the northerly trenches? Fuck, Jules had a set time before she triggered the devices if gunshots were heard.

Tommy's kit bag was in his hand, a rifle in the other. He was lagging behind Baka. Each time Tommy ran past the entrances, he became vulnerable. At least he was in a German uniform. Suddenly, the guard from the Hangar-1's office came out and faced them. Seeing Tommy looking flustered, the guard walked over to the far side pillar. I spotted the klaxon handle. I took aim but stopped when Baka changed course and leapt at him. He violently shook the guard's arm. In vain, the guard shouted and hit Baka. Baka bit down on the assailant's windpipe like the Sumatra Tiger had on Setiawan. One of the search lights went on from the far corner. They couldn't direct the beam as far round as us, their mistake.

Getting up, I ran across to Baka and released him from his duty by gesticulating him off. I dragged the choking German back around the hangar's edge and dumped him against the side. Tommy mumbled what he had said to the horse and then put the soldier out of his misery with a knife. Whilst I ran back across the field, I spotted Seagal at a slower speed. He was clutching his left shoulder. Diverting to him, I put my arm around under his armpit to help him along. He groaned. He had lost his German hat and had a nasty gash across his face. The blood was heavy on his neck and uniform.

Reaching the sandy plate, two screwdrivers were wedged on each side of it. Scrap was waving at me from the entrance of the junk. Baka sat panting. Scrap took my Bergan from me and passed it into the entrance he had made. A pair of hands dragged it through. I helped Seagal down and Scrap took him from me. Crawling in, I followed them through the mass of metal and timber from a path that Scrap had made. Baka was the last man.

A hole had already been cut in the fence. Bergan and kit bags on, I took over point-man and followed the trail of sticks that poked out of the minefield. Scrap had marked the area of my old footprints. Reaching the end, I turned to see the line of lads watching where they placed their feet. All on a safe footing, Seagal told everyone to stop making a fuss of him. I ordered Baka to lead the safe way through the cut barbed wire fences, and for Titan to keep watch for any unwanted followers. He tapped his grenades and then smiled.

The fence was easy. We had made it look slick. On the edge of the tar trench, we waited for Titan to get his huge frame under the last wire. He cursed that it was made for a skinny runt. I searched for the stones, but they had sunk. Scrap was the first to look at his watch. As if reading my mind, he tore off across the trench, with us in hot pursuit.

It didn't matter that the sand tore at our boots, the race to get to the LUP was on. Obviously, Baka took the lead; although, he was running in an unorthodox way. With the prison in sight, I shouted for everyone to hit their red torches. Hopefully, the Foreign Legion had remembered the drill and would not engage the Lewis.

As fit as I was before this mission, I was breathing and sweating hard.

Dumping off my Bergan, I gritted my teeth and sprinted the last hundred metres to the rocks. Just as I reached the corner, Baka was sitting in front of the Lewis. The gunner, Sameer, looked confused, as much as I did that he had returned. However, I didn't have time to ask. I spotted Jules leaning over her equipment.

'Noooooo,' I yelled.

She immediately took her hands away from the controls and looked up.

'Do not arm the explosives,' I said, out of breath. 'Disarm it until I say so.'

I jogged back to help Seagal, but Tommy was helping him. The others were keeping watch for any enemy, so I picked up my kit.

As soon as we were all back at the LUP, I gave the orders for Titan to attend to Seagal's shoulder gunshot injury and face knife wound. Before they went off to the back of Truck-2, I asked Seagal to translate to Tommy that he needed to attend to Baka who was frantically trying to rid the sand and tar from his paws.

Whilst the camp was being prepared to evacuate, I checked on each French soldier. Every one of them got a hard kick for being asleep. Captain Cock had come to and was fit to burst under his gag and restraints, so I left him. Sameer was still behind the Lewis, so I went over to praise him.

'Why have you returned?' I asked.

'I will tell you. I feel bad going home. I look after French soldiers for much long time.'

'You're a brave kid. I respect that.'

'You are crazy British men. When is big bang to kill men, tanks, planes?'

'When we're out of the area.'

In record time, the camp had been pulled down and all the vehicles had been loaded. Seagal said he was fine to carry on. I told them we would all discuss what had happened at Target-2 once out of the area. Tommy had removed the tar off Baka's paws with some medical solution. I called everyone in, except two of the fittest Foreign Legion who were to keep watch. The rest of the exhausted and malnourished French soldiers were sitting in a circle. Titan manhandled over Captain Cock. Not surprisingly, Captain Cock had now decided to remain calm. Tommy was hugging Baka and giving him lots of praise. I had to do this for our unit. First, though, we needed to get to a safe-zone to detonate.

'Right, lads, we need to head back to Ismailia. Sadly, we're going to have to take these froggies with us.'

'But what about the secret weapons base?' Scrap asked.

'We need to destroy that if we're to defeat the Hun,' Titan added.

I didn't believe there was such a base, knowing we were about to destroy the remaining army at Target-2. Yet, something Sameer had said was niggling me.

'Well?' Seagal said.

'On the raid, did any of you see any train parts?'

The lads shook their heads. The French soldiers looked baffled, so I turned to Sameer.

'You mentioned earlier, when you had discredited my plans, that there were "locomotives". None have been seen in the hangars.'

'Ottoman Empire build big locomotive to destroy British Empire.'

'And how do you know this? Where is it?' I anxiously quizzed.

Captain Cock was trying to say something under his gag. I nodded at Blister to release it.

'I see photos,' Sameer boasted. 'Parts go on lorry and locomotive to Zin Valley. It fires many big shell over desert.'

'So, it's not at Akaba like we had been told,' I said. Was this a ruse from General Rowe to throw our squad off track?

'He is telling the truth,' Captain Cock said. 'Now untie me. I will have you shot...'

'Shut the fuck up,' I barked. 'Don't you think there's been enough shot.'

He didn't reply, but turned to his men, atrocities in their eyes. I quickly got out my map and pin-pointed the new area to everyone.

'Jules, can you ride a Trusty?'

'Yes, boss.'

'OK, lads, these are the choices for a Chinese parliament. Please translate for Tommy, Seagal. One: we all leave now and take the knackered froggies back to Ismailia. Two: we leave only enough supplies and ammo in Truck-2 and let them head back on their own whilst we find this secret weapons base and somehow destroy this train. I don't...'

'You cannot destroy it,' Captain Cock interrupted. 'Its armour is too thick. Its guns are too...*puissant*,' he interrupted, again.

'What did Captain Cock say?' I asked Seagal.

Tommy laughed, as Seagal was still translating.

'*Puissant* means powerful,' Seagal said.

'Lads, you have ten seconds to decide.'

'Plan two,' Blister chose first—one by one, the rest agreed.

Not surprised, I ordered them to write down the new coordinates. Next, I instructed them to strip Truck-2 but leave just enough rations for twenty-four hours for all the froggies. Also, to limit their Lewis' ammo as we needed it.

It enthusiastically began. Captain Cock put up his objections saying there wasn't enough supplies. I reminded him what regiment he belonged to, and that they had already survived months in the prison. It shut him up.

Ten minutes later, we broke the chain link of unloading and loading. Tommy made sure the truck had enough fuel. All but one of the Foreign Legion came over and thanked us: Captain Cock. I ordered everyone to immediately evacuate.

Scrap and Jules were to get the Trusty warmed up and stay to detonate the explosives in T-minus ten-minutes. I looked back at our teammate, sorry to see Truck-2 leave. It had been an amazing asset and it deserved to make it back in memory of Flash-heart and his team.

Heading at top speed directly east, the pinky had to go at a slower speed behind. The last thing we wanted was a puncture whilst towing the cannon. I imagined the explosions and damage at Target-2 whilst Titan was giving me a minute-by-minute countdown. On the minus two-minute mark, I slowly came to a stop and killed the engine. Blister eventually brought the pinky alongside. At the same time, we all debussed. We either took off our head scarves, balaclavas, or goggles, and listened in the direction. We were about six klicks away from the LUP. Suddenly, a siren barely audible wailed: the klaxon. Where were the explosions? Why were they waiting to detonate? I wasn't the only one to think it as we eyed each other. We all checked our watches.

T-minus zero…

Nothing…

T-minus negative two seconds…

A huge light shattered the black night, followed by an array of colours, iridescent shimmering, and streaks…

T-minus negative ten seconds…

Nothing…

T-minus negative seventeen seconds…

BOOOM…BOOOM…BOOOM!

Back at top speed, we had not hung around to watch the incandescent light show and destructive sonic booms. With Titan navigating, he ordered me to stop. This new RV had been designated at fifteen klicks directly east. Tommy rolled up the canvas and sat back behind the Lewis. Baka trotted off and blended into the night. Seagal sat behind the Vickers with one arm still in a sling. Me, Blister, and Titan headed off in different directions. I found a shallow scrape and brought my weapons to bare.

Thirty-five minutes into the stag, I was exhausted. My eyes were desperate to shut. Where were Scrap and Jules? They should have been here ten minutes ago. I began to fear that the aftershocks had injured them. Time check: 03:27 hours.

A breeze from behind blew across my back. I got a whiff of my own body odour mixed with chemicals and tar. I really wanted to get out of this black-ops gear and have a wash and a good sleep. A negative thought entered my mind: had Scrap and Jules headed off to find the secret base without us? Was he still going after Lieutenant Thomas White? I couldn't let him kill this Australian soldier as it could be my link to getting back to 2013. There was also the fact that if Thomas were a direct grandfather of Ocker, this would mean Ocker would never be born. Ocker had saved my life. Why was Jules picked by Rowe? Was she here to help? Or to find Sikes and retrieve the gold? Shit, I was becoming paranoid. I needed some R&R.

I opened my eyes suddenly on hearing something. Baka had raced off into the distance. Annoyed I had fallen asleep, I slapped my face and then pulled my Enfield tight into my shoulder. I scanned the blackness. Baka appeared from nowhere. Sitting down next to me, he faced my direction and crossed his legs. I ruffled his dusty coat.

At last, the Trusty could be heard. A little while later, it came into view with the red-light jittering. Seeing them both, a sense of relief came over me. Turning off my torch, I slogged back to our vehicles. Scrap came alongside on the Trusty with Jules hanging onto him. Getting off first, he then gentlemanly took her hand and helped her off whilst still holding onto the bike.

'Were the fuck have you been?' I asked.

Jules removed Scrap's *shemagh* and goggles that she was wearing and handed them back to him. She pleasantly thanked him and then went around the back of our truck and got in.

'Well?' I asked.

Eyes streaming, Scrap tapped his watch. He then took off his balaclava and swapped it for the headgear.

With the last of the lads in the back, and Titan next to me, I ordered Scrap to find a decent LUP up ahead. As he rode off, the breeze had picked up. Twenty minutes later, I thumped Titan on the arm. It startled him awake. I told him to keep an eye out as we set off.

Approximately three klicks later, on auto-pilot, Titan yelled at me to stop. I had not seen Scrap racing towards us at speed. Jumping down, I slapped my cheeks.

'I hope you've found somewhere, as I could sleep for a week,' I said.

'Be careful what you wish for,' Scrap said.

I couldn't be bothered to find out if he had meant anything funny by his remark.

'If you had fallen asleep, you would have driven off a huge cliff. One klick ahead is a sheer drop. I have combed the area. There is a road that leads down to another level where we can get shelter from the sun, and this wind that is picking up.'

'Good work, Scrap.'

Keeping in a slow and tight convoy, I followed his rear wheel to the start of the slope. As I trailed, the truck's wheels were barely on the edge. I was gripping the wheel with my nerves jingling at the sheer drop. A few times, Titan cursed me when I had scraped the wall with the stones and shingle having fallen on him. It was either that or we went over the edge. I now wished I had chosen to drive the pinky towing the cannon.

Scrap was walking back up the slope. I pressed harder on the already binding brakes. I couldn't get out and he couldn't come to the side. He shouted for Titan to watch the tight bend at the bottom, and that everyone else should get out of the back. Titan clambered over the bonnet.

'Don't fuck this up like the last slope,' Titan said.

Chapter Twenty-five

'Wanker,' I said.

Inch by inch, back and forth, I manoeuvred the truck around the bend. At times I caught my breath when screamed at to stop. What made it worse was the wind howling up the precipice. I now had to watch the hand signals of both Titan and Scrap. Surely the enemy did not use this road. If you could call it a road.

Once conquered, the slope levelled out, appearing even narrower. Titan climbed up the bonnet and in.

'Not bad,' he said lamely. 'Make sure you keep tight to the cliff on your side.'

Every time the debris had landed on me, Titan laughed. A few times, large thuds could be heard from behind, and smaller ones on top of the canvas roof. Those in the back had sworn at me.

At last, we hit a large rocky plateau. I couldn't wait to get out. Scrap walked towards me. Instead of congratulating me, he strolled by. I turned to see him helping Jules down. Everyone else walked by me and entered the huge concave mountain side, like the sea had eroded it away for thousands of years.

'Yeah, cheers, boss,' I mumbled.

Both vehicles were parked end to end and side-on tight against the precipice. Everyone went around doing their tasks. The hardest job was the camouflage netting as the blustery wind made it hard to fix to any point. Not being able to put the poles in the solid ground, they were binned. After lots of arguments and blaming, the net was tied off to jutting rocks and around the wheels. With the cliff overhang, we were protected from the sun and planes. The worry was the falling rocks.

With no sand to fill up the sandbags, we opted to watch the area from the safety of the truck and pinky. On the first stag was Scrap and Titan. They had seen my order as being petty for their childish banter about my driving—perhaps. With dawn breaking, I took a sip of water under the truck with Baka and Seagal. Jules and Blister slept above. Stripping down to our shorts, I checked Seagal's wounds under torch light. Satisfied, I pulled over my blanket and ignored who smelt the worst. Within seconds, I was out.

'Boss…boss. Wake up, Johnny.'

I pulled my pistol from under the blanket and pointed it at Blister's face that was lit up from the dusk coming through the gaps in the armour plating. Had I been asleep the entire day?

'What?' I barked.

'You need to come and see this,' he said.

'Is it urgent?'

Baka shuffled backwards as Blister left, not even appearing tired. I achingly crawled out and adjusted my eyes. Everyone was on the road watching something. Their clothes rippled in the strong wind. Directly above the cliff overhang, the sky was pure-blue and full of birds flying in the same direction of the gale. Walking towards the lads, the background was a mix of grey, black, and beige. They all faced me with concern.

Joining the spectators, the stunning scenery of mountains, rocky formations, and plateaus spread across the Negev Desert was being consumed by the scariest and incomprehensible sandstorm I have ever seen. And, at a furious speed.

'Fuck,' I said. 'In the truck.'

In a rushed panic but weirdly in control, we made sure all the canvas was tight and secure. Scrap passed me three respirators and then closed off the rear top tarpaulin on Baka, Jules, Tommy, Scrap, and Titan. I crawled under to Seagal. He was trying to unroll the side sheets from the plating, gritting his teeth and gasping as he did. Blister was doing the other side. The front skirt had already been pulled down and tied off. Lastly, I unravelled the rear lower tarpaulin and rigidly fixed it. With our three packs against the firing slits, I lay with my back against the last one.

At first the wind gradually gained in speed. Things began to rattle and flap. The light faded. Then, as if in a car experimental wind-tunnel, everything went crazy. The pressure, the noise, and the sand blowing in. It didn't matter what position I got in to hold down the protective skirt, the grit blew in. It stung whatever part of skin it touched. At least the underwear covered my bollocks. In the dust cloud, I put on my respirator, a relief for my breathing. I then managed to wrap a blanket around my near naked body. Strange creaking, ripping, and thumps filtered in between the howling and sandblasting. Just when I thought it was slowing, another evil blast came in. Above, Scrap shouted at someone to calm down.

Day had turned into night. I only knew this by checking my watch under the torch. At that point, I caught the tired and fearful eyes of Seagal and Blister. The sand had built up around the skirts, forming a barrier. Yet, a lot had rolled in. At least we could remove the respirators.

The sandstorm eventually slightly relented its power, just enough for us to hear each other making sure we were all right. Even though we had finished all the gritty rations from our backpacks, I told them it would be over soon. When it had eased up further, Titan passed down some water and rations. We quickly tied up the tarpaulin. In that brief time, the air was filled with dust, again.

On the second day of the storm, any sleep had been interrupted. To keep morale up, I praised each one of them for their commitment and success of Target-2. Each member got to tell their event of what they had found in each hangar. With the help of Seagal translating, all of us enjoyed Tommy's sense of humour and the way he described things. He had entered Hangar-3 with Baka leading and silently took out two pilots that were checking over the planes. Tommy said there were rows and rows of fighter planes and bombers. Around the edges of this football pitch sized hangar were stacked shelves of different bombs. Luckily, both of them were able to squeeze behind the racks. Further jokes came in about how lucky Titan and Scrap had not been tasked for this hanger, being too fat. With Baka having sniffed out the guard room and the further staff that had patrolled, it had taken them a lot longer to place the explosive on the petrol bowser. Apparently, it was the size of a train carriage. I believed he was telling the truth.

Seagal had boldly walked into Hangar-2 and was confronted with three blasé mechanics. Just another German to them. He had sharply disabled all three with vicious martial arts and his knife. Of course, Titan bantered there had been only one scrawny young lad, and he wasn't impressed with Seagal's boxing. I knew the wind-up, and it had worked. Seagal retorted that it was Chinese martial arts. I had told my squad about Ocker constantly winding me up about my karate.

When Seagal had worked out it was banter, he went on to tell us that there had been ten armoured tanks and seven cannons. At the rear there was some sort of armoured car with a flamethrower fixed, like that of a HMG. Both had weaved their way in between the troop carriers, diving under when someone had come. Both had managed to lay the explosive successfully on a store of thirty or more acetylene bottles.

Seagal had fought a Turk guard at one end of the gantry, being a knife fight so as not to alert the base. It resulted in the guard being killed, and a nasty wound to Seagal's face. At the other end, Seagal had been spotted by the other sentry as Seagal went to attack. Seagal had taken a round to the shoulder. Although injured, Seagal still had managed to throw the guard off the gantry. Fortunately, the round had only torn through the upper arm muscle.

Scrap had managed to stay unnoticed from the point I had last seen him running along the security fence. Putting significant risk to himself, he had found the three underground AA bunkers and pushed in the wedges before returning to the scrapheap. There, he made a clear route through it, including the minefield. I let Blister tell our side of the story. Yes, it got quite a bit of the "bullshit" mockery from the others.

By the beginning of the third night, we had become prisoners. We also had to find whatever we could to have a shit and piss in. Even though hygiene was priority, us on the bottom bunk found it highly amusing when Baka had a shit. I agreed to Tommy lighting the joss sticks.

The squad began to get ratty. Scrap, registering this, started a new conversation about his personal life. It emerged that his mother was a drunk and used to abuse him as a child. When his father had left her, Scrap had run away to an uncle until Scrap was eighteen. He then joined a charity to save endangered animals. A long way down the road with no siblings, his father dying in a car crash and his mum taking an overdose, he stayed in the jungle as much as he could to avoid people.

Jules was next: she was your standard girl from a hardworking family but wanted to get out of the slums. She joined as a nurse to start with, but it was lucky she had an older brother who was an officer. Jules was enlisted as a signaller. This was her first tour. She had lost two brothers, one at Passchendaele and the other at sea. Blister felt her rawness.

Tommy had been through orphanage after orphanage. He was abused mentally and physically. Religion and hope kept him going. His companions were Baka and Rudi, as he didn't like making new friends, except us. He admitted there have been times he could have killed Sergeant Rowe. Everyone agreed but me.

Seagal came from a rich family. His parents were of mixed nationality. He was always seeking adventure as a kid. He would mentally and physically push himself further. From a young teen he has had a high sex drive. It must have been killing him on this mission. Titan and Blister teased him about fucking the local goats whilst on sniper duty—it didn't go down well.

My turn: I started by telling everyone that I was from the future. Those who didn't know, mocked, and laughed; until, Scrap had blurted it was true. Scrap also admitted that he had come from the same era. This was unified by Titan and Blister. I skipped the part of how I had got here. Instead, I just kept it short by saying I wanted to return to my world and see my family, friends, and squad. It went quiet. Blister was looking sorrowful. Above us, Jules asked if Titan was OK. Forgetting the bond that we had, I felt like a bag of shite.

Seagal broke the silence; well, the sound of the wind and sandblasting. He asked Titan and Blister to tell of their past. Knowing their stories, and that Seagal was going to throw back the mud in bucket loads, I turned over into a ball. Sand fell onto my face from the blanket. I got to the part where Blister was upset about missing his dog and pregnant wife, when the sounds drifted off…

Heavy coughing woke me. I peered through the sunbeams that blazed through the gaps. Oddly, it was lovely just to hear snoring and heavy breathing. Even a fart, most probably Baka. I shook the sand from my watch and undid the leather cover's popper. The small sound alerted Blister who sat up and hit his head. I laughed. Time check: 06:59 hours. I mouthed for Blister to go back to sleep. I shut my eyes, still not content with the best sleep I'd had in ages: ten hours.

Again, waking up to no sandstorm was strange. The only thing that hit me this time was the stench and humidity. Time check: 11:54 hours. Stiff, I half-sat up and looked at the amount of sand and rubbish. All that was missing were the girls and empty alcohol cans and bottles from our bachelor pad; although, it had been the furthest from the word 'party'.

'Rise and shine you lazy fuckers,' I yelled, then grimaced, remembering I was behind enemy lines.

Being the first at the rear tarpaulin, I dug my way out of the sandpit into the fresh air. I found it difficult to adjust to the sun. Wiping my eyes, I then stretched upright and staggered down the drift. I was amazed that there wasn't one area of stone ground to be seen. It was as if we had been transported back to the desert. Alarmingly, the sand on the truck was like a layer of snow. The camo paint had been stripped back in places to its original. Walking around to the pinky with the warm sand under bare feet, it was the same. Shit, this was going to take some clearing, and the cleaning of our kit in the back.

Knowing there wouldn't be any enemy close by after that horrendous storm, I strolled out to the road's edge. I kept back as I wasn't sure how stable it was. The view was spectacular, like many parts of hostile places in the world. Such as Afghanistan. Different coloured rock formations, ravines, and canyons formed as far as the eye could see. Mountain peaks starkly rose into the pure-blue sky. A line of green shrubbery snaked on the bottom of the plains. Some had high banks marking the route.

I must have been standing there for five minutes before Seagal was first over. He was still brushing the sand that had stuck to his face and shoulder bandages. Under his arm was his wooden chest.

'Hey, leave the sand on, it's great bandage camo,' I said.

Surprisingly, he threw the box over the edge. We both peered over and watched it smash into many pieces on the way down. Pieces of cloth scattered.

'I do not need that anymore,' he said.

'You're over the nightmares then.'

'No, I have a new set to deal with after taking this fucked-up mission with you chaps.'

I smirked. 'I see you've stopped talking in that Victorian lingo and are more like us.'

'Fucking exactly. I feel like following the box down.' He walked off.

One by one everyone clambered out, shocked at the level of sand and damage to the vehicles. According to Jules, the worst sight was that I was only in my pants. She added how cold it must be. Jesus. One person had to stay nice and pure, I thought.

Baka took guard at one end of the road before the bend. I sent Seagal to the other end where it travelled further down to the valley floor. He took a book and a pair of binos, making a quip about needing a holiday. Grabbing the chance to top up the white bits, everyone stripped down to their underwear. For some reason, Scrap was very defensive about us ogling Jules' fine assets. What has changed since seeing Batgirl's alpaca?

The rest of us stripped out the pinky and the truck. We then cleaned the sand from the kit and re-stocked it after. Next was the cannon. Once excavated, we left Blister to maintain it. I dug out the poor old Trusty that had fallen over, wishing Flash-heart was here to service it. Instead, I asked Jules to clean it and get it started.

Each vehicle was tested and repainted. All the weapons were checked. Lastly, we bagged up all the empty food containers full of excrement, along with the rubbish. Titan had kept out some disinfectant and soap, so we sparingly used the water to wash ourselves. Tommy handed out some German Nivea Crème to each person.

Sitting on my office rad in my robe and *shemagh*, my sunburn soothed from the lotion. The rest sat around me in the shade from the overhang. Scrap came out with his notepad and handed it to me, taking his place next to Jules.

'Right, listen in,' I said. 'Today is Friday the thirteenth…'

'One more night to Saturday's beer, curry, and shenanigans,' Blister interjected—everyone had starry eyes.

'These four days of the storm…'

'You did say you wanted to "sleep for a week",' Scrap interrupted me.

'He fucking never,' Titan said.

Blister groaned. 'You know he's a Jonah.'

Tommy started praying.

'Switch on, guys, this is serious,' I said. 'With these four days and what the froggies ate, our food stock and water levels are dangerously low. Perhaps not lasting the journey back to Ismailia.'

'I thought you were trained in the Elite to survive the harshest environment. Including live off the desert,' Scrap said.

'You're very keen to finish the job, aren't you,' I sternly insinuated. 'Perhaps the Egyptian gold or killing Thomas White is on the top of your list instead of the safety of us lads.'

'Fuck off, Johnny.' Scrap took himself off to the back of the truck.

'That was harsh,' Tommy said—the others nodded.

'I'm here to keep you alive,' I said. 'We've got no camouflage netting, and you've seen the terrain.'

'British Arabist and adventurer T. E. Lawrence mentions that the Zin Valley extends to the east. It was created from the River Zin which…'

'Get to the point,' I interrupted Seagal.

'The valley created the Dead Sea. It didn't carve this area out of the desert rock by water erosion, but natural springs are at Ein Avdat and Ein Akev.'

'You mean the shrubbery along the bed,' I said. 'OK, we can dig for water, but the extra food calories needed for the next target is one thing. Yet, to get inside the base or destroy this elusive armoured train is another.'

'We have the cannon and mortar,' Blister said.

We're not even sure where it's situated. We could drive around for days using the last of the petrol.' I let it sink in. 'Scrap,' I shouted, 'pull your kid's socks up and get your arse back here.'

Scrap came back and sat in the pinky seat, folding his arms in a huff.

'Time to vote. Hands up who wants to head back?' I said.

No one moved, and as if right on cue, a train's whistle had blown from far away. Everyone was beaming knowing we were close to the last target.

'Bollocks,' I said, and sighed.

On the very edges of the different maps and photos, we studied the most likely area. Then, the most unlikely area. The Dead Sea was approximately forty-three klicks east from our LUP and Zin Valley. Target-2 had already been inside the five thousand square miles of the

Negev Desert. With everyone agreeing on the possible area for Target-3, I dismissed the briefing.

Before we set off, I was having an argument with Tommy about getting off the Trusty. He wouldn't budge, playing he couldn't understand my English. Seagal came over. Even after translating, Tommy stayed defiant. Tommy went on to say that today was very unlucky from the story of Jesus: last supper and crucifixion where thirteen people sat. Even Seagal joined in with a story of The Knights Templar. I stopped them there and told them I wasn't interested in the Friday the thirteenth superstition. I then walked off, wondering if this is what Tommy and Seagal had conjured up between them.

CHAPTER TWENTY-SIX

I loathed moving in the daytime, but it would have been too risky to drive down the precarious and sand covered track to the valley bottom at night. The worst part was sitting next to a smug Blister who had decided to drive. Even Titan, Scrap, and Baka in the rear were saying how smoother the ride had become now that I wasn't driving. Perhaps I should have argued more about Tommy taking the Trusty and becoming point-man heading in the direction of the train's whistle; although, I knew it wouldn't be as the vulture flew. Maybe I just wanted a bit of freedom away from this lot. My own space. Even the mission that had been successful up until the last extraction in Afghanistan 2013, it had been nice to find a bit of 'me time' as it had progressed. Tiredness, hunger, and thirst can turn the littlest of a quip into something worse. Time check: 16:36 hours.

Dead on the set RV, Tommy was waiting under the shade of the wadi bank as it curved around to the left. Blister parked into some shade of a few trees and bushes. Jules kept tight behind in the pinky. Forcing my way through this little paradise, the sand fell off like snow.

'Sit rep,' I ordered.

'Sit?' Tommy sat and crossed his legs.

Was he joking? I tried to hide my amusement.

Scrap came over and said, 'Can we have a hot lunch and drink?'

'Sure, keep one in the spout,' I said, remembering Bruce had said it to me in the trenches about keeping the rifle loaded. I missed Bruce.

'Did you hear what Tommy did when he was told the same on stag back at base by Sikes?' Scrap said.

'No, what's that?'

'Tommy brought along the metal kettle and asked what goes in the spout.'

Scrap started laughing and then strolled off. Tommy was blissfully smiling.

'You're one in a million, Tommy. Perhaps a billion,' I said. 'Go grab some scoff.'

'I not tread in shit twice. Yes?' he said.

I walked back with him, patting his shoulder.

With the cookers making the tea and stew, I ventured out from the cover of the shrubland and walked the two hundred metres towards the rock peninsula at its lowest point. The humidity was low, guessing it to be twenty-five degrees. The sides of the ravine had been baked, but at the base the crust fell away. The sand under was soft and cool.

Nearer the top of the slope, the stones and solid surface caused havoc with my already sore and puffy fingers. I should have worn my gloves. Managing to scale my way up to a ridgeline, I followed it up thirty metres onto the peak to an ascending flat area of about two metres wide. Taking in as much air as I could, I pushed on to the highest point of the undulating section.

At the top, I stood like I had just climbed Everest. I was in awe of the views. Apart from looking the same in every direction ahead, the focus point was a pyramid on the south horizon. Through the binos it was even more magnificent. Like a Bedouin or even Obi-Wan Kenobi, I sat down cross legged. Closing my eyes, I took in the tranquillity and emptied the memory file of the shit I had seen so far. I had learnt this from my psychologist, having worked with him after his tours of Afghan and Iraq.

I must have been in a zone as I was disturbed by a knock to my thigh. Focusing, I was sitting in Scrap's large shadow. He gave me a mug of tea, only half full where he had spilt it on his climb. He then handed me a billy can of stew, slopped over the edge.

'Thanks,' I said.

He sat next to me whilst I took a sip of the sweet tea—amazing.

'Fantastic here isn't it,' he said.

'Apart from the war, yes. Like most places in the world.'

'Are you thinking about home, your parents, friends, and wife?'

I went to put a spoon of stew in my mouth, but he held back my wrist.

'Perhaps wait till we have finished talking instead of spluttering your remnants over me and yourself.'

'What do you mean?' I asked.

'Do you really miss home? Your old squad and job? Family, Ocker, Trevor, Simon, Will, and all the people you have met?'

Blimey, this was deep for him, I thought. 'I do, Georges. You?' I grimaced.

'I have no such loving memories I am afraid, Johnny. Oh, except those since we joined up at Lake Danau Singkarak. The adventure and people I have met since has given me a real purpose. The meaning of friendship. You know…the bond.'

I did know, but I had a massive guilt as I was still torn between leaving this lot or not returning home. I nodded and then patted his shoulder.

'I'm sorry things have got a bit messy between us,' he said.

'It's bound to in this environment, but it's all train under the bridge.' I scoffed.

He got up, the dust falling in my tea and stew. 'If Ocker hadn't saved you in Operation Last Assault, then I would probably still be captive or dead in the poachers' camp. Even if I had escaped, would I still be living a solitude life in the jungle? Wherever you end up, good luck, my *bru*.'

He walked back. I went to say to stay, but I was flummoxed by his poignant speech. Also, a little emotional, too.

A roar came from the direction of our old LUP. I twisted, knocking over my mug. A squadron of seven fighters headed this way at speed. Their machine guns echoed. Then they split. At their height, I couldn't see if they were friendly. Even if they were, they couldn't tell what side we were on.

I quickly made my way back down the ridge, the stew slopping over me. Another fleet raced across from the west adding to the firepower. The small amount of smoke rising from the camp's bushes was a massive concern. So was the thought of falling as I tried to race back. Reaching the camp, weird buzzing and engines screaming joined the cacophony of machine guns. Smaller explosions rose from the desert. Blister was on the Vickers. Titan was sat behind the truck's Lewis. Tommy had moved to the wadi's bank overhang with another Lewis. Scrap and Jules were together, each with an Enfield.

Squatting against the bank, I moved up to Tommy. I didn't say anything but watched the aerial dog-fight. I was still unsure who was who and which side was winning. One of the planes heading east poured with smoke. Another one followed, but was shot down by one behind that. Then, that one turned back west. A pom pom gun fired from somewhere beyond the cliff in the direction of our old LUP. Fuck, ground troops, I thought.

'We need to evacuate,' I said.

Tommy took off his bead necklace and placed it in my hand. 'You live to go home.'

'I don't want it…'

Tommy hadn't stayed to listen.

With the aerial battle over, we quickly packed away and made sure we had not left obvious signs. Tommy was the first on the bike. I was about to remonstrate, but Blister tapped me on the shoulder.

'Why is it that a simple sunbathe for you, can attract so much trouble?' he asked.

'Ha ha, very funny.'

'And when are you going to stop eating like a three-year-old with its hands tied behind its back?'

'When are you going to grow a proper beard?' I said, and tugged it.

With no choice but to follow the winding riverbed, I dreaded that we would be in sight from the cliff edge if anyone were searching. There was also the concern that the plane that had limped back east was German, and could report our smoke if it had been seen.

We slowly passed our first plane wreckage, still with a pilot and gunner in. The second one a little while later had no occupants. There was no sign of the bailed crew. Tommy returned and reported that he had found two British pilots crumpled in the desert on the higher plains. Tommy didn't have time to bury them. I reluctantly told him and the others that we didn't either, but we would mark on our maps. Tommy handed over the tags and logbook of each RFC pilot. I gave them to Titan who sat next to me, and then ordered Tommy to go find an excellent LUP in an area that I had indicated on the map. We only had a half an hour left of daylight.

The sun was replaced with the moon. The stars twinkled through the clouds that were forming. We eventually came out of the long canyon. The mountains now looked strange and sinister anomalies.

We had only travelled about six klicks south before we started to head slightly back on ourselves east. I called a halt. With everyone now around my office, I asked them to grab some binos to search for Tommy's red light. Baka was on the front of the bonnet. After pulling back the canvas shelter, I stood on the seat.

'Boss,' Jules said.

I looked at where she was pointing and then raised my binos at the weird lights in the sky. I feared they might be a group of fighters or bombers. Scrap stood next to Jules on the pinky.

'Fires,' Scrap said.

'In the sky?' I asked, then realised my stupidity.

Chapter Twenty-six

'That's our LUP on the mountainside,' Scrap said.

'Six in total,' Jules added. 'That means quite a large unit.'

'Fucking stupid Jerries,' Blister said.

'Or Turks,' Titan added.

'Both dumb-fucks for giving away their positions,' Blister added.

'Could be Bedouin,' Seagal said.

'You still got those gold sovereigns?' I asked him.

'Two less, thanks to you. Let's hope they don't mind being short-changed from the fifty they expect.'

'At least we've left no trail we've been here,' Titan said.

BOOOM!

The immediate after, everyone was down behind something with weapons raised. Listening. Not saying a word. The explosion had been about a klick in the direction we were facing. No fireball rose into the air and no smoke could be seen.

'That wasn't a mortar or cannon,' Blister whispered.

'No planes overhead,' Scrap hushed.

'To loud for a Mills Bomb,' Titan added.

Suddenly, Baka whined and jumped down. He then raced off into the blackness.

'Shit,' I hissed. 'It's Tommy.'

'Bloody mines,' Jules said.

'Do you think the Bedouin heard?' Seagal asked.

'Fuck the enemy, what about Tommy?' Blister ranted, and ran to the pinky.

'No, Mark,' I said. 'Seagal is right, we have to think that whoever is up there might have heard it. They could be sending out a search party.'

Blister revved the engine.

'Mark, you can't just take off into a no-go-zone until we've established where the mines are,' Titan added. 'I know you're worried, but I'm concerned as well. Especially about my best mate now driving off into the unknown.'

'What are we going to do, boss?' Blister asked, and killed the engine.

I hated what I was going to say, but the importance of no one else getting injured was overriding going to see if it was Tommy.

'Well?'

'We extract slightly back to where the gorge opened out and set up a defensive ambush on any followers.'

'A donkey leg ambush,' Blister said proudly.

Titan looked at me, trying to hide his smile. 'That's right, Blister.'
Blister proudly smiled.

Titan turned away and raised his eyes—there are times you don't take the piss.

With the 'dogleg' ambush set, I put on my Bergan. I was carrying water, snacks, and ammo. I had not even changed into night-op gear. Titan heaved his own on. He was carrying all the med-kit and equipment that there was, as we had left the main surgical kit with our original ambulance. And, perhaps stupidly, I had sent back the best surgeon we had—no disrespect to Titan. There was a disinclined foreboding feeling as we left. Scrap made an emotional good luck.

Even though Titan's hunch was that mines could not be set off by foot, I couldn't help but watch where I placed my feet. Allegedly, personnel mines had not been invented; well, by the British, according to Seagal.

The fires were still glowing in the far distance. No sound travelled, only our boots in the soft sand. There was no chat between us. Perhaps Titan had visions of what we might find, like I did.

Keeping away from the centre track in the riverbed, in a circle we covered around three hundred metres. I was still making a mental note of my footsteps when Titan went down on one knee and held up his fist. Weapon raised, I stood and scanned. My foot was still forward, ready to move or take the recoil—nothing. Cautiously, I made my way over to him and searched the area that he had sighted. As I tapped him on the shoulder, he went prone, and I went on one knee. In between the clouds moving and a light breeze, something reflected at forty metres. Without the moon and wind, it wouldn't have been seen. Unconsciously, Titan gradually pulled out his binos whilst I kept the object in my sights. Instead of mouthing what it was, he took the strap from around his neck. With minimal movement, he handed them over to me. He then took control back of his main weapon. Focusing and waiting for the moon to appear felt like a lifetime. Eventually, the object registered: a square plate hanging from something.

Handing them back, I gestured for Titan to watch me as I went forwards. Moving crouched to the right, I scanned foot by foot. The wind was whipping up the sand. Once I had stalked about thirty metres, a small clinking noise sounded, like the goat's chain on the bottles at the Somali pirates' stronghold. I regripped my Enfield, mentally looking for somewhere to take cover if it went noisy. I instinctively knew exactly where my grenades, mags, and second weapon was. All the positive was backed-up by knowing Titan would unleash controlled firepower and move towards the threat, rather than staying defensive.

Moving in quicker, I registered a new object that was leant over. I relaxed seeing it was a short post. My boot snagged on something; it pinged back. I knew it was a barbed wire fence without even looking. Searching the area first, I then poked the end of the barrel under the plate. It spun over, showing the minefield warning. Not being sure what side the danger area was, I looked at my barely noticeable steps. Holding the sign still, I faced it towards Titan and signalled him over. Gently letting go of the plate, I searched the direction of the fence. Most of it had been covered by a sand drift, or the posts and wire were missing. I didn't believe it had been destroyed by vehicles; instead, by the recent storm. Maybe we could see any mines that had been unearthed. With the enemy in the mountains, no decent day camouflage, and limited rations, our unit had to keep moving.

Titan had traced my steps to me.

'I'm guessing the minefield is on the other side of the fence. The way the sweep of the river continues,' he said, close to my ear.

'And we're on a higher level.'

'Do we go in?' Titan said.

'If we stick to…'

'Yes, or no?' he impersonated me.

If I was honest, I had no idea. But, I had to decide, not be the limbo man.

'Yes, or no?' he repeated.

'No, we wait till dawn. We need to see what we're heading into. Just in case there's a huge enemy base wanting to greet us.'

'What about Tommy?' he said, quickly grimacing. 'Perhaps it was a rogue camel that had set it off,' he tried to remonstrate.

It didn't make my guilt feel any better.

Sleeping was almost impossible, both waking each other as we had sighed or rolled over. Many times, I had stared at the stars and listened for Tommy's motorbike to return. It filled me with blame. It had been strange how he wanted to ride the Trusty on this superstitious day and had given me his lucky beads. If he had hit a mine, would I have made the same mistake being point-man? As far as I had seen, the cordoned minefield was barely visible.

'Where do you reckon Baka is?' Titan said quietly.

'No idea. Get some sleep.'

Closing my eyes, yet again, I jiggled into the sand to get comfortable. I decided to rest my head on my rifle stock.

'If we find Tommy dead, we can't bury him in a minefield,' Titan muttered.

'Look, he could be alive. Camping out.'

'Perhaps he's injured, so why the fuck are we just lying here?'

I sighed and rolled over. My stomach also turned. Titan punched the ground. Huffing, he also rolled over with his back facing me.

'Yet, you want to carry on to Target-3,' I said. 'Don't you think we've fucking been through enough.'

It wasn't helping the situation or our bond. He didn't answer.

In the moody atmosphere of the early hours of the morning, I worked out that tomorrow night, Sunday, would be three weeks since we had set off on Operation Baka. My thoughts wandered off thinking of all that had happened. There were similarities to my previous missions in or out of the British Army. We were using modern day warfare tactics, but without modern day weapons and kit. It was like the comparisons were all merged into one. Even though Blue Halo had lasted longer, about five and a half weeks as from first Chinook insertion, this seemed a shit load longer.

'You all right, pal?' Titan said.

'Yeah. You?'

'Sure.'

That's all that was needed.

As morning started to break, we were on our bellies scanning the area over the drift. Deciphering clumps of grass and bushes was challenging as the rising sun portrayed the objects as something different. Each time we had agreed that it wasn't Tommy. In the end, we waited for the sun to set properly to get a view of the background.

'PIDed Baka,' Titan said.

My heart gave a little flutter as he pointed east. Through the binos, Baka was sitting upright. The object next to Baka was lost in the mirage of heat. Facing each other, I gave a little nod. We both picked ourselves up and placed a foot over the fence.

CHAPTER TWENTY-SEVEN

Keeping to the edges of where the fence used to be, I also watched for any movement whilst we patrolled. We came to a crater, like a miniature sinkhole to the one I had been in earlier. This one was only six metres in diameter and four metres deep. The eroded ledge was perfect to stand on and view.

After both helping each other down onto the ledge, my priority was to check on Baka. He was now only a hundred metres away. Before I had the chance to view him in the binos, he started to bark. When he came into the optical view, he was chasing away nearby vultures. Close by were robes in a human form. I couldn't see the head, but by the way Baka had gone back to guard, it had to be Tommy.

Titan whispered for me to pan eight metres left. As I did, I spotted the Trusty without its front wheel and forks. It was sad to see another member down. The explosive crater was a further distance away. Titan swung around his rifle and cursed the vultures as they hovered above. The ones that kept landing, Baka would chase them off.

'It was me who let him ride on it,' I said. 'I'll go.'

'It was me who said to carry on, so I'll go.'

'We'll go together. I need someone as strong as me.'

Leaving my Bergan, Titan carrying the medic gear, he followed me over the top. Instead of looking down my sights, I tried to spot if any mines had come to the surface. Within twenty metres, Baka turned and started to growl and show his nasty weapons. Titan, who had been in my footsteps about ten metres back, caught up my frozen stature.

'Baka, it's us,' I said, taking further steps forward.

Baka stood; his hackles raised.

'Baka, it's me, Titan.'

Titan took down his *shemagh*, clearly upset. I quickly did the same.

Baka continued to look menacing, even though he was tired and dehydrated.

'Tommy,' I shouted.

I gradually walked a little more. Baka started to loudly bark and snarl, almost setting off in an attack. Titan pulled me back and continued backwards about five metres using the exact way we had entered. Baka stopped growling and sat proudly next to Tommy.

'How are we going to save Tommy?' Titan asked.

I looked at the mangled bike and debris, and where the impact had happened. I then calculated the distance between Tommy and the bike.

'It's too late, Jason,' I said.

'How do you know? Let me try and get nearer,' Titan angrily demanded.

I put my arm across him and said, 'If he were alive, Baka would let one of us help him. This may be to warn us of the mine danger. But most likely a pride thing of losing his father, wanting no one to touch him.'

'So, what do we do?'

'I'll try once more,' I said.

I pulled out Tommy's beads from my trouser pocket and stared at them. Holding them out, I returned in the same prints. Baka sniffed the air. For a second, he looked as mournful as us, before going back into a defensive mode. This time I didn't stop. The barking became more furious. I knew I couldn't go any further as he would attack me. Such was his passion. Instead, I threw the beads, and they landed a couple of metres in front of him. Baka's malevolence ceased. Hackles still raised; he attentively took the beads. Baka sauntered over to Tommy and dropped them on him, nudging him after. Tommy didn't respond, and Baka desolately stared at me. I knew we had lost another two fine lads, and the last brilliant Trusty.

Not wanting to see anymore, I turned away. Titan lowered his rifle from Baka. I couldn't have a go at Titan for wanting to protect me from Baka. Passing Titan, who still watched the sorrowful scene, I regrettably made my way back to the sinkhole. Collecting my gear, I retraced my steps. Occasionally, I would look back at Baka, wanting him to race after me. However, he continued to guard. Sometimes he would look our way or chase the vultures. Titan was having difficulty dealing with his emotions as he trudged behind at distance.

Waiting at the fence, I took his huge hand and helped him over. We partially looked at each other and then both of us took a huge breath in and out.

'Will Baka re-join us?' Titan asked.

'No, his allegiance is to his master.'

'I'm not fucking giving up. Not coming all this…'

He put his face into his hands. I embraced him, sharing our loss. Pushing me away, he then clenched his huge fists.

'Fucking Kaiser cunts,' he boomed. 'Fucking Turk twats. Fucking Bedouin bellends.' He cocked his rifle and spat at the ground. 'I'll kill the fucking lot of them.'

I couldn't help but find a little humour among his resolute passion. I had to. 'Just like Planet,' I muttered.

'Johnny, can you tell the lads. I haven't got the courage.'

I nodded.

Plodding back to the ambush site, all the memories of Tommy's ways and sayings came flooding back. As we walked into the mouth of the valley, a mini dust storm forming in the distance dissolved those feelings. I tried to signal to Titan, but he had his head down. I gave a quick sharp finger whistle. He looked up and I gestured to the danger. Without hanging around, I ran west. With the cliff blocking my view, I sprinted towards the base. I mentally worked out the distance and speed from the advancing possible threat. The only cover was a group of boulders by a clump of palm trees.

Between a crack, I aimed my rifle. Hooves echoed across the landscape. Our ambush base was hidden by the mass of rocks that had fallen. I hoped the lads would keep their nerve. Just as Titan dived behind me, the first horse and camel trotted into view: Bedouin. Slowly, we pulled around our other weapons. Mine was the submachine gun. Titan's was his Niro Express.

'You say anything about this being a shitty shotgun, and I'll compromise us by putting a fucking great big hole in that hollow head of yours.'

I didn't reply.

The leader, all in white, held up his spear. A smaller person who was totally covered from the harsh elements sat behind him. Once the dust had settled, the army was about sixty strong. They had extra horses pulling loaded carts, a cannon, and a Gatling-gun. This must be the same tribe that Seagal had seen back at the ERL.

Two of the Bedouin at the back went to the front. Huge urns bounced off each camel's gut. After a brief chat, they came this way.

'I've zeroed in on the target pulling the Gatling-gun,' Titan whispered.

Tucking in tighter to the rocks, I couldn't see what the two riders were doing beyond the palm trees. Titan was solid, not moving a muscle as he peered through the crack with his hessian covered Nitro. I had to have eyes on the threat rather than them coming around and stabbing us. Inch by inch I crawled on my elbows. Lifting a few inches up, the two camels were tied to the palm trees about seven metres away. The two riders, armed with spears, had gone down to a small water pool, and were collecting water. The angle was tight. So acute, that if they went another couple of metres to the other side of the water, we would have surely been seen.

My weapon had no hessian, the MP-18's black-holed barrel plainly obvious out here. I mentally cursed and carefully slid it back. Peering through my *shemagh*, they both took off the face scarves and splashed themselves. One found it funny to splash the other. As he wiped his eyes, he faced this way. His eyes were like the actor Marty Feldman's. I was unsure if he was looking directly at me. Perhaps he thought my head was a rock? My shallow breathing stopped; beads of sweat ran down my neck. A shout from the tribe shook both to return their headgear and pick up the churns. Tying off the water containers to the ropes around the camels, Marty started to pull his camel this way. I slid my hand in for my knife. The camel objected, wanting to follow his hairy mate who had been turned around. Marty smacked the camel and the flies swarmed. Marty was too scrawny to argue with the camel and was dragged back. I released my grip on the knife. Titan let go of his breath.

Peering back through the gap in the boulders, the two camels had formed in the line. The leader looked this way with his eyes barely visible. The little guy dismounted and started to search the tracks ahead. The chief signalled for everyone to go by. Once again, when the dust had settled, he was still looking this way. I knew Seagal also had the leader sighted, but I hoped Seagal wouldn't take the head off the serpent this time.

The shorter person was helped back up. Baka's barking put a stop to the leader staring. The leader half-twisted towards our base, nearly knocking the pillion off. His feet jerked and the horse started to follow the route of the others.

'I'm getting too old for this shit,' I muttered.

Managing to get into a more comfortable position, we waited for the barking to cease. It went on for five minutes when suddenly it stopped. Ten minutes later in the scorching sun and with both water bottles empty, the minefield area had remained quiet. My intuition told me that the Bedouin had gone because they had only just left the camp in the mountains. I ignored the gut feeling that Baka had been speared to death. Time check: 07:59 hours.

After checking our area was devoid of life, except the vultures circling, Titan stayed in position whilst I ran back to the camp—his choice. Reaching the rockfall, I noticed movement from a rock ledge about five metres up. Seagal was wearing his fancy daytime camouflage with his arm free from the sling. He put his thumb up, so I beckoned him down. The lads came out of hiding carrying heavy weaponry.

'Where's Scrap?' I asked.

Jules looked to the side.

'We heard Baka barking. Is Tommy alive?' Blister asked.

I waited for Seagal and Scrap to be present, still staring at Blister.

'Oh fuck,' Blister raged.

Blister kicked the rear panel of the pinky and then punched the side of the truck. Was my facial expression and body language that easy to read?

'Did you get the chance to bury him?' he asked.

Come on Scrap and Seagal, I thought.

'Fucking wanker Jerries,' he continued.

'For the second time, Jules, where's Scrap?'

Jules had tears in her eyes. Blister went around kicking more of the truck.

'He's gone,' Seagal said.

'What do you mean, "gone"?'

Seagal removed his coloured headgear, his bandage seeping with blood and his injured arm still holding his sniper rifle.

'Well?' I pressed.

'Is Tommy dead?' he asked.

I nodded, then swallowed.

Seagal stared into nothing for a couple of seconds, and then took himself off to around the back of the truck. Blister kicked the pinky, limping after.

'We're not fucking aborting this mission,' Blister said.

'Mark,' I rebuked. 'Stop fucking taking it out on the other team members. They got us here. Now get a fucking grip. Go and sit with Titan. And don't go busting anymore body parts on the boulders out there.'

Blister, still vexed, snatched his weapons and kit bag, and then limped off.

'And don't upset Titan anymore,' I said.

'I'm going for a scout,' Seagal said.

Seagal climbed up the mass of rocks. People took tragic news in unusual ways. It was how they continued forwards with it that mattered.

'Jules, make us both some breakfast and meet me over there to tell me what has gone on,' I said.

In what little shade there was, I took off my Bergan. Next, my boots and stinking socks. I started to clean my weapons, making sure no parts fell on the sand. Concentrating hard on what I was doing, I tried not to let Tommy's death on Friday the thirteenth get in the thought process. Yet, I wasn't winning the battle within. Also, I had thoughts of what Jules was going to say about Scrap leaving. Where had he gone? And why? Had he had another fight with Blister? Perhaps he had just gone off to cool down. Scrap's moods had recently been up and down.

Putting the kit away, I remembered how he had changed since Jules was on the scene. He had recently become deep about his admission to his past. And when I was meditating on the ridge, his recognition that we had become his family, the bond.

Jules came over with a mug and a billy can. My stomach rumbled. I took it from her. She tied her red hair in a bun and put her helmet on. I sipped the coffee, tasting burnt.

'Take a seat,' I said.

She sat down next to me, putting her rifle next to her. Appearing nervous, she confirmed it by wringing her hands.

'Thanks for the pilchard and date sandwich between the indestructible biscuits,' I said. 'I'll leave it for a while. But thanks for the coffee. So, what's gone on in camp whilst I was away sunbathing?'

'Georges and I are in love,' she blurted.

I coughed the coffee from the back of my throat.

'It is true,' she said. 'Since we met in the hospital, our eyes have not been able to part.'

'I wasn't expecting that. I can see why my joke about your assets hadn't gone down well with him.'

'What was that about?' she quizzed.

'Erm...so, what happened?'

'After setting off the explosives, we rode across the desert. We stopped to look back. In the tantalising excitement, we made passionate love under the fireworks and stars.'

'I didn't mean what happened that night,' I said. 'Even though you're on a serious warning for breaking the code. But what happened *last* night?'

'Oh. I am not sure. Georges had gone distant. As we sat together, he gave me this.'

She delved into her breast pocket and handed me something. I marvelled at Ocker's cartridge.

'What did he say?'

'He said to tell you that friendship is worth more than any amount of gold in the world and the death of one enemy.'

'Where did he go?'

She took a few ladylike sniffs and said, 'He told me he loved me, and we would meet again one day. Georges then walked off.'

'Where? What did he take?'

Jules pointed south in the direction of the pyramid. I spotted Titan and Blister who were making their way back.

'He took nothing with him,' Jules said.

'For fuck's sake, did no one try to stop him?'

'I heard him say to Blister and Seagal that he was going to the bog. Bog meaning lavatory.'

I drank the last of the burnt coffee and looked at the files that were feasting on my breakfast. Jules got to her feet and smartened herself as Titan and Blister were almost upon us.

'What time did he leave?'

'Just after nine o'clock,' she said.

I thought of Scrap's emotional good luck when we went to find Tommy, now knowing it was a farewell. Baka started to bark; birds flew into the air. At least he was alive. If only we had Baka to send out to look for Scrap.

'Sorry, Johnny,' Blister said.

'It's not your fault you left Jules to make breakfast,' I whispered, and pulled a sickly face.

'I meant for Tommy,' Blister retorted.

'I know.' I raised my eyes.

Titan sniggered.

'You've heard then about Scrap,' Blister said.

'Does this mean we get to share Scrap's stuff?' Titan asked.

'Fancy a date with me, Jules?' Blister said.

Jules stomped off with my uneaten food, clearly upset.

I covered my face in my hand and said, 'You two have really changed.'

After coaxing Jules to make a cup of tea, I called us all in for a briefing. Jules handed out the coffee and then went back. Seagal mouthed where was the tea. I gave him a little shake of the head. Jules returned and handed out the billy cans. Proud of herself, she sat down and tucked into hers. Blister pulled a face. Titan then sniffed his. Seagal dripped what looked like watered-down rice pudding with lumps in. They all looked at me. Again, I gave a tiny shake of the head. Stirring mine, trying to make it thicker, I spotted what looked like nuts, prunes, then bits of biscuits. The extra evaporated milk oozed to the top. Feeling brave, I tried a spoonful.

'No P and A jam?' Seagal asked.

'What's that?' I mumbled, unsure what to do with my mouthful.

'At the Somme, all we had to eat was bloody plum and apple jam.' He tipped the breakfast back. 'I'd rather go back to that than this slop,' he muttered.

I laughed, spitting out the small amount in my mouth. Jules sharply looked up. I picked the bits of sardines off my lap.

'I see your manners haven't improved, boss,' Titan said.

'Oh, as you come from an aristocratic background, please show us peasants how to eat,' I said.

Titan looked at us and then Jules who was keen to see. Slowly, Titan put it to his mouth but pulled it away.

'Is there something wrong with my cooking?' Jules meekly asked.

'Come on, Titan, we know you have a huge appetite,' Blister said.

Blister tipped his billy can into Titan's. I passed mine around. As did Seagal. Blister slopped it all into Titan's, almost now at the top. Titan's tan seemed to drain into his dusty beard. Jules looked as if she was going to cry.

'Come on, Titan, she's just lost her lover,' Seagal said. 'At least boost her morale.'

Titan munched on a small bit. He smiled at Jules. She beamed back and then began finishing hers. Quickly after, Titan gagged, and hid the full billy can behind him. He then stretched and rubbed his belly as if he were full—it was hilariously pathetic.

As soon as Jules returned after washing up, we hid our own snacks from her.

'Right, listen in,' I said. 'I don't have to ask if you want to carry on. I know you have thought that none of us may return. I am only continuing to make sure you guys survive.'

'And that you want to find the link to return to your era,' Titan added.

'Now that you've brought that up, let's get it on the table,' I emotionally said. 'Who's upset by me leaving this era?'

Everyone shook their heads nonchalantly.

'Whatever,' I said, and waited till the sniggering stopped. 'The new plan is, I will head out on foot to try to find Scrap whilst...'

'He set off over twelve hours ago,' Blister butted in. 'Why are you heading out on foot?'

'Because I'm not sure how far the mines go south.'

'But that would mean for the rest of the mission east that we go on foot,' Seagal added.

They had a point. If it was going to happen, it would, even if we limited the chances the best we could.

'Good call, lads,' I said. 'I'll take the pinky south. I want you to wait here until I return. If I get into trouble, I will let off a flare.'

'What about Baka?' Jules asked.

'On my return, we'll head to the minefield and try to get Baka to leave Tommy. He can't survive much longer without food and water.'

'What about Tommy, boss?'

'I know you want to do the right thing, Titan. We all do. If we can retrieve his corpse, we will, and give him a right proper burial.'

'And a swig of rum?' Blister meaningfully asked.

'Yeah, why the fuck not.'

An hour later with the cannon unhitched and the rear emptied, the camp had been tidied and everyone was around the pinky. I waved at everyone as I headed out. I opened the small hessian bag between my legs that Blister had secretly given me. Inside were dried fruit, mints, boiled sweets, and one of Tommy's blue crystals.

CHAPTER TWENTY-EIGHT

The midday heat was draining with no canopied roof. It was at least thirty degrees. I was sweating under my robe and headgear, and that was without any uniform underneath. With a lighter payload, I did try to gain speed where I could get some breeze. When the terrain became impossible in a straight line, I stopped to let the engine cool, and I took on plenty of water. Water was not so much of a problem now that the Bedouin had exposed the water pool. Munching on Blister's leaving gifts, I placed the crystal on the dash. Perhaps there was a soft soldier side to Blister—I scoffed.

Five klicks later on another pitstop, I stood on the bonnet. The sand crunched on the new paintwork. Viewing the surrounding area, it was difficult to see some areas as they were undulated or had thickets. I tried to put myself in his shoes, working out how far I would have got walking at a normal speed between seven and nine kilometres per hour. Yet, in the dark and with the difficult terrain, a lot less. Was his walk a plod? Did he rest? What was his plan and his mindset? Had he had a breakdown? I quickly took myself out of that mindset as I had been there before. There had been some that hadn't noticed mine when I had let the black dogs in. However, a part of me didn't believe he had PTSD. It just didn't fit right.

Studying the stunning mountains with the pyramid's point just visible, I remembered he would have liked this type of scenery. He would have seen the pyramid when up with me on the ridge. Was he thinking of leaving then? The mountains and pyramid were a good focal point to head for without a compass, which I doubted he had taken. Yet, the distance at night and through the baking sun over this unrelenting harsh terrain, he wouldn't get far without plenty of water and food. I had to hold onto the positive he was a good tracker and survival expert.

Driving down into a wadi, I parked under a few trees that were clinging onto the edge for dear life. I also felt the same dehydration as I got out of my sweat pooled seat. The perspiration quickly evaporated from the leather seats. Seeing the dirt worn off it, I had forgotten they were supposed to be green. I scoffed.

According to the map, time, and compass, I had travelled forty-five klicks. Considering I had stopped every hour for five minutes, and the lie of the land was good and bad, I had been averaging five to seven miles per hour—crap. To make it worse, I had seen no signs from Scrap, not even a personal item discarded. There was a good chance I had missed him. Perhaps he had fallen into a ditch or a sinkhole, or he lay under a bush. I had tried to look when zig zagging across.

I was now very tired, especially from last night's lack of sleep. Sitting under the bank, I squeezed into the fragile roots. With my little burner, I made hot tea in my billy can. I chucked in the hard biscuits. After five minutes, I tipped in loads of sugar and mixed it. I smirked thinking of what Jules was rustling up for the lads. She was a shit cook.

A small lizard shot across from the other bank and scurried into a hole under the root. The feeling of *déjà vu* flooded me. I remembered the amazing feeling of seeing a lizard in a hole under a tree overhanging a wadi in Afghanistan. My vehicle back then was a convertible Pak Suzuki Jeep that I had bought from the ex-Mujahideen fighter, Ghulam Rasool. I recalled the handbrake didn't work, along with everything else. But, I suppose I had only paid two hundred quid, being a wealthy sum of about twenty thousand afghani to him. It had also got me to Kabul, unbelievably.

Something startled me by running up my leg. I dropped the empty billy can as I opened my eyes. The lizard scarpered. Rapidly, I looked at the time: 19:27 hours. Bollocks, I had fallen asleep thinking of Haleema in Kabul. It must have been all that talk of romance and sex earlier with Jules. Standing up quickly, I checked to see how far the sun was setting. Shit, not long to go. I kicked the sand because I had fallen asleep. I wouldn't have minded driving in the dark with a quarter of the way to go, but not after having passed so many craters and wadi's mid-way. At least I had enough rations and kit to stay the night; plus, it was not raining. Blister's voice entered my mind calling me Jonah. I quickly checked the night's sky.

Being mindful of critters, snakes, and goats, I then made a decent bed in the back. I watched a shooting star, but didn't believe in the superstitious bollocks that it was good luck.

Morning quickly came after one continuous dream. I had only been awoken by the sun on my face. I was so relaxed watching the blue sky, that for a moment I could have been on holiday. Yet, the thought of Scrap entered my mind. Stiff as a stone, smirking after lying on Tommy's crystal, I stretched out and then searched the area. Trying to put the thought of a holiday hotel's full English breakfast and a huge glass of fresh orange juice, I opened a tin of corned beef. It didn't taste right, so I washed it down with a gulp of warm water.

Getting into the driver's seat, not being the patio furniture that should have gone with the breakfast dream, I decided to head back. However, the pyramid was tempting me to check it out. Perhaps Scrap had taken a couple of water bottles and some dried fruit. Maybe by a miracle, he had got a camel lift from a local. I might be able to see some tracks further on. I estimated the distance to the pyramid to be twenty klicks.

Travelling halfway to the pyramid, the distance still looked further away than the ten klicks it should have been. I was still unsure if what I had been doing was right, knowing the lads were going to kick off when I returned. The rations had already been seriously low in camp, and the same for me here.

The anxiety was growing, along with my speed. I spotted something unusual in the middle of the wadi. Pulling alongside it, I stopped and leant out of the vehicle to pick it up. It was an army issue water bottle. The cap was off, and it was empty. Scrap's footprints had disappeared. I sat there contemplating. Water started to form around the tyres. The banks were low enough for me to see over each side. Standing up, I shouted his name over and over—dangerous. As the engine was becoming hot after a few minutes, I sped off, excited that I might find him alive.

Reaching the top of a gradual hill, the pyramid imposed its mysterious persona. I braked hard as I went over the cusp and then let the pinky roll backwards. Out of sight from the people below, without revving too much I turned it around and then killed the engine. Grabbing my rifle, I crawled back up to the brow. Through the binos, a man in pristine white robes, a red jerkin, with a hat to match was standing by a water's edge. A boy was messing about in the water. A herd of four sheep and three goats drank nearby. A small woman, perhaps a teenager, was dressed in a clean red and white chequered robe with the hijab matching. From behind the well-maintained animals, two young children appeared. Both wore immaculate white skull caps. One wore a mustard robe and the other a blue. The man was telling a boy to get out of the water and held up a clean blue towel. The kid was saying he had not finished washing—both spoke in Arabic. Assuming they were friendlies and very wealthy locals, I still checked for possible concealed weapons, including the near vicinity.

The river, or canal, was about twenty metres in width with long grass growing at the edges. Further left and right in the distance were different types of trees. The pyramid was now only three hundred metres southwest. The adventurer in me was being drawn to climb it.

The lad in the water held up something. Murky water dripped from it. The father placed out his hand and the kid waded in. My heart missed a beat as the father held up the object: a boot, the same type as mine. He then slung it on a pile of something.

With the family gone, I sprinted thirty metres down to the area. Immediately I was drawn to the pile of items. They were Scrap's uniform, including his underwear. I stared at the water, and then sat, pondering. Fuck, another friend gone. I threw Ocker's cartridge in.

Searching through his clothes revealed nothing. Underneath them all was a folded blue towel and a small and ornate box. Feeling and smelling the soft and fresh cloth, I then opened the lid. Inside was a small bottle of something like vinegar, and a porcelain bowl of what looked like cream. The smell inside the bottle was amazing. Obviously left by the family, it would be rude not to use it. However, I could not use the perfume out here.

Stripped off, with the water I lathered up from head to toe. I became aware how much muscle mass I had lost, including the array of bruises, lacerations, and bites. Scrubbing my heavy beard and scraggly hair, I ran into the middle of the river and went under. I swished all the soap off. Taking a huge breath and then relaxing under, I unloaded all the recent mind shit. Scrap, drowning, entered my mind.

Eventually, I came up to the surface. I waded to the bank, a new man. After drying on the exquisite towel, I ran back to the pinky with my bundle of rank clothes. I was cut to the core that I had not found Scrap. I couldn't return to base and tell the others the terrible news. We had too much of that recently. I would have to lie.

The journey back became numbing, going over everything we had been through since finding him kidnapped in the jungle, including his own admission to his upbringing.

Halfway, I had to fill up, using more fuel. We were already running exceptionally low; although, we now only had two vehicles to worry about, not the incredible fleet we had started with.

My head and facial hair had become frizzy, made worse by the wind as I drove as fast as I could. Arriving at camp, the lads' faces said it all as I drove in alone. Seagal kept watch for any unwanted followers. As Jules went to ask, I told them all I would give them all the good news in a while.

Taking a piss at the back of the truck, I punched a boulder. Titan came up and patted me on the shoulder, not realising I was taking a slash.

'Hey, it's the first time you've returned from reconnaissance and don't stink like shit,' he said.

'Yeah, I'm fine. Nice to see you, too,' I said sarcastically—was this becoming a ritual?

'You look different…clean. Have you had a bath or a shower?' He ruffled my frizzy hair.

I thought of Ocker secretly showering on Sameer's boat on the way to Hordio. 'Don't be daft,' I said. 'Where would I?'

With their sitrep of nothing to report in the briefing, not even hearing Baka barking, it was my turn to tell them what I had seen. I first had to ignore the teasing about me looking like a 1900s' porn star but without the attributes, apparently. Because I had been away so long, I had to exaggerate my story. I said I had found quite a few dead enemies along the way, obviously being killed by Scrap. This lie went on to say that I had followed a set of vehicle tracks all the way to a canal by the pyramid. There, I set up an OP till dawn. I continued that a few soldiers were dead in the water next to a jetty mooring and canal boats. I finished with how brave Scrap had been to sail to Cairo to get reinforcements. Jules widely smiled. The others patted her on the back and then encouraged her to get some sleep whilst they sorted the pinky.

As she climbed in the back of the truck, I tipped out my late lunch of boiled mutton and ox tongue, all bound together with oats and fruit. Whilst I started to eat crackers with a smearing of olive oil and cured meats, Seagal closed his book.

'That's weird,' Seagal whispered. 'According to my research, the canal only runs from Ismailia to the Gulf of Suez.'

'I didn't think Scrap took any weapons, very strange,' Blister insinuated. 'How were the enemy killed?'

'A lone pocket of Germans sat right out in the Negev Desert with a car. Hmmm?' Titan hushed.

Pulling them away from the truck, I told them the whole truth. Their quietness screamed of the fading hope he was alive. Titan and Seagal took themselves off, clearly emotional. Blister said I needed to be shot at dawn for falling asleep at the wadi—the timing was terrible.

Packed to leave, another fleet of planes flew from north to southeast. We were unsure if they were enemy because of the height. Perhaps they were a British recon team taking photos of the destruction we had caused. Were they looking for us? We could do with a quick reaction force.

This latest flyover caused an argument to stay put. The other side argued we had to leave now because we could not drive in the dark across the minefield. It became heated until I ordered everyone to shut up. To settle it, I said we would travel across the minefield now, and once on the other side we would find an LUP for the night if more planes flew across.

Arriving around the sweeping bend, the area filled me with dread. I had decided to take the pinky toeing the cannon on my own and lead the way to find a safe path. Obviously, no objections came in. The trail of hoof prints and dung were a huge relief, being remarkably close to the outskirts of the area.

Three hundred and fifty metres later, we were in a wadi opposite where the tragedy had happened. I stood on my seat, my view just above the row of bushes. I first spotted a spear in the ground some thirty metres away, the red cloth gently moving. Beyond the motorbike, Baka was sitting like the sphinx, and next to Tommy. Baka's eyes were closed. Two dead vultures lay a few metres away. Suddenly, my view was blocked by something too close. I lowered them to see Jules walking out and holding something in each hand. Calling her didn't stop her. Blister tiptoed over.

'What the fuck is she doing?' I asked.

'She's going to try to get Baka back by tempting him with water and food,' Blister said. 'I'll be amazed if even Baka likes her cooking.'

'You can stop tiptoeing as you are lighter than the traffic that's already been this way,' I said.

'I had better warn the fat bastard Titan.'

I scoffed.

Baka opened his eyes and wearily got to his feet, slightly shaking. It didn't stop him showing his teeth. Within ten metres, Baka started hoarsely barking. He looked ready to attack. Someone pulled the bolt-action on their rifle. I was still compelled not to see who had. Without flinching, Jules carried on walking at a slower pace. Either stupid or brave, she placed the two billy cans within three metres of Baka, who was still going berserk. She stood with her hands on her hips for twenty seconds before turning and retracing her steps as if she was leisurely strolling along the beach. Baka quickly laid, exhausted.

As Jules stepped over a wire that ran parallel to the bushes we were behind, we all raced over to her and congratulated.

'Is he dead?' Titan asked.

'Baka will be after eating Jules'…'

Titan smacked Blister around the head.

'Sorry, guys,' Blister said.

'Yes, he has passed away,' she said, and held her nose—we all pulled a grim expression.

'Can we say the Lord's prayer?' she asked, teary.

I nodded.

Whilst she recited it, I lifted my bowed head and stared at Baka. He was looking at me, and he had not even touched the rations. I was filled with sorrow.

Back in the lead, I followed the left bank which ran into a tight wadi going slightly downhill. Behind, the sound of the truck scraping the sides was worrying, especially when it bounced over the half-buried rocks. If the truck were damaged, it would be perfect mud to throw back at Titan who was driving. Every dog has its day, I thought, and then cringed at the timing of the saying.

Without warning, a bang vibrated, and I was jolted left and right. I stopped and swivelled around expecting to see Titan had rammed me. He was seven metres back, and the cannon was tilted to the side.

'Bollocks,' I said.

Titan and Blister stood up in the stationary truck. Why did it have to be them two? Jules and Seagal were asking what was going on as they couldn't see due to being packed in by the bank on either side. Climbing over the kit, I jumped down. Titan and Blister climbed over their bonnet. The cannon wheel had been sheared off. I made a stupid attempt to replace the wheel upright—no chance. I looked up at Titan and Blister who were deadpan with their hands on their hips. The silence from them was killing me.

'Not bad,' Titan said.

'Oh fuck off,' I said, taking the bait.

Blister looked up at the changing colour of the sky. 'Looks like we're camping here tonight,' he sardonically said. 'Best LUP ever.'

'Piss off.'

Jules peered over the top of the canopy, but quickly ducked—sniggering. Seagal came out from under the front of the truck.

'Right, we need to get this thing moved,' I said, 'so stop dicking about and help lift the main body up.'

'That's not going to work,' Seagal said.

'Not with that fucking attitude,' I barked.

'It's too dangerous to drag it out of this rocky dried river at night,' Jules said. 'Why don't we set up a sentry at each end and one on top until the morning.'

'Fuck me,' Blister blurted. 'I think Johnny should stay here, and you come with us, Jules.'

It had been another chance to throw some mud back on me after I said it to him at the ERL.

Taking the kit and weaponry from each vehicle in the fading daylight, I moodily walked down the wadi and left the others to sort out their own positions. I set up a barricade of scavenged rocks and dead branches. Around my sentry position, I made a wall of sandbags. The work had taken my mind off the fuck-up with the cannon wheel coming off. Not that it was my fault. Even if Flash-heart were here, it couldn't be fixed. It was a strategic weapon to lose, especially against this armoured train.

A couple of hours in, I sat behind the Lewis and sucked hard on a few mints. My thoughts turned to who we had lost, the deception of the gold and bounty on Thomas, and the task ahead. I don't know why I had listened to them as we didn't have enough manpower and firepower to take on this secret base and indestructible train. We should have headed back to Ismailia. But then, I wouldn't find the link to get back to my world. Had I become selfish to continue? Before the negativity spiralled, becoming infectious to the lads, I had to think positively and not end up like Sikes or my former self with the black dogs.

I began to think of those who had and still do look up to me as a leader, a friend, and a soul mate. The list grew. Thinking what these bloody heroes had achieved from the first time I had met them, they all deserved medals. Perhaps even the key to their town. I smiled thinking back on Bruce, slightly sad he couldn't be here right now. I closed my eyes, thinking of those who I'd had the pleasure of serving with since I joined the British Army, including missions from Will and both Great Wars. I laughed at all the twats who had mocked me, filling me with strength.

CHAPTER TWENTY-NINE

I had a dream about the Chinook coming fast and low towards our LZ, giving off its eerie blue halo glow. The marvel happens when static electricity forms a dust-flickering radiance, whipped up by the Chinook's twin rotors; a magnificent out-of-this-world sight. The Chinook circled us. As always, the last seconds of descent looked as if the hulking beast was going to belly-flop, but instead the aircraft floated to the ground. These past life-like dreams were increasing as Operation Baka went on.

As dawn broke, I began to dismantle my defences. I purposely chucked it on the bank so I couldn't see if Baka had died. Briskly, I headed back to the others. Abruptly waking them, I ordered for the coffee and breakfast to be made by Blister and Titan. Jules was to clean the camp. Seeing the strong mood that I was in, they got to work with no complaining. After redressing Seagal's wounds, his movement in his shoulder was better. I ordered him to help me move the ramps from under the truck.

As I drove the pinky, the cannon axel skidded along the two ramps. As the hub came near to the end, I stopped and waited for Seagal to pick the last one up and place it in front. A few times the ramp had flicked up because we placed it over a rock. After several manoeuvres, we swapped positions for me to do the demanding work.

Two hours later, including a rest with water and snacks, we had successfully made it through the tight wadi. It had been a monumental three hundred metres. It felt a lot more. Although exhausted, the finished task's endorphins gave us a high. Seagal took some painkillers before helping me shove the cannon aside. Eventually, it fell into a ditch. I high-fived him, but he left me hanging. Reversing the pinky, I explained what the high-five had meant. I thought back of the time I had to explain to Bruce the Dab gesture.

At the LUP, Blister said we were in for a surprise as he handed out the mugs first. Returning, he had kept whatever it was behind him under a hessian cloth. The coffee was cold but deliciously strong, something new to taste. I was just about to ask where he had got it from when he produced two billy cans from under the cloth and handed them to me and Seagal. At first, I smelt it. Not to be rude, but he had surprised me before with goat and horse dishes. Seagal tasted his first. Straightaway he went into an orgasmic mode shovelling it in.

'Fucking manners,' I said, and attentively took a spoonful. 'Oh my days, food porn,' I spluttered.

It tasted of beef, vegetables, sweet crisp croutons, and spices such as salt, pepper, and paprika. I licked the mixture at the bottom of seasoned onion and garlic soup with fat. I licked my lips and surrounding facial hair. Seagal licked the bottom of his can.

'What do you think, fellas?'

'Blister, that was the best meal I've had since visiting Titan's parents' mansion,' I said.

'It's even better than the Savoy,' Seagal said.

'Jules could be one of the Savoy ladies of the night,' Blister said.

Jules gave Blister a whack.

'Where did you get the ingredients?' I asked.

'I found a ration box at the bottom of the supplies labelled Volle Portion. All the rations have funny writing on them.' Blister pulled around a tin and showed me the label.

'That's Austro-Hungarian Army rations,' Seagal said. '*Kaffeekonserve…* coffee.'

'Tommy,' I murmured.

Blister lifted another cloth and held out half a litre of wine and a 36-gram pack of tobacco.

'Smoking is a definite no,' I said, and snatched the tobacco pack.

'What about the wine?' Titan asked—everyone held their breath.

'We haven't had the rum like you promised,' Jules sulkily said.

'Pull your school socks up on the last remark?' I said.

'Yeah, just ignore her, boss,' Titan said, creeping.

'I suppose this means the shit will stop about losing the cannon wheel,' I said.

They all nodded—pathetic.

'OK, one each.'

An ecstatic low cheer went up with fist pumping and nodding. Seagal went to high five Jules, but she left him hanging—Jesus, were they that desperate?

Searching through the boxes at the back of the truck whilst they each took one gulp, I found some dog treats and toys. There were also crystals and more Hungarian rations. Taking a small jar of rum out, I uncorked it and took a long swig. I mentally said my goodbyes to Baka and Tommy. I thought of Flash-heart and Batgirl. Hopefully, Matilda had survived. I raised another small drink for them. Then came the thought of Brat and Sikes, so I took a tiny sip and left it at that. Putting the cork back, I realised I had forgotten Scouse and Wade. I quickly toasted them with another swig. Shit, this was getting nice. I had to stop.

Heading northeast had become dull and featureless. Seagal had been quiet since we had left an hour ago. A few times he blissfully smiled. Perhaps he was having good memories of Tommy and Baka. I envisaged Sameer going back to Khalasa. It boosted my morale, until I pictured his grandparents telling him that they had been tied up at gunpoint. Had Captain Cock and his men stayed with Ra or headed back to Port Said? Perhaps a bounty had been put on my head. I sneered.

Seagal woke up. I looked across at him and then at Jules happily driving behind me. Blister and Titan were asleep next to her.

'Are you drunk?'

'Just happy,' Seagal slurred.

'I said one…' I paused. 'You've had one bottle each instead of one gulp, haven't you lot. Perhaps two each.'

He smiled.

'Blister,' I grumbled, then scoffed. 'Just like Shrek at the bar, always wanting to get the rounds in.'

I was becoming bored of the seventeen klicks of tedious desert. I had not even seen a camel dung or track. It was then I spotted an object and made a detour for it. It was a leather satchel. Excited, I put my toe down. Just for fun, I shook the pinky from left to right. Seagal awoke and grabbed his rifle. He rubbed his eyes and then checked behind.

'What did you swerve?' he croaked.

'A fucking huge hangover,' I said self-righteously.

Getting out of the vehicle, I left Seagal gulping water. I smiled at the three others doing the same. Dusting the sand off the baked satchel, I undone the strap. Believing it wasn't a trap but a message drop, I pulled out the paper. The lads joined me whilst I read it.

'What does it say?' Jules asked.

'British cannon wheel found. Telegram me for details,' Blister said.

They all chuckled.

I sighed. 'It's a reward for capturing or killing three insubordinate soldiers who were drunk on duty.'

They all looked shocked, then got the joke, and possibly the message.

'It reads,' I continued. 'Soldiers, the General has recited that you are not to return without Sergeant Rowe. If you fail, you will all face the firing squad. Including the dog.'

'Wanker,' Blister said.

'Hold on there is a bit at the bottom in different handwriting,' I said. 'Lads. I hope you are safe and well. Matilda has passed away from his injuries. Infection beat him. He had told me he was thrilled with every moment to serve with the best. News is spreading about what you have achieved. Trish sends her regards and cannot wait to make love to you, boss. The cocktails are on hold. Matron.'

'Read it again,' Titan said.

'Just the bottom bit,' Seagal added.

I did, then passed it around. Each person touched it or sniffed it. I missed the base and normality as much as them. I also felt the sadness that Matilda had died without us by his side.

Five klicks back into the journey, another satchel was found. Blister had got to it first. He read aloud that Trish had changed her mind and wanted to make love to Titan as he had a bigger penis. I snatched the letter to read, but it had the same message as before.

Continuing to the area of Target-3, a train track was sighted coming from the west and disappearing into another gorge. Bringing the pinky alongside the track, Seagal leapt out whilst I kept the engine running. He viewed the easterly mountain range with the binos. Because we were lower than the incline, the track dipped out of sight.

'Bedouin have been here. The shit has dried out,' Seagal said.

'Which way were they heading?'

'Their tracks have split, boss. The majority are heading north. The others follow the rails.'

'Which way do the wheels head?' I asked.

'Impossible to tell?'

'Go tell the others the sitrep, whilst I think what to do.'

Jules sat back in the passenger seat next to me. Seagal had decided to be gunner on the rear of the truck, perhaps sensing something like I had. I drove parallel to the tracks. The further we went, the more my sixth sense battered me of an ambush. SOP would be to use a leading 'V' advance formation as a great tactic to screen the ambushers in their flanks. However, without the manpower and lack of vehicles, we couldn't.

'There,' Jules blurted.

I took my stare from the mountain edges and looked right to the south. Bringing us to a stop, Jules aimed the Vickers at the lone object. With the engine running, I got out. Titan pulled the truck sideways so that Seagal could face Lewis the way we had come. I ordered Blister and Titan to remain. Walking in and out of the surging sand dips gave me good coverage. Yet, it also would give any enemy the chance to hide. I had pulled around my submachine gun.

Lying on the last ridge before the desert plains, like I had a shell-hole on the Somme, I scanned the whole area with the binos. Eventually, I brought the view back to the object. It was a motorbike. A Trusty.

I sprinted to the bike that was lying on its side and part buried by sand. I checked the area around it for potential booby-traps if moved. My mind was screaming at whose it was. I brushed the sand off the side satchel, proving myself correctly having seen the beige paint. Sweeping more off the frame confirmed it was one of our team members. Where was the sidecar? Where was Sikes? Immediately, I looked closer in the vicinity, imagining a hand sticking out of the sand holding a pistol like I had at the Somme when walking with Bruce.

Carefully digging further revealed the sidecar had been unbolted. Heaving the old member to its wheels, I checked the satchels. They were both empty, including the fuel tank. The motorbike was in a shitty condition. The faring filters were blocked. One tyre was flat. Sand had blown into the tank as the cap was off. Oil had leaked from the engine. It was a sad way to end up. How long had it been here? How the fuck had Sikes travelled all this way? Maybe he hadn't, an enemy had taken it from him.

Still hyper alert as I reached our convoy, I told the lads the news. I then drove off at a low speed. The train tracks continued for another five hundred metres before turning through a wide cut out in the ridge.

Bang!

I stopped as the sound echoed weirdly from the other side of the basin shaped ridge. Jules was out. Moving position, I brought the Vickers around to bear. Jules jumped the tracks and continued the twenty metres up the gradual slope. A large flock of crows followed by vultures had taken to the sky. On her stomach she peered over the ridgeline. The only sounds were both vehicles. She turned and gestured for binos. Blister was behind the rear wheel facing the other way, so I signalled for Seagal to go. Titan then took up position as main truck gunner.

Seagal and Jules were whispering between themselves and rechecking whatever they had seen. The wait was killing me. In the end, I turned off the pinky and gestured to Blister to do the same. At last, Seagal motioned that it was safe for us to advance. Grabbing my Enfield, I raced up the hill with Blister, with Titan not far behind. Silently joining the others, I lifted Tommy's binos over the edge. I was perplexed and horrified at what I saw. There was so much to take in. Movement caught my attention: a soldier was cutting off part of a decaying camel, many to choose from. I immediately thought of the Elkhaba. Scanning the remaining bodies, they were a mix of German, Turks, and Bedouin. All headless. What kind of battle had gone on?

'Sikes,' Seagal hissed.

I panned back to the lone soldier heading around the back of a German truck which had been closely parked sideways to the precipice. The huge sixty metre sheer face went around in a bowl shape. It was approximately three hundred metres across and filtered down onto our level at each furthest point. The mountains were set back half a klick in the background, only letting the sun reach the middle of the bowl.

'It's definitely Sikes,' Seagal said.

'Are you sure?' I whispered.

'British uniform, messy black hair and sideburns, and a club attached to his waist belt.'

'Give me that,' I said.

I took Seagal's sniper rifle. Titan took my binos as I scoped the area. The magnification was a little improved, but I had lost the potential Sikes. Different tracks were scattered about, all crisscrossing. A set came from the right and headed to the camp. In the shade from a tarpaulin was the front half of a British plane with its main weapon partly showing. Was that the damaged plane that limped off from the dog fight? Where was the pilot and gunner? Looking to the foreground, I counted the mass of camels, two horses, four Turks, six Bedouin, and eight Germans. Each macabre body was a different stage of decay. The crows and vultures had also had a feast. How many other soldiers were in there with Sikes? I found it difficult to believe that Sikes had made it this far. Also, annoyingly unfair that some of my lads had paid the ultimate price or had to return to base.

'What's that?' Titan quietly said.

I followed his finger. Seagal gripped his rifle as he wanted his weapon back. The train tracks were barely visible under the sand as they led to the rockface. Squinting, Titan's unidentifiable object became clearer: a huge portcullis gate.

With everyone itching to know, I pulled the group back out of sight and told them what I had seen. Theories were put forward and challenged to what had gone on. Also, why were Sikes and his men camped?

Cooking smells wafting over the ridge stopped the meeting.

'One of us has to go down to see the camp. Blister?' I said.

'Bollocks, I'm not that mad.'

'Titan?'

'I can't, boss.'

'Why's that?'

'I'm a vegetable.'

'Oh, you certainly are, Titan. But you meant vegetarian. Seagal?'

'My injuries have flared up,' he said, and rubbed his shoulder—pathetic.

'I will,' Jules said. 'Who is this Sikes?'

'General Rowe's nephew. Horrid, horrid, hard bastard,' Blister said.

'You mean Sergeant Sean Rowe. I retract my offer,' she said.

'For fuck's sake,' I muttered, 'it can't be that bad. Surely he will recognise me.'

'Yeah, yeah, you're right,' Blister said.

Carefully, I drove across the train tracks with everyone pushing behind.

'Careful not to lose a wheel,' Jules said.

'Don't you end up like these fucktards,' I retorted.

'Don't get caught in the sandy slope on the way down,' Seagal said.

'Piss off,' I said.

'Let's hope Sikes doesn't see you as a filthy Arab, again,' Titan added.

'Or a 1900's porn star,' Blister said.

I gripped the wheel and looked forwards from my cold stare. The front wheels had gone over the sandy edge.

Driving slowly down the slope, I thought about a remark that Titan had said about being seen as an Arab. I rapidly undid my *shemagh* and hitched up my robe. When it was at chest height, I let go of the wheel and started to pull the garment over my head. The first rounds whizzed above my head. I panicked to get off the rest. The next hail of lead seemed closer. Half-strangled by my robe, I ducked. Hitting the accelerator, I turned sidewards. Crunching gears, the traction spun. I raced right, trying not to slide down. The rounds rained above. In a pause in the onslaught, I turned back up to the ridge, hoping I wouldn't get stuck—oh, the embarrassment of that.

Spanking the crest, I wondered why the lads weren't returning with killer firepower. I looked across to their position. They weren't spread out on the edge taking immediate action. Instead, the group were walking back to the truck, slapping each other, and holding their sides. Blister fell to his knees pissing himself with laughter. Angry, I sharply jerked the steering wheel and raced back, my mood hotter than the engine.

Getting out as they reached the truck, the laughing hadn't stopped. Blister was almost sick. I ranted abuse. It kind of stopped the mockery, until Jules started pointing. Hysterically laughing, she couldn't finish her sentence. Fuming, I looked down at my half-naked body with dirty pants and just boots. I hadn't bothered to put my uniform on under my robe. I was not impressed; however, it had become infectious. The more I had told them to stop, the more I began to giggle. This led Titan to sit behind the Lewis and exaggerate himself firing. Blister had stripped off to his pants and was now overdoing his running around like a headless chicken. He then held his arse as if shitting himself. I let go, laughing with them. What Sikes and his men thought was beyond me.

Once it had calmed down to the odd snigger, I got my uniform on. Not wanting any more silliness, I left the *dishdasha* and *shemagh* off, but it started them off. We had to switch on. As we regrouped as professional soldiers, we all seemed lighter and human again—weird. There was humour in their eyes as they told the story. They had seen me half-naked and struggling to drive blind as someone had opened fire with the HMG from the plane. As the first rounds had been fired, it had surprised them. Apparently, the rounds had been way above my head, as if a warning. That's not how it felt for me. Seeing me bouncing out of my seat, they had found the funny side as I raced across the slope. The pinky hadn't taken a round. That seemed more important to the others than me living, or that's how I perceived it. It had only been one HMG firing.

Light was fading. We couldn't stay out in the open due to the attention that attack might have caused. Also, even the undulating sand dunes couldn't hide the truck and pinky from aerial attacks. I ordered Jules and Seagal to go back and observe the camp.

Once they had cleared us to advance, we re-joined them.

'What's the plan, boss?' Titan asked.

'May I speak?' Blister asked.

'That's normally not like you to ask,' Seagal added. 'And why the silly accent?'

'I did not want to overshadow the brilliant and forward planning of Signaller Julie Richardson. Me being less military educated,' he continued in a gentlemanly voice.

'Go on then,' I dreaded saying.

'As the busty redhead has not mentioned this, perhaps not foreseeing, I will. Over there is a rock jutting out with a shallow cave behind. We can hide behind that.'

'Well done, Blister,' I said.

'Fuck me,' Blister impersonated me. 'I think Jules should stay here whilst you come with us, Blister.'

She sighed.

'Why did you say that in an Italian accent?' I jested.

'Piss off,' Blister said.

'You were nearly cleverer than Jules,' Seagal said. 'That "jutting rock" is a sea stack. It is a geological landform consisting of a steep and often vertical column or columns of rock in the sea formed by wave erosion.'

'Oh do fuck off, egghead,' Blister said.

'You can stop that silly voice now,' I added. 'Right, let's go in a wide semicircle and head to the LUP.'

As much as we all needed the humour and relief, we had to switch on to finish the job and go our separate ways. Hopefully, 2013 for me.

CHAPTER THIRTY

With little light due to heavy clouds, I studied what was on the end of my spoon. I then smelt the fishy smell from the billy can. Jules had soaked some raw kidney beans and mixed them with some fish, porridge, and water. Not only were the beans a little hard, but it also just tasted wrong. However, I couldn't keep refusing meals as I was very hungry. After eating it, I went around and checked on everyone. I was the only one not to have binned the dinner, including Jules. They had all opted to eat basic rations.

After discussing the plan that I was to go across at dawn on my own, Blister began to set up the mortar. I ordered one man on stag, changing every three hours. Tucking in behind the Truck's Lewis, I pulled up the brown blanket.

I had an awful sleep with griping pains. At one stage I had to go to the rear of the cave for a bad shit. During my stag for the last two and a half hours, yesterday's meal had repeated on me from both ends. Pulling back the blanket revealed I was covered in Baka's hair. They had stuck to my sweaty skin, even though I was very cold last night.

I was lightly equipped: sub, pistol, and knife. After testing the sub's light, I set off under the watchful eye of the lads. Time check: 05:15 hours. Keeping close to the bay's wall, I thought of the sea erosion that had caused this shape millions of years ago. My nerdy thoughts were interrupted by my churning gut. Nausea settled in. Although a little apprehensive of meeting Sikes and his men, I couldn't put it down to that. Perhaps I had Deli-belly after swallowing the canal water.

At the portcullis gate, I quickly shone the light into the shadows that formed under the rising sun. The stomach pain had worsened, and I doubled over trying to disguise the vomit that followed. With some slow breathing, I gripped the cold iron and straightened up. I wished I had brought some water to wash the taste.

Manning-up, I tucked into the wall and moved on. I was shocked to see a decomposing RFC pilot who sat inside the Trusty's sidecar. Already queasy, I turned away from the rotting stench. I only let go of my breath when I was a good six paces towards the camp. As soon as I heard it, I was down on one knee. I tried to stop my weapon from trembling. Closing my eyes to listen harder to the speech, I started to go dizzy by the weird lights in my eyes. I quickly opened them and squatted a few metres forward to listen.

'We dare not go over the top, lest perchance we should fall to our death,' someone hoarsely said.

There was a pause…

'I'll thrash you to the end of your life if you do not take my fucking orders, like I had Lieutenant Taylor,' Sikes said.

Seconds went by…

'We will be slaughtered,' the first person said.

A weapon was cocked…

'I will shoot you like a sick dog, like I had Second Lieutenant Bridge. This fuckery stops now, Major Smith.'

'But…'

'I am in charge of this one hundred metre frontline,' Sikes interrupted. 'Do you rabble understand me?'

'Yes, sir,' a high-pitched voice said.

'Do not call me "sir", Private L'Estrange.'

My heart fluttered. What the hell was he doing here? He can't be.

'Don't you make a sound, you filthy Bedouin,' Sikes bellowed.

There were a few grunts and groans.

I snuck in further towards the camp to see what was going on as none of this made sense.

'I've told you to put that away,' Sikes said. 'You should be standing on the fire step watching the Hun across no man's land.'

Thump…thump!

'My eternal apologies, Sergeant,' a Frenchman said. 'I was trying to portray some love, not…'

'Poets write bollocks,' Sikes interrupted. 'It's revulsion, not love.'

I thought of the French Foreign Legion prisoners we had rescued. I scratched my head, inflaming my blinding headache.

A fire was stoked, the ashes and smoke rising up. Embers formed a shadow on the tarpaulin. Pans began clanking.

'London Dogs, get skinning those rats,' Sikes ordered.

The London Dogs were here as well? This was becoming absurd.

Wiping the sweat from my forehead and ignoring the sickness, I pushed into the wall and crept around. I found it easier to stoop over to rid the spasms. Flicking the switch to get in the zone wasn't working. The stench from the camp was awful. Not just the new cooking smells, but rotting flesh.

I reached the rear of the Bristol Scout. Rounds had penetrated the main canvas body and blew apart the red, white, and blue tail rudder. A shadow loomed from behind me, my neck hairs bristled. I turned around. Sikes stood right behind me, tapping his club in his other hand. He looked a wreck, and he stunk worse than the shit I was bringing up. He stepped in closer, his bloodshot eyes ablaze. I took a few steps back.

'Where the ruddy hell have you been, Corporal Vince?' Sikes yelled.

'I…I've come from…'

'You took your bloody time, laddie.'

He kept walking. I was moving back quicker than him. Just as I thought about raising my weapon, something tripped me up and I scrambled back. Sikes lifted his foot off my MP-18 and picked it up.

'Boche,' he said. 'Is this what you brought back from the Boche trench raid? Where are the two prisoners I ordered you to capture? I hope you have the fucking plans of their trenches.'

I hadn't taken my glare of the rotting, magot infested RFC pilot's corpse leant against a German ammo supply crate. I lowered my eyes from his forehead wound to staring at his billy can of decaying food. He had his hand through a mug of tea, a skin of dead flies on top.

'Major Smith, this is Corporal Johnny Vince. Next time, move your legs in so he doesn't trip.'

Sikes walked over and kicked them. He then leant over to me, the rum still on his breath.

'No darling has ever had a square bashing,' he whispered.

I blinked fast to rid the sweat and blurring. My hand slid slowly down to my holster.

Sikes slowly swept around the end of the sub, his finger clearly on the trigger.

'You remember your billeted squad, Vince? Private Adrian L'Estrange. You named him Bruce. He still calls me sir at times to mock me. Isn't that correct?' Sikes paused, as if listening to a reply.

'I do,' I said.

'Not you,' he barked.

Sikes made a quick dash over to a grey blanket and lifted it off. A swarm of flies clouded. What the actual fuck? I turned away from the hole-ridden young German soldier sitting with a rifle across his lap.

'You can't hide, L'Estrange,' Sikes seethed. 'I think you want to feel the wrath of my cudgel. Hmm…yes, that's better, laddie.'

Again, I wiped the sweat and then placed my hand on my stomach.

'Remember Bombardier Mark Morrison? Blister you named him. He has now learnt not to be so insubordinate.'

Now what the fuck? I thought.

Sikes shouldered my weapon and took a few steps backwards. He then ripped down a grey blanket. I slightly lifted over a three-foot sandbagged wall to see a German slumped across a mortar.

'Sorry, Bombardier, did you mutter something? No, I thought not. But if you do it again, try saying it like a man and not a yellow belly.'

'Fuck,' I whispered.

Sikes pointed his club at the truck. 'Remember medic Jason Bentley? Titan you named him. As you can see, he has at last shaved off that monstrosity. What, Bentley? Oh, you want to remind Corporal Vince where the CCS is.'

In the shadows, a large Turkish soldier lay with his head on a German HMG. His uniform was peppered with puncture marks.

'Jesus,' I muttered.

Sikes faced me, looking at my sweaty hand on my pistol. He swung the sub around and strode over to the German transporter, lifting the tarpaulin side.

'Perhaps the London Dogs have cooked us a fine rat stew. How about it, Dogs?'

I didn't want to look but was compelled by the madness. Four dead Bedouin were sat in a circle with the help of rope. Their heads were bowed.

'Say hello to the London Dogs, Vince.'

I wondered if there was going to be a negligent discharge from Sikes' weapon still facing me, or that I would end up in the pot.

'Are you hungry, Johnny?' he tenderly said.

I stayed silent.

Sikes lifted a piece of hairy, rotten meat from a pot between the Bedouin. My body shuddered with another pain spasm.

'Well?' he menacingly said.

'Thanks, Sergeant Rowe, but I've eaten.'

Sikes chucked the joint back in the pot that wasn't even cooking. I needed the next opportunity to take him out, as I felt I was winning the trust of this psycho. Yet, he turned and faced the weapon at me.

'I'm glad you have remembered how to properly address me,' he said.

'Yes, sir.'

'If those filthy Bedouin try to escape like our Boche prisoner had escaped the custody of L'Estrange, you have my permission to shoot them.'

He pointed behind me to the far corner. Grimacing, I turned slowly to see two naked men back-to-back and bound by rope. They had suffered many beatings. I faced back and looked at Sikes' club. There was no way of winning Sikes' trust. He had *become* the black dog.

'And last of all, this blithering wet behind the ears French poet Private Edouard Boivin,' he said.

Sitting under the Bristol's double wings was a young lad in a French uniform. He was holding a book in one hand and a fountain pen in the other. His throat had been cut. Where had he come from?

'What?' Sikes bellowed. 'I've warned you to only speak in English.'

I grimaced at what was coming next. Sikes stomped over and snatched the book. He then threw it on the embers. I covertly undid my holster.

'Oh stop crying for your mummy, Boivin,' Sikes said.

'Sergeant…Sean…you need my help,' I dared say. 'We can make you better and get you home to sort your shit out. Remember our conversation in your quarters?'

Sikes looked at me. Tears filled his eyes. He searched around at the camp, the carnage reflecting in his sad eyes.

'I am a failure,' he muttered.

'No. Look what you have achieved in the Boer War and the Somme.' I went to get up.

'Sit down,' he growled.

It was as if a switch had been flicked, his face snarling in disgust in me. I looked at the end of his trembling machine gun that he pointed towards me.

'Not so fucking loquacious and obnoxious now, are you,' he said.

I held onto my guts, wishing I had slotted him when I'd had the chance.

'Well?'

'What?' I croaked, desperate for water.

'What Boche trench news do you have for me? I need to report back to the orderly room.'

He really must think he is still on the Somme, I thought.

The sun caused his shadow over me as he just stared at me. Flies danced in the beams. He was becoming more agitated, so he moodily lifted a lid on a wooden box.

'I saw you touch my telephone in my quarters,' he said. 'I could phone to have you marched away by the MPs.'

I gritted the gut pains away, and said, 'The Germans have three concrete bunkers, each fitted with a heavy machine gun.'

'What was my nickname?'

I didn't reply.

'Perhaps you're a fucking traitor like Taylor and Bridge. Fucking useless darlings.'

He stomped off and out under the netting. Dizzy, I reached down for my pistol and brought it onto my lap, hiding it with my other hand. Voices and weird movements from the dead bodies in camp confused me. I staggered up; the pains continued. As I reached the edge of the camp, Sikes was dragging someone and arguing with him. Blinking hard, an object was racing across the flats.

'Field Marshal Georges Demblon wasn't a darling,' Sikes said. 'He was a liar. Impersonating an officer carries the death penalty by firing squad. His real name was Private William Hewitt from the South African Heavy Artillery.'

Sikes put the pistol to the dead soldier's already mashed head and fired. He then let the corpse drop to the ground.

'Where's Corporal Vince, Private Hurst?' he asked me.

'You need stopping, Sikes.'

'Is that right, laddie? And what fucking army is going to?'

Taking a deep breath and standing tall, I aimed my pistol. Although shaking, everything became clear. The pains and nausea subsided. Sikes raised his weapon at me. He gritted his teeth, food remnants in between. My finger slightly pressed the trigger. Thoughts entered of me putting the pistol to my head when in my house because of the PTSD. I shook them. The blinding pain worsened.

'This fuckery stops now, Hurst.'

Thud!

Blister threw the spade. Swinging his sub around, he stood aiming over Sikes who lay groaning on the floor.

'No, Mark,' I ordered.

'Are you sure you don't want me to finish this piece…'

'Stand down.'

Reluctantly, he did. I sank to my knees, crippled in pain. My thumping head was lifted, and I drank from the water bottle.

'Call the others over,' I gasped.

'Are you OK, boss?'

'It's not nice in there,' I mumbled, thumbing over my shoulder. 'There's a double of you.' I tried to laugh.

'Tell me you didn't eat that dinner,' Blister said. 'The kidney beans weren't perfectly cooked. And the pilchards were off, having been open since the last meal.'

My guts contracted. I followed through like I had in the Nissan with Rabbit.

'Don't worry, fella, we'll get you right,' he said.

Shaking on the floor, I held onto the water bottle for comfort, staring across at Sikes who was shivering with the infamous thousand-yard stare. The pinky arrived. Jules was holding a scarf to her nose and mouth. I wasn't sure if it was because of my diarrhoea. Titan kicked Sikes and started to rant. I ordered him to stop.

'Lads,' I croaked, 'unload the pinky with enough fuel and rations for Jules to head back to Ismailia with Sikes.'

'But...'

'That's a fucking order,' I interrupted Jules.

'Johnny, you have a high fever and you're delirious,' Titan said.

'I've remembered my promise to get Sikes back and right in the mind. Make sure he does. I let the back dogs in once, and without intervention ...' I stopped, forgetting where I had got to. 'Tie him up,' I slurred.

'Oh fuck,' Seagal said.

Gasps went around.

Opening my eyes, the lads had taken up defensive positions. Shading the sun, I looked at the line on the cliff top and panned the whole basin. I staggered to my feet and held onto the pinky. Like a scene from the movie, *Zulu*, hundreds of soldiers on camels and horseback watched down on us.

'What do we do, boss?' someone said.

'Stand down,' I said, barely audible.

'No way. I'm not going without a fucking fight,' Seagal said—everyone agreed.

'Maybe a bit of hearts and minds might win the fight,' I said.

A lone figure dressed in a white robe and holding a spear rode towards us on horseback. Slowly dismounting, leaving a smaller person on the horse, the figure walked over.

'Bedouin,' I muttered. 'Do not open fire. Wait to be engaged.'

Titan sighed, then lowered his Nitro. I blinked, trying to study the fighters on the cliff edge. None of them were bearing arms this way.

'Make your body language passive,' I muttered. 'I hope you have got those sovereigns, Seagal.'

My face planted the soft sand.

CHAPTER THIRTY-ONE

Weird lights, smells, and tribal people confused me. I wasn't sure what were nightmares and what was real. Was this the Indonesian tribe at the lost city that had found me dangling on the rope?

When I had been awake with the agony, the room had been a blur. The nightmare seemed to go on for days. I would be startled with another bout of sickness or fever. Hands would touch my clammy body, eyes peering through their masks. The voices had been inaudible, except a woman's smooth, broken English. It always had been sharply exchanged for Sikes. I would wake again thinking that it had been a nightmare.

I opened my eyes to darkness. A light came across to me and softly illuminated the woven branches covered by clay. There was a tiny hole at the top of the roof. A star shone through. Behind the flame was a person in a white robe. I waited for the next evil part of the dream. He lit the candles on the floor around my thatched straw bed. I was lying naked under animal skins.

'Where am I?' I croaked.

'You are safe,' the lady caringly said.

'Khalida?'

'Yes.'

I went to sit up but was very weak. I slumped on the straw and felt my inverted belly.

'You are lucky to live,' she said.

I smiled and shut my eyes.

Leaning on my elbows, I half-sat. The piercing light came from the hole in the tepee-shaped roof. The smell was perfumed. I looked around for the lads, but it was empty. Had meeting Khalida with the candle been a dream? Different bowls lined the edges of the circled hut I was in. Beams of light strobed through the crude timber door.

Surprisingly, it was cool in this clay like oven. I swung my legs out from the sewn together skin blanket and took a sharp breath as the blood surged to my feet. I was very skinny and had strange drawings on my body. Trying to work out what they were, the door opened, and a waft of heat followed Khalida in. More females entered carrying jugs. All wore different masks to Khalida's. They began to stare at me, too long. I covered my tackle. Khalida waved them away. They bowed and disappeared, shutting the door. Khalida took off her mask. Once again, I was stunned by her beauty.

'You need to wash,' she said.

Having been in the same embarrassingly naked situation before with the stunning Haleema, it had now given me some balls. I stood up and held my arms up, ready for my clean. I went dizzy.

'After you have eaten,' she said.

I quickly sat down, just before I was going to faint—or was it that I felt an idiot? Khalida handed me a tiny bowl of green leaves with a date on top.

'Please, eat,' she said.

'I need more than that after a few days.'

I started to cram the leaves in, swallowing hard. Then my stomach started to growl going into spasms. She smugly smiled.

'Being here for ten days, you need to slowly build your strength.'

'What? "Ten days"? Are you joking with me, Batgirl?'

'No. I prefer you call me Khalida now that I am back as the leader of the Bedouin.'

'That was you on that horse by the minefield.'

'Yes. You hide badly.'

'That's because there wasn't a big enough boulder to hide Titan,' I joked.

I caught her beautiful smile just before she leant back behind her. I picked the remnants that I had spluttered and put them back in my mouth. She held out a chalice like the one at Ra's. I sipped the water, disappointed it wasn't the same fruity wine.

'Who was the kid on the back behind you?' I asked.

'One of my many children, Jamil Seif.'

'He's your kid?'

'You save him from death. My husband, Ra Seif, very happy.'

'Hold on, you're married to Ra? I thought you were married to Imam. Not your horse, I mean.'

'I have many husbands.'

'Batgirl is a slut,' I joked.

'Is slut good word?'

'Oh yeah,' I said sarcastically.

Khalida took the food bowl and chalice from me. Again, I stood up, ready for her to wash me. She handed me the water churn and a piece of cloth. I was disheartened that I had to do it instead of her.

'Where're my clothes?' I asked. 'I want to get back to my unit.'

'You rest for a couple of days.'

'Where are the lads?' I insinuated.

'Safe.'

'Did you spare our lives at the morbid camp because we had saved your lad?'

'No.'

'Oh. It must be because me and Scrap saved your delicate arse from the sinkhole.'

Khalida sighed and opened the door. Two Bedouin outside looked in. I covered myself with the churn.

'Did you save us because you missed the squad?' I pressed.

'No. We need you to kill underground enemy, so we can get Egyptian gold back.'

She shut the door.

'Once a pikey, always a pikey,' I yelled.

For the next three days, I got used to the servants bringing in a variety and accumulating in portion size of food. The hotel service didn't stretch to alcohol, which was a shame. Even my look-alike cider piss that had amassed in small vessels seemed tempting. I had turned my ground level apartment into a gym, using whatever objects I could to rebuild my strength. I was desperate to get back to my lads, hoping they were surviving on the remaining sparse and dull rations.

In that R&R period, I had wondered if Khalida had let Sikes live. Let alone agree to Jules taking him back. If it had been granted, had Jules made it back OK? Surely reinforcements were on the way.

Finishing off my bowl of meats and vegetables, I changed into my washed uniform and then slid over my robe. Due to my constipation, I gulped down the third glass of fruit juice. Fitting my dependable watch that had served me well since the Somme, I checked the time. It had stopped working. They could have at least wound it up in the five-star accommodation, I thought, and smiled.

It was quiet outside. Maybe the whole village was waiting for me.

Perhaps they were going to cheer and clap. I hope not. Opening the door for the first time exposed nothing but the empty desert—how dejecting. Directly in front, a woven branch fence circled my mud like bread oven. Pampas styled grass sprigs were spaced every metre. Where the hell was everyone? Perhaps they had gone to Bedouin church because it was Sunday.

I checked over the fence and into the bland desert in every direction—nothing. At least the shimmering sea in the furthest background was inviting. I should have complained to the manager for not having a proper sea view—it kept me amused. How was I supposed to get out of here? Wherever here was.

I stared at the camel, my Bergan by its feet.

'Oh, you've got to be shitting me,' I said. 'No fucking way am I getting on that.'

I found the map, compass, and a parcel of dates that Khalida had left inside the top of the Bergan. I had eventually managed to get on the bloody thing. My horse-riding skills were already shit, but better than the camel riding. It was sad that Matilda wasn't here to take the piss.

There had been no trail left from the tribe. The Bedouin camp had been situated close to the Dead Sea; an 'x' left on the map I had presumed where the huge basin was. I made a mental note to bollock Khalida for marking the map, like I had Shrek in the Hangar-2 briefing room. The RV's distance was only ten klicks west. Easy, but with no weapons, not so.

Heading west, I was about three hundred metres from a small smoke plume. It blended into the mountains in the background. I fixed the binos on a flash at the top of the bay's edge. Recognising the signal, I slid down. The camel grunted. Sifting through my Bergan, I found the square piece of polished aluminium. I pictured Flash-heart handing them out.

After returning the signal, I got the go ahead that I had been acknowledged. I was most probably being watched by Seagal's sniper rifle. After a few goes at mounting, I rode slowly down to the camp at the stack. This fucking hairy beast didn't understand my kicks to go faster.

The smoke had gone. Blister and Titan appeared exhausted. The camp consisted of Truck-1 nose to nose with a German truck. Where the heck had that come from? I was happy to see our team member again. Both had the sides rolled up with a HMG facing out. Immediately, I looked across at Sikes' camp. The haunted camp and graveyard had gone. Titan gingerly climbed out of Truck-1. I ungracefully dismounted and wearily walked over.

'You're looking well,' Titan quietly said.

'Thanks, dude.'

I waved Seagal down from his position. Blister barely managed a wave and his eyelids tried to stay open as he plodded over. Again, it wasn't a huge welcome home. For me, it was amazing to be back. Yet, I began to feel a little guilty of their survival compared to my luxury R&R.

'Good to see Jules didn't kill you off with her cooking,' Blister lethargically said. 'Bloody worse than that nerve agent.'

'Are you guys OK?' I said.

Titan sat down and said, 'Barely, but we're in the Elite. This is what we had trained for.'

Seagal came running down full of pride and enthusiastically said, 'Johnny, I thought you bricky mofo would survive.'

I didn't care about his mix of modern and strange Victorian sayings. His quick hug and back slapping nearly knocked me over. Perhaps he had been at the medical drugs cabinet.

'Good to be back, you church-bell,' I greeted.

'Although it is good to see you catching on with the Victorian lingo, I don't think you understand that "church-bell" means a talkative woman,' Seagal said.

'Sorry, I meant bellend.'

'I didn't miss your non-humour,' he said. 'I'll get a brew on and tell you all that has happened and how well the Bedouin have looked after…'

'Ahem,' Titan interrupted.

Titan's eyes went wide with a little shake of the head. Seagal stared at him for a few seconds and then went all exhausted and almost sat down. Blister sunk his face in his hands.

'You had one job, Seagal,' Blister said.

'Oh fuck off,' I said, 'I saw the campfire. And I bet if I ask Khalida if you've been looked after.'

They remained quiet, so I walked around the back of the truck to see loads of new provisions and recent pits in the ground. And surprisingly, a new cannon.

'You need to get up earlier to try to wind me up,' I said. 'Now get a brew on and tell me what's happened.'

The camp was very relaxed considering where we were. It was as if a Sunday at our Ismailia base when we were winding down and chatting about the previous Saturday night's mess do. In fact, once leaving my clay oven this morning, I'd had a strange feeling of the date 29th April. I couldn't reason why, but it was growing inside.

Blister started the conversation off with a bit of banter about me being so fat and unhealthy. I had missed him. Then, he began at the point where he had whacked Sikes with the shovel and nearly put "two into his head, to make sure he was dead". That was until I had ordered him to stand down.

Once I had collapsed, the Bedouin leader revealed who she was under her *shemagh,* and so had the horse pillion. However, seeing Sikes, Batgirl had drawn her curved dagger and briskly made her way over. Titan had restrained her. The tribe on the ridge had become restless. Blister had warned her that if it kicked off, she and Jamil were the first to go. Seagal had his weapon sighted on the lad. After a tense few seconds, Batgirl stood back and put her knife away.

It had been agreed that Jules took Sikes back. After the pinky had been loaded with Sikes bound, she was given a map and compass.

'Did Jules make it back?' I said.

'I followed her on horseback for five klicks to make sure Batgirl wouldn't go back on her word,' Seagal said.

'His fanny was like an empty headlock when he returned,' Titan said.

Seagal threw a tin of herring. 'Piss off.'

We all laughed.

'Any more news on Jules or Sikes?'

'No, boss,' Blister said.

Apparently, I had been taken away on a stretcher behind a camel. A few of the women tribe and Batgirl had entered the psychotic world that Sikes had been living in. The Bedouin had taken Sikes' 'friends' away. A distant fire had been seen later, with a wretched odour. The remaining tribe had cleared the site, including towing the plane away. Our lads had set up the stack LUP come OP with both trucks. They had also been feasting with food service from the women. Batgirl had ordered that the cannon and artillery shells remain here. Between them, the plan was discussed. Then, the whole tribe had left last night.

'So, what's the plan?' I said.

'We are to go in and kill the enemy. Finally, bring out the gold,' Seagal said.

'And if we don't, we'll be on the Bedouin menu at their next banquet,' Titan said.

Chapter Thirty-one

'Plenty of leftovers from you for Egypt,' Blister said.

Titan gave him a dead arm.

Leaving them to their banter, I stared at the portcullis gate whilst throwing away the dregs of my black tea.

'We could dig under it,' I interrupted them.

'We've tried that. There's an iron block under the sand,' Titan said. 'And before you say about blowing the rails, Batgirl said the train has to transport the amount of gold.'

'Not Ra's donkey and cart,' Blister added. 'Batgirl also wants to do a deal with the British Army for the locomotive, sell it to them.'

'Pikey,' I said. 'We could wait till the enemy came out, and then rush in.'

'I doubt there are many enemies left to come out. Except a few on the locomotive,' Seagal said.

'Why's that?'

'Four troop carriers had left at the stroke of midnight. We and the Bedouin tailed into the desert and attacked them,' Titan proudly said.

'What?' I exclaimed. 'And you forgot to mention this.'

'Didn't want to make you feel left out and useless whilst you were sunning it up, boss,' Seagal said—the three of them sniggered.

'Twenty-seven dead. Two seriously injured. And one young survivor unharmed,' Blister said. 'The passenger had pissed himself whilst hiding in the cab's footwell.'

'Couldn't blame him, Blister,' Titan argued, 'he was barely thirteen.'

I remembered the frightened lad, Heinz Otto Fausten, in the German underground communication bunker. 'Did you let him live?' I said.

'We're not fucking savages,' Titan said.

'Batgirl wanted to torture the lad, but we got chummy with him,' Blister continued. 'Offering our hospitality and sweets, we found out the layout of the bunker and who was remaining: six German officers and four Turks. The locomotive leaves Tuesday night for Ismailia, and then onto Cairo.'

'And the German lad?' I asked.

'Batgirl had ordered a few of the tribe to take him back to her husband, Ra. The rest of the Bedouin were tasked to scour the town to kill off the remaining enemy who were supposed to meet there Tuesday morning. The German lad had spilled the beans. He also said that the enemy we had ambushed and killed were heading to the town to form an army of tanks and vehicles to assist the locomotive.'

'Let's hope the Bedouin had stifled the enemy in the town,' I said.

'What's the plan, boss?' Seagal said.

I looked beyond the eager faces, not really having a clue. I then spotted the piles of shells and mortars.

'Well?' Titan said.

'At dawn, we blow the fucking gate.'

CHAPTER THIRTY-TWO

Dead on the sunrise, Blister towed the Bedouin cannon into position. Me and Titan circled the edge in Truck-1 towards the portcullis. Seagal had set up in his camo suit directly opposite, keeping his sniper rifle aimed at the entrance.

We parked right of the estimated five-tonne iron bars. Titan handed me a mortar projectile. I placed it in the rock channel behind the gate, hoping to blow it out and not collapse the precipice above. Finishing at the top arch, I stopped and climbed down. Titan handed me another artillery shell as he reckoned it needed more. This continued till I had done the whole arch.

A little quiet spat followed about Titan wanting more on the left, as not to unbalance the explosion to stop the gate buckling instead of toppling over. Whilst Titan climbed the left side, I continued to run back and forth for more explosives. Running out of explosives, he said we had to use the grenades. I looked at him, wondering if he was obsessed. He whispered that there was only a foot left to go. I gave him half a bucketful as we need to keep some back for the attack. Wedging tight the grenade handles, he pulled the pin on each.

Sneaking back to the truck under the watchful eye of Seagal, I signalled him to retreat. Blister had parked the German truck almost back in the LUP cave. I hid our truck close to the enormous stack. With thumbs up all around, I pulled down my loaded Bergan from the truck.

'Fucking ammo up, lads,' I said.

I laid behind the Lewis, three metres from the right of the cannon. Blister was making a few final adjustments to it. I held tight the stock in my shoulder, then ducked my face into the sand.

'Stop fucking around and hit it,' I said.

'It's because it's a fucking German cannon,' he said.

'Just press the fucking trigger.'

'"Press the trigger"? Dickhead.'

He pulled the cable.

BOOOM!

I hadn't replaced my head down as the cannon shot backwards into the desert. I was covered in the back blast.

BOOOM!

A huge shockwave trembled below. A gust of sand raced up the slope and over me, pushing me deeper into my shallow grave. Even my shout of 'What the fuck?' was drowned out.

Lifting my eyes over my arm around my nose and mouth, I couldn't see Blister through the haze. The cannon had almost disappeared. Thuds like at Target-1 started to rain around me. A wave of heat warmed the top of my head and back.

'Blister,' I shouted.

My voice seemed not to go beyond the debris blizzard.

It was approximately five minutes before the cloud started to disperse. The only noise was the granules landing on the Lewis' peeled beige-painted barrel. I checked the edges of the cliff as I still couldn't see if the gate had been blown away. Blister came crawling over, coughing.

'Did you miss my arm around you for comfort?' he asked.

'No. You really…holy shit.'

'Now I should get the medal for best explosion,' he said.

'You're only supposed to blow the bloody doors off,' I said in my best Michael Cane impression.

'Why did you say that as Henry Asquith?'

'Who?'

'Prime Minister…'

'Contact,' I interrupted.

I squeezed the trigger. My rounds had no stopping impact on the German armoured car as the chained wheels punched through the rocks. It collided with the mangled gate that laid eight metres away. I quickly changed mags. Blister was firing through my cordite smoke with his Enfield, trying to take out the driver through the slits. The shutter plating closed. I fired controlled bursts at the solid rubber tyres that were trying to rock off the gate—no effect. I switched the firepower to the turning main turret. Sparks gave me an indication I was dead on target. The noise inside that car must have been hell. Blister fired onto the side gun behind the passenger's door. Both HMGs battered our positions.

Blister heaved his Bergan backwards whilst they suppressed us. I slightly lifted and returned fire.

'Set up the fucking grenade launcher,' I yelled.

'The distance is too far.'

'Fucking mortar them then before it comes off that gate.'

Blister ran back to the LUP. Rounds whizzed over his ducked head. I slapped another round mag on and shuffled further left. Just as I blitzed the turret, it faced my direction. The truck bounced off the gate. Fuck. In a plume of exhaust smoke with all three weapons firing, it groaned this way. I had nowhere to go but hide behind the stationary cannon. Instead, I unclipped my grenades. Suddenly, a new weapon sounded: two powerful shots. The armoured car's main gunner turret stopped firing. A huge calibre weapon flashed from the right cliff's edge, then another slightly left. The enemy armoured car stopped.

Another exact vehicle came out of the tunnel entrance. Seagal continued to fire his German anti-tank weapon. Titan with his Nitro Express. There was no point in me wasting ammo. As much as the driver weaved, chunks of metal flew off it. The vehicle had no chance. Seagal had reverted to his John Rigby hunting rifle. Perhaps to conserve ammo or give his body a rest. The second armoured car ceased.

Smoke gassed at the entrance. Then, further ones dotted along, one after the other. Through the smoke screen, a substantial number of Turkish soldiers advance at speed. I began to mow-down the ones who directly ran towards me. They should have taken cover behind the disabled vehicles—idiots. A few managed to return fire at my position, splats of sand showered me.

Sighting those that had taken cover on Car-1, one soldier opened the door. His red mist sprayed from behind and he slumped to the floor. Those who had worked out he had been taken down from above started to return fire at Titan, Seagal, and his three 'mates'. The edge sent shards over them; the real lads crawled back. I fired a burst into those stupid enough to come out.

BOOOM!

A grenade had been thrown. Even though I was out of its range, more followed. It made those hidden behind Car-2 difficult to see. Another smoke barrage clouded whilst I ripped off a mag to replace a new one. Shockingly, five Turks were now screaming out of the tunnel with bayonets fixed. Another armoured car came racing out and ran over the dead or injured. Slapping a new mag, only three remained charging.

Another slumped forward, as if in slow motion. Pissed off Seagal was taking the sniper glory, I dropped the other two.

The new armoured car turned sideways to the cliff and pummelled the edge. The lads were unable to return fire. I fully opened-up the Lewis on the side gunner that faced me. He returned fire, but then stopped. The rear gunner swivelled around and unleashed his firepower. I was just out of its arc. The top turret faced me and opened fire. Slightly left, he then fired too far right. Just as it had me bracketed, a large spark shook it. The gunner stopped.

Titan and Seagal seized the opportunity and put it out of action with a ferocious barrage of continuous firepower, one after the other as the other reloaded. Low on ammo, I pulled around my Enfield and took down the enemy that came out of hiding. I knew there were a few still waiting in the vehicles. A few dared to poke half-out to return fire. It was short lived, like them.

The haze lifted; an eerie stillness followed. Where the hell was Blister? I was still lying in the shallow scrape that had formed. I brought up the grenade launcher coupling. A recollection came of Blister, Titan, and Bruce taking the piss in our quarters at the Somme. This time I had got the correct modified Enfield and kit. The joyous reunion was ruined when the infamous mechanical rattle came from the tunnel. My arm hairs bristled.

'Oh fuck,' I muttered.

First into view in the tunnel was another tank, like the one I had hid in at the scrapheap. The two-man cockpit, twin tracked tank nimbly moved. It stopped just under where the gate would have been. Perhaps the driver was surveying the carnage, fearful of what it was up against. The front flap opened. The front stumpy weapon moved left to right and then up and down, but with minimal movement. What was it doing?

Bang…

The sand erupted over me as the thirty-seven-millimetre cannon calibre round buried in close by. I shimmied backwards…

Bang…

I shouldered my weapon and picked up my Bergan as it continued to try to blow me apart…

Bang…

A lighter machine gun followed me. I back tracked into the desert, hating taking my eyes off the tank. Hearing Titan and Seagal return fire, I went prone and set out the bi-pod. The tank unleashed its main gun towards the cliff. Yet, the vehicle was too near. It drove forwards with its turret facing behind. So, the top turret could move 360—degrees, not good for us.

I squeezed off the Lewis trigger, hitting some that had ventured out of the tunnel. I followed up on those that had run back in. Titan's weapon wasn't stopping the tank. Seagal sent two rounds into the turret. The T-Gewehr reverberated from the holes it had blown into the armour. He had done it very quickly, considering each cartridge had to be manually removed and then reloaded. The recoil must have been hell for his injuries.

Like a scene from some crazy Japanese game show, more Turkish soldiers followed another light tank out. They were all firing their weapons as they ran for the nearest cover. The shooting was indiscriminate, useless. Mine wasn't, dropping many that had decided to try to find a shallow scrape or a dead body to hide behind. Why were so many coming out like this? And why all Turks?

The light tank continued to move at speed, running over those who got in its way. Eventually, it was put out of action. Just as well as it had nearly made the slope. I quickly took a sip of water.

Through my binos, there was nothing left of the three Papier-mâché mates. Titan was blowing holes in people who weren't hidden well. I looked at Seagal. He was looking through a pair at me. Half-lifting his huge rifle, he then gave the signal he was out of ammo. Bollocks.

Concerned at the new sound, I peered back into the tunnel. A beastly tank straddling the rail tracks entered the arena. Fuck. Titan stopped shooting the soldiers and instead hit the top of the tank—no effect. The flap on either side of the front weapons opened. Through one square aperture, a pair of hands gripped the rim. His wide eyes stared at the battlefield. The other soldier was looking through a pair of binoculars, the sun glinting off the lenses. He nodded at me. I lowered mine, wondering why. I nodded back. The flaps were closed, and the beast moved forwards under great exhaust fumes. Jets of flames spewed out from each side.

Raising the binos, four sticks of Germans began to run up the tunnel. Smoke grenades launching from the tank disguised the infantry as they branched left and right. A handful had stayed behind it. The Germans had used the barricades of vehicles to hide, including the dead, like sandbags. Turks were being pulled out of their hides and thrown forwards for the Germans to take their place. Had the Germans planned the carnage so they could use the barricades to take cover?

Titan and Seagal shot the disorientated and scared Turks. Both then came under sustained fire from the rear tank gunner. The tank wasn't stopping for no one. It ran over the gate, the dead, and the injured. I started to hit the tank with controlled bursts, having no impact. Then, I got the dreaded click. I was perplexed that I had used the spare twenty-two pan-mags. Yet, with the Lewis' rate of five hundred a minute and the carnage that I had inflicted in the intense battle, it should have been understood.

The tank's main gun fired. The whole arena joined in from every direction—it was ludicrous. I fired two grenades over, blind almost. I peered at how far away they were landing—well short. Fuck. Blister had been correct at the launcher's distance. Titan and Seagal had stopped lobbing the grenades down. The tank was making good ground. The soldiers started to shoot and scoot, covering each other. It went against all my training and backbone, but we had to quickly extract. The fear was that we had nowhere to go but the open desert or back to the LUP. Perhaps we could get the vehicles away before the tank mashed them. I raced to place my Bergan on, thinking about the time it would take for Titan and Seagal to return. They were now only taking the odd shot. Were they almost out of ammo?

Anxious about the advancing noise and leaving the Lewis, I sent up a flare to signal a withdrawal. Weirdly the battle stopped. I lifted my eyeline above the ridgeline. That pause seemed to enhance the enemy that they had taken control, or that's how I perceived it. We had little time left to live.

Plop…

I searched the sky…

Plop…

The enemy were also doing the same…

Plop…

BOOOM!

The eighty-one-millimetre high-explosive mortar tore up those huddled next to the tank. It covered it in sand and body parts…

BOOOM!

The tank rolled through the mass. I quickly fired at those alive lying facedown…

BOOOM!

With no trenches or shell-holes to lie flat in, it was over for many.

The infantry decided to come to life at last, as did the tank. With all our squad finding a new lease of life, Blister had found his range. The tank had taken a direct hit. It stopped clunking. More mortars landed close. As I picked off targets, the tank jerked forward with all its machine guns firing. Every flame thrower spewed. Panic must have set in as their soldiers caught alight. Another direct hit blew the insides out of each hatch and hole. Fire now raged through the top vents.

Quickly changing an Enfield mag, I aimed and fired. I repeatedly slid the action-bolt back and forth. The speed and accuracy quickened with the thought of taking back control. My Bergan took some flak. A voice from the past shouted, "Unleash the mad minute." It was pleasing that Sikes had mentally joined the battle.

Blister continued to rain the mortars, at least seven per minute. I now know why he had bragged he was the best Bombardier ever. On every minute mark there was a pause from him, so we opened fire. Then his designated landing target would change. Even though this four-man squad was decimating the enemy, the enemy weren't cowering.

I was down to two mags. One of the light tanks exploded, sending many around it to their death. Two Germans decided to take the long run back to the tunnel but were quickly dropped. In the killing-zone, many more started to run. Some the wrong way. Some left their weapons. A new mortar exploded above the tunnel sending rocks outwards onto the first group of runners.

Getting to my feet, I ran down the slope. Every five metres, I got on one knee and fired a shot at the petrified enemy. Zig zagging at the incoming, I reached the first immobilised light tank. Dark liquid had pooled underneath the main body. Well concealed, I took aim. Another mortar exploded. Seeing a white flag waving, I locked onto it. A whistle streaked across the sky.

BOOOM!

The explosion had stopped echoing off the walls. The sound was more intense down here. I scanned my arcs. Three other flags came up from the recent pockets of resistance. Spotting movement through the fire's haze to my right, I swung my weapon around but released my finger off the trigger.

Titan's large stature was running along the edge. He jumped over Seagal who was still lying behind his sniper scope. I began to shake. Catching my breath, I had not realised how dry my throat and mouth had become. Weird smells choked my senses. I waited behind my weapon, pushing it down on the track to stop it trembling. The number of dead targets and unidentified parts didn't bother me, for now.

We had defended the ground for five minutes whilst the white flags were still up, but they had stopped vigorously waving. The familiar sound of Truck-1 came across the flats. Turning side on, it stopped. The side was lifted on the main fixed Lewis. I slowly moved forwards with my Enfield tucked into my shoulder.

BOOOM!

I laid flat on the floor. Screams and a fire raged from an armoured car that had been smoking for some time. I waited to see if my lads opened fire.

Gingerly, I returned to advancing. The flags vigorously waved. Perhaps those enemies on the blindside thought we had started again. Like the Elkhaba war, I stepped over the dead soldiers and swept the area. A few were moaning, so I made sure they had no weapons in close vicinity.

Reaching another armoured car, I moved the shredded body slumped on top of it. There was no doubt that another was dead as he had no legs. I swivelled back to our truck, Titan and Blister menacingly by its side.

'*Heben Sie Ihre Hände*,' I shouted to the enemy.

The enemies' hands slowly raised; the white flags waved. I gestured for the lads to watch the surrendering soldiers.

'*Langsam aufstehen*,' I shouted.

None of them stood up. The enemies' cries became louder. Again, I shouted for them to stand up slowly.

'Will you kill us?' a German soldier shouted.

'*Nein*,' I shouted. 'You have my word if you comply.'

Cautiously, the first person rose from behind the sunken wheel. The officer was petrified. More began to rise with hands raised above their heads. One soldier desperately tried to lift his blooded arm. He looked at me for acknowledgement. I nodded and waved at him to lower it. I glanced across at the other three groups, one existing of a young lad.

'Tell all your soldiers to move over to the British truck,' I calmly ordered.

'*Männer. Umzug zum britischen fahrzeug*,' he shouted at his men.

I backed up quicker than they walked and headed back to the safety of Truck-1. Again, I was careful where I trod, ignoring a hand that went up for help. Reaching the truck, I patted the rad's plate. Both Titan and Blister kept guard. The officer stopped, the nine soldiers did. All were frightened. Thinking back of the Jews getting tricked into being rounded up in front of armoured vehicles with HMGs, I guessed this was what they were thinking. Titan slowly moved the Lewis between the soldiers. Blister lifted his sub as he sat in the driver's seat. The youngest turned to our sniper, and then back to me. His eyes were full of remorse.

CHAPTER THIRTY-THREE

'Titan, get down and search these men,' I ordered.

Seeing that Seagal and Blister were covering, I placed my Enfield on the truck and drew my pistol. Titan had checked the nervous soldiers, some intimidated by his huge physique. He gave me the nod that they were clean. The officer appeared slightly confused as he searched the ridgeline and then onto a sand ridge towards the stack. I walked over to him, bringing his confused stare back to me.

'You are now men, not soldiers,' I said. 'How many medics do you have?'

'*Zwei*,' he answered.

'Show me.'

He looked across the dishevelled line of soldiers and pointed at each medic. Both looked terrified, possibly wondering what they had been picked for.

'*Wir sind nicht wilde*,' I said to our prisoners.

'Hey, we're not savages is my saying,' Titan said. 'Get your fucking own, Johnny.'

'Titan, take the two medics. Only save those who you can with the limited medical equipment. Blister, cuff the rest of these men and help them in the back of the truck.'

'Yes, boss,' they said simultaneously.

'What about me?' the officer asked.

'It's your duty to put those suffering that we cannot help, out of their misery.'

I unwound the pistol wire and then handed it out to him. He took his drained gaze from it and stared at me. Blinking away his tears, his shaking hand took it from me. I pointed in the direction of Seagal, who raised his hand. The officer had got the message he was being zeroed.

The grim task had been done. Back at the stack LUP, everyone seemed shell shocked. If honest, us as well. The Stokes mortar's plate had sunk into the ground. The sand in the blast ring was smooth. We had only managed to save two soldiers, now just simple men. The rest wouldn't have survived twenty-four hours without excruciating pain or infection setting in, let alone the trip back to Ismailia. When the officer had used all my rounds, he had sought permission to use another pistol.

Seagal had returned, freaking out the men because of his camo suit and Vaseline covered wound, blood seeping through his face paint. We had kept the reunion jubilation down to a back slap because of the prisoners. Titan gave Seagal morphine for his pain.

Blister made an amazing late lunch consisting of stew with biscuits as dumplings. The hard biscuits had been soaked in cooking oil and an array of spices. It went down well, including the rum and wine. The men had started to chat to us in broken English. However, we slightly kept our distance, casually holding our MP-18. One of us would always cover the other when we had to get near, ready to use lethal force if necessary.

The new prisoners' nicknames didn't work as they didn't get it, so we kept to their first names. The officer still looked concerned. Did he think this was a trick? Perhaps the last supper? I went to top up his mug with a bit of rum, but he put his hand on top.

'Like I said, Günter, you're safe if you comply,' I said.

'Where are the rest of your army hiding?' Günter asked—it stopped the general chit chat from his men.

I scratched my dirty and overgrown beard.

'Where is the officer in charge?' he asked.

'This is it. And I'm in charge.'

The officer appeared shocked. I wasn't sure if it were because he couldn't believe I was the boss, or we had no other army. He looked across at the battlefield and then gulped down his rum. He tried to swallow what he had regurgitated, the spew coming through his lips and nose.

'Better manners than you, boss,' Seagal said.

'Better than having a face like a punched lasagne,' I bantered. 'Perhaps your new nickname should be Scarface.' I grinned.

'*Nur vier von euch?*' Günter mumbled; head bowed.

'Not just the four of us, Günter. Four of the Elite,' I bragged.

'And we have plenty of rounds left for the Kaiser,' Titan said. 'That's if you're getting any fucking stupid ideas.'

Blister tapped his weapon and smiled.

'Are you the British Elite who…err…'

'Caused havoc to the station and hangars? Yep,' Titan interrupted Günter.

'And derailed the locomotive on the bridge,' Seagal boasted.

'Yeah, it nearly landed on Vince's head,' Blister added.

'Yeah, all right,' I said. 'So, how many soldiers are left inside with that train?'

Günter smiled, and then gestured a zip across his mouth.

I faced the MP-18 at him.

He shrugged.

'Tie them up and put them in the trucks,' I ordered.

Titan and Seagal started to react as Blister kept watch. I led the young lad around the other side of the stack and gave him my mug of rum.

'*Sprechen Sie Englisch,* Heinz?' I asked.

'*Ja*, but my name is Reiner.'

'So, Heinz, tell me about the bunker and train.'

He frowned. 'I am Reiner.'

'So, Heinz, tell me about the bunker and train.'

'Six officers remain.'

After a few slurps, I started asking him more questions. He began to freely flow the layout of the underground complex where the remaining officers would be billeted. He answered about the train details and about the gold.

Helping him back to the lads, they were annoyed I had given him so much of our rum. With Heinz tied up and asleep with the others, I called the last briefing. First, we fleetingly went over the battle. I also made sure each of us were mentally and physically in check. No one was to bottle up any emotions or dark thoughts, with everyone's door open to discuss anything. Blister said he was annoyed with the kid with the pissy slacks they had found hiding in the German truck's footwell. The lad had lied about the numbers and vehicles. Blister now wished that Batgirl had tortured him for the truth. This led to a bit of camaraderie about Seagal losing his papier-mâché 'mates'. All being as useless as Seagal's shooting skills, and how his own face didn't look much better than what was left on the cliff edges.

As the mud started to come my way, I jumped off the office radiator.

'Right, listen in. This is the end of the mission for you lads,' I said, and then waited for the expected arguments to die down. 'There's no Chinese parliament on this. I'm going in alone.'

'How the fuck are you going to stop the remaining enemy?' Titan asked.

'Yeah, and the train?' Blister added.

'And how are you going to get the gold out on your own?' Seagal jumped in. 'The Bedouin will skin us.'

'I have a cunning plan,' I impersonated Baldrick from *Blackadder.*

'Stop the shit acting like L'Estrange,' Blister said. 'Think about what you're saying.'

'I have. This is the end for me. Either way, I won't be coming out of there as I think this is where I return to 2013,' I sadly said. 'Anyway, once everything has been disabled, you can take the gold and share some of it with Batgirl.'

Blister stood up and threw his mug at the stack. He then disappeared up the slope. Titan looked as dismayed and went after him. Seagal got up and patted my shoulder. He then lifted the bonnet, fiddling with nothing of any significance. It hurt me more than I thought it would. Yet, I knew the attraction that was drawing me in that cave was the main reason I was here.

Loaded with extra MP-18 magazines, pistol ammo, and grenades, I decided to leave my Enfield and grenade launcher. I also ditched my Bergan. My pun about sharing my gear out when I was dead had gone down like a shit sandwich. All three had a face like a ballbag as they lined up. Titan slightly shook his head in disapproval.

'So, that's it,' he blurted.

'What are we supposed to do now?' Blister added.

Seagal was lost for words.

I cleared the lump in my throat and said, 'Jason and Mark, it's been an honour to serve with you two at the Somme. I will never forget. In time, I hope the atrocities we have endured will fade with only the good times remaining. Especially those epic months spent before Operation Baka.'

Both stared at the ground.

'Seagal, it has also been an honour to have you in the Elite squad.'

His head had bowed forwards, and the end of his boot made an arch pattern in the sand.

'All four of us have gone beyond what was expected on this insane mission. It's time for you all to return home to England. Rest your minds. Marry and settle down. Have kids. Enjoy the rest of your lives.'

I felt sick as I first embraced Seagal. His good arm slapped my back. Releasing him, he walked away. Facing Blister, I ruffled his matted hair and told him to get it cut before he returned to his wife and dog. He didn't lift his chin. As I went in for a bear hug, he turned away and instead held out his hand. With a quick shake, he returned to the camp. Titan put his hands in his pockets like a sulky kid. I tugged at his beard as he looked at my feet—no reaction. Eventually, he lifted but stared beyond my shoulder. Tears ran down his dirty cheeks. Patting his shoulder, I told him to say hi from me to his amazing parents. It was too much for him and he strode off.

Walking through the damaged vehicles and shell-holes, I wiped my eyes to see where the dead lay. A good percentage of me wanted to turn back to my new squad, my best mates. I felt as if I was abandoning them after all that they had sacrificed. I argued back, muttering under my breath about not putting them at risk anymore, potentially saving their lives. That's all I had to remain optimistic. I also told myself that if I managed this last part of my mission, and there was no link to return, I could walk back to them and brag about it. I stopped and thought about my old SBS squad, Ella, and my friends and family. It was a horrible feeling not knowing what to do. I had always decided. Yet, it seemed both decisions were wrong. Perhaps if I die here this would be the final decision.

I reached the tunnel entrance and admired Titan's explosive destruction. I looked back, unsure of why. With the sun setting, I could see nothing. Not even a silhouette or a torch waving.

Tucking in tight to the wall, I firmly placed the MP-18 in my shoulder. I flicked on the underslung torch. Moving at a good pace, I became hyperalert. On both sides of me were two dugouts. Moving to the centre, I swung right and then sharply left. My heartrate had increased. Walking into the left dugout, I turned the beam around the corner to peer down the direction of the main bunker. I had choices to make: right passageway, or the one I was in? I decided to use the current one.

My sweat had turned cooler due to the conditions. The silence was ear-splitting. My mind tried to play tricks as the beam wavered. However, I had become wiser over the years, trusting my sixth sense.

Arriving at the first blind bend, I turned the light off. It plunged me into complete darkness at first. A low light crept around the corner, along with a slight breeze on my face as I had not opted for a balaclava. Tilting my head around the bend, I sniffed the air. I smirked at the thought of Baka. I wished he were here with his amazing senses. The odours were like the station sheds.

The ground was wet as I continued down the rock corridor. The light coming from the end reflected in the water on the ground. Kneeling, I placed my glove and then smelt it. It didn't register the chemical smell I had thought it would.

Watching I didn't slip on the uneven surface, I reached the end and was stunned at the view: a ginormous cylindrical area carved into the rock. The incredible cavern narrowed the further it went up. I could see what looked like a star. Dead centre on the tracks was an intimidating beast of a train. It wasn't even painted in desert khaki, but blue, black, and white. Perhaps arrogantly that it didn't need to be camouflaged because of the size, armour plating, and weaponry. I wanted a better look. However, going out into the high lamp lit area was too risky. Instead, I followed the damp walls around to the left and snuck down behind a stack of huge shells.

So imposing was the train, I wanted to take notes to show the others. Realising I wasn't going back, my shoulders dropped. The front of the train had two huge rams that stuck out of an arrow shaped heavily armoured front scoop low to the tracks. Behind the plating were four domed turrets. The front had a pom pom weapon. The other three had high-calibre weapons. The next box section had five portholes, each closed with a steel door from the inside. On top of this steel fortress was a handrail. The main cannon was the biggest and scariest fucker I had seen in this era. I touched the intimidating twelve-inch diameter shells that stood in front of me.

I moved tight to the next rows of ammunition. There was a cannon enclosed in a turret before a new carriage. Poking out the roof were three large mortars, like the large diameter one I had seen in the German trenches back at the Somme. Dead centre was the main engine room, all enclosed in thick steel with portholes. The rear of the train mirrored the front. Even the hundreds of wheels had plating right down to the track. It could be driven in any direction. I wasn't permitted to destroy this locomotive or the track. Then, the many steel doors that lined up in the rockface gave me the answer to how to stop this deadly beast from leaving: kill the crew.

Click…

I knew what the threat had been as I used the same sort of rifle. Peering slowly behind, a German officer squinted at me from under his black with red band peaked cap. His gold buttons glinted under the lamp above him. My hand slid down onto the dangling MP-18.

Ahh-ooo-aaah…ahh-ooh-aaah…ahh-ooh-aaah…

The klaxon was louder in this sinkhole than the ones at the station.

Feet running on a gantry clanged downwards. I turned to make a sprint back to the corridor but stopped when another German was standing with the same weapon as me. I turned to those standing around the walls. Five in total and all having me in their sights. The horn died out, along with my chances of escaping. Bollocks, I had been too mesmerised by the train.

Standing tall, I lowered my sub. The smooth, chisel chinned officer came over and grinned annoyingly. He was mature, possibly in charge. He had red collars and a German cross hung down from the top button. He took my main weapon. Taking my pistol, he then cut the wire to the holster.

'You can get all mardy about it if you like,' I said, 'but I was just out for a bit of trainspotting.'

'Remove your clothes,' he ordered.

The officer behind me prodded me in the back. For a split-second, I contemplated turning and seizing his weapon like I had with the lookalike gnome, Tybalt, at the airport.

Being hit harder made the officer in front smile his perfect and white teeth. I was then forcibly stripped to my underwear. The soldier behind quickly took my clothes and boots away, and my last bit of defence: grenades and a knife. However, I still had my martial arts and extreme hand to hand combat skills.

The main man asked for someone to come forward. I turned to see a stocky lad in a sling, and limping. He looked familiar to the England Rugby player Chris Robshaw, but with a lesser physique.

'*Ist er das?*' Robshaw asked his superior.

'Yes, Robshaw, this is me who annihilated your army out there,' I said.

I received a hit around the back of the head. My temper was rising, but I must play the game.

'We knew you would come,' the officer said. 'Where is your commanding officer and army? Perhaps they send in a *schmutzige ratte* first.'

'I might be "dirty", but I only kill "rats",' I said. 'By the way, you smug bellend, I am the CO of the four-man squad.'

This time I got a butt to the back of the knee. It sent me to the floor—I really was shit at RTI.

'Only "*vier mann Kader*",' he loudly said—his men exaggeratedly laughed.

I was getting bored of this bullshit. 'Did Lieutenant Thomas White make his escape?' I said.

Chapter Thirty-three

He frowned inquisitively. 'Your name and rank?'

'Corporal Johnny Vince.'

'*Sperrt ihn in das Gefängnis,*' he said to the two officers now behind me.

'Prison?' I said. 'Not even a cup of tea?'

I got the whack I deserved. The main officer came right into my face and snarled his disgust. He then grabbed at the back of my hair and yanked it back. I pulled my head forwards, ignoring the stinging scalp.

'After you see our latest weapon leave at dawn with a convoy of trucks and tanks, you will be shot.'

'You won't win this war,' I said.

'Our Empire has destroyed two of your ships: SS *Donegal* and...'

I smiled thinking that Matron had not taken the assignment to join the same ship. He hadn't liked me grinning and not paying attention. I was ordered to be taken away. Good, the plan had worked.

In cuffs, I ignored the insults about being a scared, little British soldier. Set away right at the back was a single heavy fortified door. It was heaved open. The stench wafted out. A sharp stab to the back shuffled me forwards. I had a flashback of the two German tank drivers doing the same at the reservoir in Poppy Pride.

Dirty and damp straw lined the floor. I was manhandled over to an iron ring and then secured to it. The door was slammed. Searching the complete blackness, I guessed the smell to be excrement.

'Welcome to Bondi Beach. Have ya got a smoke?'

I tried to see where the voice had come from. 'Lieutenant Thomas White?'

CHAPTER THIRTY-FOUR

It was him. After many questions, it emerged that in 1916, Thomas and a unit of his men had been tasked to locate the gold and then return to base. If he had completed the first secret mission, he had any force required at his means to return and seize it. Behind the orders was General Rowe, who would split it with Thomas and his men.

Setting out on horseback and two carts, the twelve strong unit had reached the known area. They were challenged with an overpowering force two klicks away from here. Only three of White's men managed to survive with their lives after surrendering. The horses were shot. The meat was used to feed the German and Turk soldiers who celebrated that night. The munitions and rations were taken into stock.

Stripped to their underwear, they were repeatedly beaten. The three were then marched in the scorching sun back to this underground bunker. The rest of the unit were left to the vultures. Under the ruling of the German officer, the torture continued. All three had not talked. One of the Australians, a Private Wade, had a pistol placed to his head in the arena outside. Thomas and his comrade were forced to give details of their mission and camps. If not, Wade would be shot. Thinking the officer wouldn't do it, they refused to give details. They had been wrong.

Rather than kill the remaining two, they were forced to work long gruelling hours in the underground base. The two prisoners were continually abused, verbally, mentally, and physically. However, with the appalling conditions and treatment, Private Davies had attacked a German guard five weeks ago. Davies was subsequently killed. Perhaps Davies knew this would be an easier way for him to go.

Thomas wanted to stay alive to report the deaths of his men. He also thought there might be a slim chance that he may escape or be released after the war. Thomas had kept his head down and worked like a mule, but ate worse than the animal. He had made a few Turk and German chums, regularly getting smokes and leftover food. However, that had all changed when the main unit battled with us in the arena. This morning, he had been told that the underground base was leaving with the locomotive, and that he would be shot. He admitted he was already dead inside from that statement.

Was Private Wade related to Captain Don Wade VC? And Private Davies related to Corporal Malcolm 'Matilda' Davies? It had to be, making sense why they were on this mission. Not just for the gold and WMD, but to find their brothers. I had asked Thomas if his two Australian dead mates had brothers. Both did. Their unit's disappearance was around the time Sikes had been ordered on the mission. Was Sikes aware of the failed Australian mission? Perhaps even his uncle's greed for the gold. Yet, I guessed that Sikes was here only to destroy all three targets. But, through his fucked-up mind, he didn't have a clue what was going on. His uncle was just using him.

To boost Thomas' morale, I told him of our whole mission. He was confused by my admission of our four-man squad killing the enemy outside, especially after he had heard the commotion. What had perplexed him further was that I was the only one left to stealthily kill each officer here.

After the story, he came over and fed me some food. He felt my face in the darkness. Although I was cuffed with my arms above me, I already had a picture of him in my mind: Ocker. That moment. That bond. They could not ever be taken away, even at dawn's execution.

Leaning against each other, we fell asleep. His friend, a rat called Sid, had curled up on his lap. A few times we were startled by strange noises: muffled cries and thuds that Thomas couldn't explain. Yet, he had been in this prison for over a year. The door had been rattled at one stage. I brought my knees in expecting a kicking like on other occasions as a prisoner. It had just been mind games.

I woke again to the cold. I realised that the increasing thoughts of my previous missions were the same reality I had on this mission. Even the lads' sayings and actions were the same as my old squad. A very uncanny similarity. Was this just a coincidence? Was it so I bettered myself? To understand how I worked and what I had done wrong in the past? There was something else that had been nagging me at the back of my mind, but I couldn't quite reach it. Maybe I'll never know as I guessed this was my last ever mission.

The door swung violently open and banged off the wall, shitting the life out of me. Not so much Thomas. The rat had scurried off, missed by the boot of the German officer: Erich von dem Alpers.

'Good afternoon, men. I am sorry for the late call to your deaths,' he facetiously said.

'Oh, you mean the tanks and the rest of your army didn't turn up this morning,' I said in the same tone.

A train's blast of steam roared. Erich then threw the keys at Thomas and instructed him to uncuff me. The train's whistle loudly echoed off the prison walls. Erich moved out of the doorway light. I got my first view of Thomas' face as he leant beside me undoing the cuffs. A flood of unity came over me. I smiled at his white scars under his part missing long blond hair. His blond beard looked almost bleached against his tanned and dirty complexion. Like Ocker, he had a large nose, the type you found on a wine-taster. Possibly a family trait. However, unlike Ocker, he was skinny and gaunt.

'Shall we go for it?' I whispered in his ear.

'Ya won't get past the rest waiting by the locomotive.'

'*Schneller. Schneller,*' Erich yelled.

'At least we could take this motherfucker out,' I quietly said.

My hands dropped and I grimaced in pain. Thomas rubbed my wrists. He was then ordered to re-cuff my hands behind my back. One enemy entered, aiming a sub at us. My shoulders dropped. Erich smiled. Had he guessed my plan to try to escape or kill him? The new guard was dressed in a long brown leather apron with matching leather hat. He had goggles up on his forehead.

We were ordered to our feet. With the guard behind us and Erich in front walking backwards, we entered the base. The steam and heat from the train rose to the top of the sinkhole and funnelled out to freedom. Robshaw sinisterly grinned, his only usable hand on his sidearm. He was the only one not to be wearing the leatherwear. I made a joke about not joining the bondage party. He didn't understand, but it had kept down my nerves that were already high.

Two of the original officers were missing as we were gang marched by the rest to the waiting train. Its huge presence was even more overpowering now that it was running. The shells and ammo that I had hid behind were missing. Reaching the rear, the HMG inside the turret swivelled in our direction. Thomas stuck two fingers up. I sniggered and mouthed 'fuck you' at the hidden gunner. For some strange reason, the barrel nodded up and down a few times. I was shoved in the back, and I quickly forgot about it.

Each officer in the line boarded the train. A hand came out of the centre carriage porthole with a thumb up. The last but one officer pushed Thomas hard into the metal flip-down stairs. Thomas rubbed his painful shins. He was aggressively hit and ordered up. I reacted by karate side-kicking the back of the officer's legs. Standing over him, I kicked him again in the back. I was whacked on the back of the neck, the pain sending weird patterns to my head. Swaying as I turned, Robshaw had hold of a club. Erich ordered him to stop, and to help up the officer I'd kicked. Erich aimed a pistol at my face whilst Thomas began to feebly climb the ladder.

'Thomas,' I said, 'it's imperative you survive. No matter what. Your new nickname is Ocker.'

I didn't hear his answer as he was taken by a large pair of leather gloves wearing the same leather uniform. That was the last absent officer. At the centre section of the front armoury, a solid steel door was opened. I ignored Robshaw's hand to climb up. Instead, I leant against the inside door's submarine-type wheel to assist me. The cuffs cut in my wrists.

In the confined space, the door was shut and locked. I was jostled forwards past the HMGs towards the last turret. In the dark joining centre section, a light was put on. Robshaw let Erich through first. As I was next, Robshaw was still giving me his best deathly glare—pathetic.

The train jolted forwards with huge creaking and screeching wheels. I grabbed a rail behind to hold myself up. Under a low crawl we entered the tunnel. It went pitch-black. Erich opened the front thick metal flaps and then the two smaller side portholes. I thought about the next chance to rush Erich whilst he readied the pom pom gun. He turned and smiled and then nodded at Robshaw behind me. I looked back, Robshaw had moved back to the centre section with his pistol aimed at my head. Again, it felt like Erich had read my intentions.

The low sun began to shine through the tunnel. Bloated bodies lined the track. We had not picked up speed like I had thought we would have. Just as we neared the tank wreckage, a huge flock of vultures and crows took to the air. We jolted, hundreds of wheels in reverse. Erich turned around as if triumphant that no British Army were out there. He grabbed my cuffs and moved me to the side porthole. He undid the bracelets and then reconnected them through a metal bar at waist height.

Through his binos he scanned the area. My smug comment about no vestige of a German or Turk alive got me a punch to the stomach. Catching my breath, I heard the sound he had obviously had. I peered out the port window to Truck-1 slowly coming down the slope at an angle. Behind and up close was the German truck. Erich gripped the single brass handle.

Bang…bang…bang…bang!

The noise was far worse than that when I was in the Pierce-Arrow. Shells fell at my feet as the heavy-calibre weapon continuously fired. Our truck's cab was being smashed with the driver rocking as he was hit. I screamed it to stop, but Erich didn't. Why weren't the lads returning fire or getting out of the killing-zone? Why the fuck had they come back? I fought the cuffs behind my back whilst screaming expletives. The rear German truck was being ripped apart; the driver slumped forward. I tried to kick Erich off the weapon, but was pulled back around my neck. I then received thumps in my kidneys. My yelling and struggling didn't deter Erich.

When the barrage stopped, Erich turned, smiling his perfect teeth. Two huge explosions followed.

'Oh dear, that is the best of your army,' he said.

I struggled and vented some more. I was hit hard. Too hard. I blacked out.

The cramp from kneeling awoke me. My head throbbed and my throat and mouth were dry. Opening my eyes, I was looking at the fuzzy sand. I had been tied to something around my back. Getting my legs straight to rid the cramp was difficult. Shaking away the blurriness, my head pounded even more. Thomas was also tied to a steak in the ground. Looking sorrowful, he nodded forwards. We were pegged on the cusp of the slope. Below were the two burnt-out trucks. Charred remains lay inside and out. I lowered my head and screwed my eyes shut.

'I'm sorry, Johnny,' Thomas meekly said.

'So am I. Why the fuck didn't my squad take my orders to leave?'

'Because they would die for ya, Johnny.'

'So, my little British and Australian friends,' a new voice emerged.

I half-turned to see Erich leaning against the train. My anger was as hot as the cab's boiler.

Thomas suddenly groaned. I turned to see him being subjected to punches in the ribs from the Robshaw. Thomas was then hauled to his feet. I braced myself as Robshaw came over. Holding my breath, I got the same treatment and was then harshly stood up. Erich strode victoriously over. I gripped the steak and brought my groin in.

'Bullet to the head or left to die alive?' Erich asked.

'How about a full pardon, and then ya can suck my penis,' Thomas said.

Thomas spat out the blood after the smash to the face from Robshaw. 'That's a no then,' Thomas said.

I wanted him to shut up and play the grey man as Thomas had to survive. Yet, I found it amusing what he had said, having the same brass neck as Ocker. I started to laugh.

'Funny humour. How…'

'That's because you Germans have none,' I blurted.

Erich sighed and then punched my mouth. I tasted the blood on my lips.

'Perhaps you both would like a shot to your kneecaps. You can slowly bleed to death and watch the vultures feast on you. Just think of us taking the gold and killing the British Empire.'

Robshaw placed his pistol end directly on the kneecap of Thomas.

'It doesn't matter what ya do, boy,' Thomas said to Robshaw. 'Your mother can't be proud of ya as she is being fucked by a randy Australian Waller right now. I bet your dad is bashing one out over it.'

I screwed my eyes shut thinking he was worse than Ocker. Thomas growled in his throat and then hollered for Robshaw to get on with it.

Bang!

There was no scream from Thomas. Would I be the same? I was grabbed by the hair. Opening my eyes, Erich had his pistol to my head and was frantically looking around. Breathing hard, he tried to hide behind me. Out of the corner of my eye, Thomas was full of blood splats, and was weirdly smiling and shaking. On the floor in front of him was Robshaw with half his head missing. I harshly swivelled around when a voice had shouted from the train. A body was slung out, and then another two. Both were those German officers in leather gear. The next officer scaled down the ladder and stood with his hands on his hips. He lifted off his hat and goggles.

'Blister,' I mumbled. 'What the actual fuck?'

At arm's length and directly behind me, Erich's pistol pressed hard into my neck. From the carriage's side walkway, another person in a leather uniform appeared.

'*Tötet ihn*,' Erich yelled.

I knew why the second officer to appear wasn't going to take his orders to kill Blister. Just by the size of him, it was Titan. I should have realised earlier by the huge hands in tight gloves. Instead, Titan jumped down and faced us. He took off his tight headgear and ruffled his huge beard. Both Titan and Blister had no weapons.

'Looks like ya gonna come a guster, Erich,' Thomas said.

A familiar sound filled me with joy, and I was already fit to burst. A flash of black and a growl violently took the warm barrel end from my neck. After the pistol had fired, I checked to see if Baka had been killed. Instead, he began to maul Erich. Screaming, Erich tried in vain to fight off Baka. With a short sharp whistle, Baka withdrew.

Bang!

Erich didn't move, the sand soaking up his red mist.

I was emotionally shaking to see Baka and the lads alive. The wrist ropes were cut, and I flopped to the ground.

'Have you been fucking crying because you miss your beloved truck?' Blister asked.

'Fucking pansy,' Titan said.

Thomas was untied. I sat up against the post and tapped my leg. Baka came sheepishly over as if he was in trouble. Grabbing his collar, I pulled him and gave him a hug. He had lost a lot of weight. Baka began to lick my face and then the blood from my lips. I didn't mind it this time.

'That makes the blood pack now, Baka,' I said.

'Gets more fucking praise than us,' Seagal said.

'Hey, if there's going to be any balls licking praise, I want first dibs,' Titan said.

I tried to stand to greet Seagal to thank him for shooting the last of the Germans. I was held by Titan as I went wobbly.

After much needed back slapping, we called Thomas over and I introduced him. He gave a little banter for the homosexual play, just like Ocker would. He automatically fitted in. Surreal as it was, we were sat in the desert with the indestructible train with its gold on one side of us, and the recent battles on the other. We took on food and water, joking, and laughing. The story played out that they knew I would balls it up—hopefully a joke. Blister and Titan in black-ops gear had entered the chasm and killed two of the officers. They proceeded to dress up in their leather gear and goggles, like Bruce had at the Somme. They had realised I was behind the locked prison door, but were not able to communicate for the fear of compromising.

Titan had to hide in the centre carriage with the gold due to the uniform being too small compared to the guard he had killed. Once

Thomas was inside with the other officer, Titan swiftly and silently killed the officer. It had been Blister who was behind the HMG. He said it had been difficult not to shoot me and Thomas after our rude gestures.

Once the train had started to move, the rest of the train guards were put out of action. It was Seagal who had taken out Robshaw as he went to shoot Thomas' kneecap. Finally, Seagal had put Erich out of his agony—shame.

'Who were in the trucks?' I asked. 'Not our German prisoners?'

'We're not savages,' Blister said.

'I've warned you about using my saying, Mark,' Titan snapped.

Blister gave Titan the middle finger.

'We copied Sikes' idea,' Seagal said. 'Using some of the dead Turks, we had tied them in the trucks. We had roped both trucks together for when the train came out. I let the handbrake off each and then took my position.'

'Someone had to finish the job properly,' Titan added.

'That was a croc-shit idea,' I said—Thomas enjoyed my remark.

'Why?'

'Because how are we going to get back?' I said. 'Unless you can drive a fucking train.'

'You don't think we've not thought of that,' Seagal said. 'Us four and our new digger friend are getting a lift from the Bedouin. They're looking after Günter and his men.'

Right on cue, the sound of many hooves raced across the desert. I searched the horizon, and then turned back.

'You say four of us, but what about Baka?' I said.

Baka did a funny whine.

'No offence, boss, but you wanted to leave us and stay here. So, it's *bon voyage* for us,' Titan said.

'But I haven't found the link to get...'

Blister patted me on the shoulder and pointed to the train. 'We've a surprise for you.'

In amongst the dust being caused by the tribe coming in on camels and horseback, a lone figure jumped down from the train. I had a bad feeling about this.

CHAPTER THIRTY-FIVE

Seagal helped Thomas to his feet and was told to say his goodbyes. Between handshakes and the thanks for saving his life, I tried to see who was walking between the camels and spare horses. Baka looked at me as if he already knew. Batgirl came over and asked her women to take Thomas. As he left, I mentioned again to pass down the family nickname of 'Ocker'.

Batgirl first bowed at me and then kissed my cheek. The lads looked on, perhaps wanting some of that—it had been ages. She headed back and waved at her entourage. Günter was led forward with his hands bound in front. In the background, his men and the lad held up their tied hands in a thanking gesture—I nodded. Günter acknowledged me for saving him and his men. It had been a pleasant surprise for me. Günter was then directed away.

Peering around the group, one person stood behind the last camel and was embracing Batgirl. Seagal coughed to get my attention.

'You were born to lead Operation Baka, and it was an honour to follow. Take care, Johnny,' Seagal said.

Seagal gave a short embrace, and then left. I turned back to the three of the lads. Blister wiped his eyes.

'Boss...Johnny,' Blister said. 'Look us up when you return home. Perhaps the photo of us in the hangar will be printed in a newspaper. By the way, I'm in charge now as you were shit.'

Blister sniffed, just about holding it together. He then hit me on the arm and strode away. The words I wanted to say did not come out.

'Johnny Vince,' Titan said, 'I will never ever forget you. I'm going to lead this lot home, and then change our nicknames to Planet, Shrek, Fish, and Rabbit.'

His huge bearlike arms wrapped around me, almost squeezing the life out before releasing. Titan took a few steps back and nodded at me with glazed eyes. He then turned his huge frame and walked to the awaiting Bedouin.

'You still stink, though,' he shouted.

'Why the nickname Rabbit? Scrap's dead,' I said, choked up. 'And make sure you tell HQ where all the bodies are.'

He put a hand up to acknowledge.

On one knee, I stroked Baka. He placed a paw on my knee and then nestled his head on me. As I stood, he faced the onlookers, ready to race off.

'Go, friend…go,' I said.

With the crowd getting ready to leave, I was shocked to see who it had been all this time by the horse: Scrap. I was so stunned that I had to lean against the steak. The train started to set off as he stood there appearing different.

As the dust settled, I lowered my hands from the waving lads as they headed off into the sunset. My guts churned. My chest burned. I bit my lip. Scrap waved me to follow him as he had mounted a horse. I took one last look around at the death and destruction, and then trailed him.

The horse had walked about fifty metres when he disappeared into a dip. As I reached the cusp, Scrap stood facing me with the horse tied to a peg. I walked down the slope. He was clean shaven and revitalised.

'Where the hell did you get to?' I asked.

Scrap swung down his kit bag from his shoulder and delved in. I was getting a little agitated as to why he was staying silent, or even not seeming pleased to see me. From his haversack, he handed me a pile of folded clothes. The nostalgia hit me. Confused, I smelt the British Army gear that I had worn in Afghanistan.

'I've been back,' he said. 'These are your clothes from the Bergan that you had left at the lost city.'

'What? How?'

'It is best if you sit down.'

As I did, he handed me my boots that I had left in the chamber. I studied the scuffs and bits of the sole that were missing. Remembering them well, I scoffed.

Scrap sat opposite me and crossed his muscular legs.

'What's going on, Georges?'

'I knew my time was up, so I handed Ocker's bullet to Jules. I walked endless miles until I found a river where I stripped off and waded out.

Life went black. I woke up in terrible pain, spewing gunge, and water. The old man and the perky titted woman were next to me.'

'How the fuck did you know it would work? You could have drowned.'

'I didn't know. Seizing the opportunity, I grabbed the old man and threatened to break his neck. Two fat bastards came down. Being taught by the best, I disarmed them and used the dagger at the old man's neck to walk free from the temple. Before I left the village, I had done a two-part deal with the old man, with the woman translating.'

'Dare I ask?' I said.

'One, if I returned with decent weapons and clothes, I would hunt Thomas White down and kill him.'

He delved into the haversack and pulled out a FN FAL rifle and handed it to me. I examined the scratches on the black stock and fore-stock.

'Nico's,' I said.

He nodded and then handed me a pistol. I smiled whilst staring at the high-powered 9-mm Browning.

'That is also Nico's,' Scrap said. 'He said that Tom Hardy would need these. You best get changed.'

I started to get dressed as the cool night settled in. Last of all, I laced up my good old boots. Standing up and putting the pistol in my leg holster, I felt important again in my old kit.

'You obviously fooled the old man as you didn't kill Thomas,' I said. 'But why are you giving me these weapons and my old kit?'

'That's the other part of the deal. I'm not returning to the jungle.'

'What do you mean?'

'I am in love with Jules. I want to start a family and remain friends with the lads. It's more than I had in my other life. The temple's chief gave me some really bad shit to drink.'

'But what about Thomas White?' I asked.

'Ocker was your best mate. It took me half the mission to realise what a selfish prick I had been. The gold means nothing compared to happiness. Give me your watch.'

'Why?'

'Please, my *bru*,' he anxiously said, and got to his feet.

I sighed and started to take it off. 'I want it back, though, as I never seem to keep one returning from a mission.'

'You will not be returning to Ismailia. I have told the lads. That is why they...'

'Huh?' I interrupted. 'What do you…'

'Shut up for a change, Johnny,' he interrupted. 'The last part of my deal was you would be returned to 2013. I have given them the photo from your Bergan. The one of your squad in Operation Blue Halo. Any second now, you are going to go through some nasty shit.'

I swallowed hard.

'Do you know what the date is?' he said.

I counted on my fingers, and said, 'It's May the first.'

The thing that had been at the back of my mind slapped me. It was the same fucking date before the day of the Afghan Chinook extraction. The same fucking five and half weeks on both missions.

Scrap came in and gave me a huge bearhug. 'You won't ever be able to go back to the temple or re-visit us again. Thanks, Johnny, for letting me start a decent life.'

I was stuck for words, but quickly said, 'I'm gonna miss…arghhhhh,' I yelled, dropping to my knees.

'Enjoy what you have always wanted, Johnny. I love…'

In pain like never was a feeling of nails being hammered through my whole body. My teeth seemed like they were exploding out through the roof of my mouth. Then, I felt as if I was being pulled apart. Weird sounds, smells, and lights surrounded me, adding to the horrendous contortions and the chaos. My screams stopped. I tried to catch my dying breath but choked up a putrid gunge. Then, everything just stopped.

I had been in this situation before, not knowing if I was dead or alive. As if an evil cloak had been put over me. Scarily, I had been in this state for many hours. I was frightened that this was the end for me.

Slowly, my hearing came back. A gentle breeze blew sand onto my face. Coming through the blurriness, I was still lying down in the dip in the featureless desert. The SLR was tucked into my shoulder. The night was spectacularly clear with the moon and stars shining on me. I caught the eyes of Fish looking back at me, probing for any signs of worry. Fish still looked so baby faced. Seeing the Supacat HMT400 and quad was as if I had just entered an unrivalled futuristic world.

'Fuck,' I muttered. 'No way.'

I had returned. Even though I had no watch to check under the pinhole torch like before, I knew the time to be 05:17 hours. This time, I was not anxious about dawn breaking with the approaching Chinook. I was shocked and elated to be here, but was also sad for who I had left.

I wasn't sure what to do, until I remembered I had mimicked the beer can to mouth action last time. I did it again to him.

Not wanting this to be a dream by waking up back in the Sinai Desert, I checked across to see if Shrek was here. Fuck, he was, and still guarding one of the suspected Elkhaba leaders. He stared back at me, still as calm as ever. Yet, I was breathing erratically and burping the evil gases. Holding my breath, I searched for Planet. My heart fluttered as I saw him. I knew what I had to do and made ready my pistol and rifle. A minute later, not being able to bear it anymore, I got to my feet and bounded over to Fish as he was the nearest. Running in hard, I put my arms around him. The SLR smacked his helmet.

'What the fuck, boss?' he said.

Over-emotional, I let go of him and studied his face, body, and specialised kit. Shrek and Planet came running over. Shrek threw the leader to the ground.

'I thought there was a fucking fight going on,' Shrek said. 'What goes down?'

I gave my rifle to Fish and then threw my arms around Shrek's broad shoulders. I held on tightly.

'It's not Thursday is it?' he said, and heaved me off.

'Yes, the second of May,' Fish answered.

'I meant Thursday as in the Afghan *special* Thursday.'

'Oh, ye meant when the Afghan boys dress as women on a typical Thursday,' Planet said. 'It has been nearly six weeks for Johnny.'

Holding Planet at shoulder height, I rambled off a load of details about how his nickname had come about and how we had passed selection together. Pulling away, I continued to waffle at speed about Shrek's looks and personality. Then onto Fish's good looks and brain power. Exhausted, I took in some breaths, almost hyperventilating. The Elkhaba prisoners looked at me strangely, as did the squad.

'Jesus, Johnny. What the fuck is going around ye head? What's spooked ye?' Planet asked.

'Where did you get this FN FAL?' Fish asked.

The others looked. Shit, I thought, trying to look innocent. I snatched it back.

'I swapped my Diemaco for it with Nobby before he had left on the first extraction,' I lied. 'I was having a jamming prob...'

'It's so old and battered,' Shrek interrupted. 'Why the fuck would Nobby have that?'

Chapter Thirty-five

'The crest markings are of the Rhodesian SAS, who fought…'

Shrek had punched Fish on the arm to stop him waffling on.

'Ye look different, Johnny…skinnier,' Planet said.

'That's coz you're a fat fucker,' Shrek said. 'Sorry, Scottish fat fucker.'

'I'll twist ye balls off when we get back,' Planet retorted, eyes ablaze.

I was beaming with joy, just staring at them, and loving their banter.

'Where's your *shemagh* and *Dishdasha*?'

'I took it off, Fish, as I was too hot.'

I tried not to show the cold had seeped into my bones, but pretended to be agitated by his constant questions.

'Do I have to fucking ask your permission now?' I said.

'Sorry, boss.'

'Why have you taken your NGVs off?' Shrek quizzed.

'Because I had a fucking little headache,' I said sarcastically. 'Because they're fucking damaged, you moron.'

It was tough being like this, but I had to act as if I had been with them this whole time.

I let the banter run for a short while between them, until almost simultaneously they stopped as the first sounds of the Chinook could be heard. I knew it would be hugging the contours and utilising its on-board screen technology's night enhancement package which turned night to day. Today though, this kit wouldn't have to pinpoint enemy positions on its return flight. There would be no extraction. My heart fluttered.

The lads got back into their positions with the NGVs down. Again, the prisoners were jostled to the floor, both face-planting as their hands were cable-tied behind their backs. I smirked.

At the Supacat, I slyly rested my rifle against the vehicle, flash-heart style. I patted the armoured front door before opening it. Trying to remember the procedure, I set up the satcom and made the necessary call to the Chinook pilot. I was ready to change history forever. I was excited on top of the emotional.

'Bravo November One, this is Bravo Zero Bravo, over,' I said, on tenterhooks to hear his voice.

'Bravo Zero Bravo, this is Bravo November One, received clear. Five klicks to LZ. Supacat first, you know the drill. Don't hang around guys. And Vinnie, we don't want any trouble now. I'm due my fry-up in an hour.'

My heart was beating like a piston. I nearly forgot my plan having heard his voice again, but said, 'Abort…abort. LZ is too hot. Repeat, LZ is too hot.'

'Bravo Zero Bravo, confirm abort.'

'Bravo November One, Rabbit, confirm abort…LZ is too hot. Do not take the flight path back across original insertion LZ. Repeat, do not take the flight path back across original insertion LZ. Fucking white hot area.'

'Roger that.'

I had to tell my lads to stay off the channels whilst I waited for the chatter to stop between him and his co-pilot, Ashely Kellett.

'Rabbit, we need to go for a beer when I get back,' I said.

'Err…yeah…sure,' he replied.

'I need you to do me a favour. Ask Mike to stay with Ella until I return, please.'

'Mike? You mean Smudge.'

Shit, I had forgotten to use his nickname. 'Sorry. Affirmative. Please, Rabbit.'

'As you've been so polite for once, sure.'

'Are you on open transmitter?' I asked.

'No. Why?'

'Do it, please,' I said.

A static pitch sounded.

'Steve Steve,' I said. 'I know you're out there watching for rogues, and why there is only one Chinook for a two-set extraction. I need you to contact me when I return. Hashtag urgent. Rabbit, switch me off the frequency, please.'

'Done. What the fuck was that about?'

'I'll tell you at the next fry up in Camp Bastion,' I said, knowing what Rabbit's would say.

'The other SAS blokes on the first extraction have cleared out the canteen of all hot breakfasts. Only muesli left for you guys, but I suppose that will make a nice change from all the posh dining you SAS nancy boys have been used to.'

'Don't think I didn't hear that, dickhead, it's SBS. I think a wee little rabbit will be…'

'Shut up, Planet,' I interrupted. 'You take care of your lovely wife and six kids, Rabbit. I'll see you soon.'

'Err…thanks, Vinnie.'

'Wait out,' I said.

'Roger that.'

Closing the satcom, I would never take for granted such communication and a friend. Again, I felt the side of the Supacat, realising how ill equipped those were in World War One, and how brave in the face of adversity.

'What the fuck is going on?' Shrek said. 'I've got an irritated bellend here, and I don't mean the one in my pants.'

'Lads, bring the prisoners over,' I said.

Regrouped by the vehicle, I was still trying to get my emotions in check. I told them of the unequivocal Elkhaba trap of many Toyota with mounted Dushka, including the SAM threat. The leader who I knew spoke English looked like he was going to combust with rage. When Planet had asked how I knew, I pointed at the other prisoner and lied that he had informed me. The prisoner had no idea what I had said. The leader started to struggle, venting off in Arabic. This time, though, my Arabic was better than my previous Pashto. Smiling smugly at the leader, I then asked Shrek to get out the map. I then showed the ambush positions on his map.

'Right, lads, we need to find a decent LUP for the day. Then we head for this village at night.'

'Then what, boss?' Fish asked.

'What the fuck is wrong with you, raghead?' Shrek bawled at the leader. 'Stop fucking struggling. *Togf an nadal.*'

'We finish Operation Blue Halo properly,' I continued. 'Eradicate all the Elkhaba and their leader, Tariq Sunny. Aka, Baha Udeen.'

The leader stopped harassing. He was even more shocked than the surprised lads that I had known about this information.

'Fucking ace,' Shrek said.

'Just like Blister,' I muttered. 'Fucking ammo up, lads.'

'This is what I signed up for. I love the Elite,' Planet said.

I remembered Titan saying it.

'Do you want me to get your Bergan and kit,' Fish asked.

'Arse lick,' I jested. 'No, leave that to me. You and Shrek sort your own and Planet's shit. Planet, you stay here.'

'Aye.'

I waited a few seconds and then I took a few steps backwards as if going to my kit. 'Cut the leader loose first and then the other prisoner,' I quietly said to Planet.

'Are ye…'

'Do it,' I barked.

As soon as the knife had gone through, the leader leapt for the SLR. He sharply turned to me.

Bang! Bang!
The old gaming voice had not returned. 'Threat neutralised,' I said.
Planet frowned incomprehensibly at me.
I calmly held my hands up to a returning Shrek and Fish.
'Why the fuck did ye leave your rifle unattended? That's an instant return,' Planet said.
'Could have fucking killed you, or us,' Shrek angrily said.
'Sorry, guys, I'm just tired,' I said, and picked the weapon off the floor.
'Shall we drop the other?' Shrek said.
The other prisoner was shaking like a jelly on a roller coaster.
'We're not savages,' I said.
'It was a joke, boss.' Shrek took his pistol off the back of the other terrorist's head.
'Did you catch the incident on your helmet-cam, Planet?' I asked.
'Aye.'
'Good. Right, Planet, load the jelly in the back and then get your shit together. Shrek, you take point-man on the quad.'
'Yes, boss,' they said simultaneously.
I waited till they had left and then grabbed a pencil and paper from the cab. After writing 'Turn off your camera', I put my hand over the lens and showed the note to Fish. As he did, I then placed the safety catch on my pistol and holstered it.
'Where did you get that antiquated pistol from as well? Isn't that a…'
He stopped as I had pulled out the ammo from my pocket. I started to add them back to the empty FN rifle mag. A wry smile from him showed that he had understood my actions.
'Fish, get onto the head sheds and tell them what just happened,' I said.
'Yes, boss.'
Returning to my original position, I kept my back against them pretending to sort my shit until they were loaded in the Supacat. Shrek was checking his satnav on the quad out in front. Pulling back the netting at the rear of the truck, I made out I was loading my kit. Seeing the other kit made me think back of this successful operation; also, of the friends and vehicles I had left behind in the Sinai. I looked at the dead leader on the sand.
'Not fucking making direct eye contact in the Chinook with me now,' I said, and spat. 'Or fucking grinning your toppled gravestones-like teeth like back then, are you.'

Walking around to the driver's door, my fatigue and the over-emotional state hit me. Barely able to open the door, Planet was sitting in my seat. Maybe he was waiting for me to rant, as he would always try to get in my seat in any vehicle, including the Chinook on that fateful crash. I closed the door respectfully and walked around to the passenger door. Planet looked perplexed. I got in the cramped and reeking but futuristic vehicle. Just another day in the Elite paradise, I thought. I closed my eyes; exuberant I had made it back.